HIDDEN PASSION

Once Morrigan had been mistress to a king—but now he had betrayed her. That betrayal burned in her blood as she looked at the young prince Lugh sleeping. The skin of his forearms was golden, and the sun, where it broke through the oaks, glinted off the copper arm bands he wore above his elbows. She could see how flat his belly was and how taut and hard his thighs were under his pale green tunic.

As she watched the handsome young man lying on long strands of warm grass near the soft, sweet mosses of the brook, he stirred uneasily and moved his right hand, slightly at first, then more purposefully, until it touched his manhood.

Morrigan's heart beat faster; her breath came quick and shallow. Revenge may have been what she had on her mind when it first occurred to her that she would have Lugh. But it was not foremost in her mind now. . . .

Lugh's ⬚⬚⬚⬚⬚⬚ *—as twin currents* ⬚⬚⬚⬚⬚⬚ *into the vast unk*⬚⬚⬚⬚ *the gods could fo*⬚⬚

FIRES IN THE MIST

FIRES
IN THE
MIST

by

Barbara Dolan

A SIGNET BOOK

SIGNET
Published by the Penguin Group
Penguin Books USA Inc., 375 Hudson Street,
New York, New York 10014, U.S.A.
Penguin Books Ltd, 27 Wrights Lane,
London W8 5TZ, England
Penguin Books Australia Ltd, Ringwood,
Victoria, Australia
Penguin Books Canada Ltd, 10 Alcorn Avenue,
Toronto, Ontario, Canada M4V 3B2
Penguin Books (N.Z.) Ltd, 182–190 Wairau Road,
Auckland 10, New Zealand

Penguin Books Ltd, Registered Offices:
Harmondsworth, Middlesex, England

First published by Signet, an imprint of Dutton Signet,
a division of Penguin Books USA Inc.

First Printing, May, 1994
10 9 8 7 6 5 4 3 2 1

For Clifford,

who in another age, would
have been among the roydamna

ACKNOWLEDGMENTS

To Barbara Wedgwood, Ph.D., and Ruth Nathan, I offer everlasting gratitude for having opened the gates. Audrey LaFehr has won my affection and respect for her clear-eyed, professional criticism. I stand in awe at the depth of her understanding. This is a better book because of her gentle guidance. Others who read the manuscript and offered helpful suggestions were: Don Goldman; Sid Harris; Don Harper; Chris Molsen; Margaret Richards; Alice Shepperd; Sally Kemp; Jean Sudderth; and Kate Willis. They continue to be my mainstays.

I owe much to my husband, Cliff, whose idea it was to go to Ireland . . . the first time. His support and encouragement for a book about the ancient land of my fathers has never lagged. He understands better than I, both the intricacies of my psyche and the computer. He, Margaret Cain, and George Cudworth provided the technical expertise I lack. Literally, I could not have done it without them.

I am grateful to the inspired teachers whose influence was far greater than most of them knew. Two are now departed from this life, but cannot go unmentioned: my mother, Lorna, who read literature and poetry to me as bedtime stories; and Bill Schmelzle, the best city editor a reporter ever had. The academics whose words and examples went deep are: Harriet Breeding; Joy Wilson, Ph.D.; and Fr. John Madden. The thing they all had in common was a love for the written word. They convinced me of its power.

No list of acknowledgments about a book based on an Irish myth would be complete without a nod to my Celtic forebears who bequeathed the genetic memory that was set aflame within hours of my first visit to the glorious, green island of Innis Ealga. The unselfish loan by Joe and Hazel Hickey of an heirloom volume on the history of Ireland gave me the framework I was looking for by making Lugh live for me.

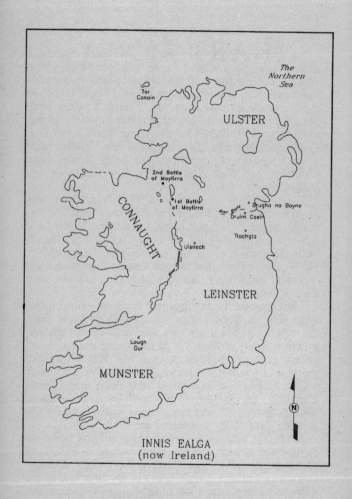

The Northern Sea

Tor
Conain

ULSTER

2nd Battle
of Moytirra

CONNAUGHT

1st Battle
of Moytirra

River Boyne Brugha na Boyne

Druim Caein

Tlachgta

Uisnech

River Shannon

LEINSTER

Lough
Gur

MUNSTER

N

INNIS EALGA
(now Ireland)

PART ONE

Then came the wise Tuatha DeDanaan
concealed in black clouds from their foe.
I feasted with them near the Shannon,
though that was a long time ago ...

—From a 1913 ballad sheet,
author unknown

Chapter One

Lugh was still breathing hard from the exertion of the hurling contest when he entered the forest and made his way to the clearing. He had reverence for the serenity he found in this beautiful glade where oaks towered overhead, their leaves trembling with birdsong, and he had need of serenity now. A clear shallow brook tumbled over mossy stones, its banks clothed in a thick cover of grass that had been a brilliant green earlier in the year, but now, with the new year almost upon them, was going to yellow.

He loved this season of the year, when all nature was coming to fruition, as Aibel was. The image of her lithe young body as she ran to make the winning goal caused him to smile. He inhaled deeply and bent to pick up his undyed tunic where he had left it beside the stream. He dropped it over his head and fastened a finely crafted leather belt, from which hung a fes and a sheathed copper knife, around his narrow hips. He regarded his leg wrappings but decided against them since he was still much too warm from the hurling. He rolled the wrappings up and put them in his fes.

No jewelry adorned the young warrior's plain garments nor were there emblems to show that he was descended from royal houses; nothing to set him apart from the other young warriors he'd just left, yet Lugh was different and it was acknowledged indirectly by all of the Fir Bolg people.

His bearing was regal even as he dropped down on his belly to drink from the stream flowing gently on its way to the mighty Shannon. After his thirst was sated he continued to lie in the grass, enjoying the warmth of the autumn sun filtering through the oak leaves onto his back.

A few turnings of the moon earlier all of Lugh's

thoughts had been of hunting, games of skill, and other arts associated with becoming a champion warrior. Now his dreams of glory were mixed with thoughts of Aibel, leaving him confounded and delighted at the same time.

She was short, like every Fir Bolg, and when she reached up to pat his shoulder at the end of the contest he had seized the moment to slip his arm around her waist and draw her close to him. The touch of her body against his had inflamed him. He cupped his hands and splashed water on his face. By the gods! She was appealing.

Well, why not? he thought, *I have sixteen summers behind me now. I'm old enough to challenge a champion or take a wife, if I choose.* His thoughts drifted back to the look of Aibel as she ran down the field, coltlike, with her dark hair blowing in the wind.

Enormous brown eyes dominated her face, above a finely shaped nose and lips as pink and delicate as a flower bud. Lugh sighed. Lately she had been more quiet than usual, but he thought her beautiful in repose.

At length he rose to his knees, wiping the cool droplets from his well-defined mouth with the back of his hand, dreaming of the day he might be both the Champion of the Fir Bolg tribe, and Aibel's lover.

A twig cracked on the forest floor. The sound was barely audible but it caused every muscle in Lugh's young body to tense. His hand flew to his knife even as he sprang to safety behind the largest tree in the grove.

The sound of the intruder's approach grew louder. There was something about it that struck Lugh as strange. If it were one of the Fir Bolg tribe, he would recognize their step. And he knew the sound of the deer, even the wolves of the wood. No, there was something about these footfalls that baffled him. The gait was foreign to him, seemingly weightless.

He strained to see who, or what, approached under the canopy of trees. His breathing was shallow and he made no sound as an old man entered the clearing. Lugh thought the old fellow didn't look like a ferocious adversary, and his fingers loosened around the handle of the knife. He could see that the man carried no weapon.

The intruder's long hair was as white as new milk, tied back in a fashion unknown to Lugh. He was stooped with age and every step was a struggle. He wore a fine woolen cloak of green, bordered in needlework of red, green, yellow, and blue, stitched into concentric spirals and geometric designs.

Lugh quickly appraised the cloak and the white woolen tunic beneath it. His eyes lingered over a huge ornament of bronze that fastened the old man's garments. It was a magnificent circle that made Lugh think of the sun; he had never seen anything like it and did not recognize the metal from which it was made. A tiny sword pierced the cloth, securing it to a metal ring with patterns engraved on it similar to those on the cloak.

The stranger appeared to be a man of high degree. Scanning once more his lined face, Lugh was surprised by the youthful appearance of the old man's blue eyes. They did not suit his ancient face.

In one hand the man held a stout blackthorn stick that bore his weight. Slowly, and with much difficulty, he dragged himself to a fallen tree and lowered himself onto it, holding one leg straight out in front of him. He busied himself with loosening the leather bindings around his cloth leg wrappings.

Lugh watched in astonishment as the old man removed his left leg and laid it gently on the ground. The autumn sun sank lower in the afternoon sky, causing the light to dance on the leg in dappled patterns. The old man unfastened a horn cup from his belt and stretched to dip it into the stream. He drank his fill then closed his eyes to rest.

It seemed to Lugh a safe time to make his presence known, so he stepped from his hiding place, saying, "Hail, stranger. I am Lugh, son of Cian the DeDanaan and Ethne the Fomorian. I am foster son to Eochy and Tailteann, monarchs of the Fir Bolgs, and am rightly of these woods. Who are you and what is your business here?" He tried to sound authoritative and bold.

The old man was not startled by Lugh's sudden appearance. His lips curled into a smile even before he opened his eyes to look at the lad. His gaze spoke of familiarity.

"Hail to you, Lugh, son of Cian, foster son of Eochy. I am Diancecht, seer and chief physician to Nuad, king of the DeDanaans. It is right well I know you and well you will be knowing me before we are done."

Giving Lugh no time to respond, he continued, "You do not know King Nuad, but your fate and his are intertwined. Soon, his boats will land in the bay and you must prepare yourself for that time. The destiny that no man can escape is on you now and upon the Fir Bolg people.

"A great cloud of darkness will come over Innis Ealga, this noble isle. It will confuse the minds of the Fir Bolgs until the land has been taken from them. You are the man who will heal the wounds of the invasion and become our champion and our king. I charge you now, Lugh, to prepare yourself through study and deeds for the great day that awaits you. My words will stay in your heart until we meet again, although I must remove them from your mind for a while. When they are needed you will remember every detail of our meeting."

The old man raised his hand in a commanding gesture. His blue eyes riveted Lugh to the spot where he stood and paralyzed his speech. Lugh felt alarm and with all of his being tried to force his eyes away from the piercing blue stare that was fastened on him.

The old man saw him tense, struggling to move.

"No!" said the old man. "Stay. The time for sounding an alarm has long since passed. Look you to it. When the time comes you must mind the Stone of Destiny. Your place in time is secure. We will meet again . . . soon. Until then, keep my charge in your heart: You will be king."

So saying, the old man reached for his detached leg. His fingers caressed its hard surface. The sunlight faded and Lugh was aware of a soft mist curling upward through the trees. Suddenly the old man was gone. Inexplicably, Lugh had not seen him go.

He blinked hard and looked again, shivering and cursing in disbelief. How could the old man have departed unseen by him? He sheathed his knife and slowly made his way out of the woods to the field where moments before he had been playing games with his childhood companions.

Dark gray clouds rolled across the sky of Innis Ealga, blowing in from the vast western sea, and the air against Lugh's damp skin was as heavy as his thoughts. He walked along the familiar path toward the compound, unseeing and unaware, until he reached the top of the Hill of Knockadoon where he encountered Aibel, seated on the ground, her back against the stone wall of the compound, waiting for him.

"What's the matter, Lugh? You look strange. Are you all right?" she asked, hopping up to greet him.

He looked at her blankly. "All right? Yes. I'm all right."

"Oh. Well, you look different. I'm excited about the Samhain festival, aren't you? It's going to be such fun. I had only thirteen summers the last time we journeyed to Tlachgta to celebrate the new year and the harvest. I think it's going to be different this time, especially since I'm going to be the chief handmaiden to the priests."

She waited expectantly, hoping Lugh would offer her compliments for having been selected by the priests to assist them in the sacred ceremonies, but he offered none.

"Will you sit with me at the feast, Lugh?" she asked, lowering her eyes shyly, her long black lashes resting against her cheeks.

"I always sit with you and Rury at the feasts, don't I?" he said slowly. "You two are my best friends."

Without warning, lightning cracked overhead, illuminating a sky that had grown increasingly dark as she spoke. Huge raindrops fell, slowly at first then faster, and faster. The change in the weather seemed to bring Lugh to his senses and he grasped Aibel's hand, pulling her to her feet.

"Come on," he shouted over a clap of thunder that tore from the depths of the churning clouds. The sky over the settlement at Lough Gur was now as black as night, though the sun had not fully set. "We've got to get to shelter."

They ran into the fortified compound through a gateway in the circular stone wall, toward the safety of their hilltop village. Aibel's family lived in the center dwelling, always the home of the reigning champion, and she dashed inside, turning to wave good-bye to Lugh through the rain that was coming down in great, soaking torrents, driven by a hard wind.

Lugh ran across the packed earthen floor of the enclosure toward his own dwelling, sending up sheets of rainwater as his feet hit the puddles, all memory of the old man in the clearing erased from his mind.

Inside the royal dwelling Lugh's foster parents, King Eochy and Queen Tailteann, were deep in serious discussion. The small brown-haired queen protested to her husband of many years, "I know, I know, Eochy. It's just that the Fomorians are our kinsmen."

"It's more than that and you know it, Tailteann. You don't want us to force the issue of the broken treaty with them because Lugh's natural mother is a Fomorian."

Tailteann wanted to protest further, but Eochy was right. She looked up at him with her bright, black eyes pleading for understanding.

"We have had him for twelve turnings of the earth, twelve summers, my love, since he was but four! Since the gods have seen fit to send us no children of our own, I am certain that they gave us Lugh for a special reason. I don't know what it is, or why we were chosen, but you yourself have heard Ard and the other priests say it again and again. Lugh was sent among us for a purpose. How dare we take action that could jeopardize what the gods have planned?"

King Eochy, his patience tried, said, "My sweet wife, surely you can see that the last raid the Fomorians made upon the clan of the Fir Galian in the north of Innis Ealga cannot be tolerated. We have to answer them or we will not be worthy to call ourselves Fir Bolgs. An attack that vicious is not just against one of our clans, it's against every Fir Bolg, the whole tribe.

"When Lugh came to us, his fosterage was our best hope for a lasting peace. But the time has come to face the fact that all attempts at peace with the Fomorians end in failure and this one has, too. If such a fosterage between us, involving the king of the Fir Bolgs, and Lugh, the grandson of the Fomorian king, has failed to secure peace, I ask you—what will?" He paused a moment, then answered his own question.

"No. The unprovoked raid upon the Fir Galians must be punished. I cannot permit my people to be attacked and killed. We will not continue to live in fear of marauding pirates who swoop down upon our coastal settlements at will, burning, looting, and raping. We are forced to strike back. When the council meets at Samhain I trust you will be with me on this."

He looked at her directly and her usually steady gaze fell beneath his challenge. She knew she must agree. The

Fomorians had to be stopped, even though Lugh was of Fomorian blood.

"I will be with you, as I always have been," she said at length. "I too, know that we must challenge the Fomorians. Since the time our tribe has lived on Innis Ealga they have been as a plague upon us, kinsmen or not. How I wish their island of Tor Conain were so far across the western seat that their curraghs could never reach us! But, husband, I fear for Lugh in the coming conflict. I cannot help it. I love him so."

The fire in the center of the round house burned brightly in spite of the hissing and snapping caused when the occasional raindrop came through the smoke hole in the thatched roof and splashed into the middle of the flames, yet the royal couple was oblivious to the storm that had blown up outside.

"I know, dear one," King Eochy said. "Let us not be at odds with one another. I love him, too." Tailteann came into her husband's arms, eager for the comfort she always found there, and laid her cheek, unpinked by ruam, against his strong chest. He lifted her chin with his fingers, and kissed her sweetly upon the lips.

"I love you with all my being, Tailteann. I pledge to you that I will do all in my power to protect our foster son, even as I must do all within my power to protect our tribe against the threat from the Fomorians."

"I know you will, and I will be by your side to help." She smiled at him, glad the disagreement was behind them.

Lugh burst into the royal dwelling and struggled against the wind to pull the door shut. For a moment he was blinded by the smoke and steam rising from the fire, then he saw his foster parents who pulled apart when he entered. Queen Tailteann put her hand on the king's sleeve, a silent warning to say nothing of their discussion to Lugh, then turned to their son.

"Come in, darling, and sit down. Let's dry you off and get you some hot broth. You are soaked through."

Lugh submitted easily to the ministrations of his foster mother, more like a boy than a champion of the Fir Bolgs. Both he and King Eochy watched Queen Tailteann with admiration as she bustled about getting dry clothes for Lugh and preparing food for him.

She was a small, dark woman in her early thirties, with black eyes and a long aquiline nose that bespoke her Iberian heritage. She had extremely dainty hands. Lugh had always loved the small white moons of her nails and the lovely pattern they made where they met her tawny skin, so unlike his own fair skin.

This evening she wore a tunic that had been dyed in a mixture of seaweed and lichen, until it was the rich purple of royalty. Her cloak had been embroidered by her women with designs of gold. The queen moved quietly around the dwelling, unaware that the men in her family thought her so extraordinarily beautiful.

She put her arm around Lugh to help him out of his wet clothing and he could smell her skin, sweetened by the oils and herbs of that day's bath. How dear and comfortable her scent was to him.

"Put these on," she said, offering him a warm woolen tunic and shoes lined with rabbit's fur. He sat down on a stack of furs piled near the fire to luxuriate in the warmth of his home and the presence of the two people he loved most on this earth. As he ate the bread and the barley soup Tailteann brought him, he had the nagging thought that he had something very important to tell them but for the life of him, he could not think what it was.

He turned to the king. "Father," he said, for he had long called this beloved king father, "something is wrong. Today I was running to the stream for a drink. It was hot, and we had just won the hurling contest. Something happened there . . . I know it . . . but I can't remember what it was. When this terrible storm blew up out of nowhere, I knew I had to get to you. I had to tell you something, to warn you, to . . . Oh! I don't know!" he cried, growing agitated, "Mother! Father! Something awful is going to happen. I know it!"

King Eochy and Tailteann were puzzled by his words. Only they and a few of the trusted council members knew of the seriousness of the latest conflict with the Fomorians. But Lugh? There was no way he could possibly know of the danger. What could he be talking about?

"You probably fell asleep by the stream for a moment and had a bad dream," the king said soothingly.

"That's exactly what happened," Tailteann said. "Don't worry about it. If it is important you'll remember what it is tomorrow, after a good night's sleep. That's always how these things work out. Come on now, into bed with you. Rain or shine, you know we'll all be up with the first rays of the Sun God to begin our journey to Tlachgta."

He let Tailteann lead him to his bed next to the outer wall of the house, where the furs for sleeping were piled high. He crawled into their midst and smiled at her as she pulled them up to his chin.

"Good night, sweet Lugh, may the Moon Goddess protect you while you sleep," Tailteann said, bending to kiss his still damp curls.

"Good night, Mother. Good night, Father. I love you," he said and turned his face away from his foster parents and the glow of the fire. The fearsome wind had stopped its howling and the rain beat down against the thatch in a steady drone as he tried once more, weakly, to remember what it was he wanted to tell them. Images of Aibel's smiling face and wondrous body soon pushed all worry from his mind as he burrowed into the furs.

The fury of the storm ended near midnight and the sudden silence awakened King Eochy. In the orange glow of the fire's embers he could see that Lugh was sleeping soundly, so he reached for Tailteann who came to him sleepily. He had need for communion with her body and her spirit. The decision he must make at the Samhain gathering was the kind all leaders dread; some of his people would suffer, even die, no matter which course of action he chose.

Lugh awoke as the first rays of the Sun God peered over the eastern horizon, all feelings of dread cleansed from his mind. His first thought was that this was the day the tribe would begin to trek to Tlachgta for the celebration of Samhain, the first and most sacred day of the new year. Who could guess what adventures might be lying in wait for him? He arose and crept across the dwelling, silently coaxed the door open, and stopped outside the royal house, full of excited anticipation for what the day would bring.

A large gray wolfhound lying next to the door stirred, with a growl trembling in his throat, but when he recognized Lugh the watchdog wagged his tail a few times, thought better of getting up, and curled lazily back into his sleeping position. Lugh grinned and stretched, emitting a slight groan. He shook his tousled curls and looked down over the settlement that was still shrouded in the last shadows of the retreating night.

From the royal vantage point on top of Knockadoon, the highest hill at Lough Gur, it was possible to see for miles in every direction. A fine mist rose from the surface of the lake at the base of the hill. The pasturelands on the hillsides were covered with thick, green grass. Neat, gray stone walls crisscrossed the fields, holding the dun-colored cows inside their boundaries. The beasts kept their heads down, moving slowly across the meadows, intent on their feeding. *Ah, it's a beautiful place I live in,* Lugh thought. *I love my home.*

The faintest suggestion of reds and oranges in the woods accented the many shades of green that lay before him. The fields to his left were a pale yellow, shorn now of their precious harvest of wheat, barley, and oats, yet still a heart-warming sign of the bounty the harvests had brought to the Fir Bolgs, proof of King Eochy's fitness to reign.

The fullness of the earth caused Lugh to think once more of Aibel. Just two days earlier he had eaten with her and Rury near the filach fiadah, the cooking pit. Both lads noticed with pleasure how the bodice of her tunic curved around her breasts. When she rose to go she had jostled Lugh's knee, and he caught the scent of her hair as she leaned down to apologize. The memory of it caused a pleasurable stirring in his body.

He knew about physical love between men and women. Like other young Fir Bolgs who lived in one-room dwellings with their parents, he had always known, but the yearning to experience such love for himself grew daily until he wondered how much longer it would have to be denied. He wanted desperately to find a way to be alone with Aibel at the festival. He thought it was a great nuisance how his friend Rury, like one of the village dogs, was always at his heels. He hoped there would be many things at Tlachgta to distract him.

Lugh heard his parents moving about inside their dwelling and realized that wisps of smoke had begun to curl up from houses across the hillside, as the settlement stirred to life. His excitement rose as he ran down the hill, eager to make his water and return to help load the carts for the journey. As he ran, he thought that this might be the year he won a championship. He had a good chance in the javelin events. Even King Eochy said so.

Rury hailed Lugh as he started back up the hill. "It's a grand day for the journey to start, isn't it, Lugh?"

In a friendly tone, Lugh said, "Yes. I can't wait to get going. I think the four days we spend getting to Tlachgta are almost as much fun as the festival itself."

"Me, too! But then, by the time the Hill of Athboy is in sight, I'm always glad the journey is almost over because I know we will soon see the other clans and catch up on all the news from around the island. Do you remember that girl we met last year from the Fir Dolman clan? The one with the heart-shaped face? I wonder if she'll remember me."

His earnestness amused Lugh. "Why wouldn't she, Rury? Aren't you one of the grandest lads on all of Innis Ealga?"

Rury blushed up to his hairline. He never knew how to take Lugh's jests; was never sure in fact, when Lugh was jesting and when he wasn't.

"I'm one of the firstlings this year," he volunteered nervously, his thick black eyebrows knitting into a frown.

"I know," Lugh answered. "I wish I could take part in the ceremony with you and the others, but because I'm fostered, I can't. Too bad, too, because Aibel is going to be the chief handmaiden to the priests." He laughed. "I wouldn't mind having her be chief handmaiden to me!"

The chief priest of the Fir Bolg tribe was Ard, Rury's father. Because of it, Rury was only too aware that Aibel had been chosen to be first among the handmaidens.

"Her selection has caused trouble enough at my dwelling," he said ruefully. "Mother has been furious with my father because my sister wasn't chosen for the honor. She says Aibel's father forced the priests to choose her. I don't know if that's true or not, because even I can see that Aibel is a perfect choice."

Lugh thought Srang, Aibel's father, was fully capable of pressuring the priests, but he thought it better to say nothing about the selection process since he found Rury's sister, Uln, to be plain and slow witted.

Rury went on. "I'd like Aibel to serve me too, I guess.

She is the prettiest girl at Lough Gur. Father said that all of the priests agreed on the choice for this year, the first time such agreement has happened since he became chief priest."

They walked a short distance and Rury said, "Father arose before dawn today to start the dousing of all the fires in the dwellings."

Lugh nodded. Yesterday the servants had brushed the earthen floors of the royal dwelling, patted them down with water, and changed the bedding straw under the furs. He had been cross about being detained by the chore of carrying out the household rubbish.

"I had to help get the royal dwelling ready yesterday," Lugh said. "That's why I was late to the hurling contest. What a bother it all is! It seems to me the only reason the fires need dousing is so the dwellings won't burn down while we are away at the celebration."

Rury looked at him askance. "You shouldn't say things like that, Lugh. Father says it is important for every fire to be completely extinguished, so that the resulting dark and cold of our dwellings will resemble the colder, shorter days that are about to come to Innis Ealga when the Sun God turns his face away from us for the winter."

"I know, Rury, but you've got to admit there are some practical aspects to what your father and the other priests do."

Lugh saw the dismay his irreverent words caused Rury and relented a little. "I do like knowing that when we return, every fire on this island will be relit with coals from the Samhain fire. It is kind of like having the God of the Sun with us all winter."

Rury brightened, relieved that Lugh could see the importance of the fire rituals.

"How long do you think it is going to take for the priests to finish the dousing, so we can get underway?" Lugh asked.

"I don't know. I hate it when the carts are loaded, and the animals are restless, and we have to wait for the priests to finish with every last house at Lough Gur, but we haven't a choice," Rury answered. "It must be done."

"I guess so," Lugh answered, though not as accepting as his friend of the tribe's strict adherence to tradition.

Suddenly, Rury blurted out, "I tried to block Aibel's

liathroid yesterday in the match, but she is so fast that she struck the winning blow before I even saw her coming."

His tone was tinged with surprise and more than a little shame. He was so good at defending the goal that he seldom got to play any other position and he had been deeply embarrassed when her ball flew past him so easily. He wanted Lugh to think well of him.

Lugh looked at his friend who was much shorter than himself and stockier. Rury had heavy, strong shoulders atop a chunky torso. His legs and arms were short but his biceps bulged beneath the sleeves of his tunic. He was as strong as a bull and occasionally bested Lugh when they wrestled. His skin was dark, less so than Aibel's, and unruly brown hair hung over his high, flat forehead.

"Don't worry about it, Rury, no one would have been able to defend against that shot. Aibel is fast all right," Lugh said, "but I hope she's not so fast that she can get away from me in the woods." He lowered his voice confidentially. "I think it's time for her to lose her maidenhood and I intend to be the one to help her do it." He grinned at his friend.

Rury's brown eyes grew wide with alarm. "But, Lugh," he protested, "you can't. She is the chief handmaiden to the priests. You know she has been sanctified as a virgin. You dare not to touch her."

"Oh, don't be foolish, Rury. We go to Tlachgta to celebrate the harvest and give thanks to the gods for their benevolence. I don't see how the gods can be offended if I harvest what they have ripened, do you?"

Rury thought Lugh's words might possibly make sense, but he was not fully convinced. Not only was Aibel now a holy woman, she and Lugh were from the same clan and such matings were not permitted unless priests had spoken holy words in the clearings, words that bound men and women together for all time.

"Well . . . I don't know, Lugh. It seems like a dangerous thing to do to me. What will happen if you anger the gods? I think you'd better be very careful; you know how vengeful they can be when mortals overstep their bounds."

Lugh chuckled at his friend's seriousness, and clapped him on the shoulder as they moved to start the loading.

Chapter Two

Far out on the Northern Sea a fleet of hide-covered curraghs skimmed over icy waves toward the lost homeland of the DeDanaan tribe, the island of Innis Ealga. The royal curragh bearing Nuad, king of the DeDanaans, was three lengths in front of all the other dark boats moving across the sea in the predawn hours.

Dagda Mor, the wisest of all the tribe, was awake wishing he were not. It was a hard crossing for an old man even though so far, all had gone extremely well.

Much more than the voyage was on his mind; he was concerned about the settlement of the island. The DeDanaan ancestors had been forced to flee from Innis Ealga many generations before by the pirate Fomorian tribe, a people feared throughout the northern climes. In the DeDanaans' long absence a small tribe, known as the Fir Bolgs, or Men of the Bag, had populated parts of the island.

Unlike Nuad, his king, Dagda had no taste for war. He lay awake thinking of ways the DeDanaan and Fir Bolg tribes might be able to share Innis Ealga. He had given King Nuad the benefit of his counsel on the wisdom of sharing the island but had been rebuffed.

He looked to the rear of the craft where the tall, blond king slept in the embrace of his lover, Morrigan. They were a fine-looking pair and deserving of one another. Morrigan was one who took all life could offer, just as Nuad did. He wondered if he might enlist her in his efforts to convince the king to seek a peaceful sharing of Innis Ealga. Surely she did not relish a battle that could wound or kill her king and lover.

Dagda moved his great girth laboriously and tried to sit up a little straighter in the rolling craft. The square leather sails were up and full of wind, obscuring Dagda's view of the captain, Mannon Mac Lir, but he knew he was at the helm steering the DeDanaans ever onward because it had been the sound of Mac Lir's voice that awakened him. Dagda wondered to whom he had been speaking. He closed his eyes again, and pulled his cloak under his chin. He would be happy to be on dry land once more. The life of a seaman with its meager rations was not for him. He went back to sleep thinking of winning arguments he might make before the king tomorrow.

As dawn spread its mantle of gold over the heaving, white-tipped waves, King Nuad slept fitfully, disturbed by dreams of his ancestors and the oath he had sworn before he and his tribe had set out to sea:

By the Sun and the Moon, water and air,
night and day, sea and land,
I swear that I will lead the people of Danu
to a home on the island of Innis Ealga.
My sword will be strong, my faith will not falter,
and I will lean upon the goodness of the gods.

The words echoed in his dream as the figure of his grandfather, a man he had loved especially well, came to his mind, "Your duty, Nuad? Have you done it?"

The king replied humbly, "As we speak, Grandfather, I do my duty. I am taking our tribe to the ancient homeland as you told me I must do. The prophecy of our destiny will soon be fulfilled. I vow to you that no Fomorian, nor any other living creature, will ever drive the DeDanaans from Innis Ealga again."

The aged apparition nodded and placed his hand on Nuad's shoulder in blessing and absolution, smiling his approval.

"Nuad, my love, awaken. You're dreaming." Morrigan shook him again. "Nuad, the dawn has come. Wake up."

He opened his eyes and was surprised to see that the hand on his shoulder was that of his beautiful mistress and not that of his dead grandfather. He rubbed his eyes and shook his head to clear away his confusion.

"Yes," he said to her at last, and brushed his fair hair from his eyes. "It felt like my grandfather was here, not like a dream at all."

Morrigan smiled the broad smile that so delighted him. "Who is to say that he was not here, my love? The gods have many ways of communicating with us. Surely, the importance of this voyage, when we are destined to see Innis Ealga for the first time, is so great that the gods may well have sent him into your mind."

"Indeed, perhaps they did." He smiled at her and pulled her to him for a morning kiss, fully awake.

Two summers had passed since Nuad's queen died giving birth to their stillborn child. Since that time he had sought comfort with several of the DeDanaan women, but none had pleased him and turned his gaze toward the future as Morrigan had. He found her enchanting and when he looked at her in the early morning light with a fine mist spraying over the curragh as it cut through the waters, his heart swelled at her great beauty.

She was tall and slim with auburn hair that hung almost to her waist. This morning, it was bound back with narrow leather thongs to keep it from blowing in the breeze. Her eyes were large, spaced far apart, and were a deep brown, like the damp earth of a newly turned furrow. Her cheekbones were high, set in a face of flawless ivory.

Nuad raised his hand and with his forefinger, traced the outline of her lips. Her mouth was large, some jealous women said too large, but to him her lips were sensuous and inviting, not to be resisted. He kissed her again.

When he released her, she spread her crimson cloak over both of them as a shield from the mist. Nuad put his arms around her and said, "When I was a lad, my grandfather loved to tell the story of how our people settled on Innis Ealga. He said they came from a place called Macedon, in a time so long ago that no man living can remember where to find it. From the cities of Galias, Gorias, Murias, and Findias, the old ones brought lore unknown to all other men: science and the magical arts."

"It's well I know that," Morrigan said with a laugh, "for my father and his grandfather before him were heirs to the knowledge of the magical arts. Father told me many times how your grandfather took delight in the conjuring tricks my grandfather could do. He said he called him before him frequently ... for private audiences as well as before royal gatherings."

Nuad laughed. "My grandfather was a great one for the magic. Wouldn't it be a marvel if the old ones, all those who have gone before, could be with us now? I'd like them to know that I, Nuad, king of the DeDanaans, am about to restore us to our rightful place upon the earth."

Morrigan smiled knowingly. "They will have such knowledge, Nuad. I'm sure of it. The gods are good." She could not yet tell him how she had such certainty. Perhaps one day she would reveal her powers, but the right time had not yet come.

He sat up and stretched in the salt breeze, his mind turning to the challenge that lay ahead. It caused a thrill of anticipation to pass through him. He loved challenges, even when it meant battle . . . especially when it meant battle. The unknown delighted him and the thought of conquering the Fir Bolg tribe that had taken over Innis Ealga in the DeDanaans' absence aroused all of his senses and set his blood racing.

He looked around him on the open sea at the fleet of curraghs sailing behind the royal craft, and was pleased by what he saw. The livestock was enduring their ordeal well, the people were beset only by seasickness and discomfort, ailments that would soon be at an end, and the gods had kept storms from their path.

"By the gods! What a grand day this is going to be!" he declared.

Morrigan smiled. "You're right about that, my love, a grand day indeed." The full face of the Sun God, rising higher and higher over the horizon in the direction from which they had come, was welcome.

"Brig!" Nuad shouted to his slave. "Bring the razor!"

"No," Morrigan said playfully, "let me. I want to prepare your face for the gods this day."

She stroked his strong jawline, cleft almost in two at the chin by a deep crease. It was covered with coarse stubble of the same golden red shade as his hair. His eyes were as blue as the sky overhead and were fringed with thick golden lashes. Lines from his thirty-two years had collected at their corners, etched there by frequent laughter, and squinting into the sun and wind.

"You, yourself are surely the work of the gods, my love, for there is no mortal man alive as fine as yourself," Morrigan whispered, guiding his hand under her cloak to her breast, so the others in the open boat could not see. He loved this kind of frankness in her, and grinned his appreciation of it.

Brig made his way over the passengers jammed into the narrow confines of the curragh, toward the place where his king slept in the stern. Dagda awoke and grumbled when the boat rocked and Brig stepped on his outstretched foot. "By the gods, man! Can't a person sleep without being trod upon like the path to the alehouse? Be careful."

"Sorry, Dagda Mor," Brig replied, placing his foot gingerly on the other side of the wise man's great bulk. The exchange was witnessed by Gobinu, the smith, who smiled sympathetically at Brig. Everyone knew that Dagda's wrath was not to be taken seriously. The spirit inside the man was as large as the body that housed it.

"Shall I shave you now, sire?" Brig asked as he reached the king.

"No, Brig. I've decided to give my lady the honor on this special day the gods have sent us," Nuad replied, unaware of the dark look Brig shot toward Morrigan, who returned it with an indifferent stare of her own.

Brig handed her the wide-mouthed clay jar full of fresh water that had hung around his neck, without hiding his jealousy. He reached into his leather fes and removed a honed bronze razor. "Be careful, my lady," he warned, "the blade is very sharp."

Morrigan took the implement. "I am skilled in handling weapons. I believe I will be able to use a barber's razor without incident," she said coldly.

Nuad addressed Brig. "See how the boats behind us lie low in the water, heavily loaded and ready to land! Before the god of light leaves the sky this day our tribe will have a home and our wanderings will be over. It's a grand day, Brig, a grand day indeed!"

"Aye, my lord. You have brought us safely over the waters from the northern climes of Lochland and it's grateful we are to the gods for your leadership." He bowed.

This time Nuad saw the look of disgust on Morrigan's face. He knew she hated toadying, even from slaves, because it was so alien to her own strong, independent nature.

"Bring us food and drink when the shaving is done," he ordered and watched as Brig awkwardly made his way to the front of the boat where the captain of the fleet, Mannon Mac Lir, stood peering intently at the horizon.

King Nuad liked his chief seaman. "Mac Lir is the finest sailor our tribe has ever known," he said to Morrigan, as she dipped the razor in the jar. "I think he's a finer sailor than his father, although some of the elders dispute that. I was well pleased with the way he undertook the building of this fleet during our seven years' sojourn in the northlands."

"Yes, my darling, he is a fine sailor, but you're going to have to stop talking or you will go before the gods on Innis Ealga with bits of seaweed all over your face to stem the bleeding from the places where I am about to cut you." Morrigan laughed and with a steady hand, finished the task of removing Nuad's whiskers.

Dagda felt out of sorts. He did not like having been awakened twice; he was worried about the tribe's future, and he was suspicious that his adored daughter was angry with him.

He had tried several times to get Brigid's attention, but she never seemed to see him when he waved to her. It had made sense to him to put all three of his children in boats other than the one in which he sailed. That way, his line could be assured of continuation even if tragedy were to befall one of them. Brigid had not liked the idea but he insisted. Now she was pouting.

"Mac Lir!" he shouted. "Mac Lir!"

The hunky seaman with the red curls turned his attention to the wise man. "Good morning, Dagda Mor. And how are you on this fine morning?"

"Poorly, very poorly," the wise man replied. "Do you think you could slow this damned curragh down enough for Cian to bring his boat alongside? My Brigid is one of his passengers, and you know the seasickness overwhelmed the lass on the first day of our journey."

Mac Lir was a kindly man but a sailor above all else. He paused to consider how much such an action might slow the progress of the fleet.

"I'll do it for you, Dagda, but your chance to speak with her will have to be brief. I have good news for the king this morning." Mac Lir smiled at Dagda while reaching for the ropes to loosen the sail.

Cian, eldest son of the tribe's renowned healer, Diancecht, sailed his craft alongside the royal curragh. "Hail friend!" Cian called to Mac Lir. "Is this to be the day we reach our home?"

"By the gods' will, it is!" Mac Lir exclaimed. "The advance scouts came before the Sun God arose. They have sighted Innis Ealga and say that we should be standing upon the ancient sod before the rising of the Moon Goddess."

"Ah, may the gods be praised," Cian said.

From her place in the back of Cian's curragh, where she was squeezed between crates of wood fowl and frightened hares, Brigid closed her eyes and tried to imagine herself as beautiful as the sisters, Macha and Neimain, who sat across from her, stretching lazily awake, like kittens in the sun. The priests taught that envy was evil, but she could not help herself; she would have given anything to be as beautiful as they were.

Throughout the voyage she had seen how Breas, the handsome blond warrior, looked at them and the raw desire she saw on his face stung her to the quick, knowing he would never look at her like that. She was miserable, and feeling seasick. She opened her eyes when she heard Cian hail Mac Lir. She could see her father in the king's curragh, and it made her angry all over again.

She had agreed with his plan to separate the family before they set sail, but as her misery intensified she had grown more and more angry with her father for his desertion.

When the sickness came, she was too ill to care, but later it was humiliating to know that the handsome Breas had been witness to her fate. She wished the sisters could know what it felt like, just once, to be as sick and miserable as she was. She directed her angry stare toward Dagda, who stood up and waved to her, calling out something she was unable to hear over the wind and the splash of the waves. She turned her head away, pretending not to notice, and closed her eyes again.

* * *

After the first meal of the day many DeDanaan passengers aboard the royal curragh had occasion to complain about being trod upon as Dagda dragged himself the length of the lurching craft toward the king. He squashed a foot here, a hand there, apologizing as he stumbled across them.

At last he reached King Nuad. "My lord"—he panted, out of breath from the exertion—"if I had nourishment enough for this great body, I might have been able to traverse this craft with more agility, but alas, rations are pitifully small and it is a famished man you see before you."

Dagda wore a heavy woolen cloak of deep brown, held at the shoulder by a beautifully engraved circlet of bronze with a red stone centered on top, just where the sword-shaped pin passed through it into the wool. The cloak barely covered his brawn.

"Have the scouts reported while I slept?" Nuan asked.

"Yes, sire. They came alongside just before the Sun God rose over the eastern horizon. They brought fresh water and good news. They have gone ashore and say there are many Fir Bolgs gathering near the Hill of Athboy about a day's walk from the bay where we will put in this afternoon. The Fir Bolg king and all of his clan chieftains will be there to celebrate the new year. A shepherd boy the scouts met told them that the Fir Bolgs count the new year from Samhain forward just as we do, and that they use this festival time to make laws and levy taxes, as well as to honor the gods. It seem propitious that our landing coincides with one of their festival gatherings."

The news of an imminent confrontation was greatly pleasing to the king. He liked the charge of two opposing forces, the clang of sword upon shield, and the sheer power of his body pitted against that of another warrior.

He had many scars that he wore proudly, scars that Morrigan, too, viewed as badges of honor. He remembered each with perfect clarity, not the blood and the pain, but the exhilarating details of the particular engagement that had left the mark on his fair skin.

The wise man understood Nuad well. He knew battle lust would inflame the king when he heard the news of the Fir Bolg festival. His own powers of persuasion were needed, as they frequently were, to cool the king's aggression.

Dagda spoke more loudly. "My lord, it bodes well that our landing coincides with the festival gathering of the Fir Bolgs. We may settle Innis Ealga peaceably."

Nuad could not keep the disappointment from his face. "Damn it to all the gods! I told you that's not what I want to do!" he said, raising his voice. "I'm not going to share land that is *ours*."

"I know, my lord," Dagda said, trying to remain patient, "but negotiation is the more prudent way." He glanced over at Morrigan, whose eyes were fastened intently on the king's face. Her smile looked more like a smirk to Dagda, and he could see there would be no help for his position from her. He sighed. He was going to have to reach deeply into his bag of diplomatic tricks to avoid the unnecessary spilling of his kinsmen's blood.

Chapter Three

The earth of Tlachgta steamed and a heavy, oppressive mist hung just beneath the oak trees, hugging the breast of the hill. From where they stood outside the royal hut, King Eochy and Queen Tailteann could see faint tinges of orange in the eastern sky, where gray clouds separated and tumbled on in a furious journey toward the sea, east of the Hill of Athboy.

They surveyed the holy festival site of the Fir Bolgs. All was still, but they knew the calm would soon shatter into a brilliant explosion of ceremony and ritual. King Eochy had his arm protectively about his queen who was shivering slightly in the dampness of the early hour. Both were dressed in their second-best ceremonial costumes. The finest royal garb was reserved for the rite of the forest; tonight, when the dark side of the god must be appeased.

King Eochy's cloak was a rich, deep purple, embellished by the most nimble fingers among the sewing women, and it fell to his boot tops. Under it he wore a newly made tunic of pure white wool, bleached for many days under the watchful eye of the Sun God. The king was a short, squarely built man, of great strength. He wore a neatly trimmed black beard, shaded now by areas of gray on either side of his chin. His eyes were dark brown and alert, set beneath bushy, black eyebrows. His hair was still a deep black but for a streak of gray on the left side of his hairline.

Queen Tailteann was dressed almost identically to him, but her cloak was crimson. Around their necks they wore golden torcs that had been formed into exquisite rams' heads where they met in the center. Bracelets of heavy gold, embossed with holy symbols, adorned their arms; Eochy's bore a large jewel of amber that had been purchased from a Phoenician trader by his father many years before.

When the queen looked at her husband, so handsome in his finery, she felt anew the love that had been born in this very festival site, so many years before.

"It was on such a day as this that we first met, Eochy. Do you remember?"

"How could a man forget a thing like that?" he asked, his mind rushing back to his youth. "Surely, the gods had our fates firmly in hand on that day. There could have been no other woman on the face of the earth for me, and I knew it the minute I laid eyes on you."

He put his face in her black hair, and nuzzled her, in the way parents touch a newborn child, with great tenderness, even awe.

She kissed his cheek.

"I knew it, too. I could feel your presence, feel you looking at me, even before our eyes met across the sacred clearing. I thought you were the most handsome man I had ever seen. Then, when I got to know you, and realized that your spirit was even more beautiful, I would have moved the stars in the heavens to become your wife."

"The gods have certainly been good to us, Tailteann. Look around us. The harvests have been bountiful every year of my reign. The people are prosperous and happy, and if it were not for the Fomorians, all would be well with the tribe the gods have entrusted to my care." A shadow of concern flickered over his face.

"Oh, Eochy. Let us not dwell on the prospect of conflict with our enemies today. Let us enjoy the ceremonies and the feasting. The forest rite and tomorrow's council meeting will be time enough for the sorrows of man to be visited upon us, don't you think?"

"I do, indeed." He smiled at her lovingly, grateful for her insistence on the moment. He didn't want to think about the upcoming events, either.

He changed the subject. "The cleansing of the animals is always fun. I can't wait to see how Lugh performs on Anovaar! Let's awaken him now and give him his surprise."

"I think your generosity is going to make him a very happy lad, Eochy. He has admired that horse from the day it was foaled at Lough Gur. I'm sure he hasn't a glimmer of a thought that you intend to give it to him."

Holding hands like young lovers, the king and queen of the Fir Bolgs walked down the hillside path to the glade where Lugh and the other youngsters who were to take part in the cleansing ceremony had slept under the priests' supervision.

There was no need to awaken Lugh, who was so excited at the prospect of the early morning ceremony that he had arisen long before the first rays of the Sun God. He saw his foster parents coming down the path and ran to meet them.

His royal festival finery still lay neatly folded in his fes, and he wore a simple, roughly woven tunic, tied about the waist with a crude rope. The cleansing ceremony ruined the participant's garments, and his good clothes would be needed later, for the feasting.

"Here now, Lugh," said the queen, "where's your cloak? It's a damp, chilly morning. You must be cold."

"Don't worry about me, Mother," he said with a laugh. "I'm as excited as though a fire burned within me." He dropped his voice and confided in them. "I am pretty sure I can win the javelin contest this afternoon."

King Eochy smiled proudly. "You must face the javelin throwers from all the other clans, son, to say nothing of our champion, Srang."

"If the others have not improved a lot since last year, I know I can best them, for you are an excellent teacher, Father."

Lugh frowned. Srang was another matter. He was highly skilled and had been the champion of the Fir Bolgs so long that he had acquired an unshakable confidence in his own ability. Lugh understood that attitude was as important as physical skill in the throwing of javelins. A steady hand combined with a clear head and single-minded concentration were the marks of a champion. He knew he had the first two attributes but felt less certain about his ability to concentrate. Tailteann scolded him often for being impulsive.

It was ill fortune to have reached the age when he was eligible to compete for the championship at the same time his desire for Aibel had grown to a point that he could think of little else. It was an added complication that

Srang, the champion he wished to unseat, was Aibel's father.

He sighed and with a bravado he didn't quite feel, said, "I think I can outthrow Srang. I did it three times last week at home. He was really angry about it, too. Sometimes he isn't a very good sport."

Eochy let the remark go by, although he felt he ought to stand up for the tribe's champion. But he knew there was truth in the lad's words. "Lugh, come and walk with us to the place where the horses are stabled," he said. "We want to inspect them before the cleansing ceremony begins."

"I'd like that . . . I wish they'd let me take Anovaar. He's the best horse in the stable."

Lugh glanced sideways at his mother to see how she was taking his remark. He knew she thought Anovaar was too powerful an animal for him. Sometimes she treated him like a child, even now that he had sixteen summers and could be wed since he was considered a fully grown man. He smiled at King Eochy, grateful that he could always count on him to talk to Tailteann into allowing him to expand his boundaries. His foster father smiled back and put his arm around Lugh's broad shoulders. The small family walked the rest of the way to the horse pens in compatible silence.

The horses were restless, pawing at the ground, as if anticipating their part in the cleansing ceremony. Inside a small corral of sapling logs were the finest horses the Fir Bolgs owned. They had been carefully bred and cared for by the most experienced grooms to be ready for this day.

"There's Anovaar," Lugh cried. "Doesn't he look grand this morning? See how his coat shines! It's as white as a pearl! His eyes are so bright they look on fire."

The two-year-old stallion walked to the fence where Lugh stood and pushed his velvety nose over the top log so Lugh's hand could caress him. He shook his snowy mane and snorted a greeting. King Eochy and Queen Tailteann exchanged a knowing, delighted look.

"He acts as though you are his master, Lugh," the king said.

"No one will ever be the master of this stallion," Lugh

said admiringly. "A partner, maybe, but never a master." He patted the horse and leaned close to its face.

"He is yours, Lugh, a gift to celebrate your sixteenth summer. We want you to ride him in the cleansing ceremony this morning."

Lugh turned to his father. "Do you mean it, Father? You are giving Anovaar to me, not just for the ceremony?"

King Eochy nodded happily, delighted with the joy shining on Lugh's face. "I do mean it, indeed. If ever a horse was born to belong to you, my son, it is this animal. I know you will treat him well. You must spend a lot of time with him, training him, working with him, if he is to become truly your steed, but I think you can handle him well enough to take him through the ceremony."

Lugh threw his arms around his father. "Oh, thank you! Thank you! I won't let you or Anovaar down. I promise!"

He turned to Queen Tailteann. "You won't be sorry, Mother. I will be careful."

"I am sure of that, Lugh. I trust you not to be foolish. May you always ride this fine horse in joy."

She hugged him, with a prayer to the gods forming in her mind for protection for her son. *Give him the strength of a man and the wisdom of a seer as he rides forth over the green hills of Innis Ealga, and always bring him home safely to his father and me.*

She reached out for her husband's hand at the same moment he reached for hers. Their eyes bespoke the deep love they held for each other and for their son. Queen Tailteann was thankful that Lugh was fostered and wouldn't be among the firstlings in the forest rite. She took a deep breath and willed herself not to think of all the other dangers he would face.

Timing was everything in the purification ceremony that had to begin when the Sun God was barely above the horizon and had to be finished before he was straight overhead.

Only unblemished animals, properly purified, could ensure the god's favor. All the clans of the Fir Bolgs would be assured of the fertility of their livestock in the new year if the ceremony went smoothly.

The high priest, Ard, felt a tingle of excitement as a

lesser priest offered him a heavily carved stone chalice filled with the holy drink of fermented wheat, honey, and sweet water drawn from the spring at the necropolis of Parthenon's people. He drank deeply from it.

When he was sated, he raised a priestly scepter of ornately carved oak high above his head with powerful arms clad in heavy copper bracelets. He waited until the eye of every assembled Fir Bolg was on him, then turned and with a firm step walked into the choppy dark waters of the lake just as the Sun God arrived at Tlachgta in his full glory.

The drummers started a slow roll on their leather bodhrans. The priest was aware of the rustle of the wind in the trees and the splash of lake water against the shore, as he waded out to his place.

Ard turned to face the people. "COME ATTEND US NOW GREAT CHROM CRUIC!" he commanded, calling forth the god who dwelt within a great stone likeness carved by the hands of Fir Bolg artisans.

Two lesser priests waded out to where Ard stood, carrying the covered form of Chrom Cruic on a small wooden platform. The idol was draped with a cloth dyed a bright saffron yellow and embroidered with solar discs of scarlet.

When the priests stopped before him, Ard lowered his mighty arms and seized the cloth dramatically. The people gasped in wonder when the gold-plated god's shining form was revealed. Ard prayed to Chrom Cruic, then invited the people to worship the great Sun God with song and rejoicing. The drummers were joined by other musicians playing reed whistles and copper horns. Suddenly, the air was alive with gaiety and the solemnity of the priest's earlier demeanor was swallowed up by the music and the sound of singing as hundreds of Fir Bolgs raised their voices to the god who had been good to them during the past year. They all knew how capricious he could be, and their gratitude at having been spared his wrath was genuine and heartfelt.

As the last strains of their joyful music faded away, the priests carried Chrom Cruic out of the lake and set him upon a tall platform constructed earlier on the lakeshore. He would be called upon again at the festival's closing ceremony in the woods when the dark side of his nature must be appeased. Until then, he would reign over the day's festivities from a place of honor.

Ard emerged from the lake and knelt before Chrom Cruic's platform and all the priests and people fell silently to their knees. With bowed heads they were left with their own prayers for a few minutes until Ard rose and shouted, "Let the day's events begin!"

With a whoop, the cowherds ran toward the pens where the cows were kept; shepherds ran for the sheep they had tended so lovingly in anticipation of this moment; and the boys who kept the pigs shouted at the others not to start without them.

"Let's go, Rury," Lugh called and the two lads laughed as they ran, Lugh toward his beautiful white horse, Anovaar, still scarcely able to believe that the animal was his. Rury was right behind him. He would ride a two-year-old mare with a gleaming chestnut coat, a fine animal but with none of the fire that was in Anovaar. When Rury heard about King Eochy's gift to Lugh, Rury had felt not jealousy, but pleasure that his friend had been so honored. He understood that Lugh and the stallion were well matched.

Aibel watched them go, jealous that she was to be left out of the fun. Being chief handmaiden was an honor, but she longed to participate in the games as she had in prior years. As Lugh and Rury disappeared from view around the curve of the lake, she heard voices inside her head for the first time. She looked around, startled, to see who had spoken.

They came again. *You can't trust Lugh,* they said in a chorus. *He cares no more for you than your father does because he too, can see your unworthiness.*

Her eyes filled with tears, the last unpleasant scene with her father fresh in her memory. All she had done was mention Lugh's name, and Srang had descended on her in a fury. He had not gone so far as to forbid her to sit with Lugh at the feast, for after all, Lugh was the son of the king. But he made it clear that if she pursued Lugh seriously, he would make life miserable for her inside the family dwelling. Sometimes she truly hated him.

The voices came again, this time from far away. She couldn't make out what they were saying. She raised her fists to her temples and pressed hard, as though trying to dislodge the voices.

"What is it, Aibel? Are you unwell?" Queen Tailteann asked with concern.

Aibel was surprised that she had been observed, for she felt as though she were alone in the world. "It is nothing, just a headache, my lady," she said, but the queen could see fear in the handmaiden's large forlorn eyes.

She slipped her arm around Aibel's shoulders. The queen had always been fond of the small girl whose intelligence shone through her dark eyes and illuminated her tiny face like a torch. Tailteann thought she understood why Aibel was unhappy. Srang was indeed a powerful warrior, but he was often unkind to his wife and children, and everyone at Lough Gur was aware of it. He had courted the wrath of the gods by being openly contemptuous of Aibel's high honor in being named chief handmaiden, even though there was gossip that he had pressured the priests into choosing his daughter. Tailteann felt sorry for her.

A din, enclosed within clouds of dust, heralded the arrival of the youngsters with the animals. There was much good-natured shouting and shoving as they prodded the beasts carefully with sticks smoothed by their own hands during the long hours they had watched over their domestic charges in the year gone by.

When they were assembled, Ard asked, "Have you all participated in other festival rites like this one?" "Yes! Yes! Many times," they all shouted at once.

Ard chose two of the oldest boys to start the cleansing rite. "You will lead the others," he said. "Pigs like to swim so you should not have any difficulty. Drive them to the point where they can just begin to paddle, then turn them to the right and circle back to shore. Keep them moving. The shepherds will be right behind you."

He then addressed the boys who would herd the cattle into the water, always the hardest part of the ceremony. Horses were obedient to the will of their riders but cattle were harder to persuade.

"Leave space between your herds and the sheep," he said. "Don't start until you see the signal from me. It is very important that each animal be cleansed in the moving waters. Do not drive them so deep into the lake that they become frightened. Let them enter slowly with no sudden movements from any of you, and stay with them! Don't let them veer off, not one, or we'll never get the horses through before the Sun God is directly overhead. Any questions? No? Let's go then."

Ard waved at the drummers. The loud roll captured the attention of the chattering assemblage. Shouting and laughter swelled into a crescendo as the crowd surged toward the water's edge. Children scampered away from their parents and jockeyed with one another for the best viewing positions.

After several minutes, the sound of the bodhrans faded away and in the silence all eyes turned expectantly toward Ard. He checked the sun's position in the sky once more, then turned to the herdsmen and gave the signal: "Purify the Beasts!" he shouted.

The youngsters drove the animals into the water with splashing and gleeful laughter. The horses pranced smartly in place, sensing their part in the drama. Anovaar shot ahead of the others and plunged in, the muscles of his mighty chest rippling as the icy waters flowed around it.

Lugh leaned over and spoke into his ear. "Easy, boy, easy. Just swim straight and strong to bring the god's favors down upon us. Sure, you are the grandest beast to enter these waters today. You bring me and my people good fortune."

Rury wanted to talk with Lugh but Anovaar was making it impossible. All of Lugh's attention had to be directed at the big white stallion whose bare back he gripped tightly with his knees. The horse's nostrils flared as he resisted Lugh's efforts to keep him under control.

"Hold on to him, Lugh," Rury said helpfully. "If he breaks away, all the horses will scatter."

"By the gods, Rury! What do you think I'm trying to do?" Lugh snapped and went on with the struggle.

With the entrance of wave after wave of animals, mud was churned up from the bottom of the lake, turning the waters into a brown, foaming froth. Frightened animals relieved themselves as they resisted the watery transit, so in the end, it took courage to enter the lake in search of

purification for the beasts. But the Fir Bolg boys perse-
vered, for they shared their tribe's belief that only in this
way could the wealth of their stock be sustained through
the dark months to come. All the while, Lugh fought to
achieve dominance over Anovaar.

Rury's heart was not in the transit he had to make in
the lake. His feelings were hurt and much of the fun inherent in the ceremony had been taken away by Lugh's
sharp retort to his encouraging words. He urged his horse
through the waters and noted that Lugh was far ahead of
all the others.

Long before Rury made his exit, Lugh and Anovaar
emerged from the lake, winded and dirty, both boy and
horse having performed superbly. As Anovaar sought secure footing on dry land, Lugh saw Aibel watching him.
He smiled and winked at her and felt again the now familiar tingle in his loins. Perhaps she would go with him
into the woods tonight, after the feasting was over, before
the rite of the forest. He prodded the white horse with his
heels and set off at a gallop to the place where he would
bathe and make himself ready for the games of combat
that were to come.

"Lugh, wait for me!" Rury called as he and the brown
mare clambered out of the water, but Lugh did not hear
him. Rury followed him, coughing from the dust kicked
up by Anovaar's hooves.

By early afternoon, there was no trace of the mist and
fog of morning, and the golden light of autumn poured
down like liquid amber on the festival site. A crush of Fir
Bolgs crowded around the level field where the triple
competition was to be held. Excited rumors circulated
that Lugh, foster son of the king, meant to challenge the
reigning champion in this, his first year of eligibility.

Srang strode nervously up and down the field, inspecting the javelins. He was angry. His stupid wife,
Lesru, never got anything right as he had been only too
glad to tell her while she helped him dress for the contest.
It's a good thing Aibel isn't as stupid as her mother, he
thought, *or she'd surely spoil the forest ceremony tonight
and bring shame upon my house.*

Slang believed that Aibel had been chosen chief handmaiden, partly for her comeliness, but mostly because of his own powerful influence. How dare that fool woman take him to task for ensuring that the so-called honor would come to the house of Srang! *Those priests,* he snorted, *they are as stupid as Lesru, only easier to bend to my will.*

He looked into the crowd for his daughter. Surely she would be here when he demonstrated his skill. He wanted her to see him show Lugh who the true champion of the Fir Bolgs was.

Srang saw Aibel coming down the path toward the field, holding hands with Lugh. They were talking seriously like lovers, not the children that they were. He felt anger bubble up within him anew. He vowed to not to allow her to associate with that young upstart, prince or not.

Although the rules of the contest allowed lads of sixteen summers to challenge established champions, it would be considered a shameful thing if one were to be unseated by someone as young as Lugh. Srang was resentful of this brazen affront to his status. He could not admit to himself that in the past year Lugh's expertise with the javelin had approached, perhaps even surpassed, his own. He felt his gorge rise as the young people in the crowd called out, "Lugh! Lugh of the Long Hand!" as the popular boy neared the contest field. Srang turned and spit contemptuously on the ground. *I'll show him a thing or two about what it takes to be a champion. I was participating in these events—and winning them—before he was born!*

Chapter Four

Mannon Mac Lir, standing in the bow of the DeDanaan king's curragh, strained his gray eyes to see Innis Ealga for the first time. The sighting could come at any moment and he was eager for it.

"Thank the gods," he said to Dagda, who had seated his bulk near the captain, "that we have had fair sailing. With all the women and children and non-sailors on board, not to mention the livestock, it has been a rough journey."

"Seasickness has been the most serious problem, I'd say," responded Dagda. "I feared it most when the Sun God was high in the sky and the wool grease that saturates the boats grew warm. Even now, I am not able to accustom myself to the stink of these craft."

"Ah, yes, it is so. The odor is awful but curraghs made of ox hides soaked with wool grease always stink. It is the price we must pay for a watertight craft. I have been a sailor all my life, as was my father before me, so it's familiar to me. Still, I have to admit there have been times, with all the livestock on board ..."

The two men watched the fleet of curraghs flying gracefully over the waves, their slender prows rising and falling with each heave of the sea. "Don't they look grand though?" Mac Lir asked. "I will never grow so old that I don't love the look of a curragh on the water, smell or no smell."

Suddenly, Mac Lir saw what they had long been seeking: a thin, gray-green strip lying atop the faint line where the sky met the sea. It had to be Innis Ealga!

"Lower the sails," he shouted, "and take up the oars." The prevailing winds blew from the southwest and only by lowering the square leather sails could they hope to make land. The able-bodied on board dipped slender ash oars into the blue-green waters and pulled them back, slicing through the waves with powerful strokes.

Mac Lir watched as the curraghs reluctantly yielded themselves to the will of the oarsmen. "I wish my beloved curraghs went upwind better," he said to Dagda. "Still, they are the best boats I have ever seen, and I am proud to be captain of the DeDanaan fleet." He rumpled his red hair with one hand, staring hard at the line on the horizon coming into focus. Then he raised his hand and pointed.

"Ho!" he shouted to the king. "There it is! Innis Ealga!"

King Nuad heard the words he had been waiting for with such intense emotion that tears sprang unbidden to his eyes. His throat felt tight and he dared not trust himself to speak. The strength of his feeling surprised him. Establishing his people on Innis Ealga had become everything to him, and they were almost home at last. There was Innis Ealga!

He grabbed Morrigan and hugged her tightly, as much to keep her from seeing how moved he was as from the joy of sharing the news.

Cian ordered the sail of the second curragh lowered and concentrated on following Mannon Mac Lir's lead. "Man the oars!" he shouted, then turned to peer at the horizon. Mac Lir must have seen land. There it was! A deep feeling of calm came over him. Their journey was about to end.

He felt a presence at his elbow and turned to look into the brilliant blue eyes of his father, Diancecht, the tribe's chief physician. The old man was frail and Cian knew that movement on board the heaving curragh was difficult for him with his hollow bronze leg.

"Father, I would have come to you if you had asked. You didn't need to make your way up here."

"I know, I know," Diancecht said irritably. He did not like to acknowledge his physical shortcomings. "I saw you lower the sail, Cian. Does this mean the prophecy will be fulfilled this day, my son?"

"It does, Father! We should make landfall sometime this afternoon, before the evening meal."

"Ah. It will be as the gods have foretold." The aged physician wavered on his artificial leg. Cian reached out to steady him and realized that the bones beneath his father's cloak had grown small and thin.

Diancecht's sharp blue eyes burned into him, as hot as any flame. "You are ready, Cian, for what lies ahead?"

Cian started to say yes but was struck dumb by the power of the old man's stare. This was no casual question from a father to his son. Even stoic Cian could feel the power of the gods at work in it. He could only nod.

"Good." Diancecht nodded. "That is how it must be. Be strong, my son, and never forget, no matter what happens, you are part of the gods' plan."

After Diancecht returned to his place on the starboard side of the craft, Cian remained as still and silent as stone in the helm, unable to decipher the meaning in his father's words. Diancecht had never spoken to him in such a tone, never looked at him with a gaze so penetrating. A shiver passed over Cian's spine. He felt relief that the holy man, Ferfesa, was on board his boat. He made the secret sign to ward off evil before he returned to the task of maneuvering the curragh across the waves, sailing ever closer to Innia Ealga.

The DeDanaan fleet put in safely at the place known to the Fir Bolgs as Slieve Anierin, in the late afternoon on the feast day of Samhain. The rocky beach was broad and spacious enough for all their curraghs.

King Nuad sent the DeDanaans ashore with instructions to call for him when all was in order. "But why?" protested Morrigan. "I don't understand why you don't want to be the first one to step onto this sacred soil. Why are you doing this?" She was impatient and did not want to go without him.

"Morrigan," he said sternly, "go ashore. Don't you think I am fighting a strong desire to be the first DeDanaan for generations to stand on Innis Ealga? I am. But I know there is need for a symbolic gesture to seal the people to this land. I knew it even before Dagda Mor suggested it, and it is the only reason I wait. Please trust my judgment in this and go with the others."

"I see. Of course. I will go, but I had dreamed of conquering this holy land, hand in hand with you. I can't pretend I'm not disappointed." She gathered up her belongings and kissed his cheek. "Hurry, my darling," she said.

She slid over the side of the boat and waded through the shallow water until she reached the rocky beach. She threw him a kiss when she reached the shingle shore, and went in search of her sisters, Macha and Neimain, who had sailed with Cian.

Nuad longed to follow her but accepted his royal duty and forced himself to remain in the curragh and watch the unloading of the other boats. They had brought stores enough for forty days, although Nuad was privately convinced that the bounty of Innis Ealga was so great they would not need to depend on the dried meats, cereals, and roots they had carried with them from northern Lochland. Soon, a small mound of their belongings rose on the beach.

Beyond the beach and as far as the eye could see, there were gently sloping green hills, dotted now and again with stands of oak, ash, beech, hazel, and rowan. In the woodland grove nearest the beach, Nuad could see the forest floor with its ferns and the last of the wildflowers, bathed in the golden light of the late afternoon sun. He knew the woods were home to all kinds of animal life that would soon grace DeDanaan cooking pots. He chuckled to himself, *the gods are kind*, he thought.

Overhead, clouds as thick as cream were pushed across a brilliant blue sky by westerly winds. Far in the distance, Nuad could see where the hills dipped to the river Boyne, just as his scouts had described.

Nuad thought about the peace delegation that Dagda insisted they send to the king of the Fir Bolgs. If they followed the river Boyne a few miles inland, it would take them to the festival place where the Fir Bolgs were even now celebrating Samhain.

On the beach, the DeDanaans worked furiously to establish a camp in the few hours of daylight left to them, all memory of the uncomfortable voyage now banished from their minds. The king had instructed Dagda to have everything removed from the curraghs. He was adamant about it, even calling him back once to repeat the order. Stacks of cargo grew tall on the rocky shore as the DeDanaans carried out the king's directions.

The herdsmen and shepherds released their animals from the confines of the tethers and wooden cages in which they had made the voyage. The young charioteer, Desheen, walked her horses up and down the beach gingerly, testing the limbs of the beasts on dry land after their days upon the waters. In truth, her own limbs were no less stiff.

Desheen was muscular and athletic. No other girl of fifteen summers could approach her skill with the horses, and her rise as a charioteer had been unprecedented in the tribe.

Brigid, a milk pail on her arm, passed her on the way to the temporary byre where the cows were tethered. "Hello, Desheen," she said agreeably, falling into step beside her and the horses, "how did the voyage go for you?"

"Oh, not bad. It was cramped for the horses though. They were glad to be set free. I know that they want to run and frolic like colts, but it's taking some time for them to limber up. See? Even now they walk like much age is upon them. How was it for you?"

"It's better not to ask," the older girl replied. "I was seasick from the first." A blush of shame rose up her cheeks. "I can't tell you how humiliating it was to be so sick with Macha and Neimain on board my curragh . . . and Breas."

The tone of Brigid's voice caused Desheen to look again at Dagda's plain-faced daughter in the failing light of evening. Breas. *Oh, I hope she doesn't love him,* Desheen thought. He was too pretty by half, and he would never look at her. Brigid was too sweet to be hurt by the likes of him, and many times better than he.

"I am sorry you were sick, Brigid," she said, "but don't feel too bad. A lot of people were. Even your brother, Bove the Red, had to put his head over the side of our curragh more than once."

"I guess that makes me feel better. It's pretty obvious that our family will never be champion sailors, isn't it?" Brigid laughed, her sunny nature reasserting itself now that she was back on dry land. "I've got to run along if there is to be milk for our evening meal. Take care!"

"I'll talk to you later, Brigid," Desheen called and

wheeled the horses around to retrace their steps down the beach.

Space had dictated that only two breeding pairs of sheep, hares, pigs, and wood hens could be brought to Innis Ealga, but horses and cows were another matter altogether. Milk was the staple food of the DeDanaans. To be assured of a steady supply of their precious butter and cheese they had brought six of their best cows, two bulls, and several calves.

Desheen knew that the cows would be grateful to see Brigid for they were lowing insistently, pleading to be milked. The bulls were tethered some distance away from the camp where four slaves would guard them until dawn. It was not likely that the wolves of Innis Ealga would dare to come into a camp where fires burned throughout the night, but Desheen knew they could not be too careful. She decided that for the first night in this strange place she would bed down next to her horses to protect them from harm.

Above the bustle and activity on the beach, Morrigan's calm, bell-like voice drifted clearly out to where King Nuad waited in the curragh.

"The gods are good," she said, cheering on their people in Nuad's absence. "Feel the soft warm air here. Such a beautiful place this island seems already and we've only just laid eyes on it! I think we will be happier and healthier here than in those cold northern climes of Lochland where we have been these past seven years."

Nuad inclined his head in silent agreement and smiled to himself, thinking her words prophetic. His people stood on home ground at last in a scene resembling a festival gathering; people who only a short time before were miserably wet and seasick, desperately turning their heads into the wind to avoid the foul odors on board the curraghs, were now talking and laughing and making plans for tomorrow.

He had done the right thing in bringing the DeDanaans here. He'd never had any real doubts, but it was nice to be shown the rightness of his decision. He grinned, wishing to be standing beside Morrigan, buoyed by her optimistic words.

* * *

As the king watched, Dagda propelled his great body through the water to the midsection of the royal curragh where Nuad waited. He said, "Sir, I think the time is right for you to make your appearance. All the cargo has been unloaded and the evening meal will soon be ready."

Nuad glanced at the driftwood fires burning brightly on the beach under huge bronze cauldrons. Some women blew at the flames, encouraging them to leap higher, while others stirred the contents of the cauldrons with large wooden spoons. He could see the many skins and furs that had been laid in protected hollows in the green grass just beyond the beach, in readiness for sleeping. The livestock was secured. *Yes,* he thought, *things are in good order so they will be able to hear me when I speak to them. May the gods grant me the gift of a golden tongue.*

"Very well, Dagda. I am more than ready to tread upon the soil of our ancestors for the first time." King Nuad bounded from the boat, splashing his way onto the hallowed land, followed by the huffing wise man.

The drummer beat out a rhythm calling the tribe to order. Their king would speak. The talking and laughing stopped as people turned expectantly toward Nuad, who had climbed atop a large boulder at the sea's edge. Only the sounds of the wind, moving in the treetops and the splash of the waves upon the shore were heard. Even the animals were hushed.

"My fellow DeDanaans," he began, "I see when I look around me that you share my joy and the anticipation of a good life on Innis Ealga. The voyage was long and unpleasant but by the grace of the gods, we lost not one person, not one beast. We landed at the spot the scouts had chosen, in time to unload and prepare a camp without hostile interference. We must conclude from all these signs that the gods are pleased by our actions. Let us fall to our knees and offer thanks."

Ferfesa, the chief priest of the DeDanaans, stepped before the king's fire, wearing the clean, bleached garment he had carried on his lap in a leathern packet for this holy occasion. He turned his eyes to the Moon Goddess who had begun her slow climb in the night sky and raised his hands to her. The bracelets of gold he wore on each wrist glinted, reflecting the firelight that danced in front of him. He planted his leather-shod feet far apart on the sand and began his prayer to the powers that lay beyond the earth and the will of man.

"Thanks be to you, oh gods of light, we offer you devotion and fealty for our safe deliverance from the perils of the sea and the winds. Guide us, and show us what you would have us do to insure your favor toward us. We desire always to feel your presence among us and to do your bidding. Accept our joyful thanksgiving." With a shy smile to the king the priest signified that his prayer was ended.

Nuad spoke. "Arise, my people. The way we conduct our lives upon this island will show the gods how truly thankful we are to be here. I have consulted with the Council of the Wise on all details of our journey; however, after my own private prayer with the gods of light, I have reached one conclusion about which the council knows nothing."

Morrigan peered at him intently. He had said nothing to her about any secret plans. Macha and Neimain were looking at her questioningly. She shrugged her shoulders irritably then looked around seeking the faces of the twelve members of the council. There was Cian the warrior, with his brother and sister, Miach and Airmead, both trained as physicians by their father. All three looked as puzzled as Morrigan felt.

A few feet away the red-haired bard, Cairbed, stood next to Brigid, Ogma the scribe, and Gobinu the smith. They glanced at one another with raised eyebrows. Swiftly, Morrigan located the other council members. Each one's attention was riveted on the king.

Alone of all the council, Dagda had been made privy to what King Nuad planned to do. He had never been handsome by anyone's account, even in his youth. His hair was a muddy blond going to gray; his features were bulbous and indistinct, but at this moment his face was composed.

In spite of Dagda's lack of physical grace his intellect, manifest in his small, squinting hazel eyes, caused all who knew him to bend their knee in respect for him. Morrigan, noting his composure, decided that whatever King Nuad had planned, she need not be apprehensive. Every DeDanaan waited for Nuad's next words.

In a loud, firm voice, the king commanded Mannon

Mac Lir to take all the slaves, oarsmen, and able-bodied warriors, to the water's edge. "I want every curragh dragged onto the beach," he said. "Do not turn them upside down in the customary way. Do not leave any portion of them in the water."

Mac Lir responded to the order, full of curiosity but not rebellion. "DeDanaans," he shouted, "come with me!" And he led the workers to the water's edge.

They strained and pulled at the boats until all the craft were lined up on the beach, sometimes two deep where the stones were too numerous to permit deeper passage. Dagda, responding to a nod from King Nuad, walked over the cobbles to where Mac Lir stood awaiting further orders.

"Dagda Mor," Mac Lir said, bowing his head slightly to the wizard of the DeDanaans, who softly stated the king's instructions. An involuntary "No!" escaped Mac Lir's lips. He could not believe what he had just heard.

"It is the king's will," Dagda replied firmly, "and that of the gods. You must do it!" The struggle flaring within the sea captain, who had overseen the construction of the fleet for seven long years, was visible upon his face. Finally, in a voice little more than a whisper, he said, "Yes, my lord," and turned to look at King Nuad with tears glistening in his angry eyes. The king nodded his resolve. The pale Moon Goddess cast her silver light weakly across the night sky.

"My people!" the king shouted. "The gods have led us to our homeland as surely as we stand upon the soil of Innis Ealga this night. Many generations will come forth on this land to grow and prosper and to make the name of DeDanaan great in these climes. We who stand before the Moon Goddess are not the first DeDanaans to claim this island. We owe much to our forefathers who kept the dream of returning here alive in us."

He smiled in acknowledgment of his debt to his grandfather, then continued. "We will, however, be the last DeDanaans to wander without a home. From this day forward our seed will flourish on Innis Ealga, this blessed island. To ensure that each of us will make the supreme effort to realize our dream, to never waver or weaken in our resolve, I now give the order to BURN THE FLEET!"

A gasp arose from the DeDanaans as though from one throat. They watched in dumb amazement as Dagda gave the signal, and a heavy-hearted Mannon Mac Lir, builder and captain of the fleet, touched his lighted reed torch to that of Cian who stood next to him in grim-lipped silence. Pine pitch ignited with a whooshing sound and blazed high. When all the torches were lit, Mac Lir turned reluctantly toward the graceful bow of the king's curragh, and set his beloved craft afire with a shaking hand.

The wool grease caught and fire skittered across the boat in irregular lines, following the seams of the ox hides where the grease was especially thick. The wicker frame inside the skin of hides caught next, then the wooden planks the DeDanaans had rested on only a few hours earlier. Light from the mast and the sail flickered in the gentle night breezes as they were consumed by the blaze. Mac Lir felt the nausea that had plagued his passengers well up in him and he turned his face away from the king and retched into the ocean until he was spent. When he straightened up, his entire fleet was afire. Flames leapt eagerly upward toward the Moon Goddess, who watched in cool detachment.

"Nuad is brilliant," Morrigan breathed to her sisters. "No other man living would have had such boldness."

"I think he suffers from the madness of the moon," hissed Neimain. "How could he have done this terrible thing to us? Now we are trapped." Fury contorted her beautiful face, so like Morrigan's but darker in every aspect.

"It probably won't be as bad as it seems," interjected Macha who frequently acted as mediator between her older and younger sisters. "We all know that Nuad is king because he has the courage and foresight bestowed by the gods. We'll have to trust him," she said uncertainly.

A loud harumph was Neimain's only reply. She knew a thing or two about the gods herself, and she believed they would surely punish a leader who could be this careless with the wealth of the tribe.

"Of course we will trust him," Morrigan declared, "he is our strength and hope." Her sisters stared at her, Neimain with anger and Macha with a growing fear that Neimain could be right.

"Now there is no way for us to get away from the fate that awaits us on this island," Macha whispered. "Even if it is evil."

Chapter Five

Lugh and Rury trotted onto the field of contest, fresh from the bathing compound. Both boys had soaked in stone basins filled with hot water and sweet herbs to remove the filth of the lake ceremony, then ate barley soup and boiled swan's eggs to restore their strength. Rury had been so eager to get to the contest that his still damp hair gleamed like the bark of an oak after rain.

Lugh sent a warm smile Rury's way to erase the hurt of his earlier sharp remark, and Rury was content to be in Lugh's inner circle once more.

Lugh lowered his voice to confide in his friend, "I told my parents that I think I have a chance to outthrow Srang."

"But he's the greatest champion our tribe has ever had!" Rury cried, unable to hide his shock at Lugh's arrogance.

"I hate the way he treats Aibel, and I hate the way he acts toward everybody else. I'd like to bring him down." Lugh looked at the ground, and made a pattern in the dirt with the toe of his boot. "I probably can't do it this time and I know it's not an honorable motive for challenging him. Still, I'd like to see if he could take defeat like a true champion. I doubt it."

"I know what you mean. Srang is strong and cunning in battle, but I heard my father say he has acquired so much pride in his championship that the gods will have to destroy him. Maybe you are the one they have chosen to do it."

Before Lugh could reply, the beat of the bodhrans called them to the contest, leaving no more time for private talk.

King Eochy came forth from the crowd to greet the most able Fir Bolg athletes, all of whom had been chosen to represent their clans. Fourteen competitors in all, they were to run an obstacle course through the woods, swim against the current of the mighty Boyne, and return to the field to throw their javelins. Speed, strength, and agility were what counted, the skills necessary to bring down a stag or a wild boar in the forest.

Lugh's heart pounded within his chest, so eager was he to be off. He removed his cloak, revealing his bare, oiled chest. He rubbed his arms briskly and shrugged his shoulders several times to loosen his muscles. As he did so his eyes met the hateful gaze of Srang which was full upon him. Exhibiting an insolence he didn't feel, Lugh returned his stare. After some moments he flashed his broadest smile at the champion and said, "May the gods take you by the hand this day and lead you to yet another championship, if it be their will."

Ignoring Lugh's words, Srang turned away and slid off his own cloak. He was shorter than Lugh and his massive chest was covered with curly black hair, as were his arms and back. He was powerful and worked hard to keep himself that way, but he was approaching his thirty-first summer, and showed a faint softening around his middle.

Lugh inhaled, raised his arms over his head, and stretched lazily. He knew his sleek, young body looked magnificent and he wanted to make sure Srang knew it, too. The king's words interrupted his preening.

"Go forth at the sound of the horn, men of the Fir Bolg clans, to engage in holy contest. Upon your prowess rests the survival of our people. The gods will be with you!"

Lugh did not look at Srang as they crouched at the line drawn in the dirt and thus did not see the look of disdain that was sent his way just as the starting horn sounded. Lugh's burst of speed put him out front by several lengths by the time Srang was away from the line.

Through the woods the competitors ran, leaping over fallen logs, dodging around trees, their leather-clad feet crushing the autumn leaves on the forest floor. Lugh startled a nest of wood hens that flew up in noisy alarm. Some part of his mind registered their flight but he took no conscious notice.

By the time he could see daylight through the trees at the edge of the deep woods, he noted that there were no competitors beside or ahead of him. He could hear the footfalls and the heavy breathing of someone behind him, very close, but not wanting to break his stride, he did not look back to see who it was.

His lungs were fairly bursting by the time he emerged from the forest. He ran by the cluster of Fir Bolg judges stationed on the banks of the Boyne and hurled his sweating body into the icy waters of the river. The shock caused a tingle of pain to shoot through him, but he pressed on. He swam with powerful strokes against the current. As he turned his head to gasp for breath he saw that Srang was swimming beside him. Stroke for stroke they kept pace with one another and pulled their weary bodies from the river at virtually the same instant.

Neither took the time to pause for breath before racing toward the javelin field. Lugh could hear the splashing of the other competitors as they entered the river. *So, it is just between me and Srang now,* he thought, and summoned all the strength he had left for a burst of speed that sent him headlong onto the javelin field ahead of Srang.

Cheers greeted his arrival but he hardly heard them. He reached down and took the top javelin from the stack, testing the heft and balance of it as he strode to the starting line. From the corner of his eye he could see Srang bending to choose his javelin. Lugh quickened his pace.

Without a backward glance he stopped before the line, then lifted his javelin to shoulder height and sprang into motion, as graceful as any deer, as swift as any eagle. With every sinew, every nerve, performing at its peak, he took aim and willed his spear to travel the distance between himself and the farthest loop of green willow hanging from the massive branches of a large oak tree. It sliced through the air, piercing the loop dead center, and plunged into the earth, the full length of a man beyond the tree. It was still quivering from the impact when Srang's spear whizzed by Lugh's ear, sailed through the willow loop, and fell a scant distance short of Lugh's record-breaking mark.

I've won, Lugh thought. *I am the new champion.* He felt only disbelief. He looked again at the two spears piercing the earth of Innis Ealga. There was no doubt. He chanced a glance at Aibel's father. He was scowling, his eyes filled with a murderous rage like nothing Lugh had ever seen. In that moment Lugh knew that in winning the game he had earned himself a dangerous enemy.

His friends surrounded him, engulfing him with their shouts of congratulations. As they carried him off the field he saw Aibel looking first to her father, where he stood glaring after Lugh, then at him. Their eyes met, and Lugh's triumph faltered at the sadness in her expression.

The Fir Bolgs came to the evening banquet tables happy and tired. As the sun set, King Eochy and Queen Tailteann stood with their hands touching, watching the people take their places at the feast. Tables were piled high with roasted meats, boiled vegetables, fish and fowl, apples and nuts. Torches flickered upon the cheerful faces in the clearing near the lakeshore, and the scene before the royal couple was a joyful one.

The high priest, Ard, approached them silently. He too, was warmed by the sight before him. "It's a grand festival, isn't it, my lord?" he asked, bowing slightly to Tailteann as he spoke to the king. "And to think that your son has won the triple contest! A most auspicious sign."

"Yes indeed, Ard. We have been most fortunate this year," said Eochy.

"Ah, holy man," said Tailteann, "and what of the year to come? What will you see tonight in the forest?" She smiled at him sweetly enough as she spoke, and her words were mild. Why then did he always think he heard a note of mockery in her voice when they spoke of signs and portents?

"The wood hens are ready for the seeing ceremony," he told her respectfully, "and the firstborn sons who have reached their fifteenth summer are abstaining from the feast in preparation for the holy meal they will eat in the forest. More than that I cannot tell you. The gods do not speak to me until they are properly called upon. Until that time I am as other mortal men, ignorant of the will of the gods." Ard bowed again, anxious to take his leave. "If you will excuse me, I must join my family. As you know, my firstborn son, Rury, has reached his fifteenth summer and will participate in tonight's ritual."

He withdrew, bowing. As he backed away, Tailteann followed him with her eyes, but it was his awkward son, Rury, who had taken command of her thoughts.

How could the priest consider letting his own son participate in the ceremony in the woods? She shivered as a cool night breeze skimmed across the lake and ruffled the hairdo her serving women had spent so much time arranging. They had oiled her long dark hair and plaited it into thick coils, fastening them at the nape of her neck with bone pins. She had allowed them to paint her cheeks with ruam and smooth her eyebrows with a paste made from oak bark because of the importance of this occasion.

"Have you seen Lugh yet this evening?" she asked King Eochy.

"No. But he should be along shortly. He was so excited about defeating Srang this afternoon that it was hard to talk with him. He was surrounded by admirers."

Neither of them spoke aloud of the concern they shared, but they had both seen the look of pure hatred on Srang's face when he realized that Lugh had defeated him in the triple contest. Tailteann, more than Eochy, understood that Srang had in that moment of humiliation, become a threat to their son. Knowing how close Lugh was to Aibel, she saw that the defeat carried within it seeds that would flower, into what, she did not know. She looked up and saw Lugh in the serving line and breathed a sigh of relief, glad that Srang was nowhere in sight.

When the feast was over, Ard gathered Aibel and the other handmaidens at the side of the clearing. He spoke quietly to them for several moments, then summoned the slaves who were to carry the torches for the procession into the woods.

Four priests bore a wooden crate containing the most perfect specimen of wood fowl that could be found. Behind them Ard would march, carrying a heavy leather bag containing the sacred ceremonial knife, honed to razor sharpness.

He sent a messenger to the king's table to say the priests were ready. Tailteann searched the crowd once more for Lugh. *Thank the gods*, she thought, *that he is a fostered child, for it is his protection from the priests.* She could see him talking and laughing with a clot of other young people. As always, he was at the center of the group.

He looked up and saw her watching him and waved

cheerily. She waved back and felt all the love she held in her heart for him leap into her eyes.

The horns sounded and Eochy and Tailteann rose and entered the footpath leading into the woods. The bodhrans were played with a slow, steady beat. Slaves fell in beside the procession to light the way into the dark forest, their bright torches keeping the wolves at bay.

It took some time for the Fir Bolgs to wend their way to the sacred place near the river where a perfect circle had been cleared of all vegetation and carefully swept into a concentric pattern. In the exact center of the circle lay a smooth, flat round stone with five human skulls taken in battle arranged in an arc at the top of it.

Eochy and Tailteann positioned themselves on the far side of the holy circle while Ard and the other priests marched into it, halting directly in front of the stone. The people spread out, two or three deep, around the boundary of the clean circle of earth. Slaves held the torches high, illuminating the holy place. The drummers kept up the monotonous roll on the bodhrans until Ard raised his powerful arms above his head to command silence.

The glow of the Moon Goddess was weak and did not easily penetrate the crush of tall trees surrounding the sacred circle. Nevertheless, Ard's prayers were all to her.

"Oh, sacred Goddess of the Moon, attend us with your wisdom. Show us the future and give us signs that will guide us in our actions for the new year. We wish only to please you and to do your bidding. Tell us now what you will have us do to insure your grace and that of your brother the Sun God, as we plant our crops and till our fields in the new year to come."

The drummers changed the pattern as they beat again on the bodhrans. The rhythm was lower, faster, more intense than before. The lesser priests moved back to places at the outer edge of the circle. All torches were extinguished except the one that illuminated the spot in the center where Ard stood.

He moved toward the flat stone and instinctively the other priests drew back again as if to make room for the god's visit. A low murmur of anticipation rippled through the crowd.

Four priests from the other Fir Bolg clans, the Fir Domains and the Fir Galians, approached Ard, carrying the wooden cage that had held several birds earlier in the day. Now it contained only one.

Ard removed the large ceremonial knife, honed to such an edge that it would have sheared through the leather bag he carried if it had not been wrapped in several layers of rabbit skin.

He reached into the cage and grabbed the single bird around the neck. It screeched and flopped violently in an effort to escape, causing Ard's grasp to tighten. He turned back to the stone, and offered the bird to the moon. He faced the Fir Bolgs and held the screeching bird before them. Then, with a deft motion, he raised the knife and slit the creature's wildly beating breast with one smooth and deliberate stroke. Silence was heavy in the night air. Red blood ran down the priest's arms and dripped onto the soft, clean earth of the clearing.

Chanting holy words, he knelt and with the tip of the knife, spilled the fowl's still pulsing entrails out onto the smooth center of the sacred stone. This was the way the gods had communicated with his people since time out of mind. Tonight the Moon Goddess would tell him what fate awaited the Fir Bolgs in the new year.

Ard felt fear grip his own innards when he saw the configuration lying before him. Never in all his years of apprenticeship and priesthood had he seen anything like it. He was confused. He knew the council of elders had agreed yesterday that the Fir Bolgs must go to war with the Fomorians even though it had not yet been announced to the people. Suffering and defeat were foretold on the stone but the signs did not speak of the Fomorians, their traditional foes, of that he was certain.

Sweat trickled into his eyes, his breathing was quick and irregular; he could not keep up the chanting much longer. The Fir Bolgs were all waiting to hear what the goddess had revealed to him. A priest who is befuddled by a message is a man out of favor with the gods, and he knew it.

He thought desperately about what to say. He turned his ashen face to the assembly who waited quietly for his interpretation.

He shouted, "Woe and destruction are written by the gods! Seven harvest seasons will pass before the Fir Bolgs will return to serenity and peace, but many more years will pass before prosperity is restored to our people. Clearly, the gods do speak and this is what they say: '*We face destruction and suffering but not at the hands of the Fomorians.*' "

Tailteann gasped, her brown eyes wide with wonder and fright. She saw the confusion on the faces of those around her as she turned to her husband. He gave nothing away with his expression, but she knew he was as startled as she was.

Lugh watched them both and caught their fear and uncertainty. He was frowning when Tailteann's eyes met his. What could it mean? If the Fomorians were not their enemy, who then? All the clans who lived on Innis Ealga were of the Fir Bolg tribe and known to one another. They quarreled among themselves all the time but it never approached anything like the fury the priest now predicted. Lugh wondered if Ard could be in error.

Ard faced the king and the assembled priests humbly. He looked at the ground in front of Eochy and held out his blood-red hands. After a long silence, King Eochy said, "Speak you more, priest. Is there nothing more you can tell us?"

"No, my lord," he said, "I can only repeat what the gods have shown me. The Fomorians are not the enemy we will face. The gods have not chosen to reveal all, but they do say that our defeat will be great and our people will suffer and die. There is nothing more. The gods are now silent."

He turned back to the sacrificial altar stone and peered once more at the entrails lying in the torchlight. The message he had seen was still there, only this time he saw something he had missed before. Plainly, the time of King Eochy's death was near.

Ard picked up the killing knife and wiped its bloody edge on the rabbit skins. He wrapped it carefully and replaced it in its fes. He knelt by the stone, uttering prayers and praise to the goddess. Then he arose and led the Fir Bolgs in a familiar chant. The drums and the voices swelled in sorrow and foreboding until the very leaves of the oaks shook in sympathy. Ard had broken a vow of his priesthood by not telling the king what he had just discerned.

Ard gestured and the group of handmaidens, twelve virgins dressed in tunics of fine white linen, advanced toward the center of the holy circle, carrying the stone form of the great god, Chrom Cruic, on a platform. He was undraped in all his golden glory. When the handmaidens reached the center of the circle, the bearers relit the torches and the gold plating on the idol's crooked back flared as brightly as the sun. Chrom Cruic represented both the good and evil aspects of the gods who ruled the sky. The Fir Bolgs had celebrated his benevolence earlier, in the warmth and light of the sun. Now, by the light of the moon, they would appease the other side of his nature.

Ard spoke, "I call upon the firstling son of each household who has reached his fifteenth summer, to come forth into the holy circle of the sun and the moon."

Even with the unnerving prophecy, Lugh had not been able to keep his attention from straying to Aibel. He had never seen her look so beguiling. She wore a pale yellow tunic under a dark blue cloak. Her face had been scrubbed until it shone and her black hair hung loosely to her waist. Her eyes, which always dominated her small face, flashed in the flickering torchlight with a brilliance Lugh had never seen there before. Her cheeks were flushed but she seemed calm and focused on her holy tasks.

He ached with longing and regret that there had been no time for him to be alone with her between the triple contest and the feast. He had not truly expected to win the competition with Srang and had been unprepared for the attention that came his way afterward. He sighed audibly, watching Aibel as she moved slowly and confidently within the sacred circle.

Rury stopped and looked back at his friend Lugh. He felt a twinge of disappointment that Lugh wasn't looking at him in this, the most important ritual of his young life. He followed Lugh's gaze toward Aibel and understood. He was smiling when Lugh's glance turned to him. Their eyes met in an affirmation of friendship.

Rury never seemed to know where to put his hands, although tonight they hung obediently by his sides as he tried to follow the directions given by the priests.

He knew he was not as quick as Lugh, but he realized

that the message the gods had just revealed to his father made the next part of the rite more important than ever. *I want to do it right and make Father proud of me tonight,* he thought.

The firstlings stood before Ard, their heads bowed, not daring to look at him. Ard looked at Rury and love surged in his heart for him. He had spent hours with his son in preparation for this holy night. They had enjoyed the time they spent together because Rury had seen early in his instruction how much it pleased his father. The lessons had gone well, although Ard suspected that Rury had not always understood what he was being taught.

Seventeen firstlings lined up in three rows to the left of the killing stone, the twelve handmaidens stood to Ard's right. When all was silent Ard addressed the figure of Chrom Cruic.

"I call for mercy upon the Fir Bolgs and ask for your forbearance. I assure you of my people's willingness and eagerness to please you in all things. As proof, we will give you the firstling of your choice. We offer this sacrifice to you with glad hearts, for as devout people our aim is always to accede to your will and not our own."

Aibel stepped in front of Ard, bearing the large oaken plate she had carried in the procession. Of all the handmaidens, her hands alone had not touched the bier upon which Chrom Cruic rested for they had been cleansed ritually, in a private ceremony with the priests. Only then had she been allowed to touch the tray with its precious contents. The white linen cloth covering the plate was embroidered with the symbols of the sun and the moon in threads of gold and silver. Under the cloth rested seventeen perfectly round oat cakes called Bairin Breac. Only one cake bore a charred edge.

Aibel uncovered the tray with its sacred food and offered it to Ard. The priest took the burnt oak cake and held it up so all could see. He replaced it, covered the tray, and rotated it twelve times to the left. Then he rotated it twelve times in the opposite direction. He handed the tray back to Aibel and faced the firstlings.

"Young men of the great Fir Bolg tribe of Innis Ealga, you have been called to the altar of Chrom Cruic to serve as our liaison to the gods. He who is chosen will receive the highest honor known to our people, the honor of dwelling forever more in the realm of the sun and the moon. Choose now the oat cake offered by the hand-maiden of the gods."

He nodded to Aibel and she stepped in front of the first boy and offered him the covered tray. He slipped his hand under the cloth and pulled forth one of the sun-shaped cakes. He held it up for Ard and the others to see. There was no charred spot on it. One by one the cakes were chosen. All were unmarked until Rury pulled his portion from beneath the cloth.

Lugh realized instantly that his friend had drawn the charred cake. He felt his heart sink to his toes. Until that moment he had been so intent on looking at Aibel as she moved around the circle he had not really focused on the ceremony. *No,* he wanted to scream, *it is a mistake. Not Rury. No, don't let this happen!*

The blackened ashes clinging to Rury's cake were visible to all present. The priest's own son had been chosen by the gods. Such a thing had never happened before.

Even though all suspense was over, Aibel continued to serve the firstlings until all the cakes were taken. Ard spoke to the boys in the silence of the night, his voice strangely hollow.

"Eat, all of you, except he who has been chosen. Consume this holy meal that was prepared for you this day by the order of the gods."

When the boys had done so, two handmaidens came to them bearing pottery beakers of holy water with which to wash down every last crumb. When they had finished, sixteen of the boys followed the handmaidens back into the crowd. Rury, alone, was left in the clearing with his father.

Lugh knew he could not shame his foster parents but he wanted desperately to stop the proceedings. He wanted to return to yesterday when he and Rury were boys gathering stones together, stringing bows, and throwing the javelin in the green fields near Lough Gur. He looked around anxiously, perhaps hoping to find an ally who would help him stop what was about to happen. There was no one. All eyes were fixed somberly on the holy circle.

Two of the lesser priests stepped into place behind Ard.

One carried a heavy piece of copper wire, coiled neatly, resting on a cloth of white linen. The other bore a dagger with a double blade honed to an exquisite sharpness, also resting upon a snowy cloth.

Ard addressed his son. "Rury, son of my loins, you of all the firstlings presented to Chrom Cruic this night, have been found perfect in every way for the purposes of the gods." He paused to swallow.

Rury was looking at him with wide, slightly surprised eyes. Ard went on, "Take this holy oat cake and eat all of it. Begin with the charred portion."

When Rury had eaten it, Aibel appeared at his side with a stone chalice containing a drink brewed by the priests in secret, meant only for the lips of the chosen firstling. Ard commanded his son to drink deeply of the brew. When Rury seemed about to stop his father implored him to drink more. "Do not leave a drop, my son," he whispered, his eyes shining with pride and regret at this moment, the holy pinnacle of both their lives.

Rury smiled at his father, or tried to but something was wrong with his muscles. They no longer did his bidding. His eyelids felt heavy and drooped until he could not see his father in front of him. He heard a roaring sound in his ears like storms upon the sea. His limbs were as heavy as oaks, and he felt rooted to the place where he stood in the holy circle of the gods.

The roaring became louder inside his head and his vision grew black and spiraled down inside him as the copper wire wielded by the first priest tightened efficiently around his neck. He felt no pain. The second priest drew the sharp blade of the dagger across Rury's throat and his life blood spurted onto the soft earthen circle, splashing the vestments of the priests. Ard caught his son, his firstborn child, as he fell.

He carried the lad's still-twitching body to the river's edge. Once more this Samhain, he waded into the moving waters that lay upon the face of Innis Ealga. He bent and solemnly kissed Rury's forehead before pushing him under the river's surface. He held him there a long time. When he spoke his voice cracked unmistakably.

"Chrom Cruic, accept this holy and sanctified offering of our most precious child, a son of my own blood. Take

him to your bosom and allow him to deflect the wrath of
the gods away from the Fir Bolg people. He is thrice dead
as you have commanded. He dwells now in the realm of
the gods and we give him to you willingly, with great awe
at your power and might. Grant us a new year, we be-
seech you, that is touched by your light and your mercy.
Great Chrom Cruic we owe you all that we are and all
that we have. May our sacrifice be pleasing to you." So
saying, he released Rury's body to the rushing waters.
The gods who dwelt within would take him to the place
of the sun and the moon.

Lugh's stomach churned and he thought he might be
ill. He forced himself to look into the night at Rury's
body as it floated away to the sea. "Farewell, my friend,"
he whispered, fighting back tears, unbefitting a champion.

The sobered Fir Bolgs processed out of the forest back
to the spot by the lake where the animals and frolicking
boys had emerged earlier in the day. Was that only this
morning? Lugh hurried to catch his parents. He marveled
at how the world and the Fir Bolgs' place in it had
changed in the past few hours.

"Mother!" he cried, seizing Queen Tailteann's hand.
She looked at him and saw on his face the same frozen
horror that she knew must be on her own.

She inclined her head toward him and whispered. "I
know, Lugh, I know. Say nothing, not a word. We will
have to speak of this later. The omens are bad, my darling, very, very bad." She squeezed his hand but did not
let go. Together they made their way toward the place of
the Samhain fire, gleaning strength and comfort from
each other, yet filled with apprehension for what the morrow would bring.

Chapter Six

The flames leaping skyward from the sacred bonfire of the Fir Bolgs were in perfect counterpoint to the flames consuming the DeDanaan fleet on the beach at Slieve Anierin.

Morrigan, Macha, and Neimain assumed a position a goodly distance back from the beach, driven there by the intense heat of the burning boats. They stood on a grassy knoll that jutted up from the sand. Morrigan was a woman easily bored and even the amazing spectacle before her failed to keep her full attention. She surveyed her surroundings and saw the Fir Bolgs' Samhain blaze lighting up the sky in the West.

"Look," she whispered to her sisters, "there in the western sky, just beyond that great stand of pines where the moon hangs overhead. Do you see it? There is another great fire on this island."

"By the gods, so there is," exclaimed Neimain.

Shortsighted Macha squinted in the direction of the orange glow. "Where? I don't see anything."

"It's there, believe me," said Morrigan impatiently. "The inhabitants of this place must have lit their Samhain fire. I'm going to tell the king."

"Wait, Morrigan, come back!" Neimain said to Morrigan's departing shadow. One did not approach the king without being summoned.

"She is too headstrong for her own good," Neimain grumbled to Macha. "I hope she doesn't bring King Nuad's wrath down upon all three of us."

Macha laughed, her brown eyes sparkling. "I don't think we have to worry about that. He is mad keen for her. Most likely, we are going to have to get used to being sisters to the queen of the DeDanaans."

"Oh, Macha. You always have been the one who finds honey in a dead bee tree. I hope you're right this time."

Morrigan walked boldly to the rock where King Nuad stood watching his fleet crumble into ashes. Involuntarily, she took a deeper breath when she looked closely at him. He was so handsome she wanted to put her hands on him, but knew that even she could not go that far in such a public place.

She sidled close to him and whispered sarcastically, "My lord, may it please you to have your humble servant speak?"

He turned toward her, his chiseled features outlined by the flickering light of the fire. He grinned, knowing full well that she was irked by his inattention. His eyes were full of affection and admiration for her. She was the most beautiful woman he had ever known and certainly one of the most interesting. Her mind was keen but he was sometimes puzzled by the way it seemed to scatter into many directions at once. More and more though, he found he was able to understand her moods. "Speak, humble servant," he said affectionately.

"I thought your lordship might be interested in knowing that there is another fire on this island, perhaps as big as yours. Look you behind us, where the moon hangs directly over the oaks. Do you see it?" she asked.

The king turned to peer into the night sky. "Of course! It has to be the ceremonial close of the Fir Bolgs' Samhain festival. By the gods! We have just made it. One more day at sea and we would have missed their festival gathering and with it our best chance of negotiating a peaceful sharing of Innis Ealga."

"You have decided then, to do as the Dagda Mor wishes and negotiate with the Fir Bolgs? I am surprised."

He could see a hint of amusement on her face. "No. I don't think you are, Morrigan. As you well know, when it comes to the DeDanaan tribe I may bluster and shout, but in the end, I will do what is best for the people, even if it means putting my own desires aside."

He leaned down and lifted Morrigan's chin with his closed fist. "I must ride to the Fir Bolgs at the first light of the new dawn for they will be preparing to disperse across the island. Come to my tent when the camp is quiet and all are asleep. I would lie with you before I ride with my warriors."

He kissed her lightly, granting her leave. As she started away he said to her, "Next time, Morrigan, allow Brig to announce you." She could see that he meant it and it irked her that he took kingship so seriously.

"Dagda!" the king called. "Come here."

When the wise man had lumbered to his side, Nuad said, "Look in the western sky. The Fir Bolgs conclude their festival. I have decided to accept your counsel. We will move up the river Boyne before dawn to talk with their king and his elders before they return to their homes. Call Breas, Cian, Ogma, and Bove the Red, together. I want them to ride with me. You, too. Tell Gobinu to prepare our horses for departure before the cock crows."

Dagda did not gloat nor breathe a sigh of relief, he simply nodded and said, "Yes, my lord," and went to do King Nuad's bidding. He couldn't wait to tell Brigid and Bove that his counsel had, once more, been accepted by their king.

The DeDanaan camp was silent but for the lapping of gentle waves upon the beach. Two guards stood watch sleepily over small fires meant to keep wild creatures at bay. Embers, all that remained of the once mighty DeDanaan fleet, glowed between the small cobbles of the beach as Morrigan stole from her sleeping furs and made her way to King Nuad's tent. The guards pretended not to notice when she lifted the skin flap and entered the royal presence, although they exchanged knowing smiles across the firelight as she disappeared from view and the flap fell shut.

Nuad was awake and waiting for her. He lifted the rabbit-skin rug lying over him and moved over on the furs to make a place for her. She slipped out of her soft leather shoes and pulled her tunic off over her head. She wore nothing beneath it. She lay down beside him and gazed into his handsome, strong face.

"Hello, my love," she whispered. His reply was a kiss that threatened to consume her entire being. He was such a big man, so strong, so demanding that their lovemaking was always a fierce thing, as much combat as love, but tonight he touched her breasts lightly and stroked her belly and the soft folds that hid his private delight with gentleness. She threw back the furs and bent to kiss his erect member. He allowed her to caress him for a short time before he reached up and pulled her down beside him again.

"Tonight, my darling, I will subdue you with gentleness just as we shall subdue the Fir Bolgs in the morning. There will be time enough for wild celebration later."

Flames from a fire newly kindled with coals from the Samhain bonfire cast grotesque, frightening shadows against the whitewashed walls of the Fir Bolgs' royal festival dwelling where Queen Tailteann lay trembling on the furs.

It had been but a short time since she had lain down next to King Eochy. She wasn't sure if she had fallen asleep or if the horror of what she had witnessed in the forest was haunting her mind. She had seen a clear vision of Lugh, flailing about in a raging river, the swift current carrying him farther and farther from her. She strained to reach him, crying out to him. In one last, desperate lunge her fingers touched his hair and his head spun loose from his body. His beautiful, expressive green eyes had turned to look at her, directly and accusingly.

She still could not catch her breath. Her heart was pounding wildly and she was close to tears. The dancing shadows on the wall were menacing and fear engulfed her. She filled her lungs and tried to calm herself. She looked at Eochy's strong brown back where he lay sleeping peacefully next to her. His presence was reassuring and she reached out to touch him. She could feel his strong, regular breathing beneath her fingers. She lay very still, letting the reality and calmness of his being seep into her body.

There will be no sleep this night for me, not after the ceremony in the forest, she thought, sitting up slowly and easing herself out of the furs so as not to disturb the slumbering king. She picked up her cloak and her fur-lined shoes and crept out of the round house.

As her eyes adjusted to the darkness of the night, she saw two figures near the fire next to the wall that encircled the royal enclosure. One of them was Lugh. She approached him, pulling on her warm cloak to ward off the chill of night.

"Lugh, What are you doing out of bed? I kissed you good night just a short time ago."

The guard looked up at the sound of her voice. "Queen Tailteann," he said and bowed to her.

"Mother," Lugh said in a surprised tone, "what are you doing out here?"

"I can't sleep. It looks like you are having trouble too." She dropped her voice to a whisper so the guard couldn't hear. "I can't get the picture of Rury out of my mind."

Lugh was astonished by Tailteann's words. He knew she had seen how disturbed he was by the sacrifice, but he had thought himself the only person horrified by what Ard had done. He opened his mouth to speak, but Tailteann held up her hand, warning him to hold his tongue.

"I wonder," she said sweetly to the guard, "would you mind fetching us some fresh milk? Perhaps a horn of nice warm milk would enable the prince and me to finish our night in sleep instead of keeping company with the stars." He took an oaken bucket and left the compound, bound for the byre to do his queen's bidding.

When he was gone, Lugh blurted out, "Mother! I couldn't stand to see my friend die like that. You know, sometimes he drove me crazy following me around like he did, always wanting me to show him how to do one thing or another, but we have been friends since we were little. And now he's gone . . . do you really think he's with the gods? I feel sick that he is not here to follow me around anymore and I wish, oh, I wish . . ."

Lugh began to weep hot, humiliating tears. Tailteann took him in her arms and rocked him as she had when he was a child. She stroked his blond hair back from his face and put her cheek against his, allowing his tears to mingle with her own. They stood like that for some time, sharing their grief.

"I think about the gods and their relationship to humans a lot, Mother," Lugh said at last, "and none of it ever makes sense to me. I can't see how Rury's death can make things better for the Fir Bolgs. Why did he have to die? The prophecy said death and destruction are going to come upon us anyway, so why did his own father have to kill him?"

"Oh, sweet Lugh. I wish I knew, but I am just a mortal woman without answers to holy mysteries. I only know that this is the way the Fir Bolgs have done things since time began. For the first time since I became wife to King Eochy, I felt like a foreigner tonight as I watched Ard push Rury's head under the waters of the river. Where I grew up, in Iberia, such practices ended long before I was born. I had never seen such a rite until I came to Innis Ealga. It took some getting used to, but I adapted in a short time . . . a surprisingly short time. I think, when everyone around you accepts something as true, that it is very easy to slip into their way of thinking."

She was pensive and still. "I do believe in augury, Lugh, although I have never seen a prediction turn out to be as bad as the priests forecast. I have seen prophecies come true too many times not to be a believer. I think it is possible that our distress is as much a result of what Ard saw on the killing stone tonight, as it is the result of Rury's sacrifice."

"What do you mean, Mother? Watching Rury die like that was the worst thing I have ever seen."

"I know, sweetheart, but we may have even harder times before us. You heard the priest. We are to face a new, unnamed enemy. How can one defend against something . . . or someone . . . we cannot identify? I worry that our disbelief, yours and mine, may in some way be connected to the prophecy. Are we contributing to it by being fearful and angry about the practices of the holy ones? I don't know. I only know that something ominous is happening to the Fir Bolgs and that you and I are caught up in it more than the others. I can feel the breath of the gods on my neck, Lugh."

He nodded. "I think I may be feeling it too, for I feel very strange, indeed."

On the morrow, the Fir Bolgs began preparations at dawn for the return to their various villages across Innis Ealga. A guard alerted King Eochy to the arrival of unknown horsemen.

"There are six strangers approaching the festival site, from the sea," he said. "They carry hand weapons only, so it might be assumed they come in peace, were it not for Ard's prophecy."

The king dismissed the man who brought the warning and turned to look at Queen Tailteann. Her lovely face was pale and there were blue circles under her dark eyes from her sleepless night. She lifted her fingers to her head and slowly massaged her temples. The guard's words added to the pain she felt there.

"So, my love. The prophecy comes to pass," Eochy said in his deep voice, uncharacteristically tinged with anguish and resignation.

Despite the fear in her heart, Tailteann tried to put a better face on it. "Perhaps the strangers are traders who have been delayed. You know there have been some terrible storms on the eastern sea crossing this summer."

"No. You know that no trader would venture across to Innis this late in the turning of the seasons, nor could the strangers be Fomorians, for I have guards on the northern coasts to watch for them and they have reported nothing. Six strangers only. They must be the new enemy that Ard foretold."

The king shook his head and placed his elbows on his knees so he could rest his chin on his fists. He thought for several moments, then said, "I will summon the council. We need all the wisdom of the tribe before we decide how to proceed."

Lugh was grooming Anovaar for the journey back to Lough Gur when he saw the council hastily enter the royal dwelling. Curious, he moved close enough to the entrance to overhear what was being said inside.

"What are you doing, spying on your father?" asked Aibel, creeping up softly behind him. She had been watching him from behind a tree all morning.

"Good morning, Aibel. I'm not really spying. I just want to see what is happening. I heard my father tell the council that there are six strangers approaching Tlachgta on horseback but they are not Fomorians."

Aibel frowned. Her voices had told her in the early hours of dawn that she would be punished for her unclean thoughts. "I have been expecting them," she said flatly, "they are the avengers coming to cleanse my defiled flesh."

"What are you talking about, Aibel? Are you feeling unwell?"

"The gods have spoken," she said, "they never lie. I knew an enemy would come. I knew it when you defeated my father." She turned and ran toward her family's dwelling as though a wild boar were after her.

Lugh was bewildered by her strange remarks, but the conversation within the royal dwelling was too serious to be ignored. *I will have to make sense of Aibel later,* he thought, frowning. He slipped inside and stood quietly beside the door, listening as the elders talked.

The king and the elders decided to send ten well-armed warriors out to intercept the riders, long before they got close enough to Tlachgta to inflict harm on the Fir Bolg people.

"See to it then," ordered King Eochy and the counselors filed out.

"What is happening, Father?" Lugh asked, approaching his parents. He could see the trepidation in his foster father's black eyes.

"The gods alone know the answer to that, Lugh. I fear greatly that the approaching strangers are the fulfillment of the prophecy in the forest last night. We shall have to wait and see. Stay here with us to await further news."

The royal Fir Bolg family moved closer together, the adults fearful and apprehensive and Lugh at a loss to understand his own feelings. A crisis was upon them, he knew that, but he felt an eagerness rising within him to see what the day would bring. He felt no fear, no sense of impending doom. In spite of the black look on King Eochy's face, Lugh recognized that he was experiencing now the same feeling that had propelled him out of the river ahead of Srang in the triple contest: exhilaration.

The six DeDanaan riders heard the sound of approaching hoofbeats before the Fir Bolg delegation became visible. Shortly afterward ten Fir Bolg horsemen emerged from the woods that separated the meadow upon which the DeDanaans rode, from the site of Tlachgta.

"The moment is at hand," King Nuad said when he saw the short, dark riders. He smiled broadly at Dagda

Mor and turned to address the others. "Anyone care to place a wager on what their answer will be?" he asked.

Only Dagda, and perhaps his brother, Ogma, and Cian, hoped for a negotiated settlement of the DeDanaan claim to Innis Ealga. The others were warriors born and bred, and warring was their reason for living. Most of their waking hours were spent thinking about and planning for warfare. Even their leisure was largely taken up with games that simulated warfare, so their wagers, as well as their hopes, were all on a negative answer from the Fir Bolgs.

"I will groom your horse until the full moon wanes to a sliver in the sky if they agree," offered Bove, a big man with a long red mustache and merry eyes, the son of the Dagda Mor.

"Ha! I will groom your horse until the full moon turns to a full moon again," countered Breas, the DeDanaan's chief warrior, known behind his back as Breas the Beautiful. He possessed a startling handsomeness composed of refined features and curly golden hair. His physique was well proportioned and muscular, his grooming perfect, his manners impeccable. He engaged in the rough jesting between the warriors but when he spoke, his words seemed always to have an edge to them, a sublayer of meaning that set him slightly at odds with them.

The scribe, Ogma, looked meaningfully at his brother Dagda, and the wagering stopped. They knew it would get out of hand if anyone attempted to best Breas's wager.

The earth of the green meadow was soft and spongy from occasional springs that bubbled up from below. The Fir Bolgs rode forth to meet the strangers but slowed to a careful walk when they reached the glen, not wishing to harm their horses.

In a place where wildflowers had bloomed all summer, Srang ordered the Fir Bolgs to a halt. He would force the six strangers to Innis Ealga to approach them.

Understanding well the Fir Bolgs' intent, King Nuad led his small band across the deep green field. They took even more care with their horses than had the Fir Bolgs, for they had no stables filled with replacements if one of their animals were to be injured. The DeDanaans would need every horse they rode for breeding stock once they were settled on Innis Ealga.

Breas had been designated by King Nuad to speak for the DeDanaans. He sat straight and tall as they reined up a respectful distance in front of the Fir Bolg party. Before speaking he lifted his chin, thrust out his massive chest a little farther, and spoke in a deep, resonant voice that was capable of bringing women to tears when he sang the old laments and love stories of his tribe.

"Hail, Fir Bolgs, I greet thee in the name of Nuad, the king of the DeDanaan people. I am Breas, son of the Fomorian, Ethalon and the DeDanaan, Eri. My king wishes an audience with your king. We come in peace and wish only to speak with him," he said.

He held up both hands, devoid of weapons, so the Fir Bolgs could see that he meant no malice. The other DeDanaans did the same. As Breas spoke, King Nuad absently stroked the sword called Claimh Solais, the Sword of Light, that hung at his side. It was said to be one of the treasures his ancestors had brought from the cities of the DeDanaans' origin. His grandfather told him that when it was drawn from its sheath no man could escape it because it became magically irresistible. He knew the sword was a special weapon because if had proven itself in battle many times.

The Fir Bolg, Srang, spoke words of greeting but received only a confused silence from the strangers. He knew but one language, his own, and he was unskilled with words even in that. He had a more pugnacious nature than the other warriors with whom he rode and he was eager for a fight after his humiliation at Lugh's hand. It made him angry that he was not understood immediately. He felt like hurling a sling stone at the intruders. He knew no good could come of this encounter. He scowled and tried again to make himself understood.

The two groups spoke dialects of the same language, for in fact, they were kinsmen sharing a common ancestor. After a few false starts, Breas and Srang were able to understand one another well enough.

Breas reiterated King Nuad's wish to speak with the king of the Fir Bolgs and Srang rode back to discuss the proposal with his kinsmen. The Fir Bolg warriors, mindful of Ard's prophecy, were confounded by the request and fearful of bringing strangers into their midst. Yet they reasoned that the strangers would be greatly outnumbered by Fir Bolg warriors, all of whom would be armed and waiting for them when they entered the Fir Bolg festival site.

Srang returned to the DeDanaans and fairly spat out the message. "We will take your king to meet our king, but he may bring only one man with him as his protector."

"I will go," King Nuad said boldly. "You come with me, Cian. The rest of you, withdraw to the woods. Breas, you are in charge. If we have not returned before the dining time, go back to the camp by the sea and alert the rest of the warriors."

The Fir Bolg escort was bewildered when the DeDanaan king announced his plan to approach their king unarmed. The surprised glances they exchanged told clearly that they thought such a move was foolish. Nevertheless, Nuad rode around in front of Breas the Beautiful, and made a show of presenting his magical sword to him with a flourish. Cian followed suit, handing his sword and knife to Ogma. Then Nuad and Cian turned their steeds toward the future and rode forth slowly to join the Fir Bolg escort that would take them to meet King Eochy, then in the ninth year of his reign over the Fir Bolg tribe in the land of Innis Ealga.

Chapter Seven

Lugh ran to the outer wall to watch the approach of the unknown riders, his heart beating hard. There were only two men. Where were the others? The scouts had reported six. He peered carefully at the strangers being led into the festival grounds.

They were dressed oddly in a fashion different from the Fir Bolgs. The younger man wore an ornament on his cloak that mesmerized Lugh. There was something so familiar about it that he almost thought he recognized it, but that was impossible. He didn't even know what metal it was made of, but he thought it beautiful. The ornament was large and circular, pierced through at its jeweled center by a sword-shaped pin, much more ornate than the utilitarian cloak pins worn by the Fir Bolgs.

Lugh was sure both of the strangers were of royal blood. Although they were unarmed and were being led by Srang and the other warriors, they had an air of confidence about them that made it clear they did not consider themselves inferior. They sat high on their horses and were so big, he wondered if they could be the giants spoken of by the storytellers.

When they stepped down from their horses, they towered over the Fir Bolgs. With golden hair falling down their backs and eyes the color of his own, Lugh thought they seemed like gods but did not fear them. Rather, he admired their beauty and strength and their bearing. Especially their bearing, for outnumbered and unarmed in the midst of a potentially hostile people, the two men were at ease.

The older man saw Lugh looking at him with unabashed curiosity and awe, and smiled at him, displaying strong white teeth and a twinkle in his eye. The younger man followed King Nuad's gaze and also smiled at Lugh, who blushed with pride at having been singled out by these golden god-men who had ridden so bravely into the Fir Bolg presence.

Within the royal dwelling, Eochy and Tailteann's fur-covered stools had been elevated on a small platform for the purpose of receiving the strangers. King Eochy wore his sternest expression. Tailteann sat beside him, her lovely face a mask of impassiveness although she was greatly taken by the beauty of the two men standing before them. Something about the strangers reminded her of her son. Was it their unusual height? Or their golden hair and light eyes? Or was it something more? She was suddenly aware of the smallness of the Fir Bolgs. Even her beloved husband looked dark and unlovely to her by comparison.

The younger stranger bent low before the royal couple and spoke. "Hail to the king and queen of the Fir Bolgs. I am Cian, son of Diancecht, royal physician to the DeDanaans. May I present our leader, King Nuad?" Tailteann gasped audibly.

Lugh was so intent on the strangers that he missed the stricken look on Queen Tailteann's face when the younger man spoke his name aloud.

King Nuad bowed his head but did not bend his knee, a slight that went unnoticed by most of the assemblage, who were still bedazzled by the appearance of the DeDanaans. Lugh, however, noticed it and marveled at the courage of the man who dared not kneel before the king. The lesser chiefs who appeared before his foster father would have had their lands confiscated or their cows impounded for such an affront.

In a strong, deep voice, King Nuad explained the presence of the DeDanaans on the island of Innis Ealga. "Long, long ago, out of the memory of any living DeDanaan, our people were forced to flee from this island by the cursed Fomorian tribe. We have roamed the northern lands for many generations, longing always to return to the home of our ancestors. This we have accomplished in the holy season of Samhain. You cannot know the joy my people experienced when our sailing crafts put in on these holy shores."

As Nuad spoke, King Eochy's brows knitted together

in a frown. He interrupted. "Surely, King of the DeDanaans, you know that this island is occupied by the three clans of the Fir Bolg tribe. What affrontery is it that makes you think you can sail in here and claim our island as your own?"

"Ah, most respected King Eochy, it is not our intention to do any such thing. On the best advice of our wise men, I come before you with a proposition for a fair sharing of this land. Our DeDanaan claim to this soil is far older than that of the Fir Bolgs and therefore, has more merit. We, however, are willing to share this land with you."

"Share it! Share our island! This is madness. Innis Ealga is the homeland of the Fir Bolg people."

"Hear me out, sir." Nuad's tone had grown steely. "Our proposal is this: Let us split our island straight down the middle, north to south. I care not which half is taken by the Fir Bolgs, nor which half is to be ours. Such a division would be a fair one."

"This is nonsense!" King Eochy cried. "Why should we share our island with strangers? It is our land, not yours, no matter what your claim. Such a division would never work. The royal residence is at Lough Gur and it would be separated from the places our tribe considers holy, Tlachgta where you stand, and the great necropolis of Parthenon's people, which was here long before Innis Ealga was occupied by you or by us."

King Nuad saw that he had an opening. The Fir Bolg king was considering the plan he had put forth, not rejecting it outright. He pressed on.

"We could appoint a joint council to work out the details and the laws under which we could live peaceably. It is my wish to avoid bloodshed in this matter, but be assured, King Eochy, that my people are prepared to fight to the death to establish our home on this island. You had best heed my words. We are here, and we are here to stay. I ordered the fleet that brought us to these shores burned. We have no way of returning to Lochland, the land that gave us temporary shelter. The DeDanaan people are proud and warlike, and I warn you, if we are denied what is rightfully ours, blood will stain the green grass of this island, and you will live to rue the day that you rejected my fair proposal."

The Fir Bolg monarch listened to Nuad's impassioned

narrative with unwavering attention. His piercing dark eyes were on the face of the stranger, this new foe who had appeared exactly as the High Priest had said he would. The future was clear, for the gods were never wrong. Eochy could see no use in trying to change a prediction made during the holy rite of Samhain. Negotiating could yield nothing because a bloody conflict with death and destruction had been prophesied last night in the sacred clearing. So it must come to pass.

In a voice so low the others had to strain to hear his words, the king of the Fir Bolgs said, "I will confer with my priests and wise men. We will study your proposition and prepare an answer for you. Do not think, DeDanaan king, that we value the island of Innis Ealga less than your people do, for it may be everything to you now, but it is and always has been everything to us. We wish no bloodshed, no enmity, but neither can we cleave this fair isle into two parts. I fear the future that your coming here forces on us. Tomorrow when the sun is at its highest point, I will send a delegation to meet you in the same meadow where they met you today. You will have our answer then."

Eochy sighed heavily and rose, extending his hand to Queen Tailteann, signifying that the audience was at a close.

"We await your decision, King Eochy. Thank you for seeing us today," said King Nuad.

He smiled broadly at the Fir Bolg king before turning his gaze to the beautiful, dark-haired queen at Eochy's side. By the gods! She was a little slip of a thing, and a beauty too. She did not look quite like the rest of the Fir Bolgs.

The admiration he felt for Tailteann was communicated to her by the quick sweep his eyes made over her body, and she found herself smiling at him, as though they shared a secret. She caught herself quickly, before Eochy had a chance to see. This stranger, after all, was a serious threat to them, handsome or not. Her response to him surprised her and she felt guilty. She gave her husband's hand a squeeze of support and affection.

When the two DeDanaans had gone, the royal house seemed darker, smaller somehow, and decidedly forlorn. King Eochy said, "Well, my friends, are we to be driven from our land without a fight? Or are we to fight and die in defense of our home? By the gods! They have taken all choice from us. We cannot maintain our honor nor our good name if we simply give up."

"No, Father," Lugh blurted out, "I think you should consider sharing the island. There may be a way we could work it out."

The warrior Srang, snorted, "Of course, we can't 'work it out.' We have been invaded and there can be only one response." He jerked his thumb in Lugh's direction and spoke intemperately of Lugh's parentage. "You cannot take advice from a fostered son who is half DeDanaan, sire, not when the Fir Bolg people are threatened by his bloodline."

Eochy looked sadly at Lugh, believing that Srang was right. If he were to follow his son's advice, he would be accused of weakness and favoritism, faults that could never be allowed to blemish his good name. Lugh may have beaten Srang at the triple contest, but he was a lad, just sixteen summers, and Srang had been tested many times in battle. His counsel had to carry the greater weight.

"I'm sorry, Lugh. The prophecy must be fulfilled. We must fight, as Ard said we would." Without waiting for Lugh's reply, he turned to Srang. "We will fight at Moytirra," he said, "since it is our traditional battleground and well known to all Fir Bolg warriors."

Srang replied, "We will crush the invaders and make them rue the day they set foot upon our island." He trusted not in the prophecies of the weak priest, a man who had never thrown an ax in battle.

King Eochy looked doubtful. Lugh was angry. It was as though he were no longer present. The king was clearly going to heed the advice of Srang and ignore his. He turned and left the royal dwelling abruptly, his cheeks flaming with emotion.

He was sure King Eochy must have forgotten the latter part of the prophecy, that the Fir Bolgs would suffer and die. It would be a battle they could not win if his father insisted on making the prediction come true.

Lugh went straight to his clearing in the woods beside the stream. He had much thinking to do. Aibel watched him go and followed him at a distance, knowing well where he often sought solace.

He was huddled beside a large stone, staring into the crystal-clear waters as though answers to his troubles might lie in the mossy streambed, when she came into the clearing.

Without looking up, he moved over on the grass to make a spot for her. She sat beside him gracefully, tucking her feet beneath her. "We were all watching," she said. "I've never seen men as tall as they are."

"They are DeDanaans, Aibel, The older man is their king. I think they said his name is Nuad. I didn't get the name of the younger one. The king said they have come to live on Innis Ealga. They want to share the island with us, but your father is arguing that we must go to battle with them and King Eochy seems to believe we have to, just because of the prophecy."

"So, why do you look so troubled? You love to fight."

"Aibel"—at last he turned to look at her, his eyes intense—"They are DeDanaans. I am the son of Cian, a DeDanaan. I came from them, the people with whom your father would do battle."

"Oh, dear. What will that mean?"

"I wish I knew."

Aibel slipped her small brown hand into his. Her touch was warm and soft. He looked at her shining eyes. He put his arm around her and drew her close.

Always before Lugh had been able to go to his foster parents for guidance and comfort. This was the first time he had ever had to look only inside himself for answers. He knew he would not be able to discuss his doubts with the handmaiden to the priests. Aibel had seen no evil in the sacrifice of their best friend.

In his mind he heard again the words he had been taught to say as a small child, "I am Lugh, son of Cian the DeDanaan, and foster son of Eochy King of the Fir Bolgs." *I am the son of a DeDanaan. I am one of those golden ones!* he thought. He felt a surge of pride to think that those beautiful, brave warriors who had looked at him and grinned, were related to him. Had they smiled because they recognized that he was one of them?

The joy of recognizing his ancestry was mitigated by a

fear of parting from his beloved foster parents. Could the DeDanaans take him away? He would never consider such a thing. His life was here, in the Fir Bolg royal family.

He realized with a start that his natural mother was a Fomorian. *By the gods! What does that make me?* The Fir Bolgs referred to his mother's people with contempt and fear, but they didn't seem to hate the DeDanaans in the same way they hated the Fomorians. He wondered how he could have been so blind to his parentage for so long. He had come to feel like a part of the Fir Bolg tribe, but now he saw that he was not really one of them.

He asked himself if Tailteann would still love him, now that the enemy who threatened them was of his own blood. She had loved him knowing that his natural mother was a Fomorian, he reasoned, and he knew then that the tears the queen had shed today were from the fear of losing him.

"Lugh! Where do you go when you shut me out like this? You haven't spoken to me for the longest time. It is as though you have forgotten that I am here," protested Aibel.

"I'm sorry," he said, "I have so much on my mind right now. I don't know what all of this is going to mean for us." He decided to pay full attention to her. He slid his hand under her cloak and felt the delicate bones of her spine where they curved in at her waist.

This was the moment he had longed for, planned for, and anticipated for so long that his body could not let it pass by. He bent and kissed her small eager mouth, surprised by the passion with which she returned his kiss.

He urged her onto her back in the grass, caressing her arms and kissing her deeply, when Aibel struggled to break free of his embrace. There was a look of horror on her face and terror in her eyes. "Stop! Stop! How dare you degrade me, a handmaiden of the gods!"

"Aibel, what is it? What did I do?" He reached for her as she rose to her knees, screaming something incomprehensible at him, and rubbing wildly at her arms.

"I am unclean, my flesh is defiled," she said, attacking him, scratching at his face. He grasped her wrists and held her off. "Aibel. Stop this! What's the matter with you? Have you gone mad?"

She wrenched herself loose and ran out of the clearing, tearing off her cloak as she ran, mumbling, "Filthy, rotting, flesh."

Lugh stooped and picked up her cloak, shaking his head in astonishment at her outburst. Something was terribly wrong with Aibel, but he didn't think it had anything to do with him. He heard she sometimes acted strangely with others, too. He sighed deeply. It seemed as though a hundred seasons of the earth had passed since yesterday morning.

He was not ready to return to the company of the Fir Bolgs so he resumed his position by the edge of the stream for further contemplation. Soon, however, the cold and damp sent him searching for the warmth of the royal family's temporary dwelling. They would not be breaking camp until negotiations with the DeDanaans were settled.

Lugh watched the next day as the Fir Bolg delegation rode out to meet the DeDanaans in the meadow. He ran in search of his foster parents, encountering King Eochy first, where he stood outside the wall looking after the departing riders.

"Father, what will they say to the DeDanaans?" he cried, seizing the king's arm.

He was unprepared for the profound sorrow in the eyes of the man who turned to face him. "My son," Eochy said, putting both arms around the young man, drawing him to his chest, "my beloved son, a cruel time is about to be visited upon us. It cannot be avoided, I fear. Only the gods can help us now. Pray to them, son, as I do, that our people will be spared." Lugh hugged Eochy tightly, unable to voice his objection to his father's fatalism, not wanting to damage their relationship.

The message Srang carried to the DeDanaans was uncompromising. King Nuad felt a twinge of remorse at not having been able to prevent a battle, but just a twinge. To the grim-faced Srang and his Fir Bolg riders, Nuad gave his answer smilingly. "We will meet you on the Plain of Moytirra at the first light of the Sun God on the day of the next full moon. May the strongest claim to Innis Ealga be victorious."

* * *

As the DeDanaans rode back to their seaside camp, Nuad said, "I noticed when we were in the Fir Bolg festival site that there were no weapons or tools made of bronze, not even in the king's own house. We can conclude from their absence that the advance scouts were right, these people do not yet have the advantage of this superior metal. They do not seem overly concerned, so they must not understand what a tremendous advantage bronze weapons will give us in a fight."

"You are right, sire," said Cian. "I, too, took inventory while we were there and saw no articles made of bronze. In fact, I saw many axes that still had stone heads. Did you see the stacks of javelins inside the compound wall, as we came in? Where the boys were tying them in bundles for the journey back to their homes? Even those festival javelins, which must have been their very best, looked to be tipped with copper. All of the cloak pins I saw were made of copper or lignite; only the queen's was of silver. The art of advanced metalworking has obviously not reached these shores yet."

Ever the thoughtful warrior, Cian went on to caution, "Still, we must not be too sure that our superior weapons alone will bring us victory. These Fir Bolg are small in stature but strong and muscular and they will be as determined to win as we are. That will count for a lot." A frown creased his handsome brow, and a shadow clouded his green eyes as he contemplated the coming fight.

"You are right, of course," said the king, "but there is no denying that we should have a great advantage over them if all else is equal. How many warriors do you estimate they have, Cian?"

"Between two and three hundred men, I'd say. If their women fight too, that number could easily double."

"No problem there." King Nuad grinned, thinking of Morrigan. "The DeDanaan women will fight, and the Fir Bolgs will be finished before the battle is begun!"

"But, sire, we will still be outnumbered. And they have the advantage of knowing the battlefield of Moytirra well, while we don't even know where it is," Breas objected.

Nuad turned to look at Breas the Beautiful. He found the young warrior tiresome and particularly disliked his reliance on his mother, Eri. Nevertheless, he had to acknowledge the man's superior battle skills. Only Cian and

Bove the Red could approach Breas's ability in the contests.

Nuad sighed. Breas was his champion, whether he liked him or not.

"Don't worry, Breas," he said, trying to keep his tone even, "I intend to know every rock and tree on the Plain of Moytirra before the day of the battle. That way we can plot our strategy."

Breas allowed his king to ride ahead of him, then turned to look back at Cian and rolled his eyes at Nuad's remark. The gesture did not go unnoticed by Dagda Mor, who felt a shiver dance down his spine. A seed of fear was planted in his heart by the brash warrior's insolent look. He glanced at King Nuad where he rode at the head of the line. *Such a strong king,* he thought, *may the gods hold him forever in their hands and prevent harm from coming to him.*

Nuad urged his horse into a canter. The others followed, eager to return to their makeshift camp on the seashore to prepare for the fighting that would determine which tribe was to have dominance over the island of Innis Ealga.

Chapter Eight

"Mother," Lugh shouted, "you are not being fair! I proved my prowess in the triple contest and I should be allowed to prove my valor on the battlefield if I am to be a true man of the Fir Bolgs. There is no good reason why I should not take up a sword against our enemy."

Queen Tailteann sighed. They had been over the same ground for five journeys of the sun. "Lugh, I have told you repeatedly why you may not participate in this battle." She rubbed her head and lifted her tired black eyes to look upon her indignant son. "You are of DeDanaan heritage and therefore cannot take up arms against those who share your blood. Why must you insist on carrying on like this? I am weary of discussing the matter with you. You may not participate and that is all there is to it. Go now, and leave me in peace."

"But, Mother, it isn't fair! I am a Fir Bolg and a good warrior. You've got to let me prove it. I can be of help to Father."

"No more, Lugh," she said sharply. "I have heard your arguments. The answer is no today, as it was yesterday, and as it will be tomorrow. Neither your father nor I will relent on this matter. You are wasting your breath and my patience with this endless badgering. I want you to stop it."

He stood glaring at her for a few minutes, knowing that his cause was futile, but reluctant to give up the fight. In frustration, he turned on his heel and stomped from the royal dwelling, fully intending to resume the discussion after the midday meal.

He went in search of King Eochy, whose position seemed less firm than Queen Tailteann's. There wasn't much time before the next full moon. He glanced into the bright blue sky where the sun was almost overhead. He decided to eat alone, not wanting to sit with the other lads. He was sick of their bragging about participating in the battle at Moytirra.

As Lugh approached the filach fiadah, Srang came up behind him and said mockingly, "So, Mama won't let her wee lad come out to play on the battlefield? What a shame."

Lugh turned on him in a rage and struck a resounding blow to the side of Srang's face, startling the older man who was sent sprawling. Lugh regretted his impulsive response immediately but it was too late to take it back now. Srang was on his feet, circling him with his fists up.

Srang's face darkened with pure hatred as he jabbed at Lugh, who ducked his blow and struck back as he came up out of his crouch. His fist connected with Srang's chin and sent him reeling.

Srang came back, snarling, "Just because you're a prince, don't think I will spare you."

His left fist shot out, splitting Lugh's lower lip. Blood spattered over the combatants. The sight of it made Lugh clearheaded and decisive in his movements. He moved in close to Srang with short, hard jabs as King Eochy had shown him. Srang tried to restrain him in a viselike embrace, but Lugh broke free and doubled Srang over with a hard blow to his midsection.

From among the crowd that gathered, King Eochy stepped forward. "Stop this at once! Lugh, Srang, there will be no fighting among our own! Stop it, I say."

Reluctantly, Lugh put his fists down and turned his bloody face toward his father. Srang sank to his knees, pausing to clear his head before trying to stand up. He was shaky as he took a few steps to where the king stood, glaring at both of them.

"What is the meaning of this?" Eochy demanded. "With an enemy facing us that could be our undoing I am outraged to find you two at each other's throats. Well? What have you to say for yourselves?"

He waited, looking from one to the other. Both stood silently, heads hung down, looking at their boots in the dirt. Finally, the king said, "Lugh, I would have an answer."

Lugh raised his head and looked into his father's blaz-

ing eyes. Lugh nursed his own anger at not being allowed
to fight, but knew he could not dishonor King Eochy . . .
even if he was wrong about Moytirra.

"Yes, Father. As you know, I am angry that I am not to
be permitted to fight in the upcoming battle and I had just
quarreled with Mother when Srang mocked me as a child
whose mother would not let him fight. I lost my temper
and hit him."

A light of empathy arose in the king's eyes. "I see," he
said. "Srang? What have you to say?"

Still unable to look at the king, Srang mumbled,
"Nothing, sire."

Eochy thought for a few moments. "I will see each of
you individually in my dwelling tonight after the dining
hour, after you have had an opportunity to calm down and
think over your behavior this day."

"All right, Father, but—"

"Later, Lugh. Go clean your face before you dine."

As Lugh walked toward the lake to do his father's bidding, King Eochy addressed Srang. "You are a man of
more than thirty summers. I am displeased that there is
such rage in your heart that you would taunt a prince
when you know well the reason he cannot fight in the
battle of Moytirra. Go from me now, and when you come
to the royal dwelling I hope you will have cleansed yourself of the jealousy that led you into this fight with
Lugh."

Srang walked away holding his head high, shaking
with anger and frustration. *The king should have called
down his wrath upon his son, not me,* he thought. *I have
served him long and well and I deserve better than being
humiliated before the people of this tribe.*

Later that day at the DeDanaans' seaside camp, when
the afternoon sun had turned the beach to gold, King
Nuad felt the need to take a respite from the plans being
made for the battle with the Fir Bolgs.

"Go find Morrigan for me," he instructed his slave.
Brig bowed low before him and went to fetch Morrigan.

Shortly, Morrigan appeared, wearing a lightweight tunic and a cloak dyed a bright cockle red. "Hello, Nuad.
Brig said you would like to see me?"

"Yes," he sighed. "We have been at this planning too

long. I will be able to think better if I leave it for a while. Were you busy?"

"Not very. Neimain and I were practicing our battle skills. I'm out of breath. May I have a drink?" she asked, picking up the bone cup that lay beside a pot of sweet water. She filled it and drank greedily from it without waiting for his answer.

By the gods! She is a beauty, he thought, watching as she tilted her head back to drink. When she had finished, he said, "Let us walk. The day is warm and beautiful. The Sun God shows us his favor, I think."

They set out over the heather-clad hills beyond the camp site. The autumn sun shone down on their backs until Morrigan was forced to slip off her cloak.

Her tunic was belted loosely with a braided leather thong from which hung a fes and her dagger. Her legs were bare, sleek, and strong as she climbed the green hills. Nuad deliberately fell behind her a few steps so he could watch her as she climbed. She moved beautifully and effortlessly, like a cat. Her heavy auburn hair bobbed back and forth across her back and the sun picked out its threads of red and gold.

With each step she took, Nuad's excitement rose. He had a desire to take her then and there. It was with the greatest self-control that he was able to wait until he could steer her into a wooded grove some distance up the hillside. Once inside the shelter of the trees they walked to a small clearing where wild grasses grew tall.

Nuad reached out and took her elbow. Without a word he turned her to face him. There were faint traces of perspiration across her upper lip and under her eyes. Her cheeks were flushed from exertion and her brown eyes shone. She saw in an instant what he wanted and melted into his embrace, returning the passion of his kisses in full measure.

They made love with abandon. The grass was soon matted down into a comfortable nest for them, softer and sweeter smelling than a sleeping pallet. "By the gods, Morrigan! You are my delight, a woman unlike any other," he said, rolling over and pulling her close to him. "I love you."

She smiled and closed her eyes. They slept for a while in their nakedness under the warmth of the dappled sun.

When they awoke they made love again, languorously, exploring sensation, enjoying to the fullest their physical pleasure.

"I want to stay here with you forever," Morrigan said later, smoothing the golden hairs on Nuad's chest into a pattern. She leaned over and kissed his pale pink nipple. Then again. This time she nipped him with her teeth and laughed.

"Again, my love?" asked Nuad, somewhat surprised.

"Again, if you're able," she challenged. "I don't think I can ever have enough of you, Nuad. You are so magnificent that I sometimes wonder if you are not a god in disguise."

He threw back his head and laughed heartily. "I an no god, Morrigan. I am just a man, but I am able!"

"Just a man?" Morrigan hooted. "Oh, no, my love, you are a god among mortal men, I promise you that!"

They would have liked to lie in their nest throughout the night, snuggled close under the warmth of their cloaks, looking up at the shining stars, feeling in harmony with all nature, but the responsibility of kingship and the cold that came with the dying of the day, finally tugged them back to reality. Reluctantly they rose and dressed, then paused to kiss one last time in their private lair, slowly and very sweetly.

Nuad spoke as he cupped her beautiful face in his strong hands and looked at her intently. "I love you, Morrigan. If I survive this battle at Moytirra, I want you to become my queen."

Her eyes grew wide and a small gasp escaped from her slightly bruised lips. When she spoke her voice was strained, apprehensive, and faraway.

"Oh, Nuad, why? Why must you ask me to be your queen? Why can't we go on as we are now?" she said slowly, her distress obvious. "I'm not sure how to answer you. I love you, Oh, yes! I do love you. But queen? I don't know about that."

He grasped her arms roughly, resisting the urge to shake her. "What do you mean, you don't know?" He spoke barely above a whisper, his teeth clenched. "You love me but don't want to be my queen? What kind of a demon woman are you?

She soothed him as best she could but the question was not resolved and the silence between them grew awkward as they made their way back to the seaside in the dark.

Why did he have to go and spoil things with an offer of queenship? she wondered. *Everything was fine the way it was. I have important work to do and I cannot do it as his queen. I wish I could explain it to him, but even if I could I don't think he would understand. Then too, I'm afraid that . . .* She hated to name her fear, even in her own thoughts, but it could not be avoided any longer. *I fear that I am barren. I have lain with Nuad too many times and still the bleeding comes with each new moon. Perhaps this is the fee the gods extract from me for the good fortune I've been given over other women.*

She glanced at Nuad. His jaw was set and hard. He was so angry with her that the silence hung between them like a sword, heavy and sharp.

"Nuad," she began, "I'm sorry. I . . ."

"Say no more, Morrigan. We will not speak of it again," he said harshly. "I won't be made a fool of twice."

Chapter Nine

When dawn came on the day of the next full moon, both sides were in position for the battle that would take place on the Plain of Moytirra. The Sun God did not appear through the thick clouds hanging low on the horizon. Fog was so thick warriors could not see the swords in their own hands. Moisture seeped from the air like tears, and gray clouds pressed down on the combatants with an oppressive weight that added to their apprehension.

Lugh stood resentfully outside the Fir Bolgs' royal battle tent, safely away from the fighting field. He liked to think that his own powers of persuasiveness had convinced his foster mother to allow him to be present at Moytirra, even though he could not fight there, but he knew that King Eochy had intervened on his behalf.

He could hear the waters moving against the banks of Lough Arrow, but the fog prevented him from seeing the lough, let alone the distant battlefield. How he longed to be among the warriors, preparing for action! But he didn't see how warriors could fight in such dense mist and fog. It would be impossible to see one another through it.

A slim brown hand reached out of the mist and grasped his shoulder. Lugh jumped, realizing that his intensity had caused him to drop his guard.

"Oh! Aibel, it's you," he said with relief. "What are you doing here?"

"It will be some time before the battle horns sound, and I wanted to tell you again how sorry I am that you're not going to get to fight. It's a shame that our first battle has to be against a tribe of your blood, because I know how much you want to be with the other warriors."

Lugh wished he could see her face more clearly. Her moods had him confused and off balance. She could turn on him as she had done in the woods, screaming hysterically, and the next time he saw her she acted as though nothing had happened. He was alert and wary with her now in ways that would never have seemed possible when they were children together.

"It feels as though I have been cut off from the Fir Bolgs," he told her bitterly. "I have lived among you all my life and now, when I could make a contribution to the welfare of the entire tribe, I am not permitted to take up arms. These old rules are stupid and have been observed far longer than they should."

Even as he spoke doubts flitted around in his mind. He had not been able to drive out the images of the tall golden ones who had come to King Eochy's tent, although he tried diligently. He did not want to deny his upbringing and the Fir Bolg parents he loved so much, but at the same time he knew well that he was one of the tall golden ones. Such conflict was almost more than his youthful mind and emotions could encompass, so he attempted to hold part of it at bay.

"Rules of the tribes were decided time out of mind, Lugh, and they are for our benefit. Have we not prospered by following them? I know it is hard for you today, but you'd be happier if you could accept it."

"Hmph," he scoffed, "I'll never accept laws just because they are old. That doesn't make good sense. Every generation has to think for itself."

"But, Lugh, have you no respect for the wisdom of the elders?"

He sighed, exasperated by the conversation, the weather, and the delay of the battle. "Why do we have to talk about these things now?"

"We don't. I just wanted to see you before the battle starts, that's all. I am going to act as a war witch today," she offered, changing the subject.

"I've heard that," he said. "Have the priests instructed you well?"

"I hope so. They taught us all the old chants and curses to scream at the DeDanaans. I will be positioned on the other side of the battlefield, in the middle. If this fog ever lifts perhaps you will be able to see me over there. Our robes are black and they might stand out against this white fog. I'll have to leave soon to get my face painted."

She waited expectantly, but Lugh was still peering into the mist as though he could see something there, and did not answer her.

After a long silence, she said tentatively, "Well, I suppose it is time for me to get back." Still, Lugh said nothing. "Lugh," she said sharply, "I'm going now."

"I'm sorry, Aibel. I just can't get my mind off what is about to happen . . . without me. This is a terrible time."

She nodded. "It is. I feel a little uncertain of how I will perform this day, but at least I get to perform."

"You'll do very well, Aibel," he said kindly. "I know you will make the priests proud of you."

He hesitated, suddenly wanting to ask about Srang, but not knowing how she would take it. She had never mentioned the fight he'd had with her father, although he knew the entire tribe had talked about it for days. He decided to let it go, not wanting to risk an emotional scene with her today of all days.

He put his arm around her and drew her to him. "Go now, my little war witch." He kissed her forehead and smiled down at her. She stood on tiptoe and kissed his cheek, warmed by his affection, then disappeared back into the fog from which she had come.

In the heavy air Lugh listened to the sound of men getting ready to fight. They spoke not at all but went about their business, arranging themselves and their weapons for battle. Lugh felt a physical pain at being outside the activity. He knew that he was more skilled than any warrior who would take the field, and he longed to be able to test it in something other than a game. And now he could not even be a spectator. The fog would prevent him from seeing anything. He felt completely closed out of the events that would soon shape the future of the Fir Bolg tribe.

Lugh could hear the low rumble of voices inside the battle tent as the king conferred with his warriors. They had been in there a long time making changes in battle plans necessitated by the fog. Lugh was curious but felt such enmity for Srang that he preferred to stand outside, shivering in the damp mist, than to be in the warrior's presence. It was too humiliating to watch his foster father leaning on Srang for advice, after his own had been rejected.

* * *

King Eochy stood with downcast eyes and a heart as heavy and cold as the fog outside as the chief priest, Ard, spoke, "My lord, I fear the DeDanaans have cast a spell upon the land. They have sent this fog to blind our eyes on the battlefield. The priests who practice DeDanaan magic are said to be the most powerful on earth. They can command the seas, the skies, and the gods of fire. We have no magic with which to undo their charms. We will have to fight in the fog."

"Tell me priest. What would the gods have me do?" Eochy cried in an agonized voice.

"The gods have spoken in veiled messages—" Ard replied cautiously.

Srang interrupted. "We must formulate a battle plan in the face of these things. You cannot trust priests to tell warriors how to fight," he said to King Eochy. "We should take the priest's words into consideration as we plan, but then choose our own actions."

Eochy glanced at Queen Tailteann, who inclined her head slightly, short of a nod, but he understood that she wanted him to listen to Srang's plan. He took a deep breath and turned his dark eyes on the warrior. "Very well," he said, "show me what you would have us do."

Srang unrolled a tanned rabbit skin upon which a detailed map had been drawn by Fir Bolg scouts, and outlined his strategy.

King Eochy listened carefully, but believed as Ard did, that the fate of his people had been sealed by the gods on Samhain. He knew that Queen Tailteann's faith wavered and she was not convinced of the outcome of the battle.

He looked at her with sadness on his face. *I love her so much it causes me great pain to know I am about to bring dishonor to her by being the king storytellers will hold accountable for our defeat. In all the years that stretch in front of us, we will have to hear of this defeat in songs and stories that will never die. Perhaps the humiliation will be less severe if I am able to minimize the slaughter.* He turned Srang's plan over in his mind but could find no defects in it.

"We will try your strategy, Srang," Eochy decided. "There are no other choices left to us now. Instruct the warriors immediately."

* * *

Srang strode from the tent and saw Lugh standing outside. He stopped in front of him and looked him full in the face. He said nothing, just smiled triumphantly, before disappearing into the fog, leaving Lugh more agitated than before.

The young prince ducked and entered the battle tent, emptied now of everyone but King Eochy and Queen Tailteann. The king was pacing in front of the queen, who sat gazing at him, her face troubled. She looked up at Lugh's entrance.

"Lugh, where have you been?" she asked, full of concern because she knew how upset he was. She was sure Lugh would never dishonor her and the king by disobeying the laws of the tribe, but she breathed a sigh of relief to see him in their presence, unarmed.

"I was just outside the tent. It got too crowded in here," Lugh said pointedly.

The king stopped his pacing and regarded Lugh solemnly before he spoke. "Lugh, there are words I would say to you before the battle commences."

The king moved to Lugh's side. The short, dark foster father hugged his tall, blond son. "Remember, no matter the outcome of today's battle, you are a well-loved prince. You have the blood of the DeDanaans and the Fomorians, but you have the soul of the Fir Bolgs. As a prince of our people you must never give in to personal rage. Act always with reason and compassion. Honor and obey the gods, and above all, honor your foster mother, Tailteann. She and I love you well and consider you our son in all ways. I am proud of you now in the discipline you have shown by not taking up arms, as hard as I know that is for you. If this day's events make it impossible for me to see you take your place as a leader, know that I will be always at your side in spirit."

Lugh felt his throat tighten. What did the king mean? As certain as Eochy was of the Fir Bolgs' defeat, Lugh had never for a moment considered that he might lose his beloved foster father to death in this battle.

Icy fingers of fear clutched at his heart, and he hugged King Eochy with a ferociousness that surprised them both. He did not want to let him go, feeling as though the love flowing between them was enough to protect the king as long as their bodies were touching. How sorry he was that he had been so angry with him.

Gently, Eochy removed Lugh's arms from around his waist. He kissed him tenderly on the forehead, then walked to the place where Queen Tailteann sat. Tears welled in her eyes at the moving scene between the two human beings she loved best on the earth.

She held out her hands to King Eochy, who took them in his and knelt before her on one knee. He kissed one hand, then the other. The emotion between them was so strong Lugh was embarrassed to be privy to it.

"My beloved husband, rise. Do not bend your knee to me," she said. "Are we not partners, even in this, as we have always been?"

She rose and stepped down to stand beside him. He took her in his arms and they clung together tightly, silently, for what seemed to Lugh an interminable time.

"We are, indeed, partners in all things, for all time. If I should not return to you today . . ." He gulped, tears filling his eyes. The thought of never holding her, never seeing her again was too painful to be borne. "If I should not return, I want you to know that my love for you extends beyond the grave. It was bestowed by the gods and has been a precious gift. You have made my life worthwhile. If the gods call me home today, I will go to them a better man for having loved you." He kissed her face, and their tears mingled.

"Eochy, my Eochy, I love you so. Please come back to me. Please. You are my life," was all she could say.

Lugh had to turn his face away, feeling that his presence was an intrusion, yet also feeling enriched by such overflowing, unselfish love.

They watched King Eochy stride away from the tent toward his waiting horse, showing not a trace of weakness. Lugh hugged his mother protectively to him, all anger at her having dissipated in his father's embrace. Queen Tailteann looked after her husband dry-eyed, her tears all spent. She was a queen who understood well her responsibility. She knew there was great risk in any battle but somewhere in her deepest soul she believed that Eochy was indestructible. Knowing how she loved him, how could the gods allow harm to come to him?

* * *

Across the field King Nuad and his chief DeDanaan warrior, Breas, sat side by side on their horses. They were clad in heavy leather tunics covered with metal discs sewn close together. Spears and javelins were meant to glance off of them if by chance they slipped past the heavy bronze shields each DeDanaan warrior carried. The shields featured a protruding circle in the exact center surrounded by seven concentric rings and embossed from the underside with smaller circles. It was a design both attractive and practical and had given the DeDanaans great advantage in other battles.

Leather caps and greaves completed the soldiers' protective attire. The creak of leather and the clank of swords, javelins, spears, and other weapons broke the silence of the DeDanaan camp, a camp as devoid of human speech as that of the Fir Bolgs, in the last few moments before the fighting began. Even the bravest men felt a fear that robbed them of speech as they approached the ultimate test.

King Nuad was deeply concerned by the foul weather. He feared it gave the Fir Bolgs, who had fought at Moytirra, on the Plain of the Pillars, many times, the advantage. He and his advisers had spent hours in preparation for this battle, and he hoped the fog would lift as the day wore on so their well-laid plans could be implemented smoothly.

The set of his strong jaw showed his determination to win. His blond hair hung across his forehead in damp waves. The fog was cold and miserable. He removed his leather cap and smoothed his wayward locks out of his eyes. The battle for Innis Ealga was at hand and he should not have been thinking of Morrigan, but he could not help it. He had lain with her just last night in the royal battle tent, as he had several times since that day in the grove, but there was now a distance between them, a barrier across which physical touching could not carry them. He thought she loved him. He could not understand why she did not want to be his queen.

He reined in his horse and stroked the magic sword at his side. *If I survive this battle . . . as I intend to do . . . , Morrigan will be my queen, reluctant or not. I have the power to insist and she must do as I command. . . .*

He pulled his horned cap down firmly over his head

and squinted into the deepening fog. "This damnable weather!" he said to Breas. "I wonder if the Fir Bolgs could have conjured it?"

Breas looked at him sharply but said nothing, causing Nuad to be ashamed of himself for such a silly and out-dated thought. Learned men did not believe in magic, nor did he. Aloud, he said, "Man makes his own fate, even in the fog. I propose that we bring glory to the DeDanaans today. What do you say?"

"A worthy goal, sire. I am eager for the battle to begin so that glory may be ours."

A rider approached through the fog, like an apparition. King Nuad and Breas were able to discern that the horned figure astride the big brown mare was Cian only moments before he rode alongside them.

"My lord," he said bowing toward the king. "Breas, I bring a message from your mother. The lady Eri would have words with you before the battle begins." There was no scorn in his tone but the look that passed between Cian and the king showed Breas that neither of them approved.

"Thank you, Cian," he said. "I will go, with your leave, my lord."

"Yes, go." Nuad said. When Breas was out of sight, the king asked, "What does she want with him at this late hour?"

"Who can say? She always has good advice for him. I sometimes think we should arm her and send her out to do battle. It looks as though all the ideas are hers. Breas supplies only the brawn."

King Nuad laughed. "You're right, but it's a good thing that he has so much brawn to supply. He's a good warrior, Cian, even you have to admit that."

Cian laughed, too. "You're right. He is good, although it pains me to say so. What do you think about this fog?"

The battle strategy devised by Srang might have worked if the clouds had not parted miraculously, exposing the two Fir Bolg phalanxes attempting to creep behind the lines of the DeDanaans. The Fir Bolg warriors were startled and confused when they realized they were fully visible to their enemy.

The DeDanaans seized rapidly upon their confusion

and set upon them with a fury. With bronze swords flashing, the foot soldiers waded into the badly divided Fir Bolg troops. Clanging sounds of metal against metal rang out over the grunts and thuds and the heavy breathing of men as the two sides did hand-to-hand combat.

The leather-clad, wicker-work shields the Fir Bolg troops carried were rendered useless by the sharp edges of the DeDanaans' bronze blades. In no time, the two phalanxes of Fir Bolg warriors were lying on the cold green grass, their blood seeping into the damp earth as their lives trickled to a close.

When King Eochy realized how badly Srang's strategy had gone awry, he led a desperate charge of mounted soldiers into the front line of DeDanaan horsemen. He himself had felled two men before he recognized the grinning king of the DeDanaans bearing down upon him with his sword upraised. King Eochy's last thought was one of wonder that the man could appear to be amused amid the slaughter that was going on around them. King Nuad's magic sword landed one powerful blow against the right side of King Eochy's neck, and sent the Fir Bolg king's head spinning into the mud beneath them.

King Eochy's body fell from his horse onto the earth with a heavy thud. King Nuad rose and turned slightly to look back at what his mighty sword had wrought. He raised his left hand to gesture to the Fir Bolg bearers to carry their fallen king out of the fray. As he did so he was astonished to see Srang, the Fir Bolgs' chief warrior, his dark visage twisted with fury, bring his sword crashing down upon his upraised wrist.

King Nuad felt searing pain and stared in disbelief at the dark blood pumping out of his arm in furious spurts where his hand had been. Then he too, fell onto the earth of the Plain of Moytirra.

Chapter Ten

Bearers somehow managed to find King Eochy's severed head amid the ferocious fighting and the staccato beat of horses' hooves. Blood and dirt clogged its ears and nose. The unseeing eyes were caked with mud. They carried it back, along with his body, to the Fir Bolg battle tent where Lugh and Queen Tailteann awaited the outcome of the battle. No DeDanaan raised a hand to stop them, for the conventions of battle allowed for the orderly removal of the dead and were observed scrupulously by both sides.

Lugh left childhood behind in that awful moment when his shocked senses told him that the grisly burden borne by the bearers was all that was left of his beloved foster father.

Queen Tailteann saw with her eyes only. She did not, could not, immediately comprehend with her conscious mind what it was she looked upon. It took an act of will for her to remain conscious at all. Slowly, very slowly, the horror of what had become of her beloved husband seeped into her mind. The pain of it was greater than she could bear. She said nothing and did nothing until the two parts of Eochy's body had been laid on the furs at her feet.

Then she knelt and lifted the filthy severed head from its resting place, cradling it next to her face. She crooned loving words to it. She closed her eyes and tried hard to remember the living, breathing man who had held her tightly in his arms only a few hours before.

"Mother, don't!" Lugh cried, reaching for her arm. She pushed him away and he did not try to restrain her again. She went on stroking the head of her beloved until finally, she could bear the cold lifelessness of it no more.

She laid Eochy's head gently next to his body on the furs. To no one in particular she said, "Bring me warm water and a cloth. I would wash my husband."

When the things had been brought to her she tenderly washed the dirt and blood from Eochy's eyes and face. Others volunteered to do the grim task but she would brook no assistance. He was her man and she would do this last loving thing for him. When she was finished and everyone in the tent was in tears, she kissed Eochy's cold, pale lips. Only then did she permit her own tears to come. She turned to Lugh and wordlessly held out her arms to him. He ran into them, eager for contact with her, for reassurance that her heart was still beating, that he was still loved, and that life could go on without the presence of the man they both had loved so well.

At the same hour in the battle tent of the DeDanaan king, the aged royal physician, Diancecht, worked feverishly to stop the flow of blood where King Nuad's hand had been severed. The king had lost so much blood by the time the bearers carried him into the tent that Diancecht doubted his ability to save him. Nuad's face had taken on an unearthly pallor and his heartbeat was weak. Diancecht applied a tourniquet of leather thongs, just above the elbow.

He turned to his children, Miach and Airmead, his assisting physicians. "Have the servants pile as much wood as possible on the fire outside. I will need the hottest flames you can make."

"I'll go, Father," Miach said and stepped outside the tent. The damp fog had kept the fire a puny one and servants had struggled throughout the morning to keep it going. It wouldn't do if they were to save the king's life. Miach called for more wood, praying that the gods would assist them, and returned to help his father.

Nuad groaned as Diancecht worked at cleansing his wound. The physician showed it to Airmead. "Look. The cut is a clean one. It must have been delivered with considerable force to have made such a straight cut. There are no rough or ragged edges."

"That's good," she said. "Which instruments will you need to start the cauterization? This small one first?"

He shook his head. "No, we have to seal this big channel as quickly as possible before we lose him. Have the largest one heated first." He glanced up. "Ah, Miach. The fire is being replenished?"

"Yes, Father. I told the servants to use all the firewood here and to go into the woods to cut more. They understand our need. It should take only a few minutes."

"May the gods be praised. When it's ready, heat the large instrument Airmead has selected. Don't let it touch the ashes or coals. When it glows white hot bring it to me, then have the servants heat the smaller rods."

He placed his pale fingers on King Nuad's throat. He could feel the big man's heart beating in thin, fluttery contractions.

"How I wish for a potion or a medicant we could give the king to ease the fearsome pain that is about to come to him," he said.

The power to shield man's mind from pain was something the gods were keeping from the ancient healer. His children had learned all they knew of medicine at his right hand, and were as sure as their father that such a potion existed. Unlike Diancecht, they felt certain that one day soon someone would take the knowledge from the gods. Each of them hoped to be the one so favored.

Diancecht glanced up at Airmead, who was moving silently, assembling instruments and medicants in anticipation of his needs. Of his children, she was the more competent technician and was steady and dependable in a crisis. He was grateful for her presence, and turned his attention back to the semiconscious king who had begun to groan.

"Where is that instrument?" he grumbled impatiently. "I need it now."

The old physician smoothed his white hair with the back of his blue-veined hand and sighed. He knew it was possible to survive an amputation, for he himself was standing beside the wounded king on an artificial leg of the skillful blacksmith Gobinu's making.

His mind raced over the circumstances of his own life's misfortune, the fallen tree his horse had not seen in time, and the sickening thud with which he had struck the ground. The pain had been so intense he had fainted. When he awoke, Miach was bending over him, whispering encouraging words. The search party lifted him onto the back of a horse and he remembered still the agony of that movement. He had fainted again but not before he had seen the long white bone protruding from his flesh. The memory caused a shudder to pass through him and he felt great sympathy for the suffering king who lay on the furs before him.

Miach brought in the largest metal instrument, glowing red and white from the intense heat of the fire.

"Here it is, Father," he said handing it to him carefully.

Without wasting time on words, Diancecht gestured to the servants to hold the king down. They took their places around King Nuad, and Airmead and Miach moved into position to assist their father.

The old physician touched the white-hot instrument to the king's severed wrist. Steam and the awful stench of burnt flesh sizzled from it. Diancecht held the instrument to the channel in spite of the king's cry. It was a howl of pain no one in the tent would ever forget. The king's body arched and he fell back limply as the pain pushed him into deep unconsciousness. Airmead monitored Nuad's pulse. It flickered, then held steady. She nodded to her father to continue. The king was a strong man.

Diancecht systematically sealed every open vessel in the same way until he was satisfied that Nuad would not bleed to death. He loosed the tourniquet, then poured thick golden honey over the wound and covered it with cobwebs before wrapping it tightly in linen bandages that had been boiled in cauldrons before the war, and hung to dry in the bright sunshine that had shone upon the DeDanaans in the days before they departed for the Plain of Moytirra.

As he finished dressing the wound, Diancecht wondered what would become of the DeDanaan tribe now. Everyone knew that a ruler could not have a bodily blemish of any kind. King Nuad's reign had ended the moment his hand was severed. Who among them was fit to follow in his footsteps? Diancecht could think of no one, for he knew that the time had not yet come for his grandson, Lugh of the Fir Bolgs, to become their king.

The superiority of the DeDanaans' bronze weapons and the disastrous division of the Fir Bolg troops in the first foray, led to the defeat of the Fir Bolgs before the sun had set in the West on the first day of the fighting. They had been demoralized early by King Eochy's death. Srang tried to rally them with the sheer force of his fury, but it was plain that the heart had been taken from them.

Finally, it became so obvious that further fighting would amount to senseless annihilation that even Srang had to admit defeat. He bitterly raised the white flag of surrender on a javelin. In utter desolation, he delivered up the Fir Bolg people of Innis Ealga to Breas, the champion warrior of the invading DeDanaan tribe.

The mist that had so confounded them during the first hours of fighting returned to the Plain of Moytirra. It silently swirled about the knees of the horses as the Fir Bolgs, exhausted and defeated, followed the victorious DeDanaan warriors from the battlefield as prisoners. A makeshift enclosure was built near the spot where the council of DeDanaan elders would determine their fate in the morning.

As he followed the Fir Bolgs' new masters to the holding pen, Srang vowed never to submit to DeDanaan government nor to permit his fellow prisoners to do so. Ideas for escape crowded his thoughts with such frenzy that he was barely aware of the fact that his body ached with weariness and was in need of nourishment.

He clenched and unclenched his strong brown hands, observing the impressive size and fitness of the DeDanaan force. He grimaced, exposing a dark gap in his teeth, a reminder of a previous battle. He was as alert as a wild animal captured by a hunter, taking in all the details of his surroundings, waiting for the right moment to make his move.

When the prisoners were safely in the holding pen, Breas conducted a personal search of each Fir Bolg. He could almost smell the hatred emanating from Srang as he approached him. The prisoner's short body was powerful and tense as though the blood lust of battle still raged within him. His black eyes dared Breas to touch him. Blond Breas took the challenge and handled Srang with more roughness than necessary.

"What is this?" he asked, pulling a small bone knife from under one of Srang's leg wrappings. "Were you not told, rat dung, that all weapons were to be handed over to your captors? We shall have to deal harshly with you."

Srang said nothing, but the expression on his face told of his defiance. Breas finished his search without turning up more hidden weapons. The other Fir Bolgs watched the encounter with interest, seeing in Srang's open contempt, the quality of leadership. They were secretly jubilant when Srang spat on the ground after the departing Breas.

"Guards, position yourselves closely around this circle of prisoners," Breas instructed. "Do not allow them to speak to each other and do not speak to them yourselves. There could be trouble from that one"—he gestured toward Srang—"so watch him carefully."

The guards suffered from physical fatigue as well as the complacency that an easy victory sometimes brings, and in spite of Breas's admonition, they were not as alert to Srang as they might have been.

The opportunity Srang was waiting for came when several DeDanaan women brought steaming beakers of soup for the guards. Srang knew the longer he and his clansmen were held by the DeDanaans, the less likelihood there would be of a successful escape, so he seized the moment.

The guard closest to him bent his head to drink and as swift as an eagle's descent, Srang stepped toward him and brought his hands upward sharply, upending the beaker, spilling its hot contents down the inside of the warrior's leather battle tunic where the steam and pain would be compounded. The man roared out in pain and surprise.

Srang shoved past the guard and ran. It was the signal the captured Fir Bolgs needed. They leaped the flimsy fence and ran, sprinting over the women, knocking some to the ground. They swerved around the DeDanaans who tried to stop them, dodging fists and javelins.

Twenty-three Fir Bolg prisoners escaped into the Curlew Mountains through the black curtain of night. Eleven others were killed, four wounded, and the rest recaptured. Such a chance for escape would never come again because from that hour onward, until their fate was decided by the council, the Fir Bolg captives were bound hand and foot and kept isolated from one another.

Without food, weapons, or adequate clothing, Srang led his followers into the hills, then northward toward the part of Innis Ealga known as Connaught, a barren, rocky, and inhospitable place where few people lived. If they were to survive there, he knew they would owe it to the goodness of the gods.

Morrigan came to King Nuad at midnight unbeknownst, she thought, to his physician. She still wore the leather tunic adorned with bronze discs that had protected her during the battle. Her hair fell in tangles about her face. Her arms and legs were smeared with dirt and sweat from the fighting and her eyes were ablaze with rage that Nuad had been injured by such unworthy enemies.

She watched and waited until the old physician stepped away from Nuad's side to go to the dining place for meat and drink, and then she simply strode past the guards into the king's tent.

Brig, ever the devoted servant, sat by Nuad's head. Without a word Morrigan gestured rudely to him to leave. He hesitated, then remembered that Diancecht had said that she was to be allowed to see the king alone if she should appear. Brig slipped outside. He was reluctant to go too far away but he was fearful of Morrigan's power, so he sat on a log on the far side of the still hot fire, where he could keep a watchful eye on the tent but would be unable to hear what was being said.

Inside the battle tent a pale yellow light came from a small fire burning in the center of the floor. Nuad lay amid the furs near the back wall, his arm bandaged with white linen. His face was as pale as death and his breathing was slow and irregular. Morrigan knelt and put her head on his chest, listening a long time for his heartbeat. It was faint but regular.

Working quickly, she pulled a leather fes from under her tunic and laid its contents out on the furs. As gently as she could, she pulled the garment Nuad wore away from his broad chest. She dipped her fingers into a pot of blue dye made from the woad plant and drew ancient symbols upon the king's skin. They were symbols so old they had long since fallen from favor, and today's DeDanaans remembered them with scorn mingled with fear, if they remembered them at all, yet she knew the power in the old religion.

When Nuad's chest was covered with the healing marks, she uttered words meant to restore him to life and

health as she sprinkled the white powder her grandfather
had entrusted to her in a circle around the furs where the
king lay. There was not much left and she did not know
how to get more. *May the gods be willing,* she thought,
let there be enough to make him well.

Looking at Nuad's still form she acknowledged to herself that she loved the man lying motionless before her
with a passion that both amused and annoyed her. She
who was so proud, was in the king's tent using up the sacred old medicines that could not be renewed for the benefit of a man who would have laughed at her had he
known of her superstition.

He said he loved her. She certainly loved him. At the
moment it hardly mattered, although it did cross her mind
that according to the ancient belief, if he recovered because of her ministrations she would own his spirit. Hurriedly, she rearranged his clothing. She laid her hand
upon his brow. He was burning up. She bathed his face
with water she found in the ewer next to his resting place
and tried to get him to drink. She kissed his cheek. She
would come again with more healing when dawn came.

She would move heaven and earth and the stars and the
sun to save the king of the DeDanaans, by summoning
the ways of the old gods. She kissed Nuad again and
slipped out into the black night, lit by pale, far-distant
stars, struggling to shine through the heavy clouds still lying upon the Plain of Moytirra.

Chapter Eleven

As chief of the DeDanaan Council of the Wise, Dagda Mor was sometimes called Ruad Rohfessa, the lord of great knowledge, by his kinsmen, but his heart was heavy and he felt anything but wise. He loved and respected King Nuad so much that it was hard for him to do his duty. But do it he must, for DeDanaan law commanded that a new and unblemished king must be chosen by the council.

Dagda sat cross-legged on the ground before a small fire, shaking his big shaggy head sadly. His daughter, Brigid, knelt next to him trying to comfort him by stroking his hair. His son, Bove the Red, sat across from him with a worried frown on his face.

"You have to do it, Da. You know you do," Bove said.

"I know, and I will do what our law commands, but, son, you have to understand that I have known Nuad since his birth. He was one of my first pupils. He had that deep cleft in his chin and those incredible eyes that seemed even then to take in everything around him. I learned to love him like a son long before either of you were born." The old man paused and sighed heavily.

He seemed lost in his thoughts and Brigid looked to her brother to nudge their father back to his duty. Bove shook his head, disturbing his red hair that was every bit as shaggy as his father's, as if to say, you must do it, Brigid, for my heart is as sore as our father's. So, Brigid of the sweet nature and plain face, spoke to her father.

"Da, I know that choosing someone to replace King Nuad is a grievous thing to you, but I also know how you respect the wisdom of our ancient ones. It is hard for us to accept it now, but their guidance has never failed us. We must trust that the gods are at work in our affairs as they have been always. Perhaps they gave Nuad the task

of delivering our people to Innis Ealga and now that he
has carried it out, they are through with him for a while.
It is not up to us to question the ways of the gods, is it,
Da?"

"Ah, me darling girl," Dagda said, taking her hand in
his and raising it to his lips for a gentle kiss, "you speak
with much wisdom. All you say is so. I know it and am
but a poor mortal for my reluctance to carry out the will
of the gods. You must never fear that I will turn from
their will, no matter how much I am dismayed by having
to carry it out. You know me better than that, don't you?"
he asked, looking first at his daughter, then his son.

"Of course, Da," they both replied.

"Ah, but I see no one, not a soul who has the ability to
establish the government of Innis Ealga and command the
respect of the tribe," Dagda worried out loud. "Cian, or
even I, could probably devise a government, but it takes
a larger presence than ours to bring the people into it and
avoid the petty squabbles that could destroy us before we
are firmly established here. We have to have a powerful
warrior who is also a wise man and, I'm sorry to say, the
gods send us very few of those."

Softly, Brigid said, "Da, I think you have to consider
Breas. It seems clear to me that King Nuad considered
him his logical successor. Remember that the king presented him with the Claimh Solais when he decided to
ride unarmed into the Fir Bolg's camp. Doesn't that say
to you that Nuad thought Breas worthy to take his place?
You said he told Breas that he was to be in charge if he
did not return."

Bove looked at his sister with irritation, then at his father to see if he understood that Brigid was hopelessly
smitten by the handsome, vain warrior. He could tell by
the woeful look Dagda bestowed on Brigid that he knew.
A more unlikely match could not be imagined, and both
of the men who loved her did not want her to be hurt.
They knew that even if Brigid were more comely and
therefore a candidate to be Breas's bride, no woman could
ever hope to compete with Breas's formidable mother,
Eri.

"Brigid, you know Breas was the one in charge when
the Fir Bolgs escaped," Bove protested.

"What of it? That could have happened to anyone. The

chaos of the battle was barely behind us. Since the prisoners had no weapons who could possibly have guessed
they would run into the mountains? I don't see how you
can hold that against him. He is a brilliant warrior; you
yourself said that he fought gallantly and well. You're
just jealous because he has every quality any warrior
could ever hope to possess."

"All save humility," Bove responded dryly. "Do you
know the other warriors call him Breas the Beautiful because he is so vain about his appearance?"

Brigid's gray eyes grew dark with anger. "Oh, well. Of
course that's what you would say. Look at you, as big as
a heifer, with all that wild hair flying about. You even
have food stains on your cloak. What do you care about
appearances? Breas has cause to be proud."

"Brigid! Bove! Stop this right now! It is a serious matter that lies before us, and I won't hear any more of this
childish squabbling. My task is hard enough without having to endure such behavior from you two."

A chastened Bove lowered his eyes. "I'm sorry, Father.
It's just that I . . ." He glanced at Brigid who looked as
though she might cry.

"I understand, my son," said Dagda.

A silence followed that grew so heavy Brigid was
forced to speak. "I, too, am sorry, Father, but Breas *is* the
man who should be king. I know what you and Bove
think of me, and I myself am ashamed for wanting Breas.
He is too far above me. I know that, but I cannot help
what I feel."

Dagda regarded her with a solemn look. "No, Brigid, I
don't think you do know what we think of you or you
couldn't say that Breas is stationed above you. No mortal
woman ever lived with a sweeter nature than your own.
You have a keen mind and I give you all due respect and
honor, and so I'm sure, does your brother." He looked at
Bove expectantly.

Bove moved to Brigid's side and put his arm around
her. He kissed her on the cheek. "I also honor you,
Brigid. I'm sorry I spoke harshly of Breas. I have doubts
about him though, and just as you cannot help what you
feel for him, neither can I. Let's not fight about him.
You know I want only what is good for you and the
DeDanaans."

She sniffed back tears, deeply touched by her brother's gesture. Bove was not a man given to open affection and she knew she had just been given a rare gift. She would take his words under advisement, even though she was sure he underestimated the true mettle of Breas. And what was so wrong with calling him Breas the Beautiful, after all? Wasn't he the most beautiful man she'd ever seen?

Shortly after the Sun God set in the sky on the day after the battle at Moytirra, the Council of the Wise met to choose a new king. Ogma, the scribe, was the second to arrive at the meeting site. He saw Dagda's face in repose and knew that his older brother was as heartsore at the thought of replacing Nuad as he himself was. He stepped softly to his side and slipped his arm about Dagda's shoulders. Dagda looked up, his eyes sad.

"We must do what we must do," he said solemnly.

Ogma nodded and answered grimly, "I know. But we don't have to like it, do we?" He smiled at Dagda who managed a weak smile in response.

"Have you seen Nuad yet?" Ogma asked.

"No. Diancecht or Airmead has been with him every moment and I have not intruded. He needs them far more than he needs anyone else just now. Do you think they can save him?" Dagda asked.

"Yes," Ogma answered thoughtfully, "yes. I am almost certain of it. His fever is down, a very good sign, and they are giving him potions to help him sleep. He needs to rest his mind now so his body can heal. His wound was terrible . . . may the gods help him! I don't know how a man like Nuad is going to get along with only one hand. You know, he may not thank Diancecht for saving him."

Dagda nodded. "I know life will be difficult for Nuad, of course, but I also know the depth of the man's courage. It will carry him through this loss, but it is surely the hardest thing Nuad has ever been called upon to face. The death of his queen and the infant she labored so long to bear have been the only major blows life has delivered to him . . ." Dagda paused in thought, then continued. "Until that point two years past, everything came so easily to him that many whispered about a charmed birth. Now we know it was not so. The gods have their own time for delivering hardship so I hope Morrigan will be able to stand by the king in the challenge that awaits him now."

"We have to stop thinking of Nuad as the king," Ogma reminded his brother.

"I know," Dagda said mournfully, patting his protruding stomach as if seeking reassurance. "But we must not worry about him too much, Ogma. Nuad is a wondrously strong-minded man."

Ogma looked skeptical. He didn't think anyone was half so qualified as Nuad to be king. Men like Nuad were rare in the history of the DeDanaans and he knew the council would be forced to choose a lesser mortal.

The decision was swiftly made, even though none of the council members considered Breas the equal of Nuad and many said so. But the fact remained that Nuad himself had presented his sword to Breas, and Breas had led the DeDanaans to victory after King Nuad was wounded. The vote, while unenthusiastic, was unanimous on the first ballot. Breas, son of Elathon the Fomorian, and Eri, daughter of the DeDanaan chieftain Utan, would become the king of the DeDanaan tribe in the winter of his twenty-fourth year.

A cold wind blew over the lake at Moytirra as the council met, chilling Eri where she sat talking with her son, Breas, in the firelight. She was wrapped in a long, luxurious cloak of soft new wool of a deep brown color that contrasted handsomely with the silver of her hair. Breas came by his beauty naturally, for even in her old age Eri was a lovely woman. Tall and slender, she carried herself with grace and dignity. She delighted in adorning her person with jewelry, and this night wore a ring on every finger of the hand with which she stroked Breas's blond curls.

"You are not to blame yourself for the escape, Breas. You did your duty by warning the guards to watch out for that dark beast of a Fir Bolg. It was they who were negligent and I think they should all be punished for their laxity. You are blameless in the entire affair and I shall make sure everyone understands that. I want you to put it out of your mind entirely."

"You are right of course, Mother. It was not my fault.

I am furious that the guards allowed such a thing to happen. I will have difficulty getting the council to agree to punish them, unless. . . . Who do you think they will choose to replace King . . . I mean . . . Nuad?"

"I have thought about it long, my son, and you are the only logical choice. The other possible candidate is Cian, but there is something soft at his center and I believe the council knows it. He is too kind and could not be ruthless enough in defense of the tribe. Remember what I have always taught you, Breas, a leader has to be as hard as the choices he faces. Kindness has never yet won a battle nor produced a champion."

Breas nodded at her familiar words, thrilled that she believed he would be chosen. Neither mother nor son was surprised a few minutes later when a courier came from the council to summon Breas to appear before them.

He rose and bent to kiss his mother before accompanying the courier. "Wish me good fortune, Mother, and bestow your blessing upon me," he whispered.

She raised her bejeweled hand and touched his forehead with two fingers. "Walk with the gods, my son," she said, her cold blue eyes shining with ambition. "I give you my blessing." Her heart raced with excitement to think of her own son as king of the DeDanaans.

"We are of one mind with regard to the conquered Fir Bolgs," Dagda said to the council. "They must be banished from Innis Ealga. We cannot be forever bothered by a people who were willing to go to war rather than share the territory. Therefore, Cian shall oversee the transport of the Fir Bolgs to the outer islands, far from the shores of Innis Ealga. Mannon Mac Lir will commandeer their boats. The Fir Bolgs will be scattered across the outer islands in groups too small to make war with us ever again. They will be allowed to take a minimum of tools and supplies; enough to sustain life, but no more."

Breas nodded soberly, but his mind was awhirl with the information, sure now that if Cian was to be in charge of deporting the Fir Bolgs, it left only himself as a candidate for the kingship. His heart raced and beads of sweat broke out on his high, white forehead. He wished Dagda would get on with it, and he wished his mother could be here.

Dagda was still speaking. "As you know, the council was faced with the difficult task of choosing a leader to replace King Nuad. We have pondered carefully and have reached the unanimous decision that you, Breas, are to receive that honor and the heavy responsibility that comes with it. Are you prepared to accept the mantle of kingship?" Dagda's voice was solemn.

Thoughts collided in Breas's mind like flotsam caught in a wildly swirling eddy. He wondered how he looked, what his expression should be. He didn't want to appear too grateful and weaken his power right away. On the other hand, he didn't want to appear haughty, making his rivals even more bitter.

"I am, your lordship," he answered, falling to his knees in a posture of humility. "I am most honored," he said in a loud, firm, practiced voice. When he rose he faced the king's council. His council.

"King Breas," Dagda began. The words stuck in his throat but he forced himself to continue. "You will be crowned formally before the Lia Fail as all of your predecessors have been, time out of mind. The sacred stone of destiny will be erected on the holy festival site used by the Fir Bolgs near the river Boyne. When all is in readiness the council will call you forth at the next full moon to be crowned as king of the DeDanaans. Until that time we charge you to carry out all the duties of the kingship in consultation with this council. May you rule our people wisely and well with the help of the gods of light."

So saying, Dagda opened his fleshy arms wide and embraced the new king, kissing him once on each cheek. One by one the other counselors approached Breas, giving him the ceremonial kiss of kinship.

The knowledge that he was acting king of the DeDanaans gave a new buoyancy and arrogance to Breas's walk. From this moment on, he had all the powers necessary to bend the people to his will.

Instead of going to his mother right away, he had a wish to be alone. He walked to the edge of the battleground where he had so recently distinguished himself and squinted as though hoping to see the future unfold before him on the still, black waters of Lough Arrow. He stood there a long time immersed in deep thought. He wanted to make the first decision of his kingship without advice from his mother. She too, was now his subject ... the prospect filled him with both exhilaration and trepidation.

At the council's request, King Breas's first official act would come in the morning when he would pay a call on the Fir Bolg queen and the prince. Of all the Fir Bolgs, they alone were not to be sent to the outer islands. They would be kept on Innis Ealga as royal hostages. It would not do to give the losers of the battle of Moytirra a rallying point, and besides, royal hostages often proved useful in other ways, ways that Breas could not yet envision.

After several hours of walking and contemplating his new role, Breas returned to the camp and the tent where Nuad lay. He paused only a moment before ducking to enter.

The royal physician, Diancecht, looked up sharply, startled to see Breas. The hour was late, and the camp had been still so long the old physician believed that he and Nuad's servant, Brig, were the only ones awake keeping vigil over the wounded king.

Breas spoke to the physician in low and measured tones. As he listened, the muscles in Diancecht's jaw tightened. To convince himself of what he had heard, he asked Breas to repeat himself. Again, Breas's voice was flat, emotionless.

"I will not move the king!" Dianchecht exploded. "This man is desperately ill and cannot be moved. Indeed, such a shock could very well finish him off. What possesses you to demand such a thing?"

"Look, old man," Breas growled, "by rights, this tent is mine now and I will have it. Don't let your loyalty to the former king blind you to the reality of our situation. I would be very sorry indeed if the move were to cost Nuad his life, but he is just one man, and I must now think about the lives of many. Don't fight me on this, Diancecht. I warn you, there is no way you can win and you will do yourself irreparable harm if you try. Remove Nuad from this tent."

Breas's last words were delivered in a manner that chilled the blood in the old man's veins. He knew when he was beaten. And he knew the council had made a terrible mistake.

Diancecht decided he must seek help from Morrigan. The time had come for him to reveal to her the powers that had been given to him by the gods. Sometimes the god-knowledge came to him in murky messages, but always, he followed it obediently even when he was not clear about where it would take him.

When he had found the blue woad marks on Nuad's chest, he knew he had been right about Morrigan, that she too understood the ways of the ancients. He believed she was the practitioner of the magical arts that he had been promised in his old age.

His heart had been so filled with plans for Nuad's recovery that he had given no thought to the process of choosing a new king until it crashed in upon him with Breas's words.

"Go," he said to Brig, "and bring Morrigan to me. She will be the one to help us remove the king to a safe place."

Brig left the tent with a heavy heart and went in search of Morrigan, where she lay sleeping on the damp, hard earth of Innis Ealga.

Chapter Twelve

Morning dawned fair with the full face of the Sun God shining down upon the Plain of Moytirra. The sky was a brilliant blue backdrop for a few puffy clouds being pushed by westerly breezes from the sea. But by the time the sun was fully over the horizon the grim task of gathering the dead from the battlefield had begun again. Bodies were stacked like firewood, into two piles at opposite ends of the plain; the DeDanaan dead on one side, the Fir Bolg on the other.

Breas the Beautiful awoke stiff and out of sorts at having had to lie on the damp ground all night like an ordinary warrior. He should never have allowed Nuad's removal to wait until morning. Now that he was king he deserved the comfort of many furs and the shelter and prestige of the royal battle tent.

"Are you awake, Breas?" Eri whispered. "Arise, my darling, and claim your rightful place." The pride she felt at her son's elevation to the kingship was boundless. "I have hardly slept a wink. I am so excited about the events of this new day. How can you lie there so peacefully, sleeping like an infant? Arise, my son."

Breas was cross and petulant. He had wanted desperately to go to Macha last night and share his honor with her, but in his uncertainty over her response, he had not acted. It peeved him that he did not know where he stood with her.

"Yes, Mother," he said groggily, sitting up and rubbing his eyes. "I didn't sleep so well, actually. Do you think the council will want me to choose a queen right away?"

"Oh, so your dreams were haunted by sweet Macha, were they?" Eri laughed. None of Breas's other choices had suited her, but this young woman was of sufficient status and beauty to at least bear consideration.

Breas grinned with slight embarrassment. "I have to admit they were. She is the most beautiful of the three sisters. She certainly has the sweetest temperament. Morrigan is far too haughty and Neimain can be spiteful. What would you think of Macha as queen?"

"It's a possibility, Breas, and a good one, but we would have to see much more of her before making a decision as important as that. Have you told her that the council has made you king?"

"No. I wanted to secure Nuad's tent before I did anything else. Perhaps I will tell her this morning if she is still at the filach fiadah when I get there for the morning meal."

"Very well," Eri said, "I shall dine alone this morning. Seek her out but please, make no mention of the queenship. I want to see how she responds to the news that you are king. She and her sisters are very close to Nuad. You know of course, that Morrigan sleeps with him?"

"Of course, Mother. Everyone knows that. It could be a problem, I suppose, although I don't think so. All three sisters seem to be independent thinkers."

Breas climbed a slight incline, away from the battle site, and made his way into the woods where slaves had dug trenches on the day they arrived at the Plain of Moytirra. He made his water into one of them, then walked down to the lakeshore and bent to wash his face, splashing the icy water into his eyes with his hands. By the gods! It was brisk. Winter would soon be full upon them.

He dampened his golden hair, causing even more ringlets to appear, framing his handsome face. He took a comb carved from bone from the leather fes he wore at his waist and tried to subdue the curls, to no avail. He wished he could see how he looked. He wanted to appear as regal as possible when the announcement was made to the entire tribe. He rose and shook the water from his long slender fingers and replaced the comb.

He carefully chose one of the hazel twigs he carried in the bag and chewed one end of it until it was soft and fibrous. He dipped it in the gently lapping lake water and brushed his teeth with it vigorously. He had straight, white teeth that were the envy of the other warriors. Teeth were a source of pain and disease for many of his kinsmen most of their adult lives, but the gods had been good to Breas. In all of his fighting he had never lost a tooth, something few warriors his age could boast.

When he was satisfied that his teeth were clean and his breath gave no offense, he smoothed his tunic and headed toward the filach fiadah. He looked eagerly for Macha in the line of people waiting to be served near the cauldrons. He hoped her sisters were not with her. The three of them were seldom apart, and it irked him that Macha made so little effort to spend time alone with him.

He found her quickly. She looked up and saw him watching her. She smiled and held up her wooden bowl, lifting her eyebrows in a silent invitation for him to join her. He was relieved to see that Morrigan was nowhere in sight. The third sister, Neimain, was only a few paces behind Macha but she was deep in conversation with another woman.

Like her sisters, Macha had long auburn hair and deep brown eyes, but freckles pranced across her nose and her full red lips were curved into a perpetual smile. She had one deep dimple to the left of her mouth. This morning she wore a simple tunic of yellow linen, under a cloak of dark green wool. She had stuck a sprig of holly in her hair, which was braided and coiled around her head. Breas thought she had never looked more lovely. She was always friendly to him, yet they were no closer now than they had been last year when his interest in her had first become aroused.

He longed for her to know of his elevation to the kingship, but should he tell her and risk being overheard, or let her wait and hear the news along with the others? He could not decide.

"Isn't it a fair day, Breas?" she called out to him as he came near. "A fitting omen after our victory, isn't it?"

"Aye, it is that," he answered. "More fitting than you know." They talked for a few moments until the line moved forward and they reached the cauldrons. Ladles of steaming oat porridge were poured into their oaken bowls. A servant dropped pats of sweet, unsalted butter, befitting their warrior rank, onto the surface of the hot porridge. They picked up beakers filled with sweet milk and made their way beyond the other early-morning diners to sit on a large gray stone that jutted up from the green grass, facing away from the battlefield.

As they ate, Breas struggled with the news he was bursting to share. Would she think him vain if he were to tell her now?

They spoke of the battle and Macha wondered sadly if Nuad would live. "He is so sick," she said, "they say he has not opened his eyes nor made a sound since Diancecht stopped the bleeding."

"I think he will be all right," Breas responded. "He is strong and not too old and he has our best healers working on him."

"Well, I don't know how much Miach or Airmead have been able to do. I just saw Miach and he seemed awfully busy with the Fir Bolg prisoners," she said.

"Yes. The council has decided to send the Fir Bolgs into exile," he told her. "It is Miach's job to see that they are fit for travel before they are deported to the outer islands. The council thinks they will never be strong enough to bother us again."

"What about those who escaped on the night of the battle?" she asked. "They were warriors one and all, and they could not be so far away. There will be trouble brewing there, I think."

"I wouldn't worry if I were you," he said. "They got away all right but without food or weapons. How long do you think they will last if they fled into Connaught? Wild beasts aside, the scouts tell us that it is a hard land where winds howl in from the sea and rain pounds it daily. The soil is poor and thin, more rock than earth, and few trees or plants can stand against the elements up there. No. They'll be lucky to survive one turning of the moon," Breas said confidently.

Just then Neimain found them and plopped herself down at Breas's feet, balancing her bowl and beaker expertly. "Good morning, Breas," she said cheerfully, "how are you after all the fighting? They say you fought bravely and especially well."

"Umm. Thank you," he said, trying to control his irritation at her intrusion. He had so little opportunity to be alone with Macha. Abruptly he stood, and muttered an awkward good-bye. *Once they know I am king, things will soon change around here,* he thought angrily as he moved away. He did not hear the muffled laughter of the two sisters as he made his escape.

He went in search of Dagda Mor and found him in line for a second helping of porridge, flirting and laughing with the female warriors. Breas asked him to delay sounding the horns for the announcement. "I want to be sure Nuad's tent has been vacated and is ready for my occupancy," he explained.

Dagda could but stare at Breas in openmouthed amazement for a few moments. Finally he said, "And what do you propose to do with the wounded Nuad?"

"I gave orders last night to his physicians. They will take care of the matter," he said offhandedly, unaware that his words were giving Dagda great offense. "I will go to the tent immediately after the announcement to receive the many who will undoubtedly wish to speak with me."

During the night when Morrigan had received Diancecht's news of King Nuad's impending move, a cold fury built in her. She vowed to have revenge for the outrage, but reasoned that Nuad needed her now as she never had before, and moving him to safety required her full attention. She felt confident that the gods would guide her when the moment for sweet revenge was right.

"There is only one other place to take him," she had said to Diancecht, "the royal battle tent of the Fir Bolgs. The queen and the young prince will simply have to be moved aside. Nuad's life is far more important than following the niceties of kingship."

Diancecht started to protest that the council would never permit such a breach of manners even toward an enemy, but she silenced him by saying, "I'll handle it. When the time comes to move him, he will have a bed in the Fir Bolg tent. I promise you that."

"I hope so," he said, "for the king's sake. There is a chance we can save him if we can keep the fever down. But we must protect him from the elements."

"One thing, Diancecht," Morrigan said. "I want a half-hour's time alone with Nuad before he is to be moved. That is my only condition, but it is not negotiable if you want my assistance in this."

Diancecht nodded knowingly. He was sure she would use the time to work some of the old spells, spells that he himself did not know.

"Yes. All right. Of course, you may be alone with him,

but I must burn new rushes to blend with the healing herbs under his bandage. Give them time to cool so I can rewrap his arm before you come."

"Thank you, Diancecht. You are a good friend," Morrigan said, her brown eyes still dancing fiercely. *Nuad deserves better than this,* she thought.

After she spoke with Dagda, Morrigan stripped off her tunic and leather battle dress and plunged into the frigid waters of Lough Arrow. She did it as much to cool her anger as she did to cleanse her battle-weary body. Now she was afire, struggling to recapture her memories of the old ways. Deep furrows creased her brow. Under her brown eyes there were faint lines, the pale blue of her veins plainly visible, bespeaking her sleepless night. Her skin was translucent.

At the first blush of dawn, she donned a dark brown woolen cloak over her undyed tunic. The day looked to be a fair one, but the chill of fear and uncertainty was upon her. The light breeze moving through the oaks behind her caused her to shiver, and she pulled the warm fabric of her cloak closer around her.

She left the camp quickly, needing more time to think, and she could not do it if she were subject to interruption.

Morrigan stood tall and straight peering deeply into her memory. Her hair blew loosely about her face, stirred by the air of Innis Ealga. Finally, the gods spoke to her. When she thought she had recaptured the old knowledge, she went deeper into the woods in search of the fruits of nature that could cast spells of protection around her beloved.

When she returned to the battle camp the fes at her waist was full, bulging with berries and leaves and rowan twigs broken into small pieces. In the pocket of her tunic were chunks of white, chalky limestone she had picked up as she walked across the Plain of the Pillars.

Morrigan entered Nuad's tent, and sent Diancecht and Brig away. When they were safely out of sight, she scattered some of the rowan twigs onto a flat stone, then set them ablaze. While they burned she ground the limestone bits into a fine powder between two hand stones. She sprinkled enough water from the beaker at Nuad's head to make the powder into a stiff paste. She poured red berries into a drinking cup and carefully crushed them, releasing their blood-red juices. She ground the charred ash of the rowan twigs into powder on the flat stone and added a few drops of water to make yet another paste.

When she was satisfied with her preparations she dipped her fingertips into the chalky limestone mixture and carefully drew ancient designs upon her face. They dried quickly. She repeated the procedure with the burnt rowan paste. Then she dipped her forefinger into the berry juice and made seven vertical slashes on each cheek. They looked like tears of blood cascading down her face.

She rinsed her hands and knelt beside the still unconscious Nuad. If anything, he looked even worse than he had yesterday. His skin had the pale blue transparency of milk with all of its cream removed. *One can almost see his bones,* she thought. She could feel the presence of death.

She had to work quickly before the others returned. She invoked the spirits of the old gods and began to chant spells, believing they were the correct ones. But her ancestors had taught her so long ago, how could she possibly remember everything? The gods spoke with faint voices.

As she chanted, she put chalk paste in Nuad's hair and decorated his face with symbols similar to those on her own. She opened his tunic and was dismayed to see that the blue woad symbols she had left there had been washed off. From her fes she brought out more woad and replaced each healing symbol. Then she added new ones of chalky limestone, ashes, and berry juice.

She rose, understanding that she could not trust her conscious mind with the holy dance she knew must come next. She willed her body to bring forth its ancient memory of the sacred movements. She emptied her mind of thought and let her bones and sinews, freed from her will, take charge.

From deep within her the old knowledge poured forth, enabling her to perform the complex dance with ease and grace. When it ended, she knelt once more in supplication to the gods and brought the healing rite to a close.

She poured water from the beaker into a basin and washed the magic symbols from her face and Nuad's. It was difficult to remove the chalk from his hair and she lingered so long over the task that she heard voices outside before she finished.

"He was so hot that I tried to cool him by bathing his face," she lied to Diancecht as he and Brig entered the tent. He merely nodded. In the dim light he seemed to notice nothing amiss.

However, Brig's sharp young eyes saw the unmistakable berry stains on Morrigan's face and the telltale signs of chalk in Nuad's hair. He knew then, for certain, that Morrigan was the witch who had left the blue markings on the king's chest. He had suspected as much, but knew his place and kept quiet. He had been shocked to find the hateful marks still on the king's chest the next day. How could Diancecht have left them there so long? With disgust he had washed them off himself, even though the old healer had not instructed him to do so.

He glanced curiously at the old physician and wondered if he knew who had painted those marks on his patient. He considered exposing Morrigan, but Brig was more than a little afraid of her. She was very powerful.

Morrigan set off on foot across the Plain of Moytirra toward the tent where Queen Tailteann and Lugh sat mourning King Eochy. She wrapped her cloak tightly over her head, hoping that if anyone noticed the lone figure striding across the green field among the body gatherers, they would not recognize her. She did not wish to be stopped. When she came to the royal tent of the Fir Bolgs it was an easy matter to convince the DeDanaan guards posted outside that she carried a message from their king. One lifted the tent flap for her to enter, unannounced.

In the dim light she could make out King Eochy's body, dressed in clean battle finery, laid out among the furs. A small woman knelt beside him with her head down, her shoulders curved under the weight of profound sorrow. She raised her eyes to the intruder and regarded Morrigan with little curiosity.

Next to her sat a young man with resplendent golden-red hair. He had stunning features but his eyes were full of grief. Morrigan was surprised by his appearance. He was obviously the Fir Bolg prince, but he did not look like the rest of the small dark people they had defeated.

"Good morning, my lady," Morrigan said, bowing deeply before coming to rest on her knees before Queen Tailteann. "I am Morrigan, consort to Nuad, king of the DeDanaans. I think you know him. He was one of the two men who called upon you and your husband before the battle." She paused, waiting for Tailteann to acknowledge her words. There was only a strained silence so Morrigan continued.

"Forgive me for intruding on your grief. I know the time is bad but I had to come now for I, too, am in grief. King Nuad was critically wounded in the fighting. He lost his hand and lies near death in the DeDanaan battle tent. The physicians labor over him night and day, but they are uncertain of the outcome," she said.

She paused once more and searched Queen Tailteann's face for a reaction. The queen's eyes were blank, frozen in their intense private grief.

"I would not come to you like this were I not desperate. Because Nuad's hand was severed he must be replaced as king. He will be ejected from the royal battle tent as soon as the announcement is made. We have no shelter for him, no place to keep him safe."

She took a deep breath. "I know it is a lot to ask, but I am before you on my knees, begging you to allow me to bring him here. Your tent is the only place we can give him the shelter he needs."

Morrigan was silent for a moment before she released uncharacteristic tears. Silent sobs racked her body. In spite of her own sorrow, or perhaps because of it, Queen Tailteann's soft heart lurched within her breast at the woman's anguish. Was Morrigan talking about the handsome, smiling man with the deep cleft in his chin? Of course. Any woman would love him very much.

Softly, Tailteann spoke, "You are aware, are you not that my husband, the Fir Bolg king, lies here before you in death?"

"Oh, yes, your majesty, I am, and I know what I ask is brazen and extraordinary. But if you only knew Nuad, you would want to help him too. His chances are not good, even if you agree to give him shelter, but without your help he has no chance at all. He is burning with fever and I . . . I . . ." Morrigan broke down again and frantically kissed the hem of Queen Tailteann's garment. A part of her brain noted that the clothing this royal woman wore was much less fine than she herself was used to wearing.

"Please, please. Help him live. I beg you. I can offer you nothing, but you have the power to spare me from the awful pain you are now feeling over the loss of your man. I know we are enemies," Morrigan gasped, drying her eyes. She looked at the lad whose green eyes were open wide, shocked by her words and her performance.

She turned back to Queen Tailteann. "The DeDanaan people will always remember your generosity if you do this. Nuad is a much beloved king. Most of all, he is loved by me." She burst into a renewed paroxysm of grief and tears splashed across the faint outlines of berry juice that remained on her cheeks.

When she felt Queen Tailteann's small hand upon her shoulder she knew she had won. "I would not will another woman to suffer as I am suffering now," Tailteann said. "If having this tent will help your man, take it. What do I want with it now that Eochy is gone?"

She looked to Lugh for his concurrence. "No, Mother!" he said angrily. "I won't have it. Where will you go? You cannot sleep on the ground."

She smiled at him, a thin, wan smile. "Why not, my darling? I have done it many times before. It's all right," she said, smoothing the frown from his brow with her short brown fingers, "it's all right." His indignation was silenced by his mother's touch, but he still managed to glare at the beautiful intruder.

Turning to Morrigan, Tailteann said, "We will bury King Eochy when the sun is at the midpoint of the sky today. You must wait until his body has been taken away."

Morrigan focused on the dead king for the first time since entering the tent and realized with a shock that his head was not attached to his body. She wanted Nuad to have the tent right away but realized in that instant that the queen and the boy were suffering greatly. She would have to settle for high noon.

"Oh, my lady, thank you!" she cried. "I vow to make this up to you. Anything I can do for you . . . anything at all . . . ever . . . please let me know. Oh! Thank you, Queen—" she faltered, embarrassed. "I'm sorry, I don't know your name."

"I am Queen Tailteann," came the regal answer, "and this is my beloved foster son, Lugh, son of Cian the DeDanaan, and Ethne the Fomorian."

Morrigan quickly cast her eyes down, shielding the surprise she felt at learning that the Fir Bolg prince was the son of her fellow warrior, Cian. After a moment, she lifted her black lashes and looked directly at the young man, smiling sweetly. "I am grateful to you too, Prince Lugh," she said. "We will do everything we can to make your mother as comfortable as possible."

Even in his sorrow and indignation the impact of Morrigan's great beauty struck Lugh and he felt shame at the stirring of his body. This woman was his enemy.

She backed out of the tent, tears still glistening on her cheeks. She could have kicked her heels together in jubilation at having gotten everything she wanted out of her visit. She was sure she must have said the right spells earlier, because the old gods most certainly were watching over Nuad. She ran back across the Plain of the Pillars as carefree as a colt, not caring now who recognized her. She had done it! It had been almost too easy to get Queen Tailteann to yield up her tent. The gods were at work. No question about it.

As Morrigan ran, her auburn hair streamed out behind her like a triumphant banner. The young Fir Bolg prince watched her from the doorway of the battle tent, unaware that she would forever change his future.

After Morrigan told Diancecht her news she went in search of Cian. She found him deep in discussion with Miach in front of the holding place of the prisoners. She tried to wait a respectful interval before interrupting, but finally lost patience.

"Cian, come over here with me," she said. "I have something important to tell you."

Cian walked over to Morrigan. He was a tall, handsome blond man with an air of perpetual melancholy. Some said it wasn't sadness at all, just his solemn, practical nature, manifest in his eyes and in his bearing, but Morrigan had always believed he held some secret sorrow deep within him. This morning his face looked weary; clearly the responsibility for the Fir Bolg's deportation rested heavily upon him.

"Good morning, Morrigan. What can I do for you?" he asked pleasantly.

"I have just come from the battle tent of the Fir Bolg king," she said, "and I learned something there that will astonish you."

"What were you doing in the enemy tent, Morrigan?" His eyes narrowed with suspicion.

"You'll know soon enough about that, just listen a moment. Do you recall the Fir Bolg royal family?"

"Of course I do," he said. "What about them?"

"There is a prince, an extremely handsome young man with regal bearing. His foster mother, Queen Tailteann, just introduced him to me. Do you know what she said?"

"Morrigan. I wasn't there. How could I know what she said?" He was irritated by her lack of directness.

Morrigan smiled at him, amused by his ignorance of what she was about to say. "She said she wanted me to meet Lugh, son of Cian the DeDanaan, and Ethne the Fomorian."

She watched Cian closely for his reaction. She could see the pupils of his deep green eyes dilate and the muscles at the edge of his mouth twitch. Otherwise he gave nothing away. He looked at her steadily for some moments.

"Does the lad know who I am?" he asked at last.

"I don't think so, Cian. They seemed to have no concern about it . . . not now anyway. They are distraught with the loss of their king. Think of it, Cian! The foster son of the Fir Bolg king is your son!"

Cian bowed his head. He did not want her to see his eyes. His heart had become a cyclone of long repressed feelings. His son. His and Ethne's son. He wanted to shout aloud and thank the gods for putting the lad in his path, but he would never share his feelings with anyone but Ethne. The thought of his lost love pierced his spirit like a javelin.

"Thank you for telling me," he said to Morrigan, all traces of emotion erased from his voice. He went back to his tasks, leaving Morrigan puzzled and disappointed. As they parted, an image of Lugh filled the minds of both the beautiful Morrigan and his natural father, Cian, but for different reasons.

Chapter Thirteen

S weet, haunting notes from the DeDanaan's bronze ceremonial horns sounded across the plain, calling the DeDanaan people back to the filach fiadah near the lake's edge, where they had broken the night's fast. The steady drone of the melody indicated an announcement of great import to their tribe.

Soon the space around the cooking area was crowded with DeDanaans. Armed guards brought the bound Fir Bolg warriors, the chief handmaiden, Aibel, and the priests, to learn of their fate. The DeDanaan council, led by Dagda the Wise, arrived. Dagda's gray eyes, from which few secrets of man or nature had ever been hidden, were full of sadness and doubt as he looked at his fellow DeDanaans. He folded his hands across his ample belly and waited for the strains of the horns to fade away.

The DeDanaans had anticipated this call to assemble as soon as word passed among them of Nuad's grievous wound. They were a people much given to storytelling, and the bitter irony of having the man whose vision had brought them to Innis Ealga, brought down in the realization of their triumph was not lost on them. It was a tale from which legends and songs would be woven for generations and generations.

They knew the king's replacement was mandated by the gods and were resigned to it. At the same time they felt that it was to Nuad they owed whatever the future might hold for them on Innis Ealga. They waited expectantly as the last notes of the horns settled softly across the green Plain of Moytirra.

"My friends," Dagda Mor began, "I speak to you on behalf of my fellow council members who have seen fit to choose me as chief councilman. You all know why we're gathered here. It is my voice you hear, but you must be mindful that the words I speak are representative of the collective will of all twelve men and women who make up the Council of the Wise. Our deliberations were guided by the gods. Breas, son of the Fomorian Ethalon, and Eri the DeDanaan, has been named as the new king of the DeDanaans!"

There was a stunned silence that lasted just a moment too long before the assembled warriors applauded Breas's selection. Macha was unable to suppress a gasp as she heard Dagda's words.

She turned to Neimain. "Why did Breas not tell me?" she demanded. "He had every opportunity this morning."

Morrigan came up behind her sisters just as Dagda spoke Breas's name. She leaned over and whispered in Macha's ear. "Does Breas the Beautiful look even sweeter to you now, my sister? Will you be our next queen?" There was a hard edge to her voice.

Macha wrinkled her nose in distaste at the idea. "Where have you been, Morrigan? We were worried about you."

Before Morrigan could answer Neimain said to Macha, "You couldn't be queen to a man who is prettier than you are, could you?"

To Morrigan, Neimain said, "It's about time you showed up. What have you been doing?"

"I'll tell you about it," Morrigan said slyly, "but you are going to find it difficult to believe. Wait until you hear how petty our new king is! Macha, I'm serious. But I want you to be his queen. We will need a strong ally close to Breas if we hope to ward off the evil he will bring down upon us."

Macha and Neimain both turned to look at their sister. Morrigan could not be ignored when she spoke with such conviction. They heard anger and cunning in her voice in equal measure.

Dagda was still speaking. " ... demonstrated great skill and courage in battle. Let us honor him with our loyalty and afford him all the dignity due the DeDanaan king. I give you, Breas, king of the DeDanaans."

Breas stepped to the front of the gathering and faced the people, his arms upraised in an expansive, welcoming gesture. The clear golden light of morning poured down over his curls and shone from the sword at his side, casting small shadows across the planes of his angular face, accenting his fine features. His sparkling green eyes reflected the triumph he felt. His beautifully formed lips parted over white teeth in a joyous smile as he met the eyes of his mother. The appellation, Breas the Beautiful, had never seemed more fitting.

The DeDanaans' cheering and clapping caused his cheeks to flush with excitement. He allowed their approval to wash over him for what seemed to Morrigan an inordinately long time. She had to admit that he looked like a young god, standing there with his gleaming locks rivaling the polished bronze of the ceremonial horns, but she knew in her heart that he was not fit to lead.

Breas wore a snowy woolen tunic and soft leather boots lined with fur. She admired the fine golden brooch and pin he wore to hold his green woolen cloak closed. Green woolen cloak? *By the gods,* she thought, *the bastard is wearing Nuad's cloak! How dare he do such a thing? How dare he?*

She looked sharply around the crowd to see if anyone else had noticed. Most were clapping and cheering in jubilation. *Traitors,* she thought. *You are all traitors, but wait. Diancecht and his children, Cian the warrior, Airmead the physician, and Miach the learned, are clapping politely, nothing more.* There were others whose applause seemed halfhearted. *Good,* she thought, *I will have allies against Breas.* A passing cloud blotted out the sun for a moment as the new king began his speech, casting a shadow on the ground. The old physician, Diancecht, spit. Was it a sign of contempt?

Breas talked a long time, describing the great coronation ceremony to be held with the Lia Fail at the next full moon. Every king of the DeDanaans had been crowned next to that holy stone and it was the tribe's belief that the stone itself uttered a shout when the man being crowned was a true king, deserving of the honor. There had been but one or two instances in all the long DeDanaan history, when the man being crowned had not had the qualities of kingship in him. The stone always knew and refused to make a sound on those occasions. Morrigan would have bet her life it would remain silent this time.

Breas talked so long that she and Diancecht, eager to

return to the wounded Nuad, became as tense as trapped
wild creatures. When Breas finally stopped speaking and
the bronze horns were blown to dismiss the gathering,
they fairly ran to the battle tent where Brig watched
over the former king of the DeDanaans.

Diancecht sent Brig out to fetch a half-dozen strong
servants. When he was alone with Morrigan, he spoke
softly to her.

"My dear, I know that you consider me an adversary,
someone outside your magic, but I wish to assure you
that I am not." He lifted Nuad's tunic and with a nod of
his head indicated that he had seen the blue woad marks
there.

"I knew that it was you who put the ancient signs on
his body and for that I was grateful. The servant, Brig, removed the first ones, not I."

Morrigan was astonished by the old physician's words.
Was he a believer too? She found herself struggling for
words.

"You have not lost the old faith?" she whispered at
last.

"I have not," Diancecht said proudly, "and it is pleased
I am to see that someone so young as yourself is a follower . . . and a practitioner. Where did you learn the old
ways?"

"From my grandfather and my father, but I am sworn
to secrecy."

"Aye. I, too, was sworn never to reveal the sacred arts
to a nonbeliever. I thank the gods for showing me that
there will be a follower long after my years on this earth
are ended. We shall work together to save this man . . .
our king."

Morrigan laughed. She felt great joy, knowing that
Diancecht could help her tap into the limitless power held
so jealously by the gods.

Nuad was lifted onto a stretcher of birch saplings and
Morrigan covered him with furs. He made no sound when
the servants lent their collective brawn to lift him up in
one smooth motion, into the waiting cart filled with juni-
per boughs. Morrigan climbed in beside him and stroked
his face. She could not bear to lose him. She whispered
an urgent prayer.

As if in direct response, Nuad's head moved slightly

and she heard a moan, albeit faint, the first sound he had uttered since the cauterization. Her heart filled with hope.

They erected a canopy of cloaks over the cart. It would not do for the people to see him in his weakened state. Diancecht checked Nuad once more, then went to check that the Fir Bolg king's body had been removed from the tent across the field.

After his speech to the people, Breas sent a messenger across the Plain of the Pillars to Queen Tailteann, announcing that he would pay her an official visit within the hour. She and Lugh left the tent at the appointed time and seated themselves on small stools of rough wood to await him.

When the newly named DeDanaan king arrived, they stood and bowed before him. Lugh hated to do it with his whole heart but Tailteann had insisted, saying, "It is his due as the conquering king, Lugh. We have no choice. If the outcome of the battle had been different it is what you and I would have expected from them. We cannot afford to offend their king for we need his cooperation if we are to bury your foster father with the honor he deserves. It must be done."

"My lady," Breas said, holding out his hand to help her rise from her bow, "may I offer the condolences of the DeDanaan people to you and your son on the death of your husband."

"Thank you, sir," Tailteann said, without looking directly at him. Lugh remained silent, glaring at the handsome young man with contempt. He felt bile rise in his throat and he fought back illness. The urge passed.

"King Breas, I would have a royal burial for my husband," Queen Tailteann said. "It is the Fir Bolg custom to lay our kings to rest on the highest hill. His people will wish to erect a great stone cairn over his grave and I ask your permission to allow them this privilege even though we are now your prisoners."

Breas looked at her intently, weighing the wisdom of loosening any captive's bonds for such a task. The memory of Srang's escape was humiliating and he did not wish for a repetition. Yet he was bound by DeDanaan custom to honor and respect a fallen foe of equal stature. He found himself strangely drawn to the small, dark woman in front of him. She had a quiet strength and authority about her that he envied. Her people had been conquered, her man killed, and her kingdom was to be taken from her, but she herself was in no way diminished. He did not understand such dignity, but he recognized and was awed by it even as he envied it. He decided to oblige her.

"I pledge that the Fir Bolg people will be freed long enough to bury your husband, Queen Tailteann. Further, I pledge that the DeDanaan warriors present on the Plain of the Pillars will assist in his burial," he told her. "We will help lay the stones to build the cairn that your Fir Bolg tradition demands."

So it was, that at high noon on the third day after the battle of Moytirra, the Fir Bolg warriors and their captors came together on the highest hill west of Lough Arrow for the purpose of laying a noble king to rest.

At the grave site, DeDanaan guards stood careful watch as the warriors who had been led by King Eochy were unbound. They reverently turned over the earth of their beloved homeland, digging a deep grave for their fallen king. When they were finished and had laid their implements down, the Fir Bolg priest, Ard, led a solemn procession three times around the grave.

Aibel felt a great black terror growing in her mind like a storm cloud. Her hands had been bound behind her so long that her shoulders ached. She wanted to be close to Queen Tailteann and Lugh. The voices in her head wailed, growing more insistent with each passing hour.

King Eochy's body had been bathed and wrapped in clean linen cloths, similarly his severed head. His earthly remains were carried upon a straw-filled battle cart draped with the royal Fir Bolg banner. Behind it walked Queen Tailteann and Lugh. Her head was held high and there were no tears. She grasped Lugh's hand tightly, so tightly that it was his only clue that the ceremony was an agony for her.

He was numb with grief. Despite having told himself that he wanted to recall this day with clarity, he found it difficult to concentrate on anything but the sight of the bandage-clad figure on the cart. It no longer seemed to him to be his father. He heard the holy words the priests said but found no comfort in them. The red-haired DeDanaan bard, Cairbed, stepped to the graveside and sang a standard lament for fallen heroes, inserting the name of King Eochy of the Fir Bolgs in appropriate places. He was accompanied by Brigid, who blew sweet notes from her whistle of tin. Lugh was touched so deeply by the singing that he had to struggle fiercely to contain his tears.

As King Eochy's body was lowered into the soil of Innis Ealga, Queen Tailteann fell to her knees beside the open grave, still clutching Lugh's hand.

He knelt with her and watched her pray to the gods for the spirit of her husband. He knew that it was expected that he too, should pray, but he could not. He was too angry, too confused to be mourning alongside his father's killers.

Lugh looked across the gaping hole at the blond king of the DeDanaans. *One day,* he vowed, *I will have revenge against these people.*

Queen Tailteann dropped boughs of evergreen onto the body. Lugh did likewise. Then the priests invited the Fir Bolgs to fill the grave with fragrant greens. One by one, they filed by to honor their king. Most were weeping openly.

When the body was completely covered with life-affirming evergreens, the earth of Innis Ealga was shoveled back into the grave and a massive flat stone cover was laid atop Eochy's final resting place. Onto it Queen Tailteann and Lugh scattered the first few stones for the cairn.

Tailteann's heart felt as cold in her breast as the stones she dropped. Over the next few days a veritable mountain of stone would be raised above King Eochy's grave to be visible for miles around. It pleased her that all who saw it would know that the body of a man of royal degree, much loved by his people, had been laid to rest in this sanctified place.

When the rite was finished, Tailteann whispered to Lugh that she wanted to remain beside Eochy's grave. "Please go back with the others, my darling, and try to understand. I need to stay here. When I am able, I will come to you again, I promise."

The thought of returning to the battle camp without her frightened Lugh. He did not trust these DeDanaans, their captors. He wasn't sure she would be safe on the mountain without him. He started to protest but the expression on her face halted his words before they were out of his mouth. He could see that she truly had a need to stay behind, to reach out to her husband's spirit. For the first time since the king's death, Lugh wondered if it were possible that his foster father's spirit had gone to mingle with that of the Sun God as the priests taught. He hoped fervently that it might be so.

As the Fir Bolgs were herded back to their makeshift prison, a sudden howl rang out, more chilling than that of any wolf that ever prowled the Plain of Moytirra. Lugh was shocked to see Aibel, her head thrown back, struggling against her captors, who attempted to silence and restrain her. Finally, she was carried away by them, shrieking and kicking, toward the place of the physicians in the war camp. Lugh wanted to go after them but felt paralyzed. He did not understand what demons possessed the girl he thought he loved.

Macha and Neimain silently made their way down the mountain from the Fir Bolg king's burial cairn, weary and burdened with their own thoughts about life and death. The screaming of the young war witch unnerved them more than they wished to admit. "I noticed that girl during the battle, did you?" Macha asked. "She was acting as a war witch but seemed so childlike that I was surprised the Fir Bolgs had given her such a task. But during the fighting I saw her change from a timid girl into a she-devil as though she had been enchanted. Her curses were so shocking that truly I felt a glimmer of fear about the outcome of the battle." Macha could feel the hair on the back of her neck standing upright now, as she listened to the wails coming from the girl the bearers carried away.

"Macha, I've been thinking," Neimain said, taking little notice of the screaming or Macha's words, "you really need to consider what Morrigan suggested about Breas. If you were his queen . . ."

"Not you too, Neimain," Macha said. "I don't want to talk about it. Why can't you accept that I feel nothing for him but friendship?"

"I've been turning the idea over in my mind and I can see many advantages to the family if you were to be his queen."

Macha looked at her, tears springing to her eyes. She felt very tired. "My own sisters would sacrifice me to a loveless marriage for political advantage?"

"How much sacrifice would it be, sister? Breas is exceedingly handsome and if his behavior in battle is any indication of how he performs between the furs, you would not find life with him so difficult. Besides, there are many things a queen may do that others among us may not. You could take a lover anytime you wanted after you gave Breas a child."

"How can you say that to me, Neimain? Even if you're jesting, it's not funny."

"Neither Morrigan nor I mean it as a jest, Macha. Our tribe is at a perilous point. We are few in number, in a strange land, about to send away every Fir Bolg who knows anything about living here. I feel fearful of our future without Nuad at our head. If you were queen it would be possible for Nuad's thinking to influence Breas's decisions. Without you at the right hand of the king, Nuad will have no influence at all, and we will be left to the whims of that brash, vain warrior."

"I don't think you're right," Macha protested. "No matter who the king is he has to listen to the Council of the Wise and they have never failed us."

Neimain nodded. "They have had great influence, of course. Still, if you were queen ... I do wish that girl would stop her shrieking. It's as though we were being circled by wolves. Can't the physicians give her a sleeping potion or something to quiet her?"

"I wish they could. She is upsetting me, too. Breas has never given any indication that I am his choice for queen. What makes you and Morrigan so sure he wants me?"

Macha was truly angry with Morrigan, but less so with Neimain. She thought they were far too willing to sacrifice her for the sake of the tribe, but even as she protested Macha knew she would have to consider their request seriously. She could see the advantage of what they were asking her to do, and there were worse fates then being wed to Breas.

* * *

"Look at that, Brigid," said the ever observant Cairbed, as they made their way down the steep and rocky hillside. "It looks like the beauties are having a falling out. Would you like to wager that it has something to do with our new calf-eyed king?"

"What are you talking about, Cairbed?" asked Brigid, whose mind was not on the sisters walking ahead of them. She was thinking of the Fir Bolg queen who was so tiny and sad as she knelt by the grave of her husband. Brigid's heart had been filled with sympathy for her and the boy by her side. The lad seemed to vacillate between childhood and manhood as he struggled to control his emotions, and she felt a desire to offer comfort.

"They are quarreling about Breas," Cairbed said. "He has been mooning about Macha for so long that I'm sure she will soon be our new queen."

Brigid forgot about the Fir Bolgs' grief as her own heart shattered into a thousand pieces at the bard's words. She had no idea that Breas desired Macha. As long as he was not enmeshed with another woman she was free to dream, but if he took a queen it would mean the end of all hope. Her eyes filled with tears and the end of her nose became red.

"Ah, what is it, my dear?" Cairbed asked, seeing her hurt.

Brigid sniffed loudly and wiped her eyes, "Nothing. Nothing at all Cairbed. Mind your own business."

"I'm sorry if I said something wrong, Brigid. I was just making idle chatter. Pay no attention to my words. They have no meaning. You know a bard likes the sound of his own voice. I'm sure I am completely mistaken."

He took her hand in his, raised it to his lips and kissed it. She smiled in spite of herself. Cairbed had always been sincere with her, although he seldom was with others, given his propensity for satire and jesting. She knew he was sorry. She hated for him to have seen her secret feelings, because she was ashamed of wanting Breas, but she knew Cairbed could be trusted never to mock her with it.

"It's all right, my friend. Of course our new king must choose a queen as soon as possible. I just didn't know it would be Macha."

"Perhaps it's not. Mine was just idle speculation," he replied, eager to leave the subject behind.

Eri assisted Breas in settling into Nuad's battle tent. She placed a small table draped with furs along the back wall of the tent and gave her son her own stool to sit on. She approved his green cloak and smoothed his curls with her bejeweled hand as he took his seat. King Breas beamed up at her, his heart bursting with pride.

"You look every inch the king, my son. I am proud of you," Eri said. She bent and kissed his cheek. "I will leave you now so that you may receive your subjects. But before I go ..." she paused then slipped a large golden ring from her forefinger and laid it in his palm. "This was the only gift your father ever gave me ... save for you ... and it is right that you should have it on this most auspicious day of our lives."

Breas looked at the ring. It was crudely made by DeDanaan standards. It had a sailing curragh of strange design embossed upon it amid foreign-looking symbols. He thought it ugly and did not wish to wear it.

"What kind of symbols are these?" he asked.

"Oh, something to do with Fomorian lore. I don't know."

He sighed. "Well, thank you, Mother. I shall wear this ring ... because you gave it to me."

His weak response disappointed Eri. She had expected to be praised lavishly for her generosity and sensitivity to tradition. She frowned and regarded her son carefully. She hoped he wasn't going to take his new position so seriously that he would no longer have a high regard for her judgment. She withdrew from his presence feeling hurt and cautious, not at all the way she had expected to feel on this day.

When she had gone, Breas held his hand out in front of him and peered at the ring. It didn't look too bad on his strong, well-manicured hand. He could wear it, he supposed, but he had to think about the problem of emphasizing his Fomorian blood. After all, the Fir Bolgs considered them their foremost enemy and DeDanaan lore was filled with tales of Fomorian barbarity. He slipped the ring off and put it in his fes, thinking he would replace it on his finger when next he met his mother.

He sent for the great Dagda Mor. There was much to be decided about the future of the DeDanaans on Innis Ealga. Breas needed to be seen conferring with the head of the Council of the Wise, and he planned to let Dagda believe he would have a say in tribal matters, although Breas intended to have his own way ... especially when it came to where people were to live.

He would build his seat of power near the Brugha na Boyne, on the high hill known as Druim Caein, far across the island from Lough Gur where he would send Nuad and those he considered too loyal to the former king.

Filled with grief for the man she had loved so dearly, the Fir Bolg queen, Tailteann, sat beside King Eochy's resting place and thought longingly of the day her spirit might fly to the heavens and once more join that of her true husband. She sat silently by his cairn until the lavender light of twilight descended, carefully going over the details of their life together. She went over the happy times and the sad ones, savoring them alike. She had loved and been loved by a good man and understood that few mortals were as fortunate. When she rose to return to the living she had reached a certain peace with the gods who had taken Eochy from her. She understood that her task was now to help Lugh conduct himself among the newcomers to Innis Ealga in such a way that honor would forever be attached to his foster father's name, and the Fir Bolgs would not be destroyed. Queen Tailteann did not fool herself into believing that it would be easy.

Chapter Fourteen

Gray columns of smoke rose from the funeral pyres of the battle slain and drifted across the Plain of Moytirra, swirling around the Fir Bolg tent as the wind shifted direction. Lugh approached the tent apprehensively, uncertain whether the wounded DeDanaan king had yet been installed. Through the smoke he could see his things and Queen Tailteann's bundled neatly and placed beside a large oak tree some thirty paces from the tent. So. The deed had been done; Queen Tailteann and he had been displaced. His heart was heavy with sorrow and anger that his mother should lie upon the ground this night.

He slumped down beside the oak and leaned his back against the trunk. He looked up through its bare branches where a few acorns still hung tenaciously to their summertime home. He sighed and closed his eyes, trying to imagine that he was back at Lough Gur, lying beside the stream. He had trouble remembering what it had been like there, when sunshine washed over him, filling him with warmth. There was only cold and death in this desolate place called Moytirra. He wondered if he could ever be happy again. Everything dear and familiar had been taken from him with the Fir Bolgs' defeat.

When he opened his eyes he found himself looking up into the piercing blue eyes of an extremely aged man with long white hair. Lugh felt only kindness in the old man's intent gaze, so he made no attempt to look away.

"Hello, lad. My name is Diancecht. I am the chief physician of the DeDanaans. You are Lugh, the prince of the Fir Bolgs?"

Lugh scrambled to his feet, understanding that to remain seated before this man would be a grave discourtesy.

"I am, sir. I am the fostered son of Eochy, the great Fir Bolg king we have just buried on the hilltop."

"Ah, yes. I was unable to attend the ceremony and for that I seek your forgiveness. I am old and walk upon a leg of bronze, and my duty lay in attending the injured Nuad, former king of the DeDanaans. You and your mother are to be commended for you great compassion in allowing us to shelter him in your tent. We DeDanaans are most grateful."

"I am not to be commended," Lugh said flatly. "I did not want to yield up the tent. My mother is in deep mourning and she should be sheltered instead of the man who would steal our land from us."

"The deed has been done, Prince Lugh." The old man sighed. "Can you not accept the fate the gods have decreed for you and your adopted tribe? It is their will, you know. We are all fated to act out their plan for us."

"Ha!" Lugh scoffed. "Such talk angers me. It is men who make war upon one another. I cannot see the hand of any god in it."

Somberly, the old man said, "The gods are at work in all things, my son. I believe that with all my being." He paused and looked more intently at Lugh. "Soon, you too will be a believer. This I know beyond any question."

Lugh was astonished to feel himself nodding in agreement. There was something so certain about the old physician's pronouncement that Lugh could not dispute what he said.

At that moment Morrigan emerged from the battle tent, looking for Diancecht. She called to him when she saw him speaking with Lugh.

"Nuad has need of you," she said to the old physician as she came near. Then she turned her large brown eyes on Lugh and smiled.

"Hello, Prince Lugh. We have made Nuad comfortable in the tent. I wish to thank you again and to remind you of my promise to your mother." She looked around. "Where is Queen Tailteann? Did she not return with you from the hilltop?"

"My mother wanted to stay next to my father's grave. She will join me when she is able."

He saw acceptance in Morrigan's face just as he had in the old physician's. He struggled to remain angry with the

DeDanaans, but he was attracted to these two people as much as he had been to Nuad and Cian on the day they came to call on King Eochy. The feeling was so strong that he almost felt as if he were under a spell.

"If your mother has need of anything during the night, please call. We'll be glad to help in any way, won't we, Diancecht?"

"Indeed. Most gladly. We want you to consider us your friends, Lugh, for that is what we are. Now, if you will pardon me, I must return to my patient." Diancecht bowed stiffly and hobbled into the tent.

"Have you eaten this day, Prince Lugh?" Morrigan asked.

"No, I haven't," Lugh replied, realizing that he was famished.

"Come with me then. I know one of the cooks at the filach fiadah and I'm sure we can find you something, even at this hour." Lugh went with her more willingly than he would ever wish Queen Tailteann to know.

Whispers and curious looks passed between the DeDanaans who saw Morrigan leading the young Fir Bolg prince down to the cooking place. By the time they reached the lake there were few DeDanaans who were not looking their way or murmuring about Morrigan's companion.

Desheen, the young DeDanaan charioteer, had gone straightaway to her horses when she came down from the mountain burial and was grooming a large black stallion when Morrigan and Lugh passed by. She stopped rubbing the horse's back with the rough oak bast cloth she held in her hand, to stare in openmouthed admiration of the handsome young man. She watched him until the neglected horse whinnied, demanding that she continue her task. She finished hurriedly, then left the corral to go to where Brigid was sorting clean wool for bandages.

Trying her best to sound casual and disinterested, Desheen asked, "Did you see the Fir Bolg prince with Morrigan just now?"

"I did," Brigid answered. "Isn't he a handsome young man? He certainly is a strange-looking Fir Bolg, though. I think he looks more like us."

"Yes," Desheen said, scarcely able to breathe. "I'm

glad he's not going to be exiled like the other Fir Bolgs. I wonder where King Breas will send him to live?"

"For that matter, I wonder where the king will send any of us to live," Brigid answered. "There is so much that remains to be settled. I will be glad when we can leave this place of slaughter and return to the rest of the tribe at the seaside camp. Won't you?"

"Huh? Oh, yes, I guess so," Desheen answered distractedly, her thoughts still on the handsome young prince who had not looked her way as he passed by.

The cooks found Lugh a meaty bone and a cup of broth, and he was refreshed by the nourishment. When he finished eating, Morrigan offered him a beaker of fresh milk and he gulped it down, wiping his lip on his sleeve.

"Thank you for bringing me here," he said. "The events of the past few days have been so momentous that I had not eaten for too long. I feel better now."

"I'm glad," Morrigan said, appraising his lean, hard body when he stood up. He was a handsome one. She thought Cian should be pleased that his son had turned out so well.

"I'm eager to get back to the tent. My mother could return at any time. What am I to call you?"

"My name is Morrigan, as I told your mother. Please call me that. I, too, am eager to get back. King Nuad has been stirring all afternoon and the physicians say he could return to consciousness at any time. I want to be there when he does. Come on, then."

As they passed the place of the physicians, Lugh saw Aibel who cried out to him, "Lugh! Lugh! Please! Don't let these people hurt me."

Lugh did not see that she was in any danger, but went swiftly to Aibel's side and took her in his arms. She embraced him fiercely. "Oh, Lugh, they are trying to kill me. They are horrid and cruel. You must take me away from these people. Please, Lugh, please."

"Don't worry, Aibel. I will take care of you. Everything is going to be all right."

"Her words are not true, young prince," said Airmead. "We have not harmed her. On the contrary, we have tried only to help her. She is very strong and has injured two of my assistants with her struggling. It is good that you have come. Perhaps you can help calm her. She—"

Aibel buried her face in Lugh's shoulder. He could feel her hot tears on his neck. Her body was trembling like that of a nestling bird he had once picked up in the woods.

"Stay with me," she sobbed, "don't let them hurt me anymore."

"Don't be afraid, Aibel. I will never forsake you. I promise." He looked accusingly at the doctor. "How did you attempt to help her? Why is she so upset?"

"I know not. She began to scream after leaving the burial place. It was necessary to restrain her and carry her down the mountain. Have you ever seen her like this before?"

"No," Lugh said, mistrustful of DeDanaan medicine.

"We have given her a sleeping potion. It has not made her sleep, but it has calmed her some. She was much worse earlier. I have seen one other case like hers and I am very interested in learning what caused her outburst. Has there been any change in this young woman's behavior lately? I mean, before the battle? Is there anything you could tell me that could make it easier for me to help her?"

"I can tell you nothing," Lugh said. Although he knew Aibel's behavior had been growing increasingly bizarre, he preferred to believe that today's spell had been brought on by the strain of burying King Eochy.

"Well, perhaps later," Airmead said, resting her hand kindly on his shoulder. "I would like to help her."

Lugh rocked Aibel gently to and fro until she grew quiet. When he felt her head grow heavy with slumber, he laid her gently back on the sheepskin. He looked at Morrigan and asked, "She will be safe here?"

"I give you my oath, Prince Lugh. Airmead is one of our finest physicians. She will see that no harm comes to your friend. Come, we must return."

To Airmead, she said, "You may send a courier across to the Fir Bolg tent with news of the girl's awakening. I will be there with your father, tending to King Nuad, and this young man will be nearby with his mother, the Fir Bolg queen. Take good care of her."

"I will, Morrigan. Have no fear." Airmead smiled reassuringly at Lugh.

As they strode across the battlefield, Morrigan asked, "Is that girl important to you?"

"She has been my friend since the day I came to Lough Gur to be fostered in the royal family."

"That's not what I meant. I want to know if she is your lover."

He blushed red, up to his hairline. The Fir Bolgs did not speak of such matters so bluntly. "Uhh, no. We-we are good friends only," he stammered, wondering if his desire for Aibel was so apparent to this beautiful woman that she felt she could ask such a thing.

Morrigan smiled. She knew well the appetites of young men. This one would be no different. "Do you know, Lugh, that King Breas will allow your mother to keep one serving woman from your tribe with her? Perhaps if this girl ... what is her name?"

"She is called Aibel."

"Aibel. Your mother could request that Aibel be allowed to stay in Innis Ealga if you wish to avoid her deportation to the islands, but you will have to act fast. The Fir Bolgs will begin their journey toward the bay from whence they will depart, at the first light of morning."

All the anguish that Lugh had felt earlier returned the moment Morrigan left him. His sorrow was deeper than a bone and cup of broth could negate. The slump of his shoulders and his drooping head told Tailteann that he had need of mothering.

Lugh leaped up when he saw her coming and ran toward her. They embraced and clung to one another with unexpected intensity.

"You are all right, Mother?" he asked.

"I am, my darling." She smiled. "The gods give us strength to bear our losses. There will always be pain in my heart, as though a part of it has been ripped out, leaving a ragged and bleeding wound, but I know that it will heal over in time. I can continue to live without King Eochy ... and you can, too ... because we must."

She paused and looked into the gloaming toward the hilltop where her husband's gray stone cairn rose against the darkening sky. She slipped her arm around Lugh and hugged him to her.

"You are made of much stronger stuff than you realize now, son. You will come through this pain. I know it."

"I suppose so, Mother, but it seems like everything I hold dear has been taken from me. Besides losing Father, the lads I have known all my life will be deported tomorrow and I will never seen any of them again."

He choked back tears and told her about Aibel. She readily agreed to ask the new DeDanaan king if the girl might be allowed to remain on Innis Ealga with them, believing that she knew what Aibel meant to Lugh.

They moved into the crude shelter Lugh had fashioned. When Tailteann had seated herself on the earthen floor, Lugh said, "It galls me no end, that you must sit upon the ground while that wounded man takes your tent ... the tent from which my father went forth to do battle with him. He has no right to be there."

Tailteann sighed heavily. She was weary beyond belief. "It is all right, Lugh. I told you that on the day I agreed to give up the tent. This man, Nuad, was the king of a superior force. I have tried to teach you the ways of kingship and if I have done my job at all well, you should understand that he was bound by his duty to his tribe when he went against King Eochy. There can be nothing personal in such conflict. Fate had both men bound tightly in its web. Don't you see that yet?"

Before Lugh could answer, a blood-curdling cry such as was never before heard on the plain of Moytirra issued forth from within the Fir Bolg battle tent. It was a howl of rage, a cry of pain, a sob, and it tore at the hearts of all who heard it. Involuntarily, Lugh's breath was suspended by the agony so apparent in the chilling sound. He felt the hair on the back of his neck stand up and had to fight off an impulse to make the sacred old sign said by some to ward off demons.

Tailteann looked at Lugh with wide eyes, but neither of them spoke. A lower and less shrill howl came from within the tent, then angry words, followed shortly by a water ewer hurled through the tent opening. It bounced and rolled, clattering to a stop at Tailteann's feet.

She picked it up and said softly, "The DeDanaan is awake and has seen how grievous is his wound. May the gods hold him in their keeping. This man will not find it easy to go on with his life, either, Lugh. We must search our hearts for mercy. It is said that hate destroys the vessel in which it is stored. The DeDanaan already suffers. Do not waste your energies on hating him any longer."

Chapter Fifteen

From the first time humankind set foot on the island of Innis Ealga, the high hill of Druim Caein had loomed over the plains of Meath like a beacon, calling all who saw it to come and worship there. The Brugha na Boyne, the great necropolis of Parthenon's people, lay all around its base, the tombs rising from the green fields in postures calculated to capture the golden rays of the Sun God.

Now, on the coronation morning of Breas, son of Ethalon the Fomorian, and Eri the DeDanaan, only thin, pale rays of winter sun could break through the gray clouds. Ice crystals that coated the fields during the night had melted little under the tepid eye of the awakening day. There remained a brittle sheen of frost in all the shaded hollows of the hill. Sea birds wheeled and shrieked in the chill wind, seeking sustenance inland from their usual haunts a short distance away on the eastern coast of Innis Ealga.

Eri glanced up at the birds as she made her way to Breas's dwelling near the center of the settlement, her heart bursting with joy. It was a good omen she thought, to have sea creatures here on this propitious day. There had been no ominous halo around the full moon last night and the presence of the birds further confirmed the promise of a fine midwinter's day for the ceremonies.

She smiled and gathered the soft woolen hood of her cloak about her face, careful not to disturb the arrangement of her hair. Her rainment was the finest DeDanaan craftswomen had been able to produce, and she knew her appearance would do her son proud on this, the most important day of his life.

She paused to look at the Lia Fail where it stood in solitary splendor, reaching toward the sky from the center of the festival site. The holy coronation stone had been carried up the hill of Druim Caein as carefully as though it were an infant. The priests unwrapped it from its straw bunting with reverence and supervised its erection with eyes as keen and critical as an eagle's. The holy stone had to be aligned on its axis to receive the rays of the midday sun as the man who was to become the king of the DeDanaans stood before it to take his vows. It was thrilling to think the gods had chosen her son to be that man. The thought of such glory coming to him, and to her, nearly caused her to swoon. Eri reached out a bejeweled hand and grasped the top stone of the low wall the priests had built around the sacred stone.

The dizzy sensation passed as quickly as it had come, and she made her way to Breas's dwelling, passing the holed stone the priests had raised outside the sacred circle of the Lia Fail. She was pleased with herself that she had thought to enlist the old physician's aid for that ritual. It would not do for her son to fail in his symbolic mating with the land of Innis Ealga. Too much depended upon the act for them to leave it to chance.

"It is I, your mother," she called, when she rapped on the door.

Breas hurried to let her in. "Mother. I am glad to see you," he said. "I'm a little nervous this morning. You're later than I thought you would be."

"Ah, Breas. You need not be nervous, for it's grand you look. Anyone would know at a glance that you are the choice of the gods."

"Thank you, Mother. This is a wonderful cloak, isn't it? I was well pleased when I saw how finely my coronation attire had been made. The sewing women did not have much time. Did you sleep well?"

"I did, although my excitement is so high that I was awake early this morning. And you, son, were your dreams of your coming glory?"

Breas laughed. "Well, perhaps! I dreamed of the woman who is to be my bride, Macha."

Eri laughed too. "That is as it should be, Breas. Just think, king and bridegroom too! My heart swells with pride on this day. I knew you would be special the day you were conceived. The gods had a hand in it, I know, for as unlikely as it was that Ethalon and I should have met, your birth had to have been their work."

Breas had no wish to speak of his mother's love affair when he had his own on his mind. He was planning carefully how and when he would ask Macha to be his bride. He meant to make his coronation day the pinnacle of his life by announcing that Macha would be his bride and the queen of the DeDanaans.

"Do you think the gods will work their will with Macha when I ask her to be my queen?"

"I have no doubt, Breas. On this day, all things will come unto you for you are now the most powerful DeDanaan of all. You have learned your lessons well, and I am very proud of you."

She took a stool near the fire and beckoned for Breas to be seated next to her. She reached into her fes, saying, "I asked Creidne to make this for you. I wanted something extraordinary to mark this occasion, and he has succeeded beyond my expectations. Use this, my darling, and think of the mother who loves you each time you do."

Breas reached out and took a small leather bag from his mother's hand. He opened it and lifted out a beautifully crafted mirror made of polished bronze. The handle had been twisted into the intricate shape of a grapevine and was attached to the round body of the mirror with such precision that no seam was visible.

He held it up and looked into it intently. His image was murky in the dim light from the fire, but was sharper than he had ever seen it before. He smiled broadly, pleased with the handsome face and perfect teeth he saw reflected there.

"Mother, you have outdone yourself! This mirror is without doubt the most beautifully crafted object I have ever seen. I thank you from the bottom of my heart that you would mark my coronation day with such a glorious memento."

He rose and kissed the top of her head. She moved away slightly, still protecting her hair. She reached up and took his hand and held it to her lips. "You deserve nothing less than the best, Breas. Are you prepared to start the ceremonies? If so, let us go forth together for your coronation."

"Yes, Mother. I am prepared. Let us go. Is Diancecht ready for me?"

"He is. He awaits you in my private dwelling, so no one will know what he is about. The Banois Rig rite is too important to take a chance that you might not be able to complete it."

Breas flushed. "Good. Let us be off, then," he said, helping her to rise. "You're sure his potion will work?"

There were those among the DeDanaans assembled for Breas's coronation who guessed that his thrusting at the holed stone might have been aided by Diancecht's potion, while others saw in the act a fusion between the mother earth and their new king. Later, at the close of the coronation, many insisted that they heard the Lia Fail shout loudly as the narrow crown, decorated with delicately wrought oak leaves, was placed atop Breas's golden curls by the Dagda Mor. Others, standing farther back in the crowd, complained that they had heard nothing. Nevertheless, feasting and merrymaking were soon the order of the day. Pipes and whistles were brought forth and dancing began to the throbbing beat of the bodhrans.

Breas waited until the dancing was well underway, near the close of the day when the twilight was suffused with a soft rosy haze, to summon Macha to his side. By then the people had thrown off all solemnity occasioned by the coronation. Drinking, storytelling, feasting, and general merriment occupied them one and all, except for the three Fir Bolgs, Lugh, Queen Tailteann, and Aibel, who stood apart as observers, feeling very much like conquered peoples. They did not know that the blemished DeDanaan king, Nuad, lay inside one of the guest dwellings, feeling as alienated and alone as they did.

From his chair on an elevated platform, King Breas looked out on the gathering with no thought of the fallen king he had replaced. He focused entirely on Macha and the question he was about to ask her.

The hills surrounding Druim Caein glowed like a thousand facets of a rosy jewel in the reflected light of the setting sun. Innis Ealga was his jewel, his own kingdom. As soon as he spoke with Macha his joy would be complete.

He smoothed his curls back from his brow and remembered the mirror in the fes at his waist. He pulled it out to inspect his visage. A stray curl hanging over his forehead was carefully arranged before he replaced the mirror in its bag. Breas's color was high, and his heart beat hard with anticipation.

When he saw Macha making her way slowly through the throng, he grinned broadly, barely able to contain his excitement. By the gods! She was a great beauty. Her thick auburn hair was bound into plaits, then twisted up into a heavy coil on the back of her head. A few stray wisps had fallen down as she danced. Her cheeks were pink from the exertion and her brown eyes sparkled. The bleached white tunic she wore clung to her body, and he could see the curve of her breasts where she had thrown back her cloak.

She wore a particularly fine silver torque around her neck. Servants had begun to light the torches as darkness approached and as she passed them, the reflection of the flames gleamed back from the shining surface of her adornments. She smiled at the new king when she saw him watching her, revealing the single dimple he found so appealing.

Breas drank in her beauty, believing her to be the most desirable woman he had ever seen. His servant assisted Macha onto the platform. She smiled cheerily at Breas, and he held out his hand to her. He was pleased when she raised it to her lips and kissed it.

"My lord. I am happy to congratulate you on your coronation. May your reign be a long and prosperous one. I am honored to be your faithful servant."

He bid her be seated on the low bench he had had placed before his chair. Suddenly, his confidence dimmed and he felt like a naughty child about to be rebuked by his mother. He was bewildered at feeling so small. He knew Eri was every bit as enthusiastic about a match between him and Macha as he himself. Why then, did he feel so odd?

Breas and Macha made small talk for some time. She told him of the antics of her sister, Morrigan, during one of the dances.

"I think she and Nuad quarreled earlier and she is dancing as though her feet might fall off, to spite him. She's a great one for the music, she is. Nuad should have known she wouldn't stay at his bedside when there was dancing and revelry in the camp."

She laughed and he joined in, as though the tale

amused him too, but his thoughts were of how different things would be for Macha and her sisters now that he was king. After they were wed he might send the other two to the colony at Lough Gur. That would get them out of his way.

They went on discussing this and that, until Breas simply blurted out his proposal. "Macha, will you be my queen?"

Her eyes grew round with astonishment. She was at a loss for words. She had considered Morrigan and Neimain's desire for her to wed Breas carefully, but his interest in her had seemed to wane perceptibly after he was named as king, so she had put it from her mind, convinced that her sisters had read more into his earlier behavior than was actually there. Now the words she dreaded to hear had been spoken and hung between them, demanding an answer. What was she to do?

"Breas," she said, her voice faltering, "I am much honored that you would consider me for such a position, but I . . ." She took a deep breath and went on, knowing there could be but one reply.

"I cannot marry you, King Breas. It would not be fair to you if I were to say yes and try to build a life based on falsehoods. I will always care deeply for you as a friend, but I cannot marry you. I am sorry if my answer causes you distress but . . ."

When Breas realized that she was saying no to the King of the DeDanaans, he felt a humiliation so great he feared his heart might stop beating. A crimson flush rose up his neck and crept onto his face. There was a roaring in his ears that made her words unintelligible to him. Shame and rage filled his head to the point where there was no room for her speech to enter. But slowly he became aware that she had stopped speaking. The words he spoke to her then were filled with hatred.

"Leave this platform now," he said icily, "I never wish to see you again. I wish to have no words from you or about you. From this moment forth you are as a dead woman to me. You will leave my court and go to Lough Gur with your precious sisters, never to return to this royal place as long as you live.

"You are to tell no one, not Morrigan, not Neimain, of what has passed between us this night. If ever I learn that you have spoken of this matter, I will have you and your entire clan put to the sword."

Macha was stunned. Her pink cheeks faded to white and all color fled from her lips, which were parted in astonishment at his venomous words. He said he wanted to take her to wife and now, only moments later, he was threatening her and her family with death. She looked closely at him. His beautifully shaped blue eyes, fringed with dark lashes so long they almost appeared feminine, were hard and determined. She knew he meant what he said.

She had faced enemies in battle and knew she was no coward, yet fear overwhelmed her as she looked into Breas's sculpted face, a face now devoid of any human kindness. She longed for escape, realizing that he could kill her gladly at this moment and feel no remorse.

Unable to wait for him to dismiss her, she turned away from his awful stare and leaped down from the platform. She could feel his hatred boring into her as she struggled through the crowd, seeking refuge in the company of her sisters. She dared not look back.

Too many DeDanaans saw Macha leave the coronation platform in tearful search of her sisters, for the incident with the king to remain a secret. The sharp-eyed, sharp-tongued bard, Cairbed, saw the king's contorted, angry face and from it deduced what had happened. He inched his way through the dancing, laughing crowd, looking for Brigid. He spotted her father, Dagda, and made his way toward him. He might know where Brigid was.

When Cairbed got closer he saw that Dagda had one of the younger milkmaids backed up against an oak tree. His eyes were bright from drink, his cheeks ruddy, as he tried to cajole the girl into going down the hill with him, to lie beside the river Boyne. She turned grateful eyes on Cairbed when he called out to Dagda. When the wise man turned to look at Cairbed, she slipped from his embrace and made her escape, giggling nervously.

"Now, look what you've done, you clumsy boar!" Dagda shouted. "I was well on my way to having a jolly time with that young one. Why was it not impossible to wait a few more minutes until I had fully made my case?"

Cairbed laughed heartily. "My lord, I do beg your pardon. Perhaps you will find what I have to say some compensation for the intrusion I have made in your love life."

There was no need to add that Dagda's amorous adventure was doomed to failure anyway.

"Have you seen Brigid?" Cairbed asked. "I want her to know what I have just seen."

"Brigid? No, I haven't seen her for some time. On the way to the feasting I saw her talking to Desheen by the horse pens, but I haven't seen her since then. What is it that you can't wait to tell?"

Cairbed grinned. "I am certain our new king asked Macha to be his queen."

Dagda took a deep breath and nodded with resignation. "Yes. I expected as much."

"Ah, but what you did not expect, nor did I, was that Macha would tell him no."

"What? She has refused the king? I am dumbfounded."

"I'm sure it must be so, Dagda. You should have seen his face, as dark as the blackest thundercloud. When Macha left his platform she was in tears, looking as though she had come face to face with a demon at midnight. She was quite shaken. Go see for yourself. I know I am right."

"I don't doubt you, Cairbed. Your information is always good." Dagda furrowed his brow. "I wonder what this will mean for her . . . and her sisters. With Morrigan so close to Nuad, King Breas's anger could have serious implications. By the gods, this is worrisome."

Shortly after the morning meal of the next day, King Breas ordered the Council of the Wise to assemble in the meeting hall. The gossip about Macha's refusal had spread throughout the DeDanaan tribe like wildfire in dry grass and as a result of all the talk, it was a nervous council that filed into the meetinghouse.

"King Breas will be as mean as a wounded boar," said Ogma to his brother as he caught up with him. "I fear his wrath."

"Aye, I too, feel fear. A javelin in his side would not have wounded him as much as this blow to his pride," Dagda replied, opening the door to the hall and holding it for Ogma to enter. "He will extract a heavy penalty from the beautiful Macha, of that we can be certain. She will live to rue the day she said no to Breas the Beautiful. The gods alone know how many of the rest of us will feel his ire. I hope he will give ear to the reasonable counsel of our fellows. We must try to understand his shame and be as accommodating as we can. Perhaps we can take some of the sting out of his anger."

"I hope so, Dagda. If anyone can persuade him to listen to reason, it is you. There's a good reason the people call you Ruad Rohfessa."

When they were seated, Airmead slipped in and took her place beside Dagda on the long low bench in the front of the hall.

"Good morning, my dear," he said.

"Good morning, Dagda. Did you get any sleep last night? The revelry went on so long that I feel as though my eyes never closed."

"I slept some, but I heard your patient, the young Fir Bolg girl who thinks she is being pursued, crying out again in the night. Is she improved?"

"She is quiet and was sleeping well when I left her, but I would not say that she has improved. The episodes come with increasing frequency and I am baffled by her odd behavior. This is the third such incident since the burial of the Fir Bolg king, and each time the spells seem to last longer than before. I wish I knew what was wrong."

"Does your father, the wise Diancecht, understand her affliction any better?"

Airmead shook her head no. There was no sense in bringing up her father's old-fashioned notions about the presence of evil gods. He was aged and it would be well if he could go to his grave with none of his colleagues ever knowing about his superstitious adherence to the old ways.

"Do you have any idea what King Breas wants from us today?" she asked. "Until Cian and Mac Lir return from their task of deporting the Fir Bolgs, we won't have a full council. I don't think we can conduct tribal business without them."

"You're right about that, Airmead," Ogma interjected. "I asked Cairbed to recite the laws regarding the council for me on the way over here, and we can take no action without twelve council members present."

King Breas swept into the meeting hall, drawing up his green cloak as he strode down the central passage past the council members. He looked neither to the left nor the right. His mind was set on one thing only and he had no wish to be deterred from it.

"Honored members of the council," he said, when he reached the front of the hall, ignoring all protocol. "I wish to discuss the peopling of the colonies of Innis Ealga this morning." His voice was hard and thin, but unwavering. "I know certain decisions were made earlier, but I have thought long on the matter and there are some changes I would make to the plan. There is to be no discussion, no modification, and not one of you is to go forth to the people complaining of my decree." He stared at them coldly, daring any to challenge him.

Dissent hummed through the meeting hall as counselors turned to look at one another with exclamations of surprise. They had agreed on a plan and now he was telling them that he and he alone, was amending the decision? This would not do at all.

King Breas took no note of their distress. He talked about the earlier council decision to let stand the divisions of Innis Ealga that King Eochy had made, and the farmsteads that already existed within them. "This I will allow," he said, "but the three sisters, Morrigan, Macha, and Neimain, shall be sent to the colony at Lough Gur. This of course, will necessitate sending Nuad there to be with his woman. And I think it only right that his physician, Diancecht, accompany him."

"No!" roared out Dagda, standing to face his king. "These things you cannot do. DeDanaan law commands that our kings act in concert with the Council of the Wise. I do not question what you wish to do, King Breas; rather, I object to your method. I demand that if this thing is to be done, it be done in accordance with the laws that have served us well, time out of mind. Not even our king can make such far-reaching judgments without first having consulted with the council."

"Hear! Hear!" shouted Ogma, and others took up the chant, angered greatly by the king's trampling upon their rights.

"Guards!" shouted Breas, "Restrain these who would defy their king."

Barbara Dolan

The guards looked confused and uncertain. Breas called out again, threatening them and their families with banishment if they did not do as they were bid. Reluctantly, the men moved to the front of the meeting hall, drawing their swords as they came, praying to the gods they would not have to use them.

"Your reign will be doomed, King Breas, if you commit such treachery," Dagda warned. "I will have no part of it."

"Nor I," said Ogma.

"Nor I," echoed Airmead.

All ten council members present acted as true DeDanaans on this fateful occasion, each refusing to turn to be a party to King Breas's actions.

"It is of no consequence," the king said. "As of this moment you are each absolved of further duty. I will see that a new Council of Elders is assembled, one that is more to my liking. You, Dagda, will go to Lough Gur. And you, Ogma, will accompany him. Say no more. I have spoken and I will brook no interference in my decision. Those who defy me can expect banishment from the royal court at Druim Caein. See that the word is spread among the people. Guards, take these wretched rebels from my presence. I wish to see them no more."

He waved his hand and stood glaring at the respected members of the Council of the Wise as they were led from the meeting hall at sword point.

PART TWO

Oxen lowing, winter snowing,
Summer passed away ...
Cold seizes the wing of the bird,
'Tis the season of ice ...

    —from the Ossianic literature

Chapter Sixteen

The heavy muscles of Srang's arms and shoulders bulged as he strained to haul a load of red seaweed up from the sea. He dumped the bounty near the rocks where it would be spread to dry and wiped his brow, pausing to note the progress of the three other Fir Bolg escapees who were laboring tirelessly.

He was pleased that the piles of seaweed were many and hoped fervently that when it was dried and burned and spread across the fields it might enrich the thin, meager soil of Connaught enough for them to raise a crop of grain in the spring. This winter they were enduring was the hardest he had ever known. Hunger and cold were constant companions and of the original number of warriors who escaped from Moytirra, only thirteen remained alive. Srang knew their number would be even fewer next summer if they could not force this barren land to yield food enough to sustain them.

He took a drink of fresh water from a shallow vessel they had chipped from a log with crude stone tools, and walked back to the edge of the sea. As he bent once more to his labor a movement far out on the horizon caught his eye. He straightened and looked hard at the dark blue line where the sea met the sky.

A curragh with a large square sail was making for the Connaught cove where they worked. Srang sensed opportunity as a sailing party would have many objects useful to the Fir Bolgs. He felt a thrill of anticipation.

"Men," he shouted, "look westward. On the horizon there sails a curragh with sail set to land on this very beach."

The men exclaimed their surprise. They had been in the wilds of Connaught for so many turnings of the moon, eking out a living from a reluctant earth and an unforgiving sea that they had grown more like beasts than men. The prospect of encountering other human beings was not altogether welcome to them until Srang described the bounty that would be theirs if they could rob the seamen of their possessions.

Srang pointed to the other side of the sea rocks, toward a deep brown gash in the field above them. "We will hide ourselves in the trenches dug when we harvested the turf. Go, Oda, to where the others till the soil. Tell them to bring all of the battleaxes and hasten here. By the gods! I mean to have real food roasting on our spit this night, not the animal fodder we have grown accustomed to. Run! I don't want those who approach to see us. Our sole advantage will be that of surprise."

From their vantage point in the bog, the Fir Bolgs watched as a party of five Fomorian pirates put in on the Connaught shore. The sailors were all short in stature and of even darker coloring than the Fir Bolgs. Instead of cloaks such as the Fir Bolgs and DeDanaans wore, the infamous pirates wore outer garments and head coverings made of animal skins. From this distance Srang could deduce that the man wearing a wolf's head must be the leader, for he shouted orders and stood aside while the others secured the curragh well upon the sand.

The sailors set about gathering driftwood from between the large boulders that littered the irregular coastline, and soon amassed enough for a large fire. Srang and the Fir Bolgs could hear the rough murmur of their voices, but their words were unintelligible.

"We'll wait to make our move until they sit down around the fire," Srang said. "We will have to be as fleet as the wind since their weapons are so much better than our stone axes, but we have them outnumbered more than two to one, so I know we can take them."

They waited, crouched in the narrow peat pit, growing damp and uncomfortable. Srang inhaled the fresh, clean smell of the turf. Cut into bricks and dried, it was all that had kept them from freezing to death in the bitter cold of the winter. It seemed fitting that it should give them shelter now, while they awaited their only chance of respite from the hardships that had come their way since the hated DeDanaans landed on Innis Ealga.

When it seemed that their limbs would not move if they stayed one moment longer in their hiding place, Srang gave the order to attack. The Fir Bolgs made no attempt at stealth, they drove straight for their prey, shrieking wild battle cries as they ran.

The Fomorian sailors were taken unaware and by the time they scrambled for their weapons it was too late, the ferocious Fir Bolgs were upon them. The Fomorian leader, Cochpar, cursed as Srang overpowered him, crushing him to his chest in a clasp as strong as a bear's. Srang held him until another Fir Bolg warrior could bind his wrists and ankles securely with thongs.

"Who are you?" hissed Cochpar, his dark eyes narrowing as he sent the words out through broken and missing teeth.

Srang caught the odor of wolf as the pelt slipped from Cochpar's head, revealing dark, greasy shoulder-length hair, streaked with gray, as was his beard.

"I am Srang, champion of the Fir Bolg people," he said proudly. "And which of the wretched pirates are you, Fomorian?"

"I am called Cochpar. I am the chief tribute collector."

Srang gave him a hard push that sent Cochpar headlong onto the sand, unable to break his fall with his bound hands. His head struck a stone, raising an immediate lump, but no blood. Srang shoved him over onto his back with his foot that was wrapped in mosses inside the remnants of his once fine leather boots.

"You will find only hardship and death in Connaught, foeman. There will be no tribute for you here. In fact, we were thinking of extracting tribute from you, weren't we, men?" Srang laughed cruelly. "We have earned tribute, I think, for having endured all of the raids and burdens your tribe has imposed on mine."

The other Fir Bolgs, standing by their captives, laughed with their leader. "What brings you to the desolate shore?" Srang asked.

Cochpar considered not answering for a moment, but a sharp blow to his ribs from the toe of Srang's shoe, convinced him to reply.

"We had no wish to come here. We were blown off our route yesterday by a storm on the open sea. We have need of sweet water and rest."

"As do we, foeman, as do we." Srang left him to the watchful eyes of the others, to go inspect the cargo on board the pirate boat. There was precious little food, but it was more than the Fir Bolgs had had during the long winter. Of most help would be the weapons. It was difficult to snare birds, catch fish, or bring down game without good weapons. Srang smiled, feeling hope for the first time, as he fingered a fine bow carved of ash. Perhaps he could begin to dream of the revenge he had long planned against the DeDanaans.

The Fir Bolgs' monotonous dinner fare had been relieved by the addition of dried meat from the Fomorian stores, and Srang reclined next to the cooking fire, sated for the first time since his escape from the DeDanaans.

"Are we to kill the Fomorians then?" asked one of his followers. "We could use their clothing and boots."

Before Srang could answer, Cochpar the prisoner shouted to Srang. "You would be well advised to speak with me privately, Fir Bolg, if you are not afraid. There is much I know that can be of value to you. If you kill us, it will be a mistake that will cost you dearly."

In the flickering firelight the man's visage was fearsome. Even bound and tied to a tree, Srang knew he could not take the treachery of the Fomorians lightly. Their cruelty and cunning had long been demonstrated to the Fir Bolgs, and Srang did not intend to let down his guard. Still, the captive's words were intriguing.

"Ha!" snorted Srang. "Me? Afraid to talk with you? Never!" To a comrade, he whispered, "Watch me closely. I will go near and speak with the tribute collector. Fling the ax if he makes the slightest move toward me."

He walked to Cochpar's side. "Well, what is it, captive foeman? What could you possibly know that could be of value to me?"

"You are the Fir Bolgs who escaped when the DeDanaans defeated you in battle Moytirra?"

Srang nodded. "We are."

"We have known you were out here in Connaught but none of our scouts has been able to find you, although we have searched for many seasons."

"You have looked for us? Why? What could you want

with a handful of Fir Bolgs who no longer have anything for you to steal?"

"Ah, Srang. You have much that is of value to us. Material goods are not all the mighty Fomorians seek. Knowledge, too, has a price. It is much better to take what one needs without force." He smiled crookedly and Srang got a whiff of his rotting teeth. He turned his head slightly away.

"Do not turn from me, haughty Fir Bolg. We can be of much use to one another. You know how to reach the DeDanaan stronghold of Druim Caein and I want to go there. If you were to take us inland to the royal seat of the tribe who defeated your people, I assure you, Srang, it would lead to many rewards for you and your men. Ultimately, if might even lead to the restoration of the Fir Bolgs to Innis Ealga. That would please you would it not?"

Srang nodded. "It would please me very much," he said. "Tell me more of what you have in mind."

On a sweet morning in early spring, Queen Tailteann felt a tug of hope for the first time in the six turnings of the moon that had passed since she and Lugh were returned to their home at Lough Gur. Slowly, the sorrowful, gray days of winter yielded to the gentle pressure of the seasons and green shoots of new grass were now pushing up through the soil.

How different it was to move along these old familiar paths in the company of DeDanaans even though the invaders were no longer strangers to her. Some were even becoming friends.

She thought of the portly wise man, Dagda Mor, as she carried a pail of water back to her dwelling. She could see through him as though he were made of mist. She saw how he treated his daughter Brigid, and how he longed for his sons who had been banished to the faraway colony in the province of Ulster. She knew Dagda was more bluster than bite, and she was pleased that he leaned on her more and more for advice about how to conduct the life of the colony at Lough Gur.

She went through the opening of the stone wall that surrounding the dwelling places on the Hill of Knockadoon and was pleased to see Dagda.

"Here, here, my lady!" he cried, taking the water pail from her. "Why isn't your strong young son fetching water from the lough? Or your serving girl? You shouldn't do this. The pail is far too heavy."

"Nonsense, Dagda. I don't mind, The young people were nowhere about, and we need water. Besides, this is a morning sent by the gods and I wanted to be out. There's a scent of wildflowers in the air that warms my winter-weary bones. Can't you smell it? I saw mayflowers along the path. It won't be long before there are blossoms everywhere. I know it."

"Ah, would that we could eat wildflowers," Dagda said grimly. "Soon there may be more of them than food. I can't understand the poor lambing season we had at Imbolc. We have a lot depending on the oat crop coming up well."

"Why hasn't King Breas called for the Beltaine festival?" Queen Tailteann asked, changing to a happier subject. "Even if word were to come today, it would be difficult to make all the preparations in time."

A deep crease furrowed Dagda's brow. He had no wish to take away Tailteann's joy on this fine morning, but he was certain there would be no celebration of Beltaine this year on Innis Ealga, not with the pitiful state of the scattered DeDanaans.

"Who knows what that young king will do?" Dagda answered vaguely and dropped the topic. "How do you and Lugh like being neighbors to Nuad and Morrigan? The people say that there are frequent . . . and noisy . . . quarrels between them."

Tailteann laughed aloud. "You know that I will tell you nothing. Why do you always tease me so? If you want to find out how they are getting along, why don't you ask one of them?"

"Because I know they won't tell me, and I keep hoping that you will slip and feed me some morsel of juicy gossip." He laughed.

She smiled and opened the door of her dwelling for him. He carried the water pail in and set it down beside the ewer and the basin.

"Will you stay and break the fast with me or are you bound for the filach fiadah?" she asked.

"I was down there already. We had to send so much in

tribute to Druim Caein that our stores are very low. The cooks are preparing only enough oats for one bowl of porridge apiece," he said sadly. "I've never seen the cold of winter last so long, or had to endure it so meagerly."

"Yes. It is unusual for Innis Ealga. But as I said, I think it is almost over. I have a new loaf of bread, made just yesterday, and some sweet butter and honey. I would be pleased if you would stay and share it with me."

His hazel eyes lit up at the thought of honey. "Why, yes," he said, trying not to appear too eager, "I could stay and keep you company for a while, I suppose." He pulled up a stool and sat down to stir the fire. "Not too much butter, please. We all need to learn to get by on less these days."

While his mother broke bread with the Dagda Mor, Lugh slipped into the woods with Aibel, hoping no one had seen them leave the cooking place. He told himself that he was tired of Aibel's constantly wanting him to come into the woods with her, but he had to admit that he was always willing to go. She pulled him by the hand, urging him to hurry.

"The queen will miss me soon, Lugh. We don't have much time. Come on."

It irked Lugh to have her ordering him about. Since Nuad and Morrigan dwelt in the house next to his, Lugh was well aware that Nuad never succumbed to Morrigan's efforts to dominate him. She was too bossy, Lugh knew, but her charms were too obvious to be ignored. Without deliberate intent, the tall, auburn-haired DeDanaan had become part of Lugh's daydreaming.

Every time he went into the woods with Aibel, it was Lugh's youthful lust for Morrigan that fueled his desire. He felt intensely jealous when he thought about what she and Nuad did in private.

He sighed, looking at Aibel and wanting to love her better. He wished it were the gorgeous DeDanaan warrior pulling him into the woods. In the clear yellow wash of morning Aibel looked very pretty, much better than when they had first returned to Lough Gur. She had not had one of her spells of terror for a long time.

"I'm glad to see you smiling again," he said to Aibel. She turned her dark eyes on him. "Now that you love me, I have something to smile about, Lugh. I always hoped I would be the one you chose." She smiled at him, her small face shining as though lit from within.

Lugh caught his breath. Did she think that because they went to the woods together he had chosen her to be his bride? He frowned, going over their conversations for anything that might have led her to believe such a thing. He had not counted on this.

"That day at Moytirra when you promised you would never abandon me, I knew then that everything was going to be all right," Aibel said. "As long as I can depend on you, nothing can hurt me."

Lugh was appalled by her dependence on him, but instead of discussing it, he silenced her lips with his own.

Morrigan helped Nuad to a low stool outside their dwelling and placed a fur across his knees. "We won't be too long, my darling. You don't mind that I'm taking Brig with me to javelin practice?"

"No," he growled, "take him. I'll be glad for some peace from you two."

"Now, Nuad. You know you need us and are glad we don't let you lie on the furs, pitying yourself. We do what we do out of love for you." She leaned down and kissed his unresponsive lips. "We'll be back in time for the midday meal." She walked off to find Brig at the souterrain where the weapons were stored.

Nuad frowned and said nothing, as he watched her walk away. She walked like a warrior, yet her swaying hips and beautifully turned ankles awoke in him the memory of the afternoon they had spent in the tall grass, before the battle of Moytirra, and he smiled in spite of himself. He looked down to the place his hand used to be and the smile faded, replaced by the grim, angry expression he had worn since he awoke from his long sleep after the wounding. *The god should have let me die,* he thought, *I'm no use to anyone, not even myself.*

A short time later, Tailteann left her dwelling, carrying a basket filled with washed yarn in need of carding. "Good morning, Nuad. Do you mind if I keep you company while I do this work? The day is so fine I cannot bear to stay indoors." She placed her stool close to his where he leaned against the wattle wall of his house. She looked at him and smiled, liking what she saw.

Nuad wore a tunic of spun brown wool, under a cloak of tanned hide. His bare legs were muscular and strong where they disappeared into boots of the same hide. A leather caplike device covered the stump of his left wrist. Self-consciously, he had drawn a corner of his cloak over it when Tailteann approached.

"Sit, if you like," he said.

His hair had gone snow white after he lost his hand, at least that was what Brigid had told her. Brigid insisted that it had once been as golden as the rays of the rising sun, and the shock of seeing his loss was what had turned it white.

Whatever the truth of the matter, Nuad's jaw was still firm, the cleft in his chin still deep and masculine. His shoulders were strong and his belly flat and Tailteann thought him a fine figure of a man. She was so close to him that she was aware of his scent and she realized that his presence was the reason her heart was beating hard. She found it difficult to catch her breath.

"I wonder where my son has gone," she said at last, forcing herself to think of something other than Nuad. "He disappeared right after the morning meal, and I have many chores for him to do."

"He was with your serving girl, Aibel. I saw them leave the filach fiadah together. Don't worry about him. Young people need some freedom from chores, for the gods know that there is time enough for the burdens of adulthood." He stared at the ground for a while before deciding that he had no call to be rude to Tailteann. He made a stab at conversation.

"Lugh is a good lad, isn't he? He does what you tell him?"

Tailteann laughed her light, bell-toned laugh, "Yes, he is a good lad. But I never try to tell him what to do for he is a proud lad as well. I try always to guide, never to push."

"By the gods! I wish I had a woman like you. Morrigan pushes at me constantly. Get up and do this, do that, don't do this, don't do that. I swear, she purposely tries to make me angry."

Tailteann looked up at him, surprised that he would

reveal such an intimate part of his life to her. It left her off balance, not knowing what to say. For the briefest of moments her eyes strayed to Nuad's powerful arms, and she imagined what it might be like to be enfolded within them. She felt a warm rush of shame creep up her neck and told herself that she should gather up her things and retreat within her dwelling, but she made no effort to move.

"Why would she do that? Is Morrigan naturally quarrelsome?"

"No. She says it is because she felt the cold breath of the underworld blowing on me after my hand was severed. She said I was being pushed toward death, and she believes that I need the heat of rage coursing through me, to feel the blood pounding through my veins, if I am to reconnect with life. I tell you, Queen Tailteann, I am exhausted from her constant prodding. She expects me to carry on as before, when I was a warrior with two good hands. She gives me no sympathy, no peace . . . about anything."

His emphasis on the word "anything" was too strong to be missed. Tailteann understood his meaning well and she felt her cheeks grow hot.

"And have you disconnected with life?" she asked gently. "If you can trust the observation of a new friend, I too see you in danger of succumbing to despair," Tailteann said. "It is understandable. A strong man like you, used to wielding so much power, must find it very difficult to have half of your strength taken from you, let alone your kingdom. Now your keen mind is at once your greatest asset and your worst enemy. Yes, I can see how hard it is for you."

He raised his heavily lashed eyes and looked at her carefully. He liked this woman. He liked her very much. She understood what he was going through. Morrigan never offered soft words. He leaned over and touched Tailteann's arm with his right hand.

The warmth and power in his hand shot through her like an arrow. She jumped back and he withdrew his hand. "I'm sorry," he said, "have I overstepped my bounds?"

"No, no, Nuad, not at all. It's just that . . . I have not felt the touch of a man's hand since the day my beloved husband went forth to battle." Her eyes filled with tears. "I miss him very much," she said. "I miss the warmth of his touch."

She stood abruptly and picked up her stool, plainly flustered. "I must go, I have work ... I will look in on you later ... check your fire for you ..." Then she was gone.

Nuad was touched by her gentleness and aware for the first time that he was not the only one who had suffered a grievous loss at Moytirra. *She is quite a woman,* he thought. *Maybe I did not lose my rapport with women when I lost my hand, after all ...*

Chapter Seventeen

The promise Queen Tailteann had seen in the may-flowers was not borne out. A persistent cold rain, part of a storm brewed over the western sea, swept over Lough Gur and refused to budge. Each day saw more cold, damp weather, and the Sun God did not show his face for many turnings of the moon. Tempers grew short among the inhabitants and faces were long in the line at the filach fiadah. Even Queen Tailteann was silent, standing with downcast eyes, cursing the wretched weather.

The watchman on the highest point of Knockadoon sounded his horn; three short, sharp blasts, announcing that riders were drawing near the colony. Warriors threw down their bowls and ran to defend the perimeters of the settlement.

Lugh flashed a smile at Dagda as he ran past him and joined the other DeDanaans as they assumed defensive positions. He was glad for a chance at action. Peering hard through the drizzle, he could make out the outline of two figures on horseback, still some distance from the lough. He did not recognize them and it was impossible to identify their sodden banner in such weather.

The riders grew closer and the watchman sounded his horn again. This time, a long, slow sliding sound came forth from the curved bronze horn, signaling that the visitors were known and friendly. Reluctantly, Lugh sheathed his knife and relaxed the hand that held his javelin.

"Who is it?" he asked Dagda. "Do you know them?"

"It's hard to be sure, but I think it's our kinsmen who took the Fir Bolgs to the outer islands. Yes! By the gods, it is!" The joy on his face at the recognition of lifelong friends, faded quickly. "I wonder if King Breas has banished them, too. Why else would they be coming to

Lough Gur? They have neither servants nor supplies with them."

Lugh felt resentment of the two men coming nigh, but he knew that they alone might be able to tell him how his Fir Bolg kinsmen had fared. He was haunted by the thought, day and night, that he was a DeDanaan and not a Fir Bolg, for he had loved the members of the darker tribe as though they were his own and he missed his friends daily.

Lugh resisted joining the battle games and contests of the DeDanaan young people at Lough Gur and spent all of his free time with Aibel. She, and his mother, were the only links he had to the past. Remembering the good times he'd had with the Fir Bolg lads was bittersweet. He wanted that kind of comradeship again but felt guilty at the thought of transferring such feelings to his DeDanaan peers.

He looked around him at the warriors awaiting the riders. *I will have to find it here, with these people,* he decided, *or I will never know comradeship again.* He sighed. Everything was too complicated.

"Let us go forth to great our friends," Dagda called to the other warriors. Glad shouting erupted and the DeDanaans ran across the soggy, muddy field to greet the riders. Lugh ran with them.

The cooks did their best to prepare an evening feast in celebration of the safe return of the DeDanaan voyagers. They were aided in their efforts by the donation of several wood hens Cian and Mac Lir had snared along their way. The drizzle stopped but a howling wind had taken its place by the time the DeDanaans gathered at the cooking spot for the evening meal.

Dagda raised a beaker high and shouted over the wind, "We offer praise to the gods for the safe return of our brothers. The colony at Lough Gur is much blessed to have them among us."

He tilted the beaker and drank his fill, leaving stains at the corners of his mouth. After toasting and a little laughter, the people ate quickly, anxious to return to the warmth of their fires.

"I'm sorry the celebration of your safe return is muted, Cian," Dagda said. "The poor weather drags our spirits down, and the gods know that in this place of banishment, they were none too high to start with. What brings you and Mac Lir to Lough Gur?"

"It is a long story, Dagda, but we too, have been exiled from the royal presence for displeasing the new king. We wish to speak with you about it privately. Have you established a council here yet?"

"Some of us meet regularly, but we have nothing official. You have no idea how demoralized we have been. We thought Nuad would act as our leader, but he has not. His recovery has been slow and although his wound seems to have healed, his spirit is not well. Ogma and I try to give some order to our affairs and the Fir Bolg queen, Tailteann, is most helpful to us. She is wise in the ways of people as well as in the ways of this place. You will like her, I think, and come to honor her as we do."

Cian absorbed the news with his characteristic seriousness. "I have no doubt that what you say is true. I have seen much to admire in the Fir Bolg people these past few turnings of the moon. They accept their fate and are making every effort to establish a new life for themselves on the islands. By the time we sailed away from them, both Mac Lir and I had a deep wish that they might succeed under very difficult circumstances. They are going to need the help of the gods out there. Some of those islands have no trees for shelter or firewood. One is covered with stones as far as the eye can see."

He shook his head in sympathy for their hardships, and Dagda could see that it had pained him to leave the Fir Bolgs there.

"Get Mac Lir and come to my dwelling, old friend. We will talk more of the things you have seen. Then you must tell me how it is that you and he angered King Breas."

Once seated around Dagda's fire, Mac Lir recounted the circumstances at the royal seat of power. "Things are not good at Druim Caein, Dagda," he began. "We were shocked to see how the people there have been brought low in the short time we were away. Their food stores are so few that the people are very worried. They are working too hard, too. Breas is building a new feasting hall, twice as large as the old one. He forces the residents of Druim Caein to do the work at a terrible pace."

Dagda frowned. "I don't understand how the stores at Druim Caein could be so low. Tribute collectors have come here to Lough Gur twice in the six turnings of the moon since we arrived, and they took more than half of what the Fir Bolgs had laid aside for the winter. They imposed a boroma of staggering proportions last time, forcing us to give them one third of all our milk, butter, and cheese, and they say they will be back regularly to collect more." Dagda paused, his old face looking more tired than wise.

"We are the ones who are worried about having enough to eat. The lambing at Imbolc time was awful. We lost more to the wolves than we were able to save. This rain has slowed the growth of the barley and oats, and I fear we will have a sparse harvest this year. No, lads, I tell you, it is not those at Druim Caein who have cause to worry. Those of us here at Lough Gur could be very hungry indeed, before the Sun God turns away from us at Samhain."

"That's when King Breas intends to have his feasting hall finished," Cian interjected. "Imagine! Thinking he can force the completion of such a place in only six cycles of the moon. He does not reason as other men." Cian frowned. "Where could all the plenty you have described gone? It certainly was not in evidence at the royal court. I'm telling you, Dagda, the people who are building this hall for him have barely enough to eat."

"That's what got us in trouble with the king," the usually silent Mac Lir added. "We were foolhardy enough to complain to King Breas about his treatment of our kinsmen and it angered him greatly. We are forbidden to return to the royal stronghold, except for festivals. But if it had not been this it would have been something else, Dagda. Breas would have found another excuse to send us away because of our devotion to Nuad . . . and to you."

Dagda took a sip of the hot beverage Brigid had prepared for the visitors and said wryly, "Welcome to Lough Gur, old friends, it seems that all the best DeDanaans end up here. We are glad of your company. With your banishment, the last of Nuad's advisers are gone from the royal presence. What manner of people does this leave around King Breas?"

"Frightened ones, I am afraid, people too fearful of the

king's wrath to give him good counsel or to stand up to
him when he is wrong. We were told that his mother is
the only one to whom he listens," Cian answered.

"There's more," Mac Lir said, "the Fomorians are raiding the coast of Ulster frequently and more successfully
than ever before."

Brigid, who had been listening quietly from her post
near the fire, gasped, and turned fearful eyes toward her
father. The same fear for Bove and Red, who lived on the
northern coast, gripped his mind.

"My friend," Dagda said, "did you hear any news of
my sons, Bove and Aengus? They were sent to the north-
ernmost colony in Ulster."

"Or my young friend, Desheen the charioteer, who
lives there too, what word of her?" Brigid asked.

"Alas," Mac Lir said, "I inquired about Bove and
Aengus, Dagda, but no one knew anything of them. Nor
did I hear anything about Desheen, Brigid. I'm sorry. Try
not to worry. From the absence of news I would take
heart. It probably means that they are not worse off than
the others, although that is not good news."

"I am sick at heart to learn of this," Dagda said.

"I'm afraid there is yet more to tell," Cian said. "The
rumor is that the Fomorian raids are so successful because the pirates are being led to our colonies by Srang,
the Fir Bolg who escaped from Moytirra with so many
others. It is said that he is willing to lead the Fomorians
to us because of a deep wish for revenge against the
DeDanaans for conquering his tribe and taking Innis
Ealga."

While Brigid and Dagda were digesting this information a knock on the door came. Brigid rose and opened
it, surprised to see Lugh and Aibel shivering in the wind.
She hesitated only a moment before asking them to enter.

"Do come into the warm," she said, "and take shelter
with us."

A blast of cold air from the open door reached the
bright flames of the fire, causing them to bend and waver
for a moment before righting themselves. Aibel clung to
Lugh's arm, her eyes cast down to the earthen floor of the
dwelling. Her timidity was in marked contrast to the
handsome young Fir Bolg prince who stood straight and
addressed the older men with assurance.

"I am Lugh, foster son to the Fir Bolg queen, and this is my friend, Aibel. Her mother was among those you left behind on the outer islands. We have come for news of her."

Cian stared hard at the young man.

Mac Lir asked, "And what is your mother's name?"

Aibel squeezed Lugh's arm tightly and looked even more intently at the floor, unable to speak.

"Her name is Elda," Lugh answered for Aibel. "Is she well?"

Mac Lir did not know the woman, although he wished he could offer something to this lovely girl who was so obviously in pain. He looked to Cian whose green eyes clouded over as he searched his memory. He could not place the woman either, but he thought a kind lie could do no harm.

"Your mother is well, indeed, Aibel. You must have no worry about that. She is on one of the larger islands that has a sheltered bay and more fertile soil than some of the others. It is my belief that she will fare well there."

Lugh looked into Cian's eyes and sensed that the words the tall blond man spoke were untrue, but the kindness with which they were offered was obvious and Lugh felt humbled, not knowing if he would have been as generous under similar circumstances.

"Thank you for the news," Lugh said. "I know Aibel appreciates what you have told her . . . as do I. We will trouble you no longer."

When they had gone, Dagda turned to his visitors.

"Do you know who that girl is? She is the daughter of the very man you were speaking of, the escaped Fir Bolg who leads the Fomorians to our coasts."

"You don't say!" exclaimed Mac Lir. "It's a good thing then, that we have not told the news about the Fomorians abroad, isn't it? It is probably just as well that his treachery remains known to only a few of us . . . until a plan can be devised to deal with it. One has to suppose that this girl's first loyalty will be to her father. You know how it is with parents and children."

Thoughtfully, Cian replied, "Yes. I know how it is with parents and children. If you'll excuse me I need to make a visit to the trough. Where is it?"

"Go down the hill and turn to the east just short of the

lake. You will see the path that leads into the woods. It is
well trodden." Dagda laughed. "Brigid, give this man a
torch."

Cian hurried from the dwelling into the dark night. It
took a few moments for his eyes to adjust to the lay of
the land in this strange place. A door opened across the
compound and in the momentary light he saw Lugh and
Aibel disappear inside the dwelling. He made his way
there and rapped softly on the door. The young prince answered.

"Lugh, I have no time to explain, so ask me no questions. I need to talk with you. Will you meet me at the
morning dining time at the filach fiadah? Bring your
horse and we will ride a distance from the settlement. The
matter I wish to speak of will brook no interruption." He
stepped back as though to go, then said, "Oh, yes. Tell
Aibel that her mother sent her a message of love. I forgot
to tell her earlier."

Lugh stood in silence for some moments after Cian
left. He was bewildered by the DeDanaan's urgent request. What would this stranger possibly have to tell him?

"Who was at the door, Lugh?" Tailteann asked when
he returned to the hearth.

"It was one of the DeDanaans who went to the islands,
Mother, with a message for Aibel." He looked at Aibel
who was reclining pensively next to the fire.

"He said to tell you that your mother sends her love."

Aibel burst into tears and Tailteann moved to take her
in her arms, leaving Lugh to ponder on the significance
of a secret meeting. As he turned the strange new devel-
opment over in his mind, he felt serenity descend on him
like an enchantment, enveloping his mind and body.
Soon, the need for sleep overwhelmed him and he slipped
under the furs, thinking not of Aibel and her distress, but
of what tomorrow would bring.

Chapter Eighteen

Icy winds howled throughout the night, chasing the rain clouds toward the eastern part of Innis Ealga. By morning the sky over Lough Gur was clear, although the air was still more wintry than springlike, and those who came to break the fast at the cauldrons were wrapped tightly in their warmest cloaks.

A chill that had nothing to do with the weather enveloped Tailteann's heart when she glanced up and saw Lugh ride into the woods with the DeDanaan, Cian. She knew that the hour she had dreaded was upon her and her knees felt weak, threatening to give up their support.

"I don't feel very well, Aibel," she said. "I'm going to go back to my dwelling and lie down for a while. I want you to stay here and finish your meal."

"Oh, no, Queen Tailteann. If you are not well I wish to come and take care of you."

"Thank you, my dear, but no. I would truly prefer to be alone for a while, but I'm pleased that you want to come. I'll be fine. Don't worry about me."

With that she started up the hill of Knockadoon to her dwelling place where she could worry in privacy, and wait for the outcome of the fateful meeting between her son and his natural father. She had known the first day the DeDanaans set foot at Tlachgta that this day was inevitable and she had tried to prepare herself for it. Still, she could not stop the tears sliding down her cheeks.

Lugh led the DeDanaan to his favorite spot by the stream, the only place he could think of where they could be alone and unseen. He reined Anovaar in and leaped down from the horse's gleaming white back.

He tied Anovaar to a tree and reached in his fes for

maple sugar. He offered a lump to the older man, who smiled and took it for his horse.

"You must be curious about why I have asked you to meet me today, Lugh," Cian began.

"I am curious. Have you learned something on the islands that I should know?"

"No, but I learned something from Morrigan that you should know. Do you remember the day after the battle at Moytirra, when she came to your family's battle tent?"

Lugh frowned. That memory would remain forever a sharp one. "I remember."

"Well, she realized during that meeting that you are . . . that I am . . . well, that you are . . . my son."

Lugh looked at the big DeDanaan carefully. He was a handsome man of middle age. His graying blond hair was cut short and close to his head in the same fashion that Lugh himself had adopted. There was a certain similarity in their appearance and in their stature. Lugh recognized the truth from the sincerity in the solemn green eyes that were fastened on him.

"I am Lugh, foster son of King Eochy and Queen Tailteann, and son of Cian the DeDanaan and Ethne the Fomorian," he whispered to himself. Why had he not seen it before? He felt as though he had been kicked in the stomach. He couldn't catch his breath and it was making him dizzy.

"You are the Cian whose name I have been taught to recite by rote? You are my father?"

"I am, Lugh. I am your natural father."

The DeDanaan put his large, square hands on Lugh's shoulders and looked into the face of his younger self. He could feel the tension in the lad.

"I know such news must be disconcerting to you. Do not be alarmed. I will make no claims on you, ask nothing from you that you are not prepared to give. I know well the esteem in which you held your foster father, and I am grateful to him and to Queen Tailteann for the tender care they have given you."

"Why did you send me away?" Lugh asked bitterly.

"My son, I did not send you away, nor did your mother. If it had been up to either of us, we would never have been separated, Lugh. Alas, it was not our choice. Let us be seated and I will tell you the story of your birth."

Lugh felt a rush of conflicting emotions. He desperately wanted to hear what this DeDanaan had to tell him but wondered if it was disloyal to King Eochy to feel the pull of Cian's personality so strongly.

"I revere the memory of King Eochy," Lugh protested.

"I understand that Lugh, and well you should. I learned from the Fir Bolgs I took into exile of his extraordinary renown. He must have been a wonderful king, and judging from the son he raised, he must have been just as fine a father. Come, let us sit down."

Lugh's desire to know more about his birth propelled him past the question of disloyalty and he allowed himself to be led to the stream's bank. The serenity he had experienced the night before settled over him once more like a cloak. He turned to Cian and waited for him to speak. One of the first curlews of the season, recently returned from a long migratory journey, sent up a whistlelike trill, and the hair on the back of Lugh's neck stood up as goose flesh spread across his skin.

Nuad was reaching to open the door of his dwelling when Tailteann rushed past him without speaking. Her head was down and her face partially covered by her cloak, but it was apparent that she was weeping. He paused, considering what, if anything, he should do. He followed the path to Tailteann's dwelling and knocked softly on the door. There was no answer. He knocked again, more insistently.

From inside, came Tailteann's muffled voice, "Please, come another time. I am not receiving visitors."

Nuad pushed the door open and went in anyway. Tailteann lay on the furs, her eyes red with weeping. Nuad said not a word but knelt by her side and lifted her up, embracing her in his strong arms. The gesture unleashed all the sorrow that had pent up in her since the arrival of the DeDanaans and she wept as though her heart would break. He held her tightly and let her cry.

When at last her grief was spent, she pulled away. She tried to speak but her breath came out in short, jerky gasps, and she gave up the effort.

He embraced her again and kissed her neck, her cheeks, her mouth that still tasted of salt tears. She was too weary, too in need of comfort to resist him. Soon, she

yielded her lips to him gladly, grateful for the power of
his presence and the warmth of his body. When his hand
slipped under her tunic to explore her thigh, she did not
stop him.

Her longing for union with another human being was
overwhelming. She felt intoxicated by the scent of Nuad,
by the strength of him, drawn by the power of his wanting her. His rough beard against her face awakened a desire in her that she thought had died forever when she laid
Eochy in his cairn at Moytirra.

Deep in her heart she believed that her dead husband
would have understood her need for Nuad. The profound
intimacy that had existed between them had manifested
itself frequently in physical expression and she knew he
would not begrudge her a new love. But Lugh . . . ?

"Stop, Nuad, stop. I can't . . . ," she whispered, pushing
his hand away. He kissed her again, probing her mouth
with his tongue. She weakened, then pushed him away
again. "I mean it Nuad. We must stop this."

He sat up, angry and hurt. "You cannot make love to a
man with one hand, is that it?"

"Oh no, Nuad! That is not it at all. I want you desperately, but I cannot have you."

"What do you mean? What is to stop us? Neither Lugh
nor Morrigan are anywhere about."

"Exactly." She looked deeply into his eyes. "If we were
to become lovers it would have to be done secretly, hiding
from the two people we love most on this earth. Soon, I
know we would come to dislike each other because we
would blame one another for our dishonorable behavior."

He regarded her with amazement. No woman had ever
spoken to him of lovemaking and honor in the same
breath before.

Tailteann took his hand and held it to her cheek. She
opened his palm and kissed it then reached for his severed limb. He pulled away but she persisted and took his
stump in her hand. She loosened the thongs that held the
leather cap over his wrist and removed it.

"No," he said, "don't do that . . ."

Deliberately she lifted his wrist to her lips and kissed
his scar. "Never, for a moment, must you think that this
makes you less of a man, Nuad. My body and my spirit
cry out for union with you, and if it were not for the wis-

dom I have acquired from the teachings of my tribe, you would lie atop me now. I want you to believe me."

She kissed the scar again and when she looked up at his chiseled face the brightness of unwelcome tears was shining in his eyes. He kissed her lips once more, slowly and tenderly, all passion gone. The gift she had given him was too great for words. What, he wondered, could he possibly give her in return?

"I love you, Tailteann."

"And I, you, Nuad."

He held her silently and comfortably for some time before he spoke. "Why were you were weeping?"

She smiled at him, pushing her hair away from her brow. She fixed her brown eyes on the fire before she answered.

"I was weeping because I allowed fear to push away my reason. No one knows better than I that love is the strongest tie we have to one another. It is like a spider's web, beautiful and intricate and woven of many strands. When it seems most delicate we must remember that each strand is as strong as an oak. Woven together over time, the web cannot be broken. I know this to be true, but I forgot. It took you to remind me of it and I thank you, dear friend."

"You know that we DeDanaans have been nomads, sojourning here, sojourning there, always searching for Innis Ealga?" Cian began.

"I do," said Lugh. "I've heard that you were last in Lochland, the big land north of Innis Ealga."

"Yes. We were there for seven turnings of the seasons after our scouts found the passage to this fair green isle, preparing to make the journey that culminated in the battle of Moytirra.

"In my youth I was one of the scouts sent to seek such a route from another far country. On my first trip, I was as excited as it is possible for a young man to be, but from the first the voyage did not go well. We had not been out on the northern sea more than a few hours when we saw a black cloud bearing down on us from the west. As it grew closer we saw the great, heaving waves being churned up by its winds and knew we were in for a terrible gale. Without our captain Mannon Mac Lir none of us would have survived the furious gale. Some who prac-

ticed the old religion swore we had somehow given offense to the gods. It was utter nonsense, of course, but I
have never seen a sea like that one before or since. We
lost two men overboard in the howling winds and crashing waves. When it was over, we had been blown many
leagues off course." Cian gave an involuntary shudder at
the memory of the awful storm.

"Late in the afternoon of the next day we saw an island
dead ahead. We had lost most of our foodstuffs and all of
our fresh water was contaminated by seawater, so Mac
Lir commanded us to lower the square sail on the curragh
and make for land. We rejoiced like fools, hugging each
other and crying that the gods had saved us. Little did we
know what lay in store for us.

"As we put in on the shingle shore I heard Mac Lir tell
his second in command that he feared we might have
come aground on the land of Conang's Tower, the home
of the Fomorians. Scarcely had we secured the boat than
we were surrounded by Fomorians brandishing weapons.
They captured us and took us before their wizard, a cruel
man known as Balor of the Evil Eye and a Thousand
Blows. I am sorry to have to tell you this, Lugh, but that
man is your grandfather."

Cian absently moved a small twig around on the soft
earth with the toe of his patched boot. "A terrible man he
was, to be sure, but so beautiful was his daughter, Ethne!
We had only a short time together," he sighed, "but she
was the loveliest woman ever born. I love her to this day,
though I have never seen her again. She defied her father's orders to speak to me and was so kind to a captured
sailor that I loved her instantly. She came one night and
slipped the bonds from my wrists, gesturing for me to follow her. She led me to a secluded cove on the island
where we stayed until the god of the dawn approached.

"We made our way back to the place where my fellow
DeDanaans were held captive. She pretended to tie me up
again, but did not, thus making our escape possible."

Softly, he said, "I have never forgotten our time together, and I want you to think well of her, Lugh, even if
her father is one of the world's most evil men and her
mother, Kathlen, is a fitting companion for such as he. I
will always think the gods made an error when they gave
a child such as your mother to the likes of them."

He turned to look into the dark shadows in the woods. "I might never have known of your existence at all if one of our party had not been recaptured by the Fomorians as we made our escape. It was many years before he managed to get away from them and make his way back to our tribe. He told me that your mother suffered terribly at the hands of King Balor when he discovered that she was with child. He forced her to name me as the father and he went into a rage that was said to last for thirty days and nights and set the sea to boiling."

Cian's eyes grew wistful and his voice dropped almost to a whisper at the thought of his beloved's pain. He looked at their son, now taller than himself and wished that Ethne could know him.

Lugh looked at Cian and said somberly, "I used to think I remembered my mother but now I can't even bring forth her image. I was just too young when I was sent to the Fir Bolgs to be fostered."

Cian nodded. "You see why Balor and Kathlen were eager to send you for fosterage? Perhaps it was a genuine effort at establishing peace, but doubtless your presence on Tor Conain was troublesome for them. I believe that taking you from Ethne was as much punishment for what she had done by loving me, as it was Balor's wish to seal a truce with the Fir Bolgs. I, myself, knew nothing of your fosterage until Morrigan told me that you were with the Fir Bolg queen."

"I can scarcely believe all you have said to me this morning," Lugh said, "yet I look at you and I know it is true. You will have to give me time to get used to the idea that you are my father. I have spent my life ... or most of it ... treating the Fir Bolg king who died at Moytirra as my father." Lugh looked at Cian curiously. "You were in the battle for Innis Ealga. It could have been you who wielded the sword that ended his life."

"It could have been, but it was not I who killed King Eochy. I thought everyone knew that it was our king, Nuad. His sword hand was still upraised from the blow when the dark Fir Bolg who escaped, struck it off."

"What? *Nuad* killed King Eochy? And Srang took Nuad's hand off?" Lugh's voice rose, and there was no serenity left in him. "How could the elders have placed my father ... my foster father's ... killer in the dwelling next to us? It sickens me to think the queen is friendly with him. If she knew, she would not stand for it." He regarded Cian who was looking at him calmly. "By the gods! His deed cannot go unpunished!"

"Lugh, my son. I ask you to consider the high price Nuad paid in that conflict. No warrior who takes the life of a fellow human being escapes from battle unscathed whether or not he receives a physical wound. We all know that when we put on our weapons and take the field. But the battlefield is where the enmity must needs be left when the fighting is over and the victor determined. Nuad fought honorably, as did King Eochy. I beg you not to let a quest for revenge corrode your own heart. Don't make life more difficult than it need to be by forcing on things that are past. New dangers face us, all of us, here on Innis Ealga, and we will need to stand shoulder to shoulder to face them."

Cian told Lugh of the renewed Fomorian raids and how the colony at Lough Gur needed to take counsel and perhaps action, independent of King Breas and his toadies at Druim Caein. He did not mention Srang's involvement in the raids. That could come later.

"If it comes to battle, as I fear it might, Lugh, you will be placed in the unenviable position of taking arms against your own blood . . . the Fomorians. As a Fir Bolg you have been accustomed to thinking of them as your enemy, but now you know that your natural mother is one of them. I see that you still think of the DeDanaans as your enemy too, but I am one of them. Many rivers empty into you, Lugh. I think it not unlikely that you are destined to become a leader among us. It is my hope that such a thing might come to pass."

Into Lugh's mind, from the depths of his being, came King Eochy's last words: *In you all three races meet. You have the blood of the Fomorians and the DeDanaans in your veins, but you have the soul of the Fir Bolgs.*

Lugh was stunned by the long-forgotten words. An echo of something else, something he could not quite grasp, hovered over that memory and he was suddenly quite sure he had a part to play in the future of Innis Ealga. He was as certain of it as though the gods had carved it in stone, and whatever it was to be, he knew this man seated next to him was not his enemy. Nuad, on the other hand . . .

"Thank you for all you have told me this morning . . ." Lugh groped for the right word. It felt strange on his tongue, but he said it. He called the tall, blond stranger father. "Would that my mother still lives and that you may one day be together again, Father."

The word hung between them in the glade, as fragile and as beautiful as the curlew's whistled song. Cian held out his arms and the two men embraced hurriedly, with a measure of embarrassment for both of them.

"I too have to get used to the idea of being with my son, Lugh. It feels awkward, I know. We must allow ourselves to go slowly and to become friends. Many turnings of the moon have passed away from us, and they can never be recaptured. But there is nothing to keep us from starting where we are and building a friendship." He smiled, revealing straight white teeth. The lines that crinkled around his eyes made him look older than before.

Lugh smiled back. "No," he said, "there is nothing to stop us from becoming friends."

"Thank you, Lugh. I am glad you hold no anger toward me. We DeDanaans are a hardy race. You can be proud to be one of us."

All the implications of his parentage struck Lugh. "Then Diancecht is my grandfather, and Airmead and Miach are my aunt and uncle?"

"Yes, Lugh. They are your family."

"Do they know who I am?"

"Yes, they know, but I asked them to let me be the one to reveal the truth of our situation to you. It has been hard for them to remain quiet while I was away, but they honored my wishes in this matter."

Lugh felt an overpowering urge to talk with Diancecht, the old physician with the piercing blue eyes. To think that they had been kinsmen all this time, and Lugh had not known it! Did this blood tie explain why he had always been drawn so strongly to the old man? Then why had he not felt the same pull toward Airmead and Miach? *Perhaps . . . No,* Lugh thought. *I will entertain no intervention of the gods in these matters. I will not.*

Chapter Nineteen

At the deepest hour of midnight Morrigan slipped under the furs that covered the sleeping Nuad, determined to reclaim their former passion. This day's quarrel had been so bitter it frightened her and she felt, for the first time, a foreboding that she could really lose him.

Once she had known he would live, she had come to see his wound and all the troubles it occasioned as something that simply had to be endured until he returned to normal. A hill to be climbed, a barrier to be crossed—all she had to do was show intolerance for his self-pity until he was forced to be well again. But today she saw the gulf that had opened between them was so wide it might no longer be possible to cross to the other side.

She molded herself to the curve of his sleeping body and kissed and stroked him. Even before he awakened she felt his body responding to her caresses and she breathed a little easier. Her love for him was so fierce she could not bear the thought of losing him.

He turned toward her and kissed her, then murmured, "Tailteann."

Morrigan froze. "What did you say, Nuad?"

He opened his eyes and looked at her in the flickering light of the fire.

"I asked you what you said." Her voice was as hard as a stone.

He closed his eyes sleepily. "What's wrong now?"

"You just called me Tailteann," she said.

How could he prefer that weak wisp of a woman to herself? He, who had once been all fire and action, and she his equal? Was this what she had used her healing magic to achieve? Fury took hold of her heart and grew in proportion to the humiliation she felt.

Nuad pulled away from her and propped himself up on

his right elbow to look down at her. "You can't hold a man accountable for what he says when he's asleep, Morrigan. Even if I said it, it meant nothing. I must have been dreaming."

"No, Nuad. I think I have been the dreamer. I was too blind to see what has been happening right under my nose. I couldn't see that you have grown so soft you prefer a woman like Tailteann to me."

"What are you talking about, Morrigan? I don't prefer her to you. You are my woman—"

"I was your woman, Nuad. You have hardly been a proper mate to me in these past few months. I have been patient because I knew you were recovering, but this insult is too great to bear. For you to prefer a woman with such pale blood over me offends my very soul. In the old days you could have crushed the likes of her in one night. She would never have been a match for you then. By the gods, Nuad . . . that's when you were still a man!"

She leaped up from the furs and grabbed her tunic from the floor where she had dropped it. The outlines of her naked beauty were painted golden by the light from the fire, and her auburn hair fell in wild disarray across her face. Nuad reached out with his good hand and grasped her arm angrily.

"Get back in the furs, Morrigan," he commanded. "I will show you that I am a man still." Roughly, he pulled her down next to him and crushed his lips against hers. In moments she succumbed, the needs of her body and the power of his, overwhelming her outrage. They made love throughout the night and she had to admit that the loss of his hand had taken none of his virility. But she did not forget his transgression, and she did not plan to forgive it.

Tailteann said nothing to Lugh about Cian, in spite of her eagerness to know what had transpired between them. She saw how heavily burdened Lugh seemed after their meeting and while she longed to embrace him and do what she could to ease his mind, some inner sense stopped her. She realized that he had to come to terms with his heritage by himself. During the days that followed Lugh's meeting with his natural father, she told him often that she loved him. It was all the balm she could offer, but she knew it was enough.

At the close of a hard workday Lugh came to Tailteann after the evening meal. "I need to talk to you, Mother. Will you return to our dwelling with me?" His eyes were clear, his face composed, although his tone was serious.

"Of course, my dear." She took his arm and they walked up the Hill of Knockadoon from the lough. As they climbed, she said, "Since the day you rode into the woods with Cian, I have waited for you to be ready to talk. I want you to feel free to say anything at all about what you have learned."

The surprise Lugh felt was apparent in the sharp glance he sent her. "You've known all this time that I spoke with Cian?"

She nodded.

". . . and you know what he told me?"

"I know, Lugh . . . or at least, I've guessed. I realized who Cian was the first day we laid eyes on the DeDanaans, and I knew you would have to know that he is your father sooner or later. I must be honest and say that my heart trembled with fear for a long time. I was so afraid that I would lose you."

Lugh started to speak, but Tailteann stopped him. "Never mind, darling, so much has happened since then that my fears have evaporated like dew upon the roses under a summer sun!"

They reached the dwelling and Lugh opened the door for his mother, first glancing at Nuad's house to see if he and Morrigan were within. The door was closed and smoke was coming through the hole in the thatched roof. He couldn't tell if they were there or still at the filach fiadah. He hoped they weren't home. He didn't want King Eochy's killer anywhere nearby while he and Tailteann talked about what he had learned.

Queen Tailteann poured water from an ewer into a copper vessel and placed it over the fire to heat. She took the lid from a small pot and shook out rose hips from last year's harvest into a beaker.

"Our tea will be weak tonight, Lugh." She held out the beaker. "Look, these are all the rose hips we have left. Tell me what you think of the DeDanaan, Cian. He seems like a good man to me."

"I think that's true, Mother, but there is a hard side to him, too. We have thrown javelins together a few times

and he is a determined competitor. He is steady and deliberate and is the kind of thoughtful fighter any warrior
would want next to him in battle. But I want you to know
that just because he has come here and told me the truth,
it makes no difference in what I feel about King Eochy.
He will always be—"

Lugh's voice broke in spite of his careful rehearsal of
what he would say to Tailteann. The feelings he had,
would always have, for the man who had raised him were
deep and true.

"I know, Lugh. We were both blessed by the gods to
have known King Eochy as we did. I know that you love
and revere his memory. You don't have to say more."

She looked at the water bubbling in the copper vessel,
so Lugh could not see the sorrow in her eyes. "I still miss
him every day of my life," she said softly.

She poured the boiling water over the rose hips and sat
back on her heels to wait for the tea to steep. Lugh
thought she looked smaller than usual and wondered
briefly if she were eating enough before letting his mind
go back to what he wanted to tell her.

"Mother, Cian told me Nuad is responsible for the
death of King Eochy." He waited for her to respond but
she said nothing and looked at him steadily, her bright
black eyes unblinking.

"Don't you care, Mother? Father's killer is in the
dwelling next to us!"

Tailteann felt her heart turn over, not from shock or
surprise, but with relief. She had come so close. Thanks
be to the gods that she had not succumbed to her desire
for Nuad. The anger and contempt on Lugh's face told
her more plainly than words how right she had been to
say no to Nuad. It would have been the one act of betrayal that could have separated her from her son forever.

"Why don't you say something, Mother? Why are you
silent?"

She swallowed hard, then reached for the beaker of tea.
Her hand trembled as she poured some into two shallow
clay bowls. She handed one to Lugh.

"I know not what to say, Lugh. I have not wanted to
know which hand did the actual deed. When battle is declared and tribesmen act according to time-honored customs, they are bound by duty to kill those on the other

side. The DeDanaans were no less bound than we were. I am deeply saddened to know that Nuad was the one who ended my husband's life, but it is of no consequence. It could as easily have been the other way around. All who engaged in the battle of Moytirra acted honorably, according to tribal tradition."

"Well, it matters to me, Mother! I can't believe that you don't care. You can't go on being friendly with Nuad, not now, not when you know what he did. I will never forgive him. Never. I'll make him pay for what he did."

"No, Lugh, don't say such a thing. Remember—"

"I *will* say it! I'll make him sorry. He will rue the day he ever set foot on Innis Ealga." Lugh's voice rose and his face turned red. "He will pay for killing King Eochy. If it is the last thing I do, I will have revenge on him for what he did to us."

Beltaine season came and went and King Breas failed to call for a celebration of the return of the Sun God to the northern skies. The people were restless and uneasy about this slight to the god and DeDanaan tradition. As though in retaliation for their failure to honor him at the appropriate season, Bel withheld his golden rays from the settlers at Lough Gur and gray days became the summer's norm.

The oats grew only so high and no more and there was great fear that when the crop was harvested and the grain stored, the yield would be insufficient for their needs.

The cattle were driven into the high pastures for the summer, but sweet grass was hard to find. Cowherds reported that the calving season had begun, with many cows delivering stillborn offspring. Their milk came in thin, weak streams, barely enough to feed the calves who survived. In the woods, flowers that blossomed in the morning were wilted by afternoon, yearning for more light. There was fear and deprivation in the once prosperous island of Innis Ealga.

Lugh moped about for four turnings of the moon, doing his tasks without joy. He was angry with Queen Tailteann because she would not take up his desire for revenge against Nuad. He noted with some satisfaction that she had put some distance between herself and his father's iller, but she still spoke to him almost daily, and Lugh ould not bear it.

The time for harvest was now full upon them. Lugh vas working in the granary glad for an unexpected burst f sunshine when Aibel approached him shortly past midlay. He knew the moment he looked at her that her demons had come back. She peered at him suspiciously, her normous black eyes wide with unspoken accusations.

"Hello, Aibel," he said, acting as though nothing was miss. "Where were you this morning? I thought you vere out helping with the work in the fields, but I looked or you and didn't see you."

"Shh," she begged, "don't let them know I'm here." he looked around wildly.

"Who, Aibel? I don't see anyone."

"No! Don't speak my name aloud. They'll hear. If they ind me, they will hurt me." She regarded him with narowed eyes. "They will hurt you, too," she said and aughed, a high-pitched, unearthly laugh that chilled ᴜugh's blood.

"They know what we do in the woods, Lugh. They say ve are unclean and our flesh is abhorrent to them. They vill make us pay for what we do. They told me so."

He thought that she was, at this moment, quite mad. "Come with me, Aibel," he said, trying to sound protecᴛive and strong, "I know a place where they cannot find ᴜs."

He took her arm but she jumped away from touch as hough his fingers were leaping flames. "Come on, ᴧibel," he said sternly, "you'll be safe where I'm taking ᴏou." He pulled her with him, overcoming her resistance.

"No," she whispered in abject fear. Her small body ᴊeemed to crumple before his eyes. "No. They say they vill punish us, Lugh. I'm afraid to go with you."

He drew himself up to his full stature and adopted the ᴄommanding voice he had heard Srang use so often with ᴜis daughter. "You will accompany me to the physicians' ᴛreatment house, Aibel. There will be no further discusᴊion."

Still whimpering, she allowed him to lead him around ᴛhe lough and up the hill to the place of the physicians. ᴧirmead was in the dwelling, mixing herbs into mediᴄants. She looked up as Lugh and Aibel entered.

When she saw Aibel's face, she knew why Lugh had brought her. Before he could speak, Airmead asked "How long has she been like this?"

"I can't be sure," he answered.

"Thank you for bringing her," Airmead said briskly seeing how much Aibel's relapse upset Lugh. "She will be all right here with me. Don't worry. I'll let you know how she is later. I know how busy everyone is, so you may return to your work."

Aibel appeared to have withdrawn inside herself. Her arms were wrapped tightly around her thin body, clasping her cloak to her as though it were of great value. Her head hung down, her eyes were dull and veiled. Something was very, very wrong with her, and Lugh was both eager and fearful to leave her.

"What is it?" he whispered, awed by the power that had hold of Aibel.

"Lugh, I wish to the gods that I knew," the physician answered. "The ancients have told of similar cases, but this doesn't happen often and none of us, not Miach, nor even my father, understands Aibel's affliction."

"The priest, Ferfesa, told Queen Tailteann that she is visited by evil demons."

"Nonsense! Don't you believe that for a moment Lugh. This young woman is ill, I know that deep in my bones. I know it with a sixth sense the gods sometimes give physicians. You must never blame her. I assure you she would prefer not to be visited by the voices she hears. I know not from whence they come, but I do know they are a terrible, fearsome thing, and they cause her more pain than you and I can possibly imagine."

They both looked at Aibel with sympathy. Reluctantly Lugh left her in Airmead's caring hands. Aibel took no notice of his departure.

He stepped out into the welcome sunlight and allowed its warmth to spill over him. He knew he had to have more of it. The ingathering would have to wait.

Lugh stretched out on the grassy bank a few paces from the crystal stream that splashed over mossy stones worn smooth by the ice masses that had once scoured Innis Ealga. How he loved the soothing sound of the water as it flowed over its silvery gravel bed. The sound ever quite lulled him to sleep, but it always cleared his mind of the day's chaos. He did his best thinking next to his stream.

He looked up through fluttering oak leaves into the strong blue sky of a late summer's day. Puffs of white clouds drifted by, casting occasional shadows on the forest floor. By the gods! This day had become what a summer day was meant to be, and he was grateful for the change.

As if in response to the fine weather, Lugh's thoughts turned to a most pleasant subject, Morrigan. Her full red lips and long, creamy-white thighs crowded out the more weighty issues confronting him and the tribe. Nothing could compete with his images of the auburn-haired beauty who he was certain scarcely recognized his existence.

He had seen her a few nights earlier as she emerged, naked and shining like a moon goddess, from bathing in Lough Gur. He thought she knew that he'd seen her, but he made no attempt to hide herself, nor had she turned away in shame. Later, when she passed him on the path, she looked straight at him and smiled. His face had been warm with embarrassment as he ran up the hill toward home. Above the songs of the larks and the curlews in the glade, he could still hear echoes of Morrigan's laughter.

Even as Lugh lay dreaming of the beautiful DeDanaan warrior, the object of his desire was only paces away from him, drying cold water droplets from her flawless body with a woolen cloth, having just bathed in the spring that gave life to Lugh's beloved stream. When Morrigan heard someone approach, she sat stone still behind a clump of flowering gorse bushes, their yellow blossoms hiding her body. She waited, her cloth poised in midair, not knowing who it was that interrupted the privacy of her bath.

Slowly and very carefully, she leaned forward to peer through the fragrant gorse. *Praise be to the gods,* she thought, *it's Lugh. He is a handsome thing!* It came to her that this was the opportunity for retaliation that she had been waiting for. Neither Tailteann nor Nuad would like what she had in mind.

Lugh's skin was tawny under the summer sun, his blond hair streaked with paler strands of gold. She could see the shadows cast by his long eyelashes, in pretty contrast to the strong, masculine planes of his face. The Sun God shone down on him in a single shaft of light, anointing his body diagonally from his head to his feet.

She could not see how green and clear his eyes were, but she knew. He had kicked off his boots and his bare feet lay near a clump of flowering wood violets. She was so close to him that she could see the hairs on his toes, a sight she found intimate and stimulating. She hoped he could not hear the pounding of her heart.

Veins protruded under the golden skin of his forearms and the sun, where it broke through the oaks, glinted off the coiled copper arm bands he wore above his elbows. She could see how flat his belly was and how taut and hard his thighs appeared under his pale green tunic.

Her heart beat faster; her breath came quickly and shallowly. Revenge may have been on her mind when it first occurred to her that she would have Lugh, but it was not foremost in her thoughts now.

As she watched the handsome young man lying on long strands of warm grass near the soft, sweet mosses of the brook, he stirred uneasily and moved his right hand, slightly at first, then more purposefully, until it touched his manhood.

Morrigan watched in openmouthed delight. So. He had loving on his mind too. She dropped the cloth she clutched in her hand and walked around the gorse, carefully avoiding its prickly surface, inhaling its perfume as she passed.

She stepped to the spot where the young prince lay, and whispered, "Will you have me, Lugh?"

At first he thought she was a shining goddess, too beautiful, too radiant to be a mortal woman, and he was overcome by the sight of her. She knelt next to him and bent to place her full, soft lips upon his, her white breasts coming to rest against his chest.

Over the next hour, Morrigan, a believer in the old spells, brought Lugh into the fullness of manhood without the aid of potions or chants. She taught him slowly and well and when the lovemaking was done, she felt deep satisfaction.

"Are you happy, beautiful Lugh?" she asked softly, twirling a lock of his golden hair in her fingers. "I know

now that you are a true DeDanaan, without doubt. No one but a DeDanaan could have coupled like that." He did not answer her, but pulled her to him once more.

Morrigan did not think of Nuad until she was dressed and well on her way up the Hill of Knockadoon, smiling triumphantly. That had certainly been the sweetest revenge she had ever tasted. She looked back to where she had left Lugh, wondering what his demure mother would think if she were to learn with whom her son had lain.

Lugh felt as though he'd been caught up in a cyclonic wind, tossed and pounded, returned to earth unharmed, yet profoundly changed. He dressed and sat down on a large stump. He was reaching for his second boot when he heard Aibel shriek like a tribe of banshees behind him. Before he could turn toward her, she was on his back, clawing and scratching, screaming unintelligible curses at him like a war witch. He was able to dislodge her only with difficulty. He grasped her arms.

"Aibel! Aibel! Stop this. What are you doing?"

Her face was purple with rage and streaked with tears. She attempted to pound his chest with her small fists. He grabbed her wrists and held her at arm's length.

"I saw!" she screamed, "I saw Morrigan leaving here not two minutes ago. You will die for this. The voices say that you must die."

"Aibel, how did you get here? You aren't well. You don't know what you are saying. Stop it." He could feel blood running down his back where she had scratched him, and he gripped her wrists more tightly.

She struggled like a trapped animal, twisting this way and that, trying to squirm away from him, but she was no match for his superior strength and finally ceased her fighting. When she was quiet Lugh could see the fury seep out of her like air from the sheep bladders the children played with at butchering time.

She fell against his shoulder, sobbing convulsively. What if she were to go back to the village and tell what she had witnessed? He wanted no one but Nuad to know that he had had Morrigan. When Lugh thought of Queen Tailteann, he felt ashamed, but in his deepest heart of hearts he knew he would have Morrigan again if the opportunity presented itself.

Even if Aibel told the truth, he reasoned, few would believe her because of her strange spells. He took a deep breath, alarmed at the thought of discovery, yet still warmed by the knowledge that he had taken the sweetest revenge possible against Nuad. Now he had to decide how . . . and when . . . Nuad was to learn of it . . . if only he could keep Aibel from telling everybody first.

"Come on, Aibel, let's go find Airmead," he said. "She will be worried about you."

Chapter Twenty

Tribute collectors sent from King Breas came riding into the Lough Gur settlement shortly after the harvest ended. The great feasting time of Samhain would be upon them in one turning of the moon, so the visit by the collectors was as expected as it was unwelcome.

It had been a fair day, with the great eye of the Sun God shining down on the settlement, as it had every day since Lugh and Morrigan's afternoon in the woods. When the collectors arrived, the setting sun cast long shadows toward the east, causing the hills around Lough Gur to shimmer in a soft blue haze.

Lugh was unable to tell if his spirits had been lifted by Morrigan, since he had thought of little else for days, or if the sunshine that followed their encounter was what warmed him through. All he knew was that the malaise that had gripped him since he learned Nuad killed King Eochy was gone, and he felt like himself again. Even Queen Tailteann remarked on the change in him.

He was ready for a new challenge when he walked forth with the others to greet the collectors from King Breas's court. On the path he overhead Dagda say to Nuad, "Too much has been asked from us already. The arrival of these tribute collectors can mean only more privation."

Nuad replied, "There is a limit to how much we will endure, Dagda Mor. DeDanaan ways do not allow us to lie down like stones beneath the feet of a greedy king. Do you not agree that we have reached the end of our tolerance?"

Lugh looked at the former king's face and caught for the first time a glimpse of the man whom the DeDanaans had willingly followed to Innis Ealga; the man who had been hidden beneath his wound from the time Lugh had known him.

The people of Lough Gur greeted the tribute collectors, all of whom were known to them. Once inside the walls of the compound the chief collector spoke, embarrassed by the demands the king had sent him to press.

"Forgive us, please," he said, "but the king commands us to ask yet more tribute from you. He says that you at Lough Gur must send an additional half share of oats from every hearth that owns a board upon which bread is kneaded."

Breas's stipulation insured tribute from each household in Lough Gur since a bread board was the one item certain to be owned by every family. Angry grumblings arose from the people and Dagda's face turned so red that some in the crowd feared for his health.

"What manner of madness is this?" he sputtered, "Would this king starve his own people? We will not—"

Standing next to Dagda as a principal adviser, Queen Tailteann laid a gentle hand on his arm, stood on tiptoe, and whispered something to him. He regarded her carefully, then nodded.

"Come, old comrades," he sighed, "you must take sustenance before our welcoming fires, and then rest. We will speak of this matter on the morrow."

His voice had acquired an edge, but the tribute collectors understood that his displeasure was directed at Breas the Beautiful, and not toward them. They went willingly to accept hospitality from their kinsmen at Lough Gur.

Cairbed the bard came to stand next to Lugh. "What do you make of Breas's latest demand?" he asked.

"The same as you," Lugh answered. "We cannot afford to give a single oat away. You worked up in the high fields with me and know how pitifully small the harvest was. To give half of our foodstuffs away would be folly. What is the DeDanaan law concerning the removal of a king?"

Cairbed gasped and looked around to see if anyone had heard Lugh's dangerous words. Brigid, a few steps behind them, looked straight at Cairbed, then down at the ground and he knew she had heard.

"Better ask your father, Lugh. Cian knows all about the law. I'm going to go talk to my best girl."

He gestured toward Brigid as a blush spread between the copper-colored freckles on his broad face. He didn't want to be involved in talk of rebellion because he was scheduled to return to the royal court at Samhain. As a bard he would have to remain there for three turnings of the moon until it came time again for rotation to a different settlement.

"Brigid is a wonderful singer," he said, "and she has a good idea for a new song that I might take to Druim Caein when I go . . ."

Lugh searched the crowd for Cian. All of the hardships had come about since Breas became king. Lugh could not help but remember how the earth had yielded up her plenty when King Eochy reigned over the island. Nothing but trouble had come of the DeDanaan invasion. He said farewell to Cairbed and went to find Cian.

The colonists at Lough Gur gathered in the feasting hall after the tribute collectors retired for the night. Morrigan was too irate to wait for Dagda to open the meeting.

"We won't yield a single oat to that thief," she fumed, "not one bit of our hard earned sustenance will we give to that greedy, vain Breas."

Macha tugged at Morrigan's tunic, urging her to sit down and be still. She had seen the rawness of Breas's rage firsthand and she was truly frightened of him. She did not want any more of his wrath to fall on her family.

"Please, Morrigan," she begged, "let someone else talk."

Morrigan shot her a look of disgust while Neiman observed the scene, detached and bemused by the contest of wills between her sisters. She had no doubt that Morrigan would prevail.

At that moment, Queen Tailteann's calm voice intruded. "I would know what options are available under DeDanaan laws to address this outrage. Since Breas is the king and he demands tribute are not we bound to supply it?"

"Of course we are, but only so long as the king's requests are just," Morrigan answered. "If our tribe is at odds with another and battle is imminent, we are required to give as much as we have; or if there is great want in some dwelling places and not in others, we are bound to give our all so the king can redistribute it equally. But to put ourselves at risk so he can have a new feasting hall? Never! It is unforgivable that he even asks."

Queen Tailteann looked around for confirmation of Morrigan's words. Cian nodded slowly. "That's right, although there is one other occasion when the people can be asked to put themselves under hardship, but it has never been invoked in the lifetime of any here present. It can be done if a plague is upon the tribe. The lore tells us that when Parthelon's people were struck by the plague he was allowed to compel excessive tribute from his people in an effort to save the tribe. The great necropolis near the river Boyne that is named for him, tells us that it did not work. Most of that early colony lies buried there."

"In my judgment, we must resist Breas on this latest matter of tribute," Dagda said thoughtfully. "It is our duty, both to ourselves and to all the DeDanaan generations who will follow us. To allow a king to disregard the law would be an unforgivable offense against the gods."

There was a murmur of frightened assent throughout the hall. Miach the physician rose to speak. "We are very newly come to these shores," he said hesitantly, "and because of that I can see much risk in taking rebellious action against our king. Would it not be better to hold back some part of our harvest and send King Breas only a portion of what we do not hide? By such a deception he would be satisfied and we would not be in the position of defying him, nor would we starve."

Diancecht and Airmead sent startled looks in Miach's direction. Deceit was not the DeDanaan way. The aged physician shook his white head and murmured, "I would speak without rising."

Without waiting for leave from anyone, he went on, "My son, my heart would be sore troubled if we were to engage in the same kind of deception King Breas practices. It seems to me that if we are to resist him successfully we must take the high ground and act honestly in all things."

Argument exploded, some taking Miach's suggestion to be the better way, others siding with his father. Cian interrupted the uproar by standing up to declare, "Wait, my kinsmen! I implore you to back up a moment and consider the first question that faces us. I submit that this is a larger issue than whether we honor King Breas's demand for more tribute.

"In light of the tremendous shortages that have befallen our tribe, do we not have to consider the fundamental rightness of this man, Breas, for the office of kingship?"

Excited voices rose from every corner. DeDanaans who had once sworn they heard the Lia Fail shout when Breas was crowned, now swore they had heard nothing.

". . . it made not a sound."

"He's not a true king!"

"Remember how the loudly the Stone of Destiny shouted when Nuad was crowned? We should have known Breas would not be a fit king."

"Did he not have trouble consummating the ritual act of kingship when he stood before the holed stone?"

"I heard that the only reason he was able to penetrate the stone at all was because Diancecht gave him a wormwood potion before the ceremony."

"No, no! Let me tell it!"

"The old physician mesmerized Breas by waving an amulet before his eyes, just before his loins were undraped."

"Yes, that's what I heard, too. The only reason he was able to plunge his member into the stone at all was because he had help. He was enchanted. He's not a true king . . . not the true king at all."

More crude and vulgar remarks were traded back and forth about King Breas until the talk petered out and people began to cast about, looking for leadership.

From the back of the hall where he had been watching the proceedings, Nuad rose with impatience and strode to the front. All eyes turned to him and every tongue was stilled, as the people watched him take his place before them with supreme confidence.

Morrigan held her breath expectantly, intuitively understanding that Nuad was claiming his rightful role as leader of the DeDanaans.

He spoke. "This holy rite that signifies union between a ruler, his people, and the land is no fit subject for ridicule," he said. "I will hear no more about it."

As king, Nuad had insisted on the dignity of ritual. He

looked at the members of his tribe for some time before
he went on.

"Cian is right, of course. The question we have to ask
is whether or not the kingship of Breas is beneficial to the
tribe. I say that it is not. The gods deprive us of the basic
stuff of life and by so doing show us Breas's unfitness for
the office. His unjust demands bring hardship upon hardship. I tell you that it is an unforgivable thing for a king
to do."

Dagda rose and said, "To this evil, I would add another. Cian and Mac Lir brought news that demonstrates
that King Breas is also unable or unwilling to protect us
from our enemies.

"The Fomorian pirates who once drove our ancestors
from this island are conducting vicious raids upon our
colonies along the northern coast. They swoop out of the
night upon our kinsmen whose lambing and harvest seasons were no more fruitful than our own. The people
there live in mortal fear of these pirates, yet King Breas
takes no action to protect them. None, whatsoever!"

A look as dark as thunderclouds passed over Nuad's
face. "This neglect cannot be allowed to stand. I for one,
say that we must march against the king. Are there any
who would join me?"

There was hesitation as the warriors looked at the place
where Nuad's left hand had once been. How could a
blemished man lead them in rebellion against the king?
Nuad's strength of character and the respect he had
earned through his long years of service were enough for
him to command their ears, but to follow him in such a
dangerous undertaking? They were not sure.

Morrigan rose and was the first to take her place by
Nuad's side. "I will join you," she said.

Cian, Mac Lir, and Ogma followed, vowing their support.

Queen Tailteann, stood and said, "And I will join you,
Nuad. I offer you my knowledge . . . and my son's . . . of
this island and the ways of the Fomorian raiders."

Reluctantly, Lugh rose to his feet, aware that every eye
had turned expectantly to him. "I will join you," he af-
firmed, the words of commitment sticking like thorns in
his throat.

"May I propose, Nuad, that before we take precipitate

action, I take a delegation to Druim Caein to see if we cannot negotiate an agreement with the king," Dagda asked in his usual reasonable way.

Nuad was slightly irritated by his suggestion. The thrill of impending conflict had taken hold in his heart and he did not welcome the idea of postponing it.

"An excellent idea," Queen Tailteann said. "It is possible that when the king realizes how hard things are for us here, he will see the error of his ways and rescind his demand for more tribute."

Nuad shook his head in disagreement. "I doubt it," he said. "And what of the Fomorian raids? I have been told that the reason they are so successful is because they are being led by one of the Fir Bolgs who escaped after the battle of Moytirra. He is eager to take revenge on the DeDanaans and he uses the Fomorians as his weapon."

The dismay on Tailteann's face made him sorry he had spoken, but there was no taking back his words. "Do you know the name of the Fir Bolg?" she asked.

"I don't," Nuad replied. "Cian, who did you say is responsible for this outrage against the DeDanaans?"

"I believe the man is called Srang, sire," Cian answered, careful to avoid looking at Aibel, who sat between Brigid and Airmead in the back of the hall.

An apprehensive buzz went around the hall. Lugh and Tailteann glanced toward Aibel, who bore no sign of awareness on her small, brown face. Her big eyes were dull and fixed elsewhere, as she faced the torment of the voices that Lugh could see were once more in residence.

Turning to address the DeDanaans, Lugh said, "I know this man, Srang. He has been my enemy since I bested him in a contest last year. He is a mean, unforgiving man, but I would caution you that his battle skills are superior. Even though he has been out in Connaught for these many moons, I am certain that it has made him if anything, a fiercer warrior."

"Yes," Tailteann said, "all that Lugh says is so. I would add that Srang's vindictive character and extensive knowledge of Innis Ealga could make him extremely dangerous, although it is hard for me to believe that any Fir Bolg could throw in with the Fomorians. I've known Srang since I came to Innis Ealga as a bride. I am heartsore is this is so."

She looked toward Aibel again and saw two empty places on the bench where Airmead and Aibel had been sitting. Only Brigid now occupied the bench, her plain, round face contorted as she fought to hold back tears. She could not understand how all of her kinsman could be so angry with Breas.

If only she could explain the king's need for a suitable feasting hall, she could make them understand. She longed to be able to convince her kinsmen of his worth, that Breas was not an unkind king driven by greed. Did not the gods love harmony and order above all things? Why, then, should not King Breas surround himself with things that would please him?

Nuad conducted the meeting as he had in the old days of his kingship, and before long it was decided that Dagda should lead a delegation to Druim Caein to seek accommodation with King Breas.

It was well understood when the meeting broke up, that if the delegation did not find King Breas forthcoming, an effort to overthrow the young king would be commenced, and that Nuad would be its leader.

Lugh felt an eagerness to take up arms such as he had not felt since the battle of Moytirra. He caught up with Cian as they left the feasting hall. "Father, will you come with me into the forest tomorrow for some javelin practice?"

The quiet warrior smiled at his son. "I'd like that, Lugh. It looks as though we do need to polish our battle skills. I doubt very much that Dagda will be able to move the king. Remember that Mac Lir and I have seen Breas recently. I don't think the others understand what a change has come over him. The king acts as though he is driven by demons. I'm sure there is no reasonableness left in him."

Chapter Twenty-one

"I wonder how much longer Dagda and the others will be away," Tailteann said. "I should have thought they'd be back by now."

Lugh looked up from stacking bricks of dried peat into neat rows next to the firewood. He was gratified that the stacks grew higher with each trip he made up the hill from the bogs. The turf would give them strong insulation against the cold of winter.

"Aye," he said, "but King Breas must be talking or they would have returned by now. I would like to take the measure of King Breas for myself. One thing is clear, if he were half the man my foster father was, there would be no threat of hunger upon us now."

"That's true, Lugh. The gods have their ways and as surely as if they'd whispered in my ear, I know Breas is not a just ruler. The proof is everywhere. The roots we dug out from under the rotting leaves today were smaller and more sparse than I have ever seen them before."

"I know." Lugh nodded with resignation. "It's like everything else this harvest season. Would you like to come down with me to fetch the last load of turf? You can ride Anovaar, if you'd like," he said, trying to introduce a note of levity.

Tailteann laughed. "Thank you very much, Lugh. Your generosity overwhelms me, but I'd rather walk and maintain the use of all my limbs." She laughed again. "You and that horse," she said. "I don't know how you handle him when no one else can. Oh, well, the twilight hour will be upon us shortly and Nuad said he'd carry all the fungi we harvested if I'd show him where it grows."

Lugh felt a stab of anger. "Ha! Is that all a one-handed man can do to help around here, when the rest of us toil

so hard? It is not enough. We do all the work and that
blemished—"

Lugh stopped in midsentence. A stricken look had come
over Tailteann's face as he spoke of Nuad and now her
dark eyes were fixed on a point just beyond Lugh's head.

He turned to look into the flushed face of Nuad who
had approached so silently Lugh had not heard him coming. Nuad stood within a few paces of Lugh, glaring at
him with eyes flashing green fire. Lugh glared back. His
words were true, what need did he have to take them back
or to apologize?

The truth was that he wanted to hurt Nuad. Not only
was this man the killer of King Eochy, but Morrigan had
gone back to his furs as though nothing had happened between her and Lugh. Joy over their encounter had turned
bitter as the days went by and Lugh saw that she did not
mean to come to him again.

"So, you think me a shirker when it comes to the well-
being of my people, do you Lugh?"

Nuad took four paces toward him, coming so close that
Lugh could feel his breath. Lugh drew himself up and
stood his ground."

"I do. You could use the hand the gods have left you
to work . . . even if it's only the work of half a man."

Lugh regretted his mean-spirited words as soon as they
left his mouth, and he saw a dark shadow of rage cross
Nuad's face. The former king reached out and grabbed
the front of Lugh's tunic. He pulled him close, until they
were nose to nose.

"I would show you, prince," he said, through gritted
teeth, "that I am more a man with one hand than you will
ever be with two, because I have no petty cruelty in
me . . ."

Lugh wrenched himself out of Nuad's grasp and
shoved him back, resisting an urge to strike him.

"No, but you would deliberately kill a man as good as
King Eochy. Do you find no cruelty in what you did to
him? To my mother? To me? You deserve to end your days
as a useless, one-handed old man for what you did to us!"

"I did what kings must do in battle, no more, no less. It
might interest you to know that my hand was severed as
I raised it to summon bearers for your father. He was worthy of honor and I so honored him that this"—he thrust his

leather-clad wrist in Lugh's face—"was my reward. How dare you mock me as half a man? You, who are as green as a spring sapling. I didn't see you taking to the field to defend your father on that fateful day, did I?"

"I may be green, but I am not untried." Lugh paused, knowing that he should weigh his words carefully. "You might ask your lady Morrigan how green I am. There is much she could tell you about that!"

"Stop! Please stop!" Queen Tailteann implored, looking from one antagonist to the other. "You are both behaving badly, saying things that should not be said."

She was frightened by the underlying threat in Lugh's furious words. Whatever did Morrigan have to do with her son? It could not bode well for any of them.

"Go now, Lugh, and fetch the last of the peat," she ordered. "The light fades even as you waste it arguing." Her delicate voice was full of authority and Lugh could not dishonor her by disobeying. He picked up his empty wicker basket and walked toward Anovaar, still breathing hard, still angry.

"Come, Nuad," she said. "The harvest basket awaits us in the forest."

She took his arm and felt the tension through his muscles. They set off down the Hill of Knockadoon, and his breathing did not return to normal until they were well beyond the northern boundary of Lough Gur.

When he could trust himself to speak, Nuad asked, "What did Lugh mean about Morrigan?"

"I know not, but let it go, Nuad, please. Hot words, spoken in anger are always best forgotten."

Tailteann saw the stern set of his jaw and knew he would not let it go. A black rook was flushed from its nesting place when they entered the woods and it flew over their heads, scolding noisily. *Oh, my son, what have you done?* she thought, thoroughly alarmed by the blackbird's portent.

The great Dagda Mor and his brother Ogma, were not well received at the court of Breas the Beautiful. They were offered no meat with which to grease their knives, nor ale with which to assuage their thirst after their tiring journey. The accommodations they were given were scarcely fit for slaves.

They were kept waiting for two journeys of the sun before they were shown into the presence of King Breas. They entered the royal dwelling angry over their treatment, and at a disadvantage before the negotiations began.

The lady Eri sat beside her son, her pale eyes glittering with hostility as she regarded the visitors from the settlement of the banished. If she could, she would have seen to it that these two brothers never survived to make this return journey to Druim Caein. She offered them no word of greeting.

Nor did King Breas, who sat on his elevated platform looking down on them without expression. Dagda and Ogma would not break tradition and speak first, and the silence in the dwelling grew into awkward hostility. At last, Dagda saw one of Breas's servants slip into the dwelling and whisper something to the king. Without looking at the servant, Breas raised one finger and inclined his head slightly. He whispered back to the man, who nodded and stood back to speak.

"King Breas, and the Lady Eri, may I present two residents from the lesser settlement of Lough Gur, Dagda and Ogma?"

"What is your business here?" Breas asked icily.

Dagda, repressing his anger over the many slights done to them, answered as evenly as he could. "We bring a petition from your loyal subjects at Lough Gur, regarding the tributes you have asked from us."

King Breas sighed with irritation. He had supposed it would be something as tiresome as this, and his mother had counseled him to stand fast in his tribute demands. He didn't understand why these irksome men had to bother him with their problems. If they only knew that the tributes he asked for were helping to protect and exalt the DeDanaans, they wouldn't be here bothering him when he had more important things to do. He looked at Eri. Her expression had not changed and Breas understood that he was to proceed just as they had discussed earlier.

"I'm sorry you have made this long journey, Dagda, if that is what you want to talk about, because the issue is not negotiable. The tribute is absolutely necessary or I would not request it from you. It is for the good of the tribe as a whole." He could see the disbelief on the faces of the brothers from Lough Gur. "That is my final word," he said.

Ogma leaned toward Dagda and whispered, "It is time to tell him of the settlement's resolve to rise in rebellion against him." Dagda looked at him and nodded.

"King Breas, it grieves me to learn that you will not even discuss the excessive tributes you ask from the people. They inflict terrible hardship upon us, because as you know, the harvests were poor and the fecundity of the livestock has fallen off severely. The risk of famine at Lough Gur this winter is very real. The people can offer you no more than they have already given."

King Breas's blue eyes narrowed in anger. "Silence! I will hear no more. I have told you that the subject of tribute is not open for discussion."

Dagda regarded him contemptuously, while he chose his words carefully. "Then, King Breas, I must speak as plainly as the people at Lough Gur have asked me to do. The anger and unrest spurred by your unreasonable demands is so great that they are prepared to rise against you in rebellion."

The king was taken aback. He looked to Eri for guidance. Her lips were set in a thin line and she tapped her bejeweled fingers against her knee, thinking of a response Breas might make. She had not guessed that the situation was this serious. She needed time to think.

She spoke for the first time to the two men from Lough Gur whom she had known all her life. "Please accept our hospitality and take nourishment with us. My son and I would be honored if you would dine at our table this day. There is time enough for such unpleasant talk." She smiled sweetly at her son's visitors, her eyes as cold as the north winds that swept across Innis Ealga.

Dagda realized that she was stalling for time. Clearly she and Breas had not been prepared for talk of rebellion. He seized the advantage. "My brother and I have satisfied our hunger," he said sarcastically. "We would prefer to continue this talk now. As everyone knows, dining is one of my great pleasures, but the health of my people matters far more than dining at the royal table." He fixed King Breas with an angry stare, to no avail.

"This discussion will be continued after we have dined," Breas said airily, then turned to the servant. "Please show our visitors to the filach fiadah."

Reluctantly, Dagda and Ogma left the royal presence.

"We unnerved them with talk of rebellion, didn't we?" Ogma asked.

"Aye, we did that. But they have unnerved me with talk of fine dining," Dagda replied. "They are very clever at identifying the weaknesses of their enemies." He looked morose. "We must be as clever, Ogma, if we are to reach accommodation with these people."

"Don't you mean with King Breas?"

"I do not, brother. Do you think for a moment he is a powerful man? It is the lady Eri who controls his every thought and deed. She is the one with whom we must negotiate and she is a formidable foe. Her mind is quick and, I fear, evil. When talk resumes, we must be very careful indeed."

After the dining hour at Lough Gur, during which Lugh remained apart from the others, he went to the dwelling of the old physician Diancecht, feeling compelled to seek him out.

Inside the round house, the old man was reclining against a yellowed fleece spread out on the earthen floor before a meager peat fire. Propped up on one arm, he stirred the lethargic flames, trying to coax more heat from them. His bronze leg lay nearby, next to his blackthorn walking stick.

"Come in"—he called out when Lugh rapped on the wooden door—"but shut the door quickly for my bones are old and a chill is upon me this autumn night."

"Good evening, Grandfather," Lugh said as he entered, "are you not feeling well?"

"It's nothing. I'm just cold, laddy. Come over here and sit close beside me. You know the gods are stealing my hearing, little by little." He shook his long white hair. "They give me years but steal my eyes and my ears," he complained. "Ach, it is beyond mortal understanding, it is. What brings you to call upon an old man this evening?" There was a knowing look in his eyes.

A small finger of flame rose courageously from the peat blocks. It flickered and waned, then flared again with renewed vigor, sending a degree of warmth into the house.

Lugh looked at the fire for a time before answering Diancecht. He signed deeply and turned to meet the old man's piercing blue eyes, bluer than the lough at twilight.

"I quarreled with Nuad today and we almost came to blows, but I don't regret a word I said, because I am in the right. He killed my foster father, and I owe him no respect."

His tone was defensive, and Diancecht understood that Lugh did have regret even though he denied it. "What did you quarrel about?" he asked kindly.

"Nuad overheard me tell my mother that he wasn't doing his part to help the settlement get through the winter. We are all toiling so hard and—"

"Whatever occasioned such a comment from you, Lugh?" Diancecht asked, knowing that the former king was, if anything, pushing himself too hard.

The young prince frowned. "Mother said he was going to help her fetch the wild fungi if she'd show him where the ones safe to eat are found. It made me angry. I don't understand how she can continue to be friendly with him. Not now, not when she knows that he was King Eochy's killer."

"So, your remark was meant to wound—not Nuad, but your mother?"

Lugh's green eyes grew round with surprise. "No! I . . . I . . . well, maybe. I guess it was," he said slowly, dismayed at himself. "For I had no idea that Nuad was anywhere around when I spoke."

"People often hurt the ones closest to them, Lugh. When we are angry or upset and need some release from our frustrations, we strike where it is safest, at those who will continue to love us anyway, no matter how badly we behave."

Lugh hung his head. He felt awful. "But, Grandfather," he protested, "I would never knowingly do anything to hurt Queen Tailteann. She is a wonderful mother to me."

"But you feel that she has betrayed you in a fundamental way, by befriending the man who killed King Eochy?"

Lugh nodded.

"Tell me why you single him out from among all the DeDanaans who took the field during the battle of Moytirra. Every one of the warriors on the field was trying to do the same thing. Why do you *really* hate Nuad, Lugh?"

"I don't hate him, exactly, it's just . . . ," Lugh hesitated. "One of the things I hate is that such a strong warrior could have been brought so low by his injury. He should have fought back harder. Nuad should have demanded to keep his kingship and not let that weak man, Breas, take his place. I would have—"

"You would have what, Lugh?"

"I don't know." Lugh looked into the fire as though to find understanding among the orange and blue flames. "I just know that I would never give up. Never. Not even if such a catastrophe befell me."

"I don't think Nuad has given up, my son. In fact, I think it is the very reemergence of his strength that has brought your anger into full flower. Could it be that you are jealous of him?"

Lugh opened his mouth in indignation, but Diancecht did not wait for him to speak. "In truth, Lugh, you are a man very much like Nuad. Perhaps when you look at him you see a rival."

In Lugh's mind a picture formed of the beautiful, willing Morrigan as she had come to him that day beside the stream, and he understood that his grandfather's words were true.

Diancecht smiled as pale shadows of the images in Lugh's memory danced in his own mind. So, the gods had lured the lad with Morrigan's many charms. He was not the first to be so tempted.

"You lust for Nuad's woman, Lugh?"

Lugh fixed Diancecht with a wary look. How could his grandfather know this thing? "Sometimes I think you are in communion with the gods, Grandfather. Can you see into my thoughts?"

The old man inclined his head toward Lugh as though he had not heard him. Lugh decided to tell him the truth. He raised his voice and said, "I'm afraid it's more than that. I have acted on my lust."

He waited a moment to see how Diancecht received the news. The old physician did not seem surprised. "Yes?" he said, waiting for Lugh to continue.

"She came to me in the glade and asked if I would have her, but I confess to entertaining such dreams long before that day. She was not unwelcome."

"No, I suppose not, Lugh. Don't you know that every man at Lough Gur has had the same dreams about Morrigan? Does Nuad know of this betrayal?"

"I owe Nuad no allegiance, Grandfather! How can you say I betrayed him?"

"Perhaps you did not, but Morrigan? Did she not owe the former king of the DeDanaans her allegiance? Has she betrayed him with you more than once?"

Lugh was ashamed to admit it, but he told the truth. "No, Grandfather, we knew each other that one time only. Now she acts as though we are strangers. Our eyes never meet and she speaks to me with indifference."

Diancecht nodded knowingly, certain now that the gods were acting through Morrigan, who had grown increasingly close to her as his own communication with them lessened. He did not know for what purpose the pairing of Lugh and Morrigan was intended, but he was certain that its reason lay beyond the ken of men.

"I would ask you to put Morrigan out of your thoughts, if you can, Lugh. It is over. You will never know her that way again."

In the darkest hour of that night, when all was still save the occasional baying of wolves at the crescent moon, Lugh and Tailteann were awakened by loud voices and the crashing of objects within the dwelling next door. Lugh knew instantly that Nuad had discovered his tryst with Morrigan. Had that not been Lugh's intent when he hurled the challenge at Nuad during their quarrel?

Queen Tailteann did not speak, but he could tell from the sound of her breathing that she was awake. Lugh couldn't make out the words Nuad and Tailteann were throwing at each other like daggers, although he strained to hear. Then, as suddenly as the shouting began, it was over. Silence prevailed for such a long time that Lugh was nearly back to sleep. He had pulled the furs over his shoulder and turned his face to the wall, when a furious pounding exploded against the door. He leaped to his feet, determined to keep Tailteann out of it. He didn't know whether to expect Nuad or Morrigan on the other side when he opened the door. Tailteann sat up in the furs, her eyes round with alarm.

"Be careful, Lugh. Don't open it until you know who is there," she whispered. "They could be armed."

Lugh snatched up his sheath, annoyed at his own reckless haste, and slipped his knife from it, gripping it, ready for action. He slipped the leather throng from the peg that held the door shut, and slowly pulled it open, shielding his body behind it.

Nuad burst into the dwelling, his large frame trembling with anger. His presence filled the house as he whipped around and glared at Lugh, clenching and unclenching his fist.

"Outside, Lugh," he ordered, jerking his head toward the open door. "We will settle this like men."

Lugh felt his battle lust rise and he said, eagerly, "Whatever you say, Nuad. You won't like the outcome, I promise you." The two men faced off, breathing hard, saying nothing.

Queen Tailteann broke the silence. "What is it, Nuad? Why do you intrude on us in our hours of rest?"

Nuad looked at her for the first time, as if shocked to find her in her own home. Her dark hair cascaded over her white shoulders where her garment for sleeping had slipped down. Her bright dark eyes shone in the firelight, and Nuad felt anew the impact of her beauty. He remembered how he had wanted her, how he wanted her still. He looked from her to Lugh and back again. If Tailteann had allowed it, he would have committed an insult almost as great as the one Lugh had committed against him.

After a long, charged silence during which neither man made a move to go outside the dwelling, Nuad suddenly threw back his head and roared with laughter.

"By the gods, Lugh," he gasped, "I meant to kill you with one hand when I came in here, but I see that I am no better than you." He laughed again. "We are two of a kind, you and I."

He bowed to Queen Tailteann. "Pardon me, my lady. I am sorry to have awakened you. Please return to your slumber." Then he turned and captured Lugh's green eyes and held them with the mesmerizing force of his own.

He ceased his laughter and said soberly, "Lugh, it will end right here. No more revenge. We are even."

Lugh nodded in agreement, baffled by Nuad's odd behavior. When the door closed behind him, Lugh glanced at Tailteann but saw only his mother, not the desirable woman Nuad had seen.

Chapter Twenty-two

It was a heavy-hearted Dagda who returned to Lough Gur. He and his companions had been unable to persuade King Breas to lift his onerous tribute demands, and the counteroffer he had proposed to them had the smell of demons all over it.

Ogma rode his gray mare alongside Dagda and asked, "When will you speak with Brigid, Dagda?"

The portly wise man turned sad eyes on his brother. "I suppose I will have to talk with her as soon as possible. When we arrive, we will say that we must bathe before we address the people. While the stones are heating, I will go to Brigid. Oh, my darling girl," he exclaimed with pain, "how can we ask this thing of her? I don't think I can do it, Ogma. It is too large a sacrifice."

"I know, I know, brother. But I see not what else we can do. The health of the DeDanaans depends on her now. I know she will rise to it, and I trust that in her sacrifice there will be blessing. We must hold that thought in our hearts, Dagda. The gods would not ask so much of her . . . and you . . . if it were not so."

"Harumph," Dagda growled, not nearly as sure of the beneficence of the gods as Ogma was.

The flurry of excitement that surrounded the travelers' return from Druim Caein blocked all conversation between father and daughter until they were finally alone in their dwelling. Brigid happily unpacked Dagda's leather bags as they spoke.

"Did you bring me something, Father?" she asked, as eager as a child, and his heart constricted with pain.

"No, lass, I brought nothing for there was nothing to bring. The court is nearly as poor as we are. All of the artisans were involved in field work or gathering in wood and peat for the winter. Everyone there bends their backs either to the fields or the erection of King Breas's ridiculous new feasting hall." He smiled at her. "I'm sorry."

The tone of his voice caused her to glance at him closely. She put down the leather bag and waited for his next words, knowing he had something to tell her.

She was astonished to see her blustery, good-natured father looking at her with tears shining in his eyes. "My child, my darling girl, I . . ."

"Why, Father, what is it? What's wrong?"

He walked to where she knelt by the fire and helped her to her feet. He enfolded her in his arms and rocked back and forth, holding her tightly, stroking her hair with his broad hand.

When his composure returned he released her and said, "My darling, Brigid, King Breas has asked for your hand in marriage. He would wed thee at Samhain."

They were the hardest words Dagda had ever been called upon to utter, and while he understood that Brigid had once found Breas desirable, now the entire tribe knew what manner of man Breas was.

Yet, incredibly, pure happiness shone from Brigid's plain, round face. Her too-small eyes glowed with joy. "He asked for me?" she asked, afraid to believe her good fortune.

The gods could make impossible dreams come true. She wanted to laugh, to run, to shout to the world that the most handsome DeDanaan of all had chosen her to be his bride. Her knees felt weak.

"King Breas wants me to be his bride?" she whispered, then looked to her father for confirmation. He nodded reluctantly.

"Oh, Father, this is something I have asked the gods for every day of my adult life. I cannot believe how they have blessed me this day. Why do you look so sad when the very thing that I have dreamed of has come to pass? Oh, Father! Please be happy for me. Just think, not only will I be bride to Breas, but I will be Queen of the DeDanaans. I am certain I can help our people. Please, don't look so sad."

For his daughter's sake, Dagda tried to look cheerful, but his heart was breaking. He understood only too well how much his own influence would be blunted by such a marriage. With his only daughter wed to King Breas, who among the DeDanaans would accept his counsel?

I have sold my daughter for a quarter portion of oats, he thought. *I am no better than the Fomorians who raid our coasts. But how else could I keep my people from starving this winter? Breas would have taken everything and returned for more.* And now Dagda's confounded daughter acted as though he had given her the moon. He hugged Brigid again with a troubled heart.

Brigid's happiness grew as her bride day came nearer. No one at Lough Gur wanted her to see their misgivings about what she was doing. The DeDanaans understood well the deal to which Dagda had been forced to agree, and had formed an unspoken covenant to express their gratitude to him and his daughter by cooperating in making Brigid's bride day as festive as possible.

"I wish my mother had lived to see me wed, Tailteann," Brigid said one morning, as she and the Fir Bolg queen sat sewing around Tailteann's hearth fire. "It would please her to be able to do this work in preparation for my bride day. She was a skilled needlewoman."

"Can you remember her, Brigid?"

"Aye, I do, for wasn't I on this earth for eight summers and eight winters before the gods called her home? She was well loved by all DeDanaans, but not physically strong. She got a chill the first year we were in Lochland and the gods took her so swiftly, my poor father was barely able to make it to her side in time to bid her farewell."

"But your father has done well by you and your brothers, hasn't he, Brigid? It must have been difficult for him to raise you along with all his other responsibilities."

"Well, Bove and Aengus are much older than I, so they were of help to him." She smiled at Tailteann, her newfound happiness irrepressible. "The three of them treated me like a princess, even though the truth about me was always apparent. I knew early that my body lacked all grace, for even as a young child I was always crashing into things, but none of them ever let on to me that I was less than perfect. It was only when I reached a certain age and the young warriors turned away from me to choose

more comely girls that I realized my father and brothers
had lied to me . . . protected me . . . all that time."

"Hush, Brigid. You are a lovely young woman. Don't
say such things about yourself. If you are to be a good
wife to Breas, you must have more confidence as you go
to your bride bed."

Queen Tailteann's forehead wrinkled in concern. She
had learned the value of Brigid's kindly character and she
wanted the girl to think better of herself than she did.

"I have no illusions, Queen Tailteann. I know full well
why Breas has asked for my hand."

Tailteann looked at her compassionately. "He has asked
for you because you are a wonderful young woman, of
good breeding, who will bring many gifts and talents to
the queenship," she said.

"That may be so," Brigid said, "but I understand that
an interest in weakening my father's opposition may have
played a part in his choice."

The queen leaned forward to press her point, but Brigid
laid a restraining hand on her arm. "Say no more, dear
friend. It is all right. I understand the situation full well
and I am more than willing to go to him. He has been my
heart's desire for so long, that it is my hope I can make
him love me. Through the force of my devotion to him,
it could happen." She paused looking into Tailteann's
eyes for hope. "It could happen, couldn't it?"

Tailteann laid her needlework aside and embraced the
heavyset girl who so resembled her father. "I certainly
hope so," she said. "Love is a powerful force, and I, of all
women, would never discount its magic."

After a strenuous practice session with the weapons,
Lugh came whistling out of the woods, toting a load of
javelins and targets. He caught up with Cairbed the bard
on the path toward Knockadoon.

"Ah, Cairbed, sometimes it feels like all we do around
here is work to lay things by for the winter. I was glad for
a chance to go into the forest and throw the javelin. By
the gods! I love it."

Cairbed brushed his stiff, red curls out of his eyes, and
looked at Lugh dejectedly. "I didn't think it was much
fun."

Lugh didn't care to have his enthusiasm diminished by

Cairbed's determined sadness. "Why do you mope around so, Cairbed? For days you have acted as though someone has robbed you of all you possess."

"Someone is about to," he replied with a sour expression on his handsome, freckled face.

He had tried to pour out his grief in song, but the words wouldn't come. Usually he could vent his feelings through his music and poetry but sometimes only a human confidante would do. He had to tell someone before he burst.

"I can't stand the thought of Brigid going to King Breas as his bride," Cairbed blurted out.

"No. It doesn't seem like a good match to me either," Lugh agreed, "but I can see why Dagda and the others think it should be done. You realize what it would mean to us at Lough Gur if the king were to take away half our supply of food for the winter?"

"Of course, I do," Cairbed snapped, "but that doesn't mean my heart is not in pain. I love her! I just didn't realize how much until Breas asked for her hand. I thought I had a long time to make my case with her. It's a heavy burden the gods ask me to bear, Lugh, a heavy burden indeed. I want Brigid for my own."

"I'm sorry, Cairbed, I didn't know she meant that much to you." Lugh had no words to ease Cairbed's anguish and even if he had, he suspected they would not be heard by his friend.

Cairbed stopped on the path and grasped Lugh's arm urgently. "It's more than my own heartbreak that concerns me, Lugh. I fear that Breas will not be good to her. I know she thinks she can go to Druim Caein and influence him with her kindness, but I understand the king only too well, and that will not be the case. No good can come of this pairing. Mark my words, it will bring the wrath of the gods down upon our heads."

Out on the northern sea, near the coast of Donegal, Srang gripped an oar so tightly his knuckles showed white. Seawater splashed relentlessly over the hull of the Fomorian curragh where he strained with all his might to pull the thin wedge of ash through the powerful waves toward the coast of the Fomorian stronghold, Tor Conain. Srang thought of the legends that surrounded this mys-

terious island. Many among the Fir Bolgs held firmly to
the belief that Tor Conain existed only at rare times in the
cycles of the gods. Others held that a barrier had been
thrown around it by enchantment and that no ordinary
mortal could ever arrive upon its shores through effort of
their own making.

Even if Srang had held to any such belief, it was far
too late to contemplate it now. He had agreed to go with
Cochpar to meet Balor, the king of the Fomorians, but
Srang wasn't sure they would actually make landfall. The
currents around Tor Conain were treacherous and they
had labored so long to bring the curragh around, that the
bulging muscles in his massive forearms were tiring and
had ceased to respond to his bidding.

Cochpar, his wolf's pelt secured under the belt around
his waist, yelled, "To the west, men! Pull your oars into
the west. That's it, now row hard, and it's straight on to
Tor Conain."

Srang felt pain ripple through his shoulders, but he renewed his effort and pulled with the other oarsmen on the
right side of the curragh until the leather craft turned.
Suddenly the threatening sea waves were sliding past
them, no longer crashing into them with deadly force. He
let out his breath and allowed his muscles to relax for a
moment before bending his back once more to take them
to the land of King Balor of the Evil Eye and the Thousand Blows.

"Set to work, men," Cochpar ordered after they pulled
the curragh onto the beach. "Unload and secure the craft
while I take our friend here"— he jerked his thumb at
Srang—"for his audience with King Balor and Queen
Kathlen."

"You mean we are to appear before your king like this,
with the stench of our labor and the salt of the sea covering us?" Srang asked, incredulous at such a lack of respect for the leader of a tribe.

"Of course," Cochpar snapped. "Why would a warrior
waste time on such niceties as bathing when he knows the
king is waiting for a report? Follow me. We will go to
him at once. I think he will be well pleased when he sees
what I have brought him."

Srang rubbed his short, dark fingers through his hair

and beard, in a vain attempt to tidy himself up. He looked at Cochpar who was pulling the wolf pelt out from under his belt. The Fomorian settled the wolf's head over his own and set off at a brisk pace over the sand dunes that stood as silent guardians of the southern coast of Tor Conain. Srang sighed and followed, knowing that as tired and dirty as he was, he did not look as bad as Cochpar did.

His first glimpse of the Fomorian king and queen told him he had been foolish to have worried that his appearance would give affront to either Balor or Kathlen. He had never seen two such filthy individuals in his life.

The Fomorian rulers sat on low wooden stools outside a dwelling so crude it looked like children had constructed it. The king was short, with a swarthy complexion, his face brown and deeply lined. He had a long nose that flared into wide nostrils above a bushy black mustache and beard. At his age it was surprising to see no gray in his wild, charcoal-colored hair. But the most startling thing about him was the large leather patch he wore over the space once occupied by his left eye.

He had a habit of frequently lifting the patch and rubbing the empty socket with his grimy fist. He did it now, while looking critically at Srang with his remaining eye. The gesture always intimidated those around him who did not wish to look upon the sight, giving Balor an advantage over them, and it temporarily relieved the phantom pain he experienced there.

King Balor's arms and shoulders were heavily muscled, like those of a smith and he prided himself on his strength. He noted the size of Srang's muscles and frowned.

"Hail, kinsman," he said at last, turning his dark gaze upon Cochpar. "What manner of visitor have you brought to Tor Conain?"

Cochpar bowed low before his king, nudging his Fir Bolg ally to do the same. Srang bowed his head slightly, unable to bend his knee before such a rude savage.

In a voice pitched high, with a metallic hint like copper in it, the short woman at the king's side, spoke. "Ho, ho, Cochpar, it's a haughty one you have brought to us. See, Balor, see how the stranger does not give us our proper due?"

She laughed a crone's cackle, with no mirth in it, and a drop of spittle glistened through a gap where two of her lower teeth were missing. She wiped it on the back of her hand, then on the dirty sheepskin she wore as a cape.

"Husband, make him bend his knee to you. Hee, hee, make him do it." Thick gray curls protruding in stubby outcroppings from under the squirrel-skin cap she wore would have given her a comical appearance but for the canniness Srang saw in her eyes.

"My apologies," Srang said and bowed low before the royal Fomorian pair. He had no illusions about Fomorians and regretted his slight. He knew he was vastly outnumbered here in the heart of their stronghold and he doubted the wisdom of having come. These people were so uncouth that even after his hardships in the wilds of Connaught, he was not sure he could deal with them. They seemed more brute than human.

"Who is this man?" Balor boomed, ignoring his queen.

"My lord, I have brought you Srang, the champion of the Fir Bolgs. He is the warrior who led some of his comrades into Connaught when they escaped from the DeDanaan victors after the battle of Moytirra." There was pride in Cochpar's voice.

A slow smile spread over King Balor's face, exposing a row of yellowed teeth as irregular as his wife's. "Well done, Cochpar, very well done indeed!" He regarded Srang more closely.

After some moments he spoke directly to him. "You have bravery, Fir Bolg, to come into the den of the bear who would devour you. You are not Cochpar's prisoner?"

"I am not."

"Then perhaps you are a fool. Why are you here?"

"I have come to discuss a proposition with you, one that could yield much of great value to both of us."

Queen Kathlen clapped her hands together. "Oh, good," she snickered, "a proposition. Make him tell us what it is, Balor. A proposition from a Fir Bolg. Hee, hee. I can't wait to hear this."

"Cochpar, go to the filach fiadah and fetch the counselor Indech to me. I would have him beside us for the hearing of this proposition," Balor ordered.

Srang saw the look of displeasure that crossed Cochpar's face and deduced that he and this Indech must

e rivals. He let his eyes go back to the king and saw the
ark beast of a man tenderly touching the cheek of Queen
Kathlen. "In a moment, my love, in a moment," he whis-
ered.

After his talk with Diancecht, Lugh could find no ease
or his spirit. He withdrew more and more from the com-
any of others, even Tailteann, as he sought answers in-
ide himself. On the night before the journey to Druim
Caein for the Samhain wedding of Brigid to King Breas,
Lugh left the safety of the compound accompanied only
by his favorite gray wolfhound.

"Come on, Cu," he called, and the tall lanky dog
bounded to his side, eagerly licking Lugh's outstretched
hand. They left the safety of the night fires behind them
and walked outside the stone wall of the settlement.

Starlight pierced the black canopy of the night sky,
casting silver shadows on the path as they made their way
down the Hill of Knockadoon. The dog wagged his tail,
happy to be with Lugh, and kept close by his side.

The lough was still tonight, its waters spread out like a
dark cloak across a low spot in the green hills. The reeds
and tall grasses growing at the lough's edge sighed softly
in the night breeze. Lugh wondered how it was possible
for him to feel so agitated when the natural world appeared to be in such perfect order.

He made his way to a dry spot at the water's edge and
sat down to think. He plucked the green stem from a plant
growing beside him and put it in his mouth. So much had
happened to him in such a short time. His life as a Fir
Bolg prince was gone, he knew that only too well. But
where was his place in this new order of things? He
struggled to make sense of it all.

Lugh lay back and gazed into the heavens, wondering
about the power of the gods who dwelt there. Did they really have time to concern themselves with mortals?
Sometimes he suspected that the gods had set the seasons
to turning, then rolled over and went back to sleep. They
certainly never seemed to hear his pleas.

As he brooded, Lugh saw movement from the corner of
his eye and turned to look into the northern sky. There, a
meteor blazed red under the sky's dome, falling, falling,
ever earthward, hurtling in a blazing fury toward a watery

death in the sea. Lugh was awestricken. *What a beautiful
thing of wonder,* Lugh thought, *and it's gone so fast . . .
just like us.* He knew suddenly that he had to make his
time upon earth count. He sensed that destiny was calling
to him, and although he knew not why, he was ready for
whatever lay ahead.

He patted the dog's head. "Let's go back and get some
sleep, what do you say, old boy?" The two of them trotted
back up the path to the stone-walled compound, Lugh's
mind filling with the details he needed to see to in the
morning before the journey to Druim Caein began.

Chapter Twenty-three

Brigid asked Queen Tailteann, Desheen the charioteer, and Macha to be her attendants on her bride day, and he was hurt and puzzled when Macha did not make the journey to Druim Caein with them. She was still asking er father about it on the first day of Samhain, shortly before it was time for her bridal toilette to begin.

"But why wouldn't Macha come? She knew how much wanted her to be part of my special day. I just don't understand why she would want to stay alone at Lough Gur, when all the rest of us are here."

"Hush, me darling," Dagda said, "I've told you that he would have come if she could. She didn't want to tay behind; you know how much she cares for you, but ou have to take my word that she has a good reason for ot coming. I don't want you to worry your sweet head bout it for another moment. The time has come to pre-are yourself to go to your"—he gulped and swallowed ard before he could say the words—"your bridegroom. he lady Morrigan will come in Macha's place to assist ou."

Brigid was surprised that the older sister would be willng to assist her on her bride day for she and Morrigan ad never been close.

"All right, Father, send the women to me. I'm ready." he smiled at him, her eyes full of hope.

"I love you, young one," Dagda muttered, his voice racking with emotion. He left the dwelling quickly to ummon the women to assist his daughter.

The bride who wended her way through the crowd to King Breas's side was as comely as loving hands could make her. Her hair had been combed with rosewater and swept up in an elaborate arrangement with wild autumn

flowers and sweet lavender tucked among the curls. Her
cheeks and lips were reddened with ruam and her small
gray eyes, framed by darkened lashes, gleamed with happiness. Her cloak of scarlet was of soft, washed wool held
at her left shoulder with a golden clasp set with a single
polished stone that had been a gift from her father and
brothers. From its opaque surface the many colors of fire
shone forth, changing hues as the sunlight fell on it from
different angles.

Her bridal tunic had been tinted a pale pink and was
embroidered with lozenges of scarlet and green. She wore
leggings of pure white, wrapped around with the soft
suede laces of her deerskin shoes. Upon her plump arms
were many bracelets of gold that matched the rings upon
her fingers. She wore beads of jet and lignite, polished to
a deep gleam and set into golden chains. Yet as beguiling
as was her finery, it was overshadowed by that of the
king.

For every gold ornament that Brigid wore, Breas wore
two, of more ornate design and even better quality. His
clothing was embroidered more elaborately, in many
more colors, and the overall effect of his rainment,
combined with his natural beauty, was stunning. The
bridegroom overshadowed his bride by half.

Breas waited for Brigid, standing regally beside an
evergreen holly bush that had been brought in from the
woods and planted on top of Druim Caein for this occasion. Beside him stood the priest, Ferfesa, in immaculate
white robes.

Cairbed lifted a beautifully made whistle of bird bone
to his lips. He positioned his fingers, and with a sad-eyed
look at Brigid, began to play the slow, sweet notes that
had called DeDanaan brides to their bridegrooms, time
out of mind. He thought his own heart would break inside
his breast as he played. A tear rolled down his ruddy
cheek as he blew the last note. The music hung over the
silent assembly, trembling slightly like the leaves of the
oak, before it faded into the thin sunshine of the day.

Breas watched Brigid approach, wishing with all his
heart that it were Macha coming to him in her bridal finery. He glanced at his mother, and she stared steadily
back at him, as though to give him courage to go through
with the rite. He took a deep breath and turned his eyes

ack to his bride whom he knew he must greet with en-
husiasm, since every DeDanaan eye was upon them.

Lugh stood in front of the holly bush, facing the king,
ut was oblivious to the drama of Brigid and Breas un-
olding before him. From the moment Cairbed began to
olay, the hair on the back of Lugh's neck had stood upright. He felt a presence so acutely, that it was as though
he gods were shouting at him to turn around. Queen
Tailteann looked at him curiously, seeming to sense the
energy surging in him as he turned around to stare at the
approaching bridal party.

Lugh's eyes swept quickly over all the young virgins
who walked with Brigid and came to rest on the face of
Desheen, the charioteer from Ulster, who walked seven
steps behind the bride.

He drew his breath in sharply. This was the most exquisite creature he had ever seen. He felt himself drawn
to her with a strange power he had never felt before in his
life.

She was a full head shorter than he and had to tilt her
chin up to meet his gaze. He liked it that this girl did not
turn her eyes away from him as most young women did.
Her eyes were blue, like Diancecht's, as blue and clear
and deep as a cloudless sky on a fine midsummer's day.
Thick, black lashes curved up toward slim arched eyebrows and Lugh could not look away from her beautiful,
compelling eyes. When Desheen passed near him he
caught the faint scent of lavender. His head spun as
though he had drunk too much ale.

Tailteann followed her son's gaze and smiled. Even
though she had only recently met Desheen in Brigid's
dwelling, the charioteer seemed a much more suitable
match for Lugh than Aibel, whose illness was masking all
hint of who she used to be. Tailteann still did not know
the details of what had passed between Lugh and
Morrigan, but she was certain her son was not experienced enough to be involved with the DeDanaan beauty.
Besides, whatever was between them seemed to have
ended the night Nuad stormed into their house to confront
Lugh. Yes, this lovely young woman from Ulster would
be a welcome distraction for her son from the troublesome women he knew at Lough Gur.

Lugh thought he was being enchanted but he didn't

care. The bridal rite seemed to go on forever when all he
wanted was to tear himself away from the crowd and discover the identity of this female creature who filled all
his senses. Finally, the lilting, merry melody of the pipes
and the bronze horns announced the triumphal end of the
ceremony.

King Breas took the hand of Brigid, his new queen
and paraded in a sunwise circle around the guests, inviting the participation of the Sun God in their marriage
When they returned to the spot in front of the green holly
the newlyweds led a procession to the place of the wedding feast.

Lugh felt rooted to the spot and Tailteann had to take
his arm and announce, "Lugh, it's time to go."

"Humm? Oh, yes, Mother."

"She looks lovely, doesn't she?"

"I've never seen anymore more beautiful," Lugh
breathed.

Queen Tailteann laughed out loud. "I meant our new
queen, Lugh."

He looked at his mother and realized that she had seen
and understood the direction of his thought. His face felt
warm, but he too, had to laugh at the intensity of his sudden passion for this girl he'd never seen before. He took
his mother's arm. "Some things cannot be explained,
Mother. Shall we go see what King Breas provides for his
wedding guests?"

On the main banquet table there was but one flank of
venison served with braised leeks and wild garlic, but
there were boiled bird's eggs in abundance, some roasted
badgers, and bowls of parsnips and carrots on the other
tables. Red apples from the recent harvest and whortle-
berries with soft curds of milk graced the dessert table,
but only King Breas and his bride were served bowls of
duilesc, a sweet lichen scraped from the surface of sea
rocks, which were gifts from the settlers of Ulster and had
been brought carefully to Druim Caein.

Some among them had argued that they should bring
no gifts at all, since Breas did nothing to protect them.
Others argued that he might look more favorably upon
them if they brought the best Ulster had to offer. In the

nd, they had been able to harvest only enough of the del-
cacy for the king and queen.

Lugh was impatient to finish his meal. His mother and
Cian and Cairbed sat around him making pleasant talk,
but he had no interest in their conversation.

"Did you notice that there is not a single hazelnut to be
had at this great feast?" Cairbed asked.

"You're right, Cairbed. Well, what would you expect?"
Cian's tone was sarcastic, an attitude not usual for him.

"I don't understand," Queen Tailteann said, "do hazelnuts have significance for the DeDanaans?"

"They do indeed, my lady," Cian responded. "As long
as I can remember the DeDanaan priests have taught that
hazelnuts are a sign of harmony between the gods and a
just ruler. They come only in abundance when the king is
good. Is it any wonder we have not one hazelnut at this
wedding feast?"

"Excuse me, please," Lugh said abruptly, rising to
leave them. He walked away with the curious stares of
Cairbed and Cian following him.

"Where is he going in such a hurry?" Cian asked.

"I think he has fallen under the charm of Desheen, the
charioteer from Ulster," Tailteann answered. "He looked
as though a bolt of lightning had struck him when he saw
her in the wedding procession. She's a lovely young
woman, isn't she? I met her when we went to assist
Brigid with her bridal rainment, and found her delight-
ful."

"Aye, she's a fine lass. She comes from a good family
of warriors and horsemen. She'd make a fine match for
Lugh," Cian answered thoughtfully, watching his son
move among the wedding guests. "I guess Aibel wouldn't
think so."

Cairbed said nothing. He lowered his eyes to his empty
plate. There seemed to be someone for everyone on Innis
Ealga, but there would never be another mate for him.
With Brigid wed to Breas he would walk these hills alone
for the rest of his days. He sighed sadly.

Throughout the meal Lugh had been keenly aware of
where Desheen was seated. He walked straight to her now
and she stood to greet him as though he were expected.

"Hello, you're Lugh of the Long Hand aren't you? My
name is Desheen."

While she was speaking Lugh was mesmerized by her mouth, the most wonderful mouth he had ever seen. Two full red lips, rows of neat white teeth, perfectly formed, a small pink tongue. Somehow he had to force his own tongue to form words and respond to her friendly greeting.

"Hello, Desheen. I am happy to meet you." He held out his hand and touched hers. He could feel calluses on her soft palm, left there by the reins of her chariot, and he realized there was strength in her to match his own. "How is it that you know who I am?"

Desheen laughed. "Well, I have seen you before. Just before we were dispatched to the various settlements, I asked Brigid who you were. Then today, I heard some of your comrades from Lough Gur saying that you are the best javelin thrower there."

Usually Lugh accepted acknowledgment of his skill with equanimity. He couldn't imagine why he was embarrassed for Desheen to point out how good he was. His skill was something he wanted her to admire, but he was unsettled by her effect on him.

She was a vision of delight in a long, green cloak over a snow-white tunic belted with a gold and silver sash. She wore a single starlike ornament in her hair and armlets of twisted silver and gold. Her dark brown hair had been braided and twisted into thick coils above each ear, leaving the rest of it to hang in soft waves around her shoulders. Her blue eyes were luminous and full of intelligence. Her lips had curved into a warm smile. He wanted to bury his face in the soft curve of her white neck where it met her shoulder. Instead, he grinned at her and his confidence came flooding back. "Would you like to come and see my horse, Anovaar? Almost everybody is afraid of him, but I think you will be able to appreciate what a wonderful animal he is."

"I'd like to, Lugh. I've been mad for horses since I was a little girl."

Her hand still lay in his and he did not release it as they went off, chattering like old friends. Aibel, who had been allowed to attend the ceremony and wedding feast, followed them so silently they did not know she was there, pausing when they paused, stopping when they stopped, and listening all the while to the voices screaming inside her head, urging her toward action.

While the DeDanaans on Innis Ealga made merry at their king's wedding, the Samhain offerings on Tor Conain chilled the very marrow of Srang's bones. He had never before seen infants sacrificed to the leaping flames of the new year fire. He would have been shocked at the drunken wantonness that accompanied the ritual, if he himself had not felt the need of prodigious amounts of ale to endure what he saw.

Not once in three days of Samhain had Balor or Kathlen drawn a sober breath and their lechery and gluttony were disgusting to the former Fir Bolg champion, who was used to seeing Samhain observed with more dignity.

It was hardly the time to discuss the details of his proposition with the Fomorian king, so he was surprised when he was summoned to the royal dwelling shortly after the close of the Samhain fire ritual on the last day of the festival.

When he was shown into the royal presence, the king and his queen were sprawled on the animal pelts they used for sleeping. Her garments were disheveled and it was obvious that they had been engaged in some kind of intimate play. Queen Kathlen sat up, and rearranged her tunic slowly, while looking Srang in the eye.

"Balor, our guest is here." She nuzzled her husband's neck and nipped him on the ear with her yellowed teeth.

"Careful, woman!" he cried out, "or I will carve you up and throw your old bones to the dogs."

He gave her a resounding slap on the rump, and staggered to his feet. He had consumed so much ale that his legs staggered under his weight. He reached out and steadied himself on Srang's arm, chuckling at his own wit.

"Come in and sit down, you old traitor," he said to Srang. "I've been thinking about your proposition and I've decided that I like it. We like it, don't we, Mother?"

Kathlen was as unsteady on her feet as her husband. She stooped and groped about the furs searching for her squirrel-skin hat. Balor patted her rump again, rubbing his hand up and down her flank in a lewd fashion. She laughed uproariously, retrieved her hat, and straightened up while pulling it down over her stiff gray hair.

"We like it," she said with a giggle, "we like your plan, Fir Bolg, but you are an evil man, aren't you? I like evil men . . . and you are the worst of the lot, Balor."

"Don't you forget it either, Fir Bolg," King Balor said, all trace of merriment vanishing. Balor's voice was cold and cruel, leaving Srang confused about whether the man's drunkenness was real or merely a ruse. He cautioned himself never to let down his guard.

"In thanks for access to the inner settlements of the DeDanaans, we shall ally with you and your men to take back Innis Ealga for the Fir Bolgs. You understand though, that the price you'll pay for our help will be high?"

"I understand that, King Balor," Srang replied. "I also understand that I will have your promise that no Fomorian will ever again lay waste to a Fir Bolg settlement."

"Of course, of course, my lad. That goes without saying." Balor winked his remaining eye, causing Srang to start at the gruesome picture Balor presented.

"The price, you remember, will be one half of everything the Fir Bolgs produce when you are restored to Innis Ealga," said Kathlen, suddenly as sober and as serious as her husband.

Srang nodded his agreement, willing himself not to waver at the punishing terms.

Kathlen cackled, her coppery laugh loud and merciless. "Good. Hee, hee. Everything! Think of it, husband: one half of everything! We won't let him forget his pledge will we? Oh, no, no. The Fir Bolg will never forget the promise he made to us. Hee, hee. No, he never will forget, never, never!"

Shortly after dawn on the third and last day of the DeDanaan's Samhain celebration, Aibel crouched behind a grove of thorn trees, watching the priests mold the wax figure they would use in tonight's sacred Samhain fire. The voices told her she must watch every detail and she kept her vigil faithfully, observing how the priests first softened the wax over the flames before molding it into the shape of a warrior.

When Ferfesa allowed a large piece of beeswax to

overheat and drop into the coals, Aibel's voices were jubilant. *That piece is for you, Aibel!* they cried. *In that little piece of wax lies your salvation. Retrieve it from the embers and carry out our instructions.*

Aibel was barefoot, wearing only a light, unbelted tunic, and her hair hung in tangled tendrils around her shoulders. She had been awake the entire night. At sunrise she had plucked tiny, sun-shaped flowers she found growing along the river Boyne, and woven them into a chain that now hung around her neck next to her fes. There was wildness on her face and in her heart, the residue of the rage and despair she felt when she saw Lugh grasp the hand of the strange girl from Ulster. At that moment the voices had begun to shriek at her, ordering her into the woods. They screamed at her all night with frenzied demands and warnings.

When the priests left the fire untended, Aibel crawled toward the dying embers on her bare knees, carrying a forked rowan twig she had found lying on the ground. She used it to fish around in the coals until she found the soft blob of wax. It was warm and pliable and she eagerly set about forming it into a likeness of Desheen, the charioteer from Ulster. Aibel worked with intense concentration, her brown eyes feverish. When she finished the figure, she concealed it in her fes and crept away from the fireside. *Well done,* her voices encouraged. *Bide your time.*

Chapter Twenty-four

Morrigan sat cross-legged by the fire, languorously combing her long auburn hair, and wearing only the light garment she had worn for sleeping. There was a smile of contentment on her face and she hummed a merry air. Brigid may have been the bride yesterday, but she doubted that the bridegroom had claimed his prize with as much gusto as Nuad had shown last night.

But for the loss of his hand, Nuad was as he had been when she first knew him. It pleased her that she had not been forced to resort to potions of purple foxglove and henbane to restore their loving after he found out about Lugh.

On the night Nuad had forced the truth from her, she had thought he would turn her out under the moon. Yet, when he returned to their dwelling from his confrontation with Lugh, he had been laughing. He was the most surprising, and certainly the most interesting man she had ever known. Just when she thought she understood him, she always came across some secret place in his spirit. He said the same about her, and she was coming to the belief that they were fated for one another.

The door opened and Nuad entered. "What? Not dressed yet, my love? The sun rises higher in the sky with each moment you linger here. Don't you know you cannot add to your beauty with the tricks of grooming? The gods have favored you such that nothing in nature can improve their creation." He bent and kissed the back of her neck. "The newly wedded ones have not emerged from their bridal nest, either. I wonder if they had as much fun last night as we did?"

"I doubt it, Nuad. There is pale blood running in Breas's veins. By the gods! I wish you could be the king of the DeDanaans once more. You alone possess the qualities of kingship. That worm, Breas, disgusts me."

Nuad frowned. The kingship was the one subject that caused his heart to twist with pain. He pondered daily on how the gods could have taken the leadership of the tribe away from him at such a crucial time. He knew he could order the affairs of the DeDanaans in a far superior manner to that of King Breas. Could the gods possibly have erred?

"Morrigan, if there is a way for the kingship to be redeemed, I swear I am as ignorant as a goat as to what it might be. Breas has bought time for himself by wedding the hapless Brigid, but something else will arise, some crisis with which he cannot cope, and he will seek to impose more punitive tributes on us. Nor must we forget the Fomorians who are emboldened and strengthened through his weakness."

"Well, let's not worry about it now, Nuad. These days of Samhain are the first respite from work we have had for a long time, and I for one, want to enjoy every minute of our leisure. Is the day fair?"

"Indeed, it is fair! The generous Sun God pours forth his warmth upon this gathering."

"Oh, good," she said, laying her comb aside and jumping up. "I'll dress quickly and then perhaps you will walk with me down to the river? I'm not quite ready to share you with the others."

Nuad smiled, pleased by her possessiveness. "Hurry then, the day awaits."

Morrigan and Nuad, hand in hand, left the safety of the royal enclosure and set off down the grassy hill, enjoying the warmth of the sun on their faces. In the distance, clouds cast blue shadows that stretched languorously across the low hills surrounding Druim Caein.

They walked in silence to the river that ran around the base of the Hill of Tara. Tall reeds covered part of the mossy bank, bending and swaying softly in the breeze. The river flowed at a moderate pace, but it was possible to sense its power as it moved toward the sea.

Nuad removed his cloak as they walked and now wore only a tunic and heavy boots of bull hide. He spread the cloak out on the driest spot they could find and Morrigan seated herself there, reaching up for his hand to pull him down beside her.

"What—" he started to say, but was stopped by her lips. It was a kiss as sweet as the first clover honey of the season, a girlish kiss full of love and tenderness. He pulled her into his lap and they sat like that for a while, her head resting on his shoulder. Nuad was surprised at how protective such a pose made him feel. Only the birdsong of midday and the churning of the river between its banks broke the stillness until Morrigan chose to speak.

"Dear one," she said, stroking her cheek with her forefinger, "the gods have bestowed a boon upon us. I hope the news of it will please you as it pleases me."

She slid from Nuad's lap, so she could look him full in the face. She wanted to read his expression, to see the joy she hoped to find there, when she told him.

"Nuad, my beloved, we are going to have a child."

Morrigan clapped her hands together gleefully, and for a brief moment seemed childlike herself. Her earth brown eyes sparkled.

Nuad looked at her with surprise, mentally calculating how long ago she had lain with Lugh. He had forgiven her transgression, taken her back into his heart, and his furs, had he not? And having done so, was he not obligated to treat the coming child as his own? Besides, it could be his child.

"By the gods! I cannot believe it, Morrigan," he said. "We have been together so long without issue that I can hardly grasp the fact of a child. When is it to be sent?"

"I have consulted with Diancecht and he estimates that six turnings of the moon will pass before our child comes."

He nodded seriously. In that case, there could be no doubt that he was the father. "I am overjoyed that we are to have a child," he said and covered her face with kisses. She was laughing, as was he, until suddenly, tears stung her eyes.

"What's wrong, my love?" Was there something else she had not told him? "You said you were happy."

"Oh, Nuad, I am, but it has been hard for me. With every moon when my bleeding came again, I felt sadness at failing you. I know I seemed not to care, but I did care . . . very much. I have lived in fear every day that you might turn from me in search of a woman who could give you a son."

Nuad's heart softened. He had never seen Morrigan expose her deepest self this way and he had a strong desire to reassure her.

"Morrigan," he said firmly, "you and I are fated by the gods to be as one, don't you know that? Even when no child was sent, I knew that we were bonded together for all time. I am sorry you ever felt a moment's fear about my turning away from you, for that could never be. You are mine and I am yours. Nothing can change that, child or no child."

She smiled at him, secure in the relief that only pregnancy could have given her. Even the old spells and incantations had failed in this matter. It was good to hear his dedication renewed.

They shared a long, loving kiss, and Nuad wiped away the trace of a single tear that had fallen down her cheek. "We will wed as soon as we return to Lough Gur," Nuad said. "I don't wish to make too big a thing of it, since I consider ourselves wed already."

Morrigan agreed. "We can have a small feast later, with my sisters and Diancecht as our guests. Can Ferfesa perform the ceremony for just the two of us?"

"We will have to have two witnesses, as the law demands," Nuad said, wondering caustically if those two people should be Queen Tailteann and her foster son. He shoved the corrosive thought aside and took Morrigan in his arms again.

Queen Tailteann was touched when Queen Brigid requested her presence at the royal table for the midday meal on the last day of Samhain. They had not spoken since the wedding toilette and Tailteann was eager to see her young friend. Brigid herself introduced the Fir Bolg queen to her new family.

"My lady Tailteann, this is my husband, King Breas," Brigid said proudly, gesturing toward the tall, handsome king. He smiled at Tailteann and she thought she saw a glimmer of interest when he said, "We have met before, under sadder circumstances."

"I remember well, King Breas, but that is behind us

now. I offer you congratulations and my wishes for a long and happy life with your wonderful bride."

"Thank you," he answered with a bland expression, "won't you sit here beside Queen Brigid?" His mother, Eri, sent him an angry glance. She would be glad when this Samhain festival was over and life could return to normal. She was certain she could assert her power over Brigid once all these people had gone back to where they came from.

"Lady Eri, may I present the Fir Bolg queen, Tailteann?" Brigid said, then added, "She has been friend to me since we made our home at Lough Gur."

Eri held her hand out for Tailteann to kiss it, as though she were the person of royal blood. Tailteann took her hand and held it for a moment before complying with the woman's unstated wish. For Brigid's sake, she bent and lightly touched her lips to Eri's hand, amazed by the display of jewelry she encountered there. When she straightened, she said as pleasantly as she could, "I am pleased to meet you, Lady Eri."

The king's mother looked at her with thinly disguised contempt. Breas could have no possible use for this queen of a defeated people. Eri had no idea how Brigid could have befriended a royal hostage, let alone had the effrontery to place her at the royal table. The girl had much to learn.

"A pleasure to meet you," Eri lied, "I have long been curious about you."

Tailteann smiled. "No more curious perhaps, than I have been about you."

Eri raised her eyebrows, surprised at such a retort from this mild-looking woman. She clapped her hands and the servants brought plates heaped with food for those seated at the royal table.

When she was served, Tailteann looked down at the plate in front of her with dismay. How could she touch all of this knowing how little there was going to be at Lough Gur this winter? It seemed a criminal waste to her even if it was Samhain. The gods could not be pleased with such greedy inequity.

"What's wrong?" Brigid whispered, "Don't you like boiled otter?"

"It's not that, Brigid. I'm just not very hungry."

Tailteann turned her dark eyes on the happy bride, feeling fear for the naive girl well up inside of her.

As night fell the servants lighted the cressets along the processional way that would take the faithful into the clearing near the river where the Samhain sacrifice was to be offered. Lugh caught the familiar scent of resin coming from the cressets as he and Desheen walked past, hand in hand, and his stomach turned.

"It will soon be time to go into the sacred circle," he said grimly.

"I know. It's a very moving ceremony, isn't it? I always feel the presence of the gods before it is over."

Lugh looked at her, surprised that she was not of the same mind about the cleared circle that he was. "I hate it," he declared. "I will never be able to come to the closing Samhain festival without pain. It was in the Samhain season when you landed on Innis Ealga, that the priests rendered one of my best friends, Rury, thrice dead and sent his spirit into the river."

"What?" Desheen asked in astonishment. "You mean they really killed him?"

"They did," Lugh replied, "and his own father was the priest who presided over the sacrifice."

"Oh, Lugh, that's horrible. How could you bear to watch such a thing?"

Lugh was confused. If Desheen felt the presence of the gods so strongly, how could she think the actions of the priests horrible?

"Did you care for Rury very much?" she asked.

"He had been my friend since I was four summers old. Sometimes he was a pest, but he was always my friend. I know it sounds foolish, but I have the idea that his spirit will be waiting for me tonight beside the river."

"Perhaps it will, but that wouldn't be a bad thing, would it? Not if you were friends."

"Rury's spirit may be angry with me. I should have stopped the priests before they sacrificed him, but I did nothing."

"What could you have done, Lugh?"

"Nothing. There was no way for me to stop it." He looked at Desheen and said, "The only other person who knows how much Samhain upsets me is my mother."

"And she doesn't think your feelings are awful, does she? No DeDanaan would ever think less of you for feeling this way, Lugh, nor do I. Our tribe has not practiced human sacrifice for many generations."

"You don't?" he asked in astonishment. "What then, is to be done when we get to the sacred circle?"

"All the boys of fifteen summers put wickerwork cages over their heads and then they jump over three holy fires. That's all. It's symbolic of the old ways when firstlings were locked in big cages and sent, thrice dead, to be consumed by the flames. The symbolic offering must be just as pleasing to the gods because they seem to favor us as much as they did before."

Lugh was dumbfounded. Why had no one told him this? In all the instruction Cian had given him about the ways of the DeDanaans he had never mentioned that their sacrifices to the gods were symbols only. Lugh felt enormous relief wash over him.

Desheen's fingers curled over his. "I'm glad you told me this," he said. "It makes going into the place of the sacred circle to call upon the dark nature of the gods much easier for me. I hope that one day all tribes will be spared, as many generations of DeDanaan boys have been already." He was thinking of the Fir Bolgs on the islands and wondering which of them would not live to see the morrow.

"Well, I've got to go get ready for the ceremony, Lugh. I don't want to be late. Where shall I meet you?"

"Mother and I will stop by your house on the way to the woods. Hurry," Lugh said, "there's not much time left."

Desheen smiled at him and ran off, knowing that he was watching her go.

Desheen worked rapidly but carefully at her toilette, combing her hair, rubbing black walnut oil into her eyelashes and eyebrows so they would gleam. She pinched her cheeks until they had a healthy pink glow, eschewed the ruam pot, and adorned herself with her best armlets and finger rings. Then, she slipped a pale pink woolen tunic over her head, being careful not to muss her hair. Her cloak was the natural warm brown color of the wool taken from the different kind of sheep the DeDanaans had found living on Innis Ealga. It complemented her fair complexion beautifully and it pleased her because she did so want Lugh to think she was appealing. She fastened her cloak with a silver pin, then left her dwelling to await Lugh and his mother.

She was surprised to find Aibel waiting for her.

"Hello," Desheen said when Aibel approached. "It's going to be a lovely evening for the Samhain fire, isn't it?"

In stark contrast to Desheen's amiability, Aibel drew near to her and seized her arm harshly. She put her face close to Desheen's, her eyes wild and angry.

"Your flesh is unclean," she hissed. "You must pay for your wickedness. The gods tell me so."

Desheen pried Aibel's fingers from her arm and leapt back in shock. "What is the matter with you?" she cried.

"If you go into the woods tonight with Lugh, the gods will take your life" Aibel whispered. "Take your life, do you hear, your *life*."

She reached out and attempted to take Desheen's arm again, but the brown-haired girl twisted away from her grasp. "Go away and leave me alone! You are mad."

Lugh and Tailteann appeared around the round house just as Desheen's alarm was becoming genuine fear. Desheen turned to them with pleading eyes.

"Oh, no," Tailteann whispered. Aibel grasped wildly at Desheen's clothing as the charioteer backed away from her. Lugh stepped between them and removed Aibel's hand from Desheen's cloak.

"Here now," he said, "what's going on?"

"I don't know, Lugh," Desheen answered. "I was just standing here when this girl—"

"You will die with her, Lugh of the Longhand. You and she must be punished for your transgressions. Tonight, in the forest, the gods will punish you." Aibel spoke now in a dull, monotone, in a voice so low it was difficult to hear her.

"Come on, Aibel. Leave this girl alone. You don't know her, she has done nothing to you. If you are angry, talk to me."

He took Aibel's hand and pulled her roughly away from Desheen. Aibel began to scream as she had on the

mountain above the Plain of Moytirra following the burial
of King Eochy.

"I'll go get Airmead," Queen Tailteann said quickly,
"she is the only one who can handle Aibel when she is
like this. Take care of her until I get back, Lugh. Be careful."

Tailteann was back with the physician in a short time,
and the two of them coaxed the still-screaming Aibel to
return to the medicine house with them.

"What was all of that?" a shaken Desheen asked Lugh
when they were alone.

"I'm sorry, Desheen. Aibel has been growing stranger
and stranger. She says she hears the god talking to her inside her head. Almost from the time the DeDanaans
landed on Innis Ealga it seems that Aibel has heard the
voices. My grandfather thinks there are demons in her
spirit, but my aunt Airmead argues that she is ill. I don't
know who is right. I only know that something is very
wrong with her and you must be careful. What did she
say to you before we got here?"

Desheen turned her big eyes on Lugh. "She said that I
would die in the forest tonight."

"Oh, Desheen," Lugh said dejectedly, "I am sorry.
Aibel has never hurt anyone before but she has many battle skills. Don't leave my side tonight, all right?"

Desheen tried to lighten the moment. She suspected
that although something was obviously wrong with Aibel,
a good part of the confrontation they'd just had was occasioned by jealousy over Lugh.

"I hadn't planned to leave your side, Lugh. I like it
next to you too much for that! Don't worry about your
friend. She is with the physician so she won't cause any
more trouble for us tonight. Besides, I can take care of
myself."

Lugh and Desheen walked to where the Samhain procession was forming and fell into step behind the priest,
Ferfesa, who chanted a prayer to the Sun God, Bel, asking him to defeat Mog, the god of evil and want, and return the DeDanaan tribe to a condition of plenty.

Upon arriving at the river, the priests ordered carts
bearing firewood and turves to be brought into the sacred
circle. Lugh, filled with his new knowledge, leaped for-

ward, eager to help lay the materials that would soon become the blazing flames of Samhain that would keep the hearths of Innis Ealga burning throughout the long, dark days of winter.

He watched the rest of the ceremony with great interest. Even though it was different from the Fir Bolg rites he had known all his life, it was similar enough that he was able to follow most of it and understand what was happening. But at the end, the priests did something Lugh had never seen done before. Ferfesa brought forth a waxen figure that had been shaped by priests, then carved into a perfect likeness of a warrior by the artificer, Creidne.

"Behold our enemy!" Ferfesa shouted, holding the figure up.

He walked around the perimeter of the clearing, holding the waxen figure high for all to see. Dark clouds passed in front of the moon, darkening the ceremonial site for a few moments. The effect caused a sharp intake of breath among the people.

"Oh, mighty Bel!" the priest cried. "Look down upon us this holy Samhain night. As you dissolve the old year and send us a new one, we pray that you will keep us safe during the interlude between the two."

The threatening clouds passed on and the moonlight emerged so bright that it was possible to see one's own shadow on the soft, clean earth of the circle. The tops of the tallest oaks barely swayed and the birds made no sounds.

"Hear us, mighty Bel!" the priest shouted as he threw the waxen image into the fire. He stood aside so all could see the god's pleasure.

Fire licked at the enemy warrior's upraised sword, consuming it quickly, causing the flames to leap higher than before. In seconds there was nothing of the waxen figure left to be seen.

"Praise be to Bel!" Ferfesa shouted.

From the back of the crowd, Aibel screamed so loudly as to be heard above the roar of the fire, and rushed straight toward Desheen, heedless of the hot, snapping flames that leaped skyward just behind the charioteer. Airmead came running down the path toward the Samhain circle in pursuit of her patient. She stopped when she saw what Aibel was doing, knowing she could not reach her in time.

Inside Aibel's head, the voices screamed like banshees, *Do it now! Now! You must destroy the enemy!*

Aibel flung the waxen likeness of Desheen that she had made into the fire. With the frenzied cry of a war witch on her lips, she bore down upon the charioteer, lunging to push her into the flames. Lugh picked up Desheen and swung her out of Aibel's path. Unable to stop herself, Aibel plunged headlong into the raging Samhain fire.

Chaos ensued. Lugh set Desheen down and ran to pull Aibel from the flames. He grasped her ankles but felt her struggle from his grasp. It seemed to him that she deliberately clambered into the heart of the enormous blaze. Only the gods could save her now, for surely he could not. He stood as one turned to stone, unmindful of his own burned hands, wondering why Aibel did not cry out as the searing flames engulfed her slender body.

PART THREE

Ours is no sapling, chance grown by the fountain,
Blooming at Beltaine, in winter to fade.

—Sir Walter Scott

Chapter Twenty-five

King Breas looked at Queen Brigid, fury blazing in his blue eyes. He stood menacingly close to her, his hands clenched into fists at his sides. His face was red; the veins in his neck stood out.

"Not another word, woman!" he hissed. "I'll hear no more from you. No more about the wisdom of your father, the great Dagda. I will run this kingdom as I see fit, without your interference ... or his."

Queen Brigid's round face was splotchy and as red with rage as her husband's. She would not back down from him. The matter was too important.

She lifted her chin and said, "Then you are a bigger fool than even I know you to be."

Breas struck her hard, across the mouth, while her words hung in the air between them. Her swollen, pregnant body reeled from his blow, but she did not fall. Blood trickled from her lower lip. Tears of pain and rage glistened in her eyes.

She looked at him with defiance and said, "You are despicable." Then she spit at him.

King Breas had just completed his toilette and was arrayed in his finest clothes in anticipation of the banquet he was about to host. To have the spittle of this pig-faced woman running into his eyes enraged him beyond all reason. He raised his mighty warrior's fist with deliberate slowness and hit her so hard he sent her reeling onto the furs stacked on the floor.

He felt no pity watching his wife fall. Marrying her to win the support of her father, Dagda the Wise, had been the most stupid mistake of his life. He smiled in satisfaction at his brutality.

Queen Brigid was stunned by the blow. She kept her face turned into the furs. She did not want to give Breas the satisfaction of seeing her weep, and she could not contain her tears. She felt her infant stir within her. Through the fog of pain came Breas's contemptible voice.

"Get up, you sniveling wench. The feast is soon to begin, and you will sit by my side in the hall as is your duty. If you disobey, I don't know what harm will befall you or your father, but I am sure I can think of something appropriate. Get up, I say, and make yourself ready to receive our guests." He grasped her arm and pulled her roughly to her feet.

The sight of her disgusted him. "I'll send in your woman," he said. "You look a fright." He stalked toward the door, pausing before he left. "Remember. No matter what happens in private, in public you will act the queen."

When the door slammed behind him, Queen Brigid gave into the pain in her face and in her heart. She sank back to the floor, sobbing softly. She buried her face in the furs so no one could hear and wept with great wracking heaves of her shoulders, lamenting for the thousandth time the day she became the bride of King Breas the Beautiful. Believing that no man would ever want her, she had been far too quick to say yes when the handsome Breas asked for her hand.

When her grief was spent, she continued to lie on the furs, her breath coming in ragged gasps. Her life with Breas was an intolerable burden. He showed his contempt for her in many ways but never before today had he struck her. She felt trapped, wondering if death was to be her only escape from him.

Her child turned over. Brigid placed her hand across her abdomen to soothe the infant, and realized that death was not a viable option for a woman who was to give birth within three turnings of the new moon.

She remembered how upset her father had been when he learned that they were to be among the banished at Lough Gur. She had not minded going there for herself, but it hurt her father deeply. Breas could have sent no clearer insult to the well-loved and respected chief of the council that had made him king.

Breas has made nice speeches, saying Dagda was to retain his title and all due respect was to be paid him, but in fact his intent had been to diminish the wise old man's prestige and influence. Brigid reproached herself now for ever believing that she could influence Breas to raise her father back to his former prominence.

She lifted her hand and tentatively touched her bruised face. She could feel her eye swelling. Tears gushed forth anew. She tried to remember the warmth of her father's comforting touch but the pain in her head blocked it. All she could think of was her miserable state as a captive queen. How could the gods have allowed her to come to such an end? Had they nothing better for her than this?

She sat up and ran her finger over her swollen lip, feeling the split. She touched it with her tongue and tasted salt. Was it blood or her own tears that she tasted? She searched in her fes for a handkerchief.

She blew her nose, and the effort caused her head to pound. She looked around, trying to focus her eyes, now sore from weeping. One eye refused to open. She felt it gingerly. *By the gods! What has he done to me?* she wondered.

The door opened and someone entered, but Brigid could not bring herself to look up. She was ashamed at having been brought so low and she hated for anyone, even her maidservant, to see her like this. She tried to cover her face with her hand.

Dagda the Wise stood looking down at his daughter, pity filling his heart. He saw a woman great with child, sitting awkwardly on the furs meant for sleeping. Her mouse-colored hair, so like his own, hung in damp tangles across her face. "What is it, my darling girl," he asked, "why do you weep?" She reluctantly lifted her face to look at him with surprise, and he saw the cause of her tears.

"The bloody beast!" he shouted. "How could he have done this thing to you? I'll kill him with my own hands."

He dropped to his knees beside her and cupped her bruised and swollen face in his big warm hands. He examined her injuries gently.

"Thank the gods," he said, "no bones are broken." The split in her lip was deep, but the blood had clotted and was drying in a jagged maroon splotch. The skin around her eye was a raw crimson, tinged with blue at the edges.

"Father! Oh, I am so glad you are here . . . but—"

"Why?" Dagda asked in a choked voice. "Why did he do this to you?"

Brigid began to cry again, and Dagda took her in his arms. He cradled her as he had when she was a small child with a skinned knee. He smoothed her hair and crooned words of comfort to her.

"There, there, my darling girl. You are safe now, my lamb. We won't let him hurt you again. There we are now. You are going to be all right, no more tears now. No more tears, my girl."

Rage shone from his eyes. The king would pay dearly for what he had done. He was brute, not man and this crime would not go unpunished.

Slowly Brigid quieted, soothed by the dear and familiar touch of her father. It was possible to believe for a little while, as she had as a child, that her father could set all things right again.

She told him of her quarrel with the king, hoping her halting account made sense. She had to struggle for each breath, so drained was she by her fit of weeping.

"Oh, Father, King Breas is even now planning to receive the wicked Fomorian king, Balor, as his honored guest," she said. "I insisted on knowing how he could consider doing such a thing and in his fury, he told me why. Oh, Father! He has betrayed the DeDanaans. He told me why he demands so much tribute from the people and it makes me sick at heart." She paused to gather her wits, now eager to tell her father everything.

"I have been deeply troubled since I came to Druim Caein and saw the tribute collectors bringing the bounty into court, yet there was no more wealth here than there was in Ulster or at Lough Gur. It made me very suspicious and even before Breas confessed his misdeed, I had guessed at what becomes of the wealth of the DeDanaans," she said.

Drawing a deep breath to prepare for the worst, Dagda asked, "What does he do with the tributes, child?"

Brigid looked at him imploringly with her one good eye. "He gives the wealth of the DeDanaans to Balor of the Evil Eye! Breas admitted to me that in the very first year he was king he tried to buy our safety by bribing the Fomorian king. He said he believed that Balor would cease the raids on our coastal settlements if he paid him a handsome sum. It worked for a short time, but soon, the Fomorians were not content with the size of the bribes, and they demanded more. Always more. Now their threats about what they will do to Breas if he does not accede to their latest demands, have grown to the point that Breas is a desperate man."

She paused to blow her nose again. "It was a Fir Bolg who led them here to Druim Caein, the heart of our kingdom. The king of the Fomorians has grown so emboldened that he and a small party intend to pay us a diplomatic visit this very day. Balor has sent a messenger with the demand that Breas set up a royal banquet for him. Breas is so terrified of him that he has agreed to do it . . . to honor the one who would destroy us!

"I begged Breas not to debase himself or our people by honoring Balor, but he would not listen. I tried to tell him what you have always taught about the health of a society being dependent upon the honor of the king, but I'm afraid it only made him more furious with me. That's when he struck me. Breas is so fearful of the Fomorian king that it is hard for me to remember that he was once a strong warrior, a champion of the DeDanaans. I hate Breas, Da! I do. I hate him!"

"I do too, my darling," Dagda said grimly. But what could he do to help his beloved daughter? What could they do together, to help the DeDanaans? He sighed, wishing he possessed the wisdom his people said he had.

"Breas says that I must sit with him at the feasting table to greet Balor, but, Da, I would rather die than dishonor my people like that." Brigid's words were still shaky from her weeping.

"Let us think on that a moment, Brigid. Who would be dishonored if you were to join him, making no effort to hide your injuries or your contempt for Balor? Your presence would shame Breas, not yourself. By refusing Balor your hand in greeting you could make it very clear to all present that he is undeserving of honor. Could you do it, my dear? Sit on the platform with the man who beat you?"

Slowly Brigid nodded yes. "I could, if it will shame Breas and bring dishonor to our enemy. Will you be in the feasting hall, too, Father? I don't know if I'm strong enough to do it alone."

"Of course, you are, Brigid. You are as strong as stone, you always have been. I will be in the hall if I possibly can be, but you know that Breas's guards will attempt to keep me out. You should have seen how I was greeted when I arrived here a short time ago. They treated me as though I carried the plague upon my back."

"You still haven't told me how you happened to come to Druim Caein, Da."

"Well, at the last rotation of the bards, the poet who had been here at the royal court came to Lough Gur and told us that you are with child. Without asking Breas's leave, I came to be with you. I have had much concern about your well-being, Brigid, as I have long sensed that all is not well."

"So Breas doesn't know that you are here yet?" she asked. "He is going to be very angry that you have come, the more so because you have seen what he did to me with his fists ... how he put his own child at risk, because of his low character. I no longer fear for myself, but you may be in danger, Father, and I have deep fear for my child. Breas can be very cruel."

By the time Brigid took her place in the feasting hall next to Breas, she was composed and regal in spite of her wounds. She had arrayed herself in her best tunic of bleached white wool and a fiery scarlet cloak. She wore a neck torque and bracelets of gold and a ring on every finger in imitation of Eri, but she had made no effort to conceal the bruises marring her plain face.

A collective gasp ran through the hall as people saw her face. Not one person was in doubt as to how their queen had been injured, for the angry shouting that came from the royal dwelling had not gone unnoticed. Their eyes flew to Breas's impassive face, then back to Queen Brigid's battered one.

She sat back slightly in her fur-covered chair, smoothing the folds of her cloak around her, satisfied that her child-swollen belly was sufficiently obvious under her unbelted tunic. But, to be certain, she patted the rounded bulge.

Dagda stood watching from the rear of the fine new feasting hall, his back against the wall. His angry eyes met the gaze of King Breas and it was apparent that the king was disconcerted by his presence. Breas set his beaker of ale down carefully so no one could see the trembling of his hand.

Chapter Twenty-six

The rays of the setting sun shone back from the calm surface of Lough Gur in a pale pink gleam. A soft breeze ruffled the tall reeds at the water's edge, then rose and wafted over the walls of the compound until it touched Tailteann's cheek where she was standing outside her round house in the sweet autumn twilight, barely aware of the beauty that lay before her. She squinted into the gathering dusk with the details of an idea tumbling around in her mind like stones before a rushing waterfall.

She saw Nuad come through the opening in the inner palisade and watched him stride toward her. Memories of earlier times were stirred as the fact of his handsomeness struck her anew. Nuad looked regal because he was too far away for her to see how threadbare his clothing was.

He was grinning broadly, nodding and speaking to the people he passed—all of whom responded with friendly greetings. It was obvious that he was still much loved and respected among the DeDanaans. There were many who rued the day he was lost to them as king. Seeing how popular he was convinced Tailteann that her idea was a good one; perhaps one sent by the gods.

Nuad came to her side, unaware that her eyes had been on him since he entered the enclosure. "Good evening, Tailteann. Enjoying the sunset?" he asked in his deep voice.

Tailteann replied so softly he had to bend toward her to hear her words. He thought she seemed to grow smaller with every turning of the moon.

"I was wondering what is keeping Lugh. You haven't seen him this evening have you?" she asked, pulling her thin, well-worn cloak a little tighter about her shoulders.

"Yes, as a matter of fact, I just left him and Cian. We have been practicing with the sling stones we gathered yesterday, but they are bound to be along shortly. Soon it will be too dark to see whether their stones find their marks. You know, Tailteann, Lugh is almost as skilled with the sling stone as he is with the javelin. I marvel at his skill as an athlete. He must have had the finest training."

She nodded proudly. "He is skilled. Since he was a small lad he was able to hunt with the men. I remember well when he was too small to even lift the heavy sling stones that he throws now with ease."

Tailteann remembered the Samhain fire that had taken Aibel's life and how far Lugh had come since then. "Diancecht deserves our deepest thanks for healing Lugh's poor burned hands. You are sure that he is as skilled with the sling stone as he was before he was hurt?"

"I am, Tailteann. I would not lie to you about so important a matter. One would never know from his performance that he had ever been burned."

"Thank you, Nuad. I do worry about him. It was all so horrible. I think it would destroy Lugh if he were to lose his ability to compete."

Nuad gave a hoot of laughter. "I don't think you need to worry about Lugh losing that! I've never seen anyone who wants to win more than he does. Lugh would never let a little thing like burned hands slow him down. I doubt if he'd even let something like this"— he held up his leather-covered stump—"stop him."

Queen Tailteann looked about them to see if anyone was near enough to overhear her words. "Nuad, I've had an idea I'd like to discuss with you. Do you have time right now?"

He glanced around the compound. Morrigan was nowhere in sight. "I do," he said. "What is it?"

"Before Dagda Mor left to go to Queen Brigid's side, he and I had a conversation in which he mentioned that it would be possible for you to be reinstated as king of the DeDanaans if you had two hands capable of movement."

"Yes, that is as true as it is impossible," Nuad replied briskly.

"Ah, but is it impossible, Nuad? I was watching Diancecht going about on the leg of bronze that Creidne,

Gobinu, and Luchta, fashioned for him, and it occurred to me that an artificial hand could be made for you. It would have to be fashioned from a lightweight material, copper, silver, or even gold, I suppose, or it would be too heavy to carry around all day."

"Of course, it would be possible to craft such a hand," Nuad said thoughtfully, "but the law requires that all of a king's limbs must have movement if he is to be considered unblemished. As skilled as our artificers are, they would never be able to breathe life and movement into a metal hand."

"I know, but I think there is a way. The artificers are very clever. Would you object if I were to discuss such a hand with them?"

Nuad smiled at the tiny Fir Bolg queen. Once she took hold of an idea, she was as tenacious as a hound.

"I was born to serve the DeDanaan tribe, Tailteann, you know that. If it were possible, I would be king once more in an instant. But it can never be. You have assumed a feat that would take a miracle to achieve."

"I know. But just suppose for a moment that Creidne and the others could restore your severed hand . . . and give the new one movement . . . would you be willing to become king if an uprising against the unjust Breas takes place?"

"Of course. But such a thing as a silver hand that moves can never be."

"I'm not saying that it can be done; it may be a foolish idea, but . . . don't laugh at me, Nuad. Dagda thought it was a good idea. I will talk to the artificers without delay. Please give my regards to Morrigan."

Nuad watched her walk away, not daring to let himself dream that his deepest desire could ever be realized. Still, the little queen had sparked his hope.

Talk of rebellion came up between Lugh and Cian on the combat field where they had thrown sling stones enough to fill a battle cart. Lugh's aim had improved with each toss of the heavy, flat stones, which were as deadly as any spear when thrown with precision.

As father and son watched, Lugh's last stone found its mark two lengths of an oak tree away from where it had been thrown.

"I'd like to send one of these stones straight at the king who oppresses us," Lugh said. "I still cannot get over the way Breas went back on his oath to Dagda about the bread board tributes. It took less than one cycle of the moon for him to break his word."

"The king's behavior is beneath contempt, Lugh. It sets me to thinking that the time has come for us to rise against him. If we wait much longer, our hardships will leave us too weak to fight him. I wish Dagda hadn't gone to Druim Caein when we need him here to help plan what must be done. Besides, Breas has shown us that he cannot be trusted and I fear for Dagda's well-being. Having Brigid in the royal household clouds her father's vision, I fear. We must form a secret council . . ." Cian paused a moment, then went on. "There are many able warriors here at Lough Gur who can be counted on to carry out the noble task of restoring harmony to the DeDanaans."

"What of me, Father? Would I be counted as a DeDanaan in such a council?" Lugh's tone was serious.

Cian turned his kindly eyes toward his son and smiled. "You are counted as a DeDanaan, Lugh. For in truth, you are one of us." Cian put his arm around his son, feeling the strength of the sinews in his sturdy shoulders. "Do you still have doubts about that?"

"No, Father. I have no doubts about it, it's just that I would never wish to do anything that would cause Queen Tailteann grief and I'm not sure she would approve of my participation."

Cian laughed. "In that case, rest your mind. Your foster mother has spoken of an uprising with me several times." His tone turned serious. "Queen Tailteann has a remarkable sense of the natural order, Lugh, and to her, the kingship is so clearly out of harmony with the gods, that there can be but one answer."

"I wasn't sure how strongly she felt about it. She is always admonishing me not to be impulsive about calling for an uprising, saying that deposing a king is such a serious matter that one must proceed slowly."

"Aye, Lugh, that we must. Would to the gods that such a task had not fallen to this generation of DeDanaans, but there it is, and we must rise to the call, I'm afraid.

"Come, let us be away to the cauldrons. There may yet

e a bone left for us latecomers and I'm hungry. Aren't
ou?"

"I'm always hungry these days," Lugh answered.

Cian looked at the young man who had been a boy
uch a short time ago yet was now willing to assume the
esponsibilities of a DeDanaan warrior in an uprising. He
knew it would not be long before Lugh would want to
ake to wife the beautiful young charioteer, Desheen. He
ighed heavily, saddened that the young lovers would not
ave a smooth path before them.

On the same evening that the new moon brought the
springtime season of Beltaine to Lough Gur, the unusual
arrival of a messenger from Druim Caein set the colony
abuzz. It was said that he bore a gift from the Dagda Mor
or his brother, Ogma.

For all the talk and excitement, when the gift was
opened it appeared to be no more than a simple art
object—a human figure carved from soft stone with hor-
zontal lines notched across its sides in irregular patterns.
Disappointed, the DeDanaans quickly lost interest and re-
urned to their daily tasks.

Ogma, alone, understood the significance of the object
he held in his hands. As children, he and Dagda had devised a method of communicating by scribing slashes,
first on sticks, and later on stones as their skill and ingenuity increased. Ogma knew the figure must bear news of
grave importance for Dagda to send a runner to Lough
Gur. He hurried back to his dwelling to decipher their
code.

Nuad and Cian exchanged glances, picking up simulta-
neously Ogma's urgency. "Cian, get Morrigan, Queen
Tailteann, Lugh, and Diancecht, and ask them to meet me
in the feasting hall. I will go to Ogma and see what this
is all about." Nuad was already walking toward Ogma's
dwelling as he spoke. Cian ran to fetch the others.

A short time later, the group Cian had assembled sat in
the feasting hall waiting for Nuad and Ogma to appear
and explain the mystery. The two men arrived and after
the greetings, Nuad assumed control of the meeting.

"It is not without reason that we DeDanaans have always called Dagda, Ruad Rohfessa," he said. "For he is,

indeed, a man of great wisdom. Hear the message he has sent to Ogma. Hear it, and let it renew in your hearts a dedication to right order."

Lugh felt his heart give a start. Nuad's words sounded like a call to action. What could have happened?

Ogma unrolled a tanned rabbit hide onto which he had transcribed the markings Dagda sent him. The scribe's deep, rumbling voice commanded attention when he spoke.

"My friends," he intoned, "it grieves me that I must pass on such a message as I have received from my brother, but you must know what King Breas is doing with the tribute he takes from us. Dagda reports that he gives it to the Fomorian Balor of the Thousand Blows, as a bribe for not raiding our settlements."

"But," sputtered Morrigan, "our settlements are continually raided!"

She looked to Nuad whose green eyes were grim, his strong jaw set in anger. Lugh and Cian exchanged surprised looks. Quietly, Tailteann said, "That explains the want we saw in Druim Caein last Samhain, why they had nothing left for themselves."

Cian rose. "I would speak, sir. Last year when King Breas imposed such a heavy boroma, I thought he had gone about as far as it was possible to go with tributes. I was willing to back away from talk of rebellion when Dagda struck a deal with him, but when the king broke his word and took from us the bread board tribute, it was enough to prompt me once more to serious thoughts of uprising. I tell you now, that the knowledge that we mighty DeDanaans are being brought to our knees in the service of the demon Fomorians is too much. We must rebel against this unjust king, and we must do it now!"

Lugh was on his feet, eyes shining, passion tinging his words. "My father is right! We must rise against Breas! We cannot allow him to take more than half of our milk, cheese, butter, and oats, and give them to the Fomorians. He will want our babies, next! I say that we must rise and unseat him!"

Diancecht nodded in agreement. "The message that Dagda sends makes it clear to me that we must rebel. To do nothing would be an insult to the good sense that the gods have given us. Breas cannot be allowed to squander what little we have on bribes to Balor, bribes so ineffective that our coastal settlements remain in constant danger."

Nuad found not a single dissenter among them. "It is agreed then, that the time has come to gather like-minded DeDanaans into a battle council to plot the overthrow of King Breas?"

When the hearty hurrahs died down, Queen Tailteann rose to speak. "A word please, Nuad. You recall our conversation about the artificers?"

He acknowledged that he did, feeling a shiver of anticipation when he saw the triumphant smile Tailteann sent his way. She turned to address the others.

"I have consulted with the artificer, the smith, and the wright, and they have consented to make for Nuad a new hand of silver. It is their belief and mine, that it can be made with movable joints."

She paused before spelling out the importance of such a deed. "DeDanaan law has no provision that the king's limb be made of real flesh and blood; only that it have movement. I propose that the artificers be instructed to begin work immediately on such a hand and that we look upon the coming uprising as a means to the restoration of a just king, more than simply the unseating of a bad king."

She sat down, her cheeks flushed. Morrigan stared at her in openmouthed amazement, a little resentful that she herself, had not had the brilliant notion.

With the authority of his advanced years, Diancecht pronounced Tailteann's idea a gift from the gods, and when the meeting broke up, a measure of hope had been restored to all those present.

Lugh alone felt apprehensive, even a bit angry. Why did Tailteann always have to look out for the welfare of Nuad? It didn't seem fair that one man should rise to become king of the DeDanaans twice in one lifetime. Events were pushing Lugh to the realization that he himself wished for a position of greater leadership in the tribe. Once more, he found himself jealous of Nuad. He left the meeting hall, wishing it were not too cold and dark for him to retire to his glade by the stream, for he had need of solitude.

Chapter Twenty-seven

"Macha!" Neimain called across a broad green glen that was littered by white ewes in various stages of motherhood. "Come, I need help. This one is going to have two!"

The wolfhound at her side pricked up his ears, looked around, sniffing the sharp springtime air, then settled back on his haunches as he recognized Macha coming toward them.

She came on the run to a hollow shaded by a thorn tree where Neimain was assisting a big ewe. The sheep's eyes were dull as she labored to bring forth her offspring, bleating as though pleading to be relieved of her burden.

Macha bent down, out of breath, and examined her. "Uh-oh, this doesn't look good. We're going to have to turn one of these lambs."

Neimain nodded. "I feared we might. Well, come on, let's do it. I don't think the mother can stand this much longer." Macha cast off her cloak and rolled up the sleeve of her tunic while Neimain put her arm around the ewe's neck to secure her for the discomfort that was to come.

Macha pushed her hand into the ewe and felt about, then grasped the legs of the lamb that was incorrectly positioned. She winced and cried out as a powerful contraction squeezed her arm painfully inside the birth canal. She waited for it to subside, then swiftly and efficiently flipped the lamb head over hoof. She withdrew her mucus- and blood-covered hand and Neimain released her grip on the panting ewe.

"Good! That ought to do it. Macha, are you all right?" Neimain asked with concern.

"I'm better than she is." Macha laughed, gesturing toward the heaving ewe. She reached for a rough cloth that had been made from the bast of the oak tree, and tried to rub the muck from her arm.

Within a short time the ewe gave birth to one of the tiniest lambs the sisters had ever seen. "By the gods! It's so little and weak, I don't think it can suckle," Macha said despairingly.

"Yes, it is too small. Take one of those cloths there and rub it clean. This mother can't take care of him herself."

Macha rubbed the lamb with a growing feeling of dismay. Even brisk rubbing was not eliciting much response from the tiny, feeble creature on the grass in front of her. She doubted that he would survive.

"Here comes the other one!" Neimain shouted and sat back on her heels to wait. This lamb was slightly bigger than the first and at a glance, the sisters could see that he was more robust.

"Now, maybe the mother can nudge this little one along. He's not responding well at all," Macha said, laying the first lamb in front of its mother.

The ewe looked too tired to hold her head up but she tried, licking at her newborn listlessly. "We can try to save it, I guess," Neimain said, "but it would mean taking it into the settlement and keeping it warm. It will die for certain if we leave it out here in the open."

Queen Tailteann drew near on her way down from helping with the lambing higher up the hill. "Our batch has all been born," she said. "Do you need any help here?"

"We have two more ewes that will deliver soon, but I think they are going to be normal births," Neimain replied. "Not like this one." She pointed to the twin lambs.

"Oh, twins!" Tailteann exclaimed. "That one is awfully small."

"We were just wondering if we should take him back to the compound and try to save him. It's not likely that we can do it even there, but he'll die for sure out here on the hillside."

"Let me take him back with me now," Tailteann said, slipping off her woolen cloak. She knelt and gently wrapped the motionless lamb in it. "He'll be beside the fire in no time. It's worth trying."

"Thank you," the sisters called to Tailteann's retreating form. "Good luck."

Tailteann walked as fast as she could, her passage impeded by the many ewes and lambs on the meadow. The little creature in her arms was awkward to carry. Even though he was too weak to squirm, his legs with their sharp hooves seemed to be sticking out everywhere, and she was glad when she reached the bottom of the slippery hill. She increased her pace and made straight for the path that led through the woods to the safety of the Hill of Knockadoon.

The towering trees, huddled so close to one another that little sky was visible, laid their shadows across the pathway, dropping the temperature inside the forest by several degrees. The queen stopped to rewrap the lamb in several thicknesses of her cloak, knowing how important warmth was to his survival.

She walked only a few steps before she was aware that something was walking parallel to her, hidden by the trees. She stopped to listen. Nothing could be heard but the sigh of the wind through the new leaves. She walked on. Again she heard a rustle of movement on the forest floor. She looked into the darkness between the trees and this time she saw several pairs of burning yellow eyes a short distance from her. Wolves!

She ran as fast as she was able but she could hear them running beside her in the shadowy places, keeping pace. Why hadn't she thought to bring a wolfhound down the hill with her? She knew better, but she had been careless and now she would pay for her lapse. She knew the clever wolves would simply wait for her to tire before the pack closed in. What could she do to save herself and the lamb? She was virtually trapped and helpless. All she could think to do was scream, hoping someone might hear, so she ran, clutching the little lamb to her bosom, screaming for help till she thought her lungs would burst.

In the clearing where Lugh, Nuad, and Cian were tossing sling stones, Queen Tailteann's cries were heard. Nuad was the first to respond.

"It's Tailteann," he said dropping his sling stone and bolting toward the sound. "She's in trouble."

Lugh and Cian threw their stones down to follow him. The terror in her cries told them she was in mortal danger. They crashed through the woods, branches snapping back in their faces as Nuad ran like a man possessed in front of them. They leaped over stones, dodged trees, trying to follow the direction of Tailteann's screams. Lugh thought his heart might explode from the effort and the fear that had it pumping so wildly.

Tailteann, weeping from desperation, was surrounded by circling wolves, salivating at the sight of the lamb. Nuad erupted out of the trees onto the path and ran toward her without slowing his pace. All she could see were the yellow curved fangs the animals bared at her, their lolling red tongues, and their eyes, their terrifying yellow eyes. There was no breath left in her for screaming.

Nuad emitted a loud cry as terrifying as that of any war witch, and raised his knife high in his right hand. He rushed heedlessly into the pack of wolves, slashing savagely at them. When the startled, snarling animals moved back from Tailteann to avoid his blows, he wrenched the lamb from her arms and threw it onto the path behind them as far as he could. The alert wolves yelped and ran after the helpless little creature, saliva dripping from their tongues.

Nuad said, "Run, Tailteann, let's go. I'm right beside you."

Cian and Lugh emerged from the woods in time to see Nuad throw the lamb to the wolves. They ran behind the fleeing pair until they reached the relative safety of the clearing that ringed the Hill of Knockadoon. No one spoke until they were well clear of the forest.

"Mother, are you hurt?" Lugh gasped, catching up to her.

Tailteann shook her head, too winded to speak. She stopped and drew air deeply into her aching lungs, holding her hand to her chest. It was then that she realized the blood of the tiny lamb was on her. She knew his scent was on her as well, and she wanted to get as far away from the woods as she could.

"I'm all right," she said breathlessly, "thanks to Nuad." She turned to look at him. "If you hadn't come when you did . . ." She burst into tears and both Nuad and Lugh moved to her side to comfort her. Their hands touched where they embraced her. Lugh felt only gratitude, with no residue of jealousy for the former DeDanaan king. His only thought was that Tailteann was alive and unhurt.

"When I think of what the wolves might have done to me ... Oh, Nuad ... I ..."

"Shh. Don't say another word. Let's get away from here before you attract any more wild beasts. What were you doing with that lamb in your arms anyway?"

"I thought I ... I ... could save ... the poor little thing," she said weakly, realizing that instead she had caused his death. They set off up the hill, Tailteann holding tightly to Nuad's hand on her right side, and to Lugh's on her left. Cian walked behind them, smiling, believing that many things had conspired this afternoon to heal the rifts within the DeDanaan tribe. It was as it had to be if they were to rise against Breas successfully. He hoped that at last, Lugh and Nuad would be able to work together.

The craftsmen sent word that the silver hand was complete on a day in Beltaine when the Sun God showed his face with a fierce warmth. It seemed an auspicious beginning for the serious undertaking that lay ahead.

Nuad asked the members of the battle council to meet in his dwelling to witness the wonder the artificers had wrought. The three craftsmen, Gobinu, Creidne, and Luchta were acknowledged masters in the arts of smithing and metalworking, so skilled that the bards often sang the praises of their work.

Nuad said what was on everyone's minds when he spoke to the three artists. "Well, men. Show us quickly, for my poor spirit can stand the suspense not one moment longer."

The lanky, long-limbed Gobinu carried a bundle wrapped in linen cloths. He smiled and dropped to his knees before Nuad, laying his bundle on the floor. With great care he untied the leather thongs binding it and parted the cloths, revealing a silver hand of such grace and beauty that a gasp arose from those assembled as though from a single throat.

Firelight danced on the surface of the hand, disclosing hundreds of intricate spirals etched into a harmony of design more beautiful than anything they had ever seen.

The craftsmen had begun with a deep silver cuff, modeled after the leather cuffs the bowmen used to protect their wrists. To that they had fastened layers of silver plates that resembled fish scales. It was in the fingers of the silver hand, however, that all the ingenuity and artistry of the craftsmen reached its peak. Each digit was made of three pieces of silver, jointed where living fingers had joints. The rivets Creidne made to bind the sections together were as small as the shamrocks that grew along shady riverbanks, delicate and fragile looking, but in reality the strongest parts of the hand. They had been inset so perfectly that none but the most discerning eye could have noticed them.

Each finger was decorated as intricately as the rest of the hand and were in themselves individual works of art. Long coiled wires of silver, originating within the hand, lay in neatly folded bundles at the top of the cuff.

"Beautiful, it is truly beautiful," Queen Tailteann breathed, eliciting a fiery look from Morrigan, who as her figure disappeared into maternity, had decided that she had endured quite enough of this woman's interest in her husband.

Nuad's eyes shone with wonder as he gazed at the hand, caressing it softly with his fingers. Finally, he raised his eyes to the smith and said, "Please show the others."

Gobinu rose and made his way slowly around the circle, letting the council admire close up, the work that he and Luchta and Creidne had done for love of the DeDanaan people.

In consultation with the physicians, a new type of padding had been devised to go over Nuad's stump in the hope that the silver hand would be comfortable to wear. Diancecht moved slowly to the king's side and said, "Hold out your arm, my lord."

The former king did as he was asked and the old physician carefully loosened the leather thongs holding the cap over his wrist. Underneath was a layer of soft, unspun wool that Diancecht removed, exposing Nuad's naked, wounded wrist. He noted with satisfaction that the scar was neat and straight. He turned to Creidne and took the new padding from him. He wrapped it gently around Nuad's wrist. When he was satisfied, he stepped aside to make room for Luchta.

The wright took up the silver hand and slipped it onto

Nuad's wrist. It fit perfectly. While Luchta held the cuff in place on Nuad's arm, Creidne and Gobinu uncoiled the long silver wires and slipped them into a tube woven of the softest wool. This they placed around Nuad's neck and arranged down the length of his right arm, securing it with flexible bands of wool at his elbow and his wrist. They allowed each strand of silver wire to dangle a short distance beyond the end of the tube. Nuad looked at them quizzically, but asked no questions.

Creidne took five silver charms in the shape of different animals from his fes and threaded the wires into openings in each of the small creatures. He tied each wire off tightly, and stepped back to admire his handiwork.

"When you wish to make the hand move, Nuad," he said, "all you have to do is bend up the fingers of your right hand until they grasp the charm that corresponds to a given finger of your new hand. A slight tug on the charm will cause that finger to curl."

Nuad's hearty laugh filled the house as he delightedly grasped one of the silver charms and utilized for the first time, the cleverness of the craftsmen's design. He chose the charm that looked like a boar, one of the most dangerous beasts in the forest.

"By the gods! It works!" he exclaimed as his new silver forefinger slowly moved. "I won't be winning any contests of skill with this hand, but it moves. By the gods! It will be my joy to wear it as I lead our people to take the kingship from Breas, the unworthy!"

Morrigan moved her swollen body awkwardly to Nuad's side and grasped his silver hand in her own two hands. She smiled broadly as she examined it.

"The gods have willed this, Nuad," she whispered. "You will once more be our king." She turned to beam at the metalworkers.

Nuad spoke to them. "Surely, the gods have guided your hands, for you have made here a thing of such beauty and utility that it is a perfect marriage of art and science. This hand may be the means of restoring health and security to the DeDanaans and for it, my wife and I shall be forever grateful."

Tears of joy were in Morrigan's eyes when she kissed Nuad full on the lips and said, "You are worthy to be king, with or without this silver hand, my husband. I am glad for the restoration of your power."

Lugh felt a shiver of excitement run down his spine. Could it be that the hand of the gods had actually been involved in making the silver hand? For surely it seemed a miraculous thing. He looked closely at Nuad, whose white hair was tied into a neat bundle at the nape of his neck. He looked much older than he had the first time Lugh saw him, but he had an aura of kingship about him that could not be mistaken.

Lugh looked at his mother, whose black eyes were fastened on the blazing silver hand as though it were an object of worship. This had all been her idea. Nothing would have happened but for her. His heart warmed with pride.

Nuad spoke solemnly to the artificers. "If we are successful in attaining the kingship, it will be to you three that we owe everything. When I am once more king of the DeDanaans, you will be richly rewarded. To the gods and to you, I give thanks."

Creidne, Luchta, and Gobinu, accepted Nuad's gratitude humbly, but it was observed that when they left the dwelling they were all beaming with pleasure and even the taciturn Creidne was talking excitedly.

Lugh's excitement and high spirits turned sour after the artificers left Nuad and Morrigan's dwelling and he realized that Nuad's public expression of gratitude was not going to extend to Queen Tailteann.

Before he took leave of Nuad he walked to his side and bent his head close to his ear to hiss, "And what do you give to my mother, the one who conceived the idea of a silver hand in the first place? Do you have not one word of thanks for her?"

Nuad was startled by Lugh's angry remark. He looked at him quizzically, then saw that Morrigan was watching them closely. He chose not to answer Lugh, regretting that there was something between himself and Lugh that was never going to allow them to rest easily.

Chapter Twenty-eight

Five days after the silver hand was bestowed upon Nuad, Brig came running onto the training field in search of his master. His usually impassive face showed concern when he spoke.

"Sire, the physician Diancecht bids you to return to your dwelling."

"What for, Brig? We're right in the middle of an archery exercise."

"It's the lady Morrigan. Diancecht says she needs you by her side."

"It isn't the baby, is it?" he asked, alarmed. "It's much too early."

Brig nodded yes. "I fear it is. Morrigan has been complaining of pain since shortly after you left this morning."

"Lugh," Nuad called, "tell the others why I had to leave, will you? My wife is ill and I must go to her."

In truth, Morrigan had felt the first pangs of childbirth in the early hours of the preceding night and had eased herself out of the furs to prepare a potion of lavender and dried primrose petals. It was the only antispasmodic she had in her collection of herbs, but it had not helped; the pangs continued. By midmorning they could no longer be denied and she was forced to summon her colleague, the physician, Diancecht.

He came to her quickly and had sent for Nuad when he realized that the birth was imminent. While the servant was away, Diancecht placed intricate woad markings across Morrigan's distended belly.

"The sacred signs are in place, Morrigan. You must have no fear, for you are protected," he told her.

Morrigan nodded. "Open the door and let the light in," she said, "I have to have the light."

She could hear the chirping of wrens and the sigh of the wind moving through the treetops, but try as she might, she was unable to feel the presence of the old gods. The small house was close and dark with the only illumination coming through the doorway as the Sun God shone intermittently through rapidly moving banks of clouds journeying to the sea.

A wave of pain engulfed her and she tried to concentrate, as Diancecht had instructed her to, on her memory of the journey to Innis Ealga across the heaving waters of the northern sea. She knew there was risk for a woman of her years to be bringing forth a firstborn, even at the appointed time. And this day was far too early. Something had gone very wrong, indeed.

She bit her lip and tried to imagine herself skimming lightly over the surface of the sea, rising gracefully with each wave as it crested, then falling back to await the next one.

The old physician bathed her brow with cool rose-scented water and said soothingly, "You do well, my dear." Yet, he wished desperately that the old ones had left him some knowledge of how to stop the birth process once it had begun.

Nuad's large frame blocked the light as he came into the house. He went directly to Morrigan's side and took her hand, trying to convey confidence with his broad grin, but she could feel the trembling in his touch.

"Morrigan, my love. They tell me that the time has come for our child to be born."

"Oh, Nuad! I'm so glad you're here. It is too soon, much too soon for this child to come into the world. Nuad ... I'm afraid." Tears squeezed from her tightly shut eyes as another contraction seized her, and she could speak no more.

Nuad had respect for Diancecht but he worried that the physician had become too frail and his medical knowledge rooted too firmly in the old ways.

"I think you need assistance here," he said to the old man. "I will send Brig to bring Airmead to you."

Diancecht fixed him with his brilliant blue eyes. "Lady Morrigan has asked that only I attend her, sir. I don't need assistance. It is too soon, I know, but the birth seems to be progressing normally." He was offended that Nuad appeared to have lost confidence in him.

"We can't be too careful when it comes to Morrigan," Nuad said, and sent Brig off to find Airmead.

"No, Nuad, please," Morrigan begged when the pain had passed. "I want only you and Diancecht with me now. Please, tell Brig not to bring Airmead."

"Hush, my darling, I'm doing what is best for you. Don't you fret." He bent and kissed her cheek, as another violent contraction gripped her.

Morrigan's breath came irregularly and Nuad was overcome with the fear of losing her as he had his first wife under the same circumstances. Was he cursed by the gods that the woman he loved should be killed by his seed? He rested his head in his hands and looked on the verge of tears.

Diancecht saw Nuad's dismay and said, "Nuad, will you step outside with me for a moment, please?"

The old physician was stern with the man who had once been his king. "We shall have none of that now, Nuad. Morrigan needs you to be strong, for as brave as she is, she is very frightened by what's happening to her. Her condition is delicate and she needs all the help you can give her. You will have time enough for fear after the birth has been accomplished. Do you understand what I am telling you?"

"Is Morrigan going to be all right?"

"I think so," Diancecht answered kindly.

"And the baby?" Nuad looked sharply at the old physician. "There's a problem with the baby, isn't there?"

"It's too early, Nuad, that's all. The infant will undoubtedly be very small, but I have no reason to think that our best efforts won't be successful. I have saved very small babies before. If Morrigan's milk is generous, we will make it. But that's not our problem yet. Right now, our task is to keep Morrigan's spirits up, to keep her from too much worry about the baby. Can you do that?"

"I can," Nuad said, ashamed of his weakness. "But this is much harder than going against an enemy one knows and understands. I am helpless here. There is nothing I can really do to help Morrigan."

"Yes, there is. You can put good cheer and confidence

back on your face before you return to the dwelling. Come, we will go to her side."

The moon goddess had risen high in the sky, casting her silver net over the stars that shone down on Lough Gur, before Morrigan was delivered. Diancecht had cause to give thanks for Nuad's mistrust because while he was swaddling the tiny infant boy, Airmead cried out.

"Da! There's another head here. Our work is not yet done."

The old physician handed Nuad his firstborn son, saying, "Here, wrap him in another woolen cloth, then in the fleece and take him close to the fire. Hold him close to your chest and don't let him in the way of any drafts."

The old man was clearly concerned because of the first infant's size, but the arrival of the second child would not await the completion of the swaddling.

Nuad stood as a man transfixed, gazing down at the son in his arms. The infant had a tiny red knot of a face and was smaller than anything Nuad had imagined. Fearful that he might hurt the baby, he took extreme care in wrapping him, a task made more difficult because of the silver hand to which he was not yet accustomed.

Morrigan screamed suddenly, and gripped Airmead's arm until the pressure of her nails drew blood. When she relaxed she had been delivered of another son, as small as the first one.

Nuad emerged from his dwelling near daybreak and was surprised to see almost the entire population of Lough Gur waiting for him around a large fire in the center of the compound. They turned to him expectantly and he realized they had waited all night for news. He felt remiss not to have sent word out as soon as his sons were born.

Sons. The gods astounded him by sending not one, but two sons to him and Morrigan. There could be no clearer indication that his life was under their guidance. If he'd had doubts before, the appearance of his second son quelled them. Twins were a rare, mystical occurrence and he was awed. He swallowed hard and cleared his throat before he spoke.

"People of the goddess Danu," he called loudly, "hear

you well how the gods have honored me this night. The
lady Morrigan has been safely delivered of ... we have
... there were two fine sons born to us!"

He would have said more about the will of the gods,
but a loud cheer stopped him. People grabbed each other
and danced in happy circles, slapping each other on the
back. They understood well that the man who would once
more be their king had been clearly marked by the gods
who sent him twin sons.

The priest Ferfesa shouted, "Praise be to the gods, for
they have sent us an omen of their favor." He fell to his
knees in front of the fire and lifted his hands to the fading
moon goddess. One by one, the others stopped their revelry and followed his example until the only DeDanaan
left standing was Nuad of the Silver Hand. His powerful
silhouette was drawn on the earthen floor of the compound by the leaping, quivering orange flames in front of
him. Then he, too, slipped silently to his knees, and gave
abundant thanks to the gods of the sky for his great boon.
He ended with a prayer of thanksgiving for Morrigan's
safe delivery from harm.

Inside the dwelling, the cheering roused her from a
light slumber. She turned her head first to one side, then
the other, gazing with an undreamed of strength of emotion for the wee sons who lay beside her.

"Diancecht, have you ...?"

"Yes, my friend. Both boys wear the holy markings
upon their chests. The old gods watch over them."

She stroked the tiny red cheek of one of the infants
with her finger. It was as soft as the petals of the wild
roses she had gathered so often in the woods, and covered
with a pale blond down.

"They're so little, so helpless," she murmured. "Promise me you will stay close to them tonight."

"You have my promise, Morrigan. Don't you worry.
Sleep now. I will stay right here beside you."

Morrigan closed her eyes and slipped once more into
slumber, wearing the age-old smile of female triumph.

One turning of the moon after the birth of the twins,
Cairbed the bard arrived at the Lough Gur settlement in
the early afternoon of a fine day. Word of the bard's ro-

ation to Lough Gur spread across the green hills so quickly that within a short time there was not a single inhabitant who did not know he was there.

The people were joyous, for Cairbed was as well liked as he was famed for his skill as a storyteller. They knew the show he would put on would take their minds away from their misery.

Cairbed could do handstands and cartwheels with ease and delighted the children who gathered around him by walking on his hands, bulging muscles rippling across his shoulders.

A mop of thick red hair fell across his high forehead, curling over the tops of his ears and down the back of his short, powerful neck. There were deep wrinkles around his gray eyes caused by the frequent laughter that had once come to him easily and often, before Brigid wed King Breas.

The law demanded that the king's court have at least one bard in attendance at all times and it had been Cairbed's misfortune to have been there during the wedding. It had broken his heart to see Brigid so sad, and now, with what Breas had done to her father, his heart was especially heavy. Tonight Cairbed meant to give his old friends a performance they would never forget. He inquired after Lugh's whereabouts, then went into the woods to seek him out.

As darkness descended upon the settlement, a parade of torches advanced from all around the lough as settlers from the outer farmsteads came to the Hill of Knockadoon. Flames flickered in the evening breeze as torchbearers lit the cressets around the filach fiadah where the bard was to hold forth.

People perched on stones, on the ground, in trees, wherever they could find a vantage point. Mothers held infants on their laps, while excited older children scampered about.

"Oh, isn't this grand, Lugh?" Tailteann asked, her face shining. "I am so glad Cairbed has come home." She paused, then remarked worriedly, "But I think he looks awfully careworn, don't you?"

"He told me he is worried about how bad things are at

Druim Caein, but he had a long journey too, and he must be tired."

"We could have waited for the storytelling until tomorrow night," Tailteann said. "We really shouldn't have insisted that he perform for us on the same day of his arrival."

"Actually, I don't think we could have stopped him, Mother. He wouldn't tell me exactly what he's going to do tonight but he has a surprise planned that he promises will capture our attention.

"I told him about the battle council, and he was pleased to hear that we will have the allegiance of the provincial chieftains when we march against Breas."

"Had he heard about Nuad's silver hand?" Tailteann asked apprehensively.

"Thanks be to the gods that he had not! Not a whisper of it has gone to Druim Caein. For once, every last DeDanaan has refrained from gossip. Cairbed laughed and laughed when he heard what the artificers have done. He really hates Breas and would be very happy to have Nuad restored to the kingship."

"Yes, but I think Cairbed's feelings are as much personal as anything. The love he holds for Brigid is as obvious as the red hair upon his head. Did he say how our young friend is?"

Lugh shook his head, his expression grim. He knew how it felt to be separated from one's love since Desheen had returned to Ulster after Samhain.

When there were no more torches to be seen on the hillside, Cairbed made his appearance. All talk and movement ceased as he walked through the crowd to the platform that had been erected for him next to a raging fire that would serve to light his performance and give warmth to his audience. When he reached the platform he stopped, then executed a perfect flip up onto the stage, landing steadily on his feet.

"Come gather round me, kinsmen!" he shouted in a loud, resonant voice. "I will tell a tale of lowly men in high places, of intrigue and deception, and the valor of the DeDanaan tribe!"

His first song was in celebration of great deeds done in bygone days: of battles won, of weddings, coronations, funerals, and treaties made. His sweet tenor voice soared above the heads of the people, rivaling the silver stars in the night sky with its brilliance. The song set the minds of the people on the glories of being a DeDanaan, plowing fertile ground for the seeds of the story he was about to sow.

When he set his harp aside, the assembly grew restive, waiting eagerly for the tale he would tell them. He picked up the bodhran and began to beat out a heavy, solemn rhythm. He did not name the people of whom he sang for there was no need. All present knew that he was singing of King Breas and Queen Brigid.

The first lines of his song were about vain beauty taking to wife a plain woman. His wit and biting satire met with roars of appreciative laughter from his audience, and frequent interruptions of applause. He paced his ballad carefully, his voice rising and falling, now building suspense, now retreating. Slowly the timbre of the tale changed and Cairbed became deadly serious, singing of a banquet in a new feasting hall of such a size it must rival the halls of the gods; a banquet where stony silence met the arrival of a queen whose face had been beaten bloody by her husband.

"Oh, no, Lugh, not Brigid. Oh! The poor girl," Queen Tailteann whispered, horrified.

Among the DeDanaans and the Fir Bolgs, only fratricide was a greater crime than striking a spouse or child, so Cairbed's song went straight into the hearts of the people whose angry voices rumbled in protest beneath the roar of the fire.

The manners of DeDanaan society were carefully prescribed, with guests seated at the king's feasting table in order of rank and behaving according to well-defined rules. So, when Cairbed's next verse concerned a rude and ignorant guest seated at the right hand of King Breas, he was able to change the mood of the crowd and evoke derisive laughter.

When he named the guest as King Balor of the Fomorians, the laughter grew uneasy then ceased altogether. Somewhere nearby an owl hooted in the dark as a counterpoint to the bodhran, and skiffs of black clouds drifted across the moon.

Lugh heard Morrigan's voice rise above the song as she

said to Nuad, "A king who raises his hand to his queen, then honors one who would destroy us, invites his own doom."

Cairbed heard Morrigan's words too, and his mind raced. He had to be quick on his feet tonight. He could feel the tension created by his song. The air around the platform grew smoky and close.

He took a deep breath and sang of how the great bronze ceremonial horns had trumpeted the arrival of King Balor as though he were a king worthy of great honor. Cairbed's gift enabled him to coax a chuckle from his angry audience by recounting how Balor and his party barged into the hall like bulls, nearly sending the door guards sprawling in the process.

He made fun of King Balor by describing his great height and girth. He said his body looked more like that of a beast than a man and that it was far too large a home for the small spirit it housed.

Cairbed laid the goatskin drum aside and stood to mime the removal of lice from a long and unkempt beard, all the while keeping one eye tightly closed. It was done so skillfully that none missed the parody of the slovenly, one-eyed King Balor. Cairbed pretended to stuff food into his mouth with both hands, wiping them on his cloak, then belching loudly.

The bard's stance and demeanor changed, and the audience understood instantly that he had become King Breas the Beautiful. He smoothed his hair, smiling into an imaginary mirror, then turned away, greatly pleased by his appearance. He drew back in alarm at the imaginary approach of the giant Balor, then held his nose and turned aside, waving frantically at the air to dispel Balor's foul odor. The pantomime drew raucous laughter and applause.

In a small obsequious voice meant to be that of King Breas, Cairbed said, "King Balor, you do me the honor of calling upon the humble DeDanaan court." He waved his fingers delicately, helplessly, in the air. "May I introduce to all here present, Balor of the Evil Eye, King of the Fomorians?"

Cairbed switched back to the Balor persona and stomped loudly to the front of the platform. He turned his back to the crowd and bent over, pulling his cloak to one side. He pretended to break wind with two mighty blasts from a pig's bladder concealed under his clothes. The DeDanaans roared with laughter and burst into loud applause as Cairbed bowed to thank them for their attention. *Now they know,* he thought with satisfaction.

The DeDanaans were slow to return to their homes after the performance. They stood around in clusters, speaking excitedly about the planned uprising against Breas. They were of one accord that the time was now. The latest affront to the dignity of the DeDanaan tribe could not go unchallenged.

"Tailteann!" Nuad called out, "I would have a word with you."

She and Lugh stopped to wait for him. "I want to talk with Cairbed in private, and I wondered if we might meet in your dwelling. You and Lugh will stay of course; I have no secrets from you about the revolt. It's just that Morrigan is weary . . . she is still weak . . . and meeting at my dwelling would not be such a good idea. We're not getting much sleep at night."

"Of course, Nuad," Tailteann said with a smile, "we would be pleased to have you, wouldn't we, Lugh?"

Lugh said nothing, but the other two went on talking as though he had agreed. "And how are the babies?" Tailteann asked, "Have you found names for them yet?"

"As you know, we had planned to call the one we expected Tadgh, but it has been hard to agree on another name. I think we have finally settled on Ultan. Do you like that?"

"Oh, I do." Queen Tailteann tried it out: "Ultan. Yes, it has a fine ring to it. Well done, Nuad."

"It was Morrigan's idea. I'm afraid I can't take credit for it. Well, if you're sure it's no bother, Cairbed and I will join you shortly."

"No bother at all. I'll just run along and set the water to boil for tea. I do have a bit of ale left that I've been saving for a special occasion. Perhaps this is the time to bring it forth?" There was a question in her voice.

Lugh looked at Nuad who obviously understood the implication in her tone. The big man nodded his shaggy white head. "Aye, Tailteann. The time has come."

* * *

The compound on the top of the Hill of Knockadoon was as silent as a cairn when Nuad and Cairbed finally left the dwelling of Tailteann and Lugh. The moon goddess was but a tiny silver crescent in a black sky from which all stars had fled. Their footsteps were guided by the reflected light of small fires along the perimeter of the wall, built to keep wild creatures away.

"Your information is invaluable, Cairbed. Without your journeys back and forth to the settlements and the royal stronghold, we at Lough Gur would remain largely ignorant of what happens there," Nuad said. "I was afraid when Dagda didn't come back as expected that some trouble had arisen, but I never dreamed that Breas was holding him prisoner."

"There can be no other word for it, my lord. Dagda repeatedly took the king to task for his treatment of Brigid and they quarreled bitterly on the night before I left Druim Caein. I left so early that the morning mist was still thick, but I am certain that I saw Dagda with a guard over him, carrying heavy bags of earth up the ditch bank that is to serve as the outer defense of Breas's new palace." He paused to let this outrage sink in.

"I have no way of knowing Breas's intentions, but he will kill Dagda with continued hard labor for which he is totally unsuited, a cup and a bowl being the heaviest things he ever lifted in his life."

Nuad smiled a bitter, wry, smile. He loved Dagda like a father and was stunned that his old friend should be treated so basely.

"He's not suited for labor, that's for certain. I feel good about our plan to dethrone the beautiful one. By the gods! I am eager to set off for Druim Caein. I'd like to go tomorrow. Soon, though, Cairbed, soon ... before the time of the next bardic rotation ... we will march upon the king, and he will be ousted. I know the gods are with us."

They reached the bard's dwelling. "One other thing before we part, Nuad," Cairbed said. "King Breas met a white hare upon his path the day before he entertained Balor of the Evil Eye. His servants reported that he was terrified when he saw it because he still believes in the old ones' sayings about a white hare portending the downfall of a sitting king."

"I thank the gods for the enduring nonsense of the old

ways." Nuad laughed. "Let us think kindly of white hares as we go about the business of deposing Breas. If he believes that the hare means his demise, it will work to our favor."

He seized Cairbed's hand, pumping it up and down, "Thank you, my friend, for what you have told us," he said. "You are a true and loyal DeDanaan. I can pay you no greater compliment than that."

"Thank you, sire," Cairbed said, humbled and gratified by Nuad's approval. In Cairbed's mind Nuad had never slipped from his regal status, wound or no wound. "May your sleep be untroubled this night."

"And yours likewise, dear friend," Nuad said, taking his leave.

He made his way through the dark toward his sleeping wife and infants, his mind not on them, but on Breas. He could not foresee whether the young king would put up a fight or go easily. Part of Nuad still tingled with desire for conflict, but the father he had become shunned it. Whatever would be was now in the hands of the gods, for the wrath of the DeDanaans had been unleashed and was abroad on the night air, riding the wind like an avenging eagle.

Chapter Twenty-nine

Thick mist rose from the surface of Lough Gur as Lugh and the other warriors followed Nuad away from the settlement of the banished toward the royal stronghold at Druim Caein. The sun was too low in the sky to tell if it would be their companion today or not. High overhead, Lugh could hear the cry of wild geese making their way north. The honking sound cheered him for it was a sure sign that summer would soon be full upon them.

Anovaar pranced smartly, lifting his hooves in a comfortable rhythm. Lugh leaned forward to stroke the shining white mane of his steed and whispered to him, "We are off then, laddy, off to restore peace and plenty to our beautiful green land."

He looked up to see Cian watching him with an amused smile. Lugh was embarrassed to have been seen talking to his horse like a youngster and he smiled back weakly, slowing Anovaar to wait for his father to catch up with him.

They rode in agreeable silence for some time before Cian asked, "What are your thoughts this morning, my son, as we ride forth on this momentous adventure?"

Lugh could see that he truly wanted to know. "Well, Father, I've been thinking about the kind of a king my foster father, Eochy, was. When I contrast him with Breas, I am filled with confidence and am eager for this rightful confrontation."

"I, too am eager for it ... to be behind us. Nothing about our task will be pleasant, and blood may well be shed, Lugh. It is likely that Breas will resist with all the power at his command."

"I know, but did you hear about the white hare he met and how it scared him? I think he'll go easily enough

hen he sees the force we have arrayed against him. Tomorrow when we meet the provincial chieftains and their
warriors at Uisnech, there will be too many of us for
Breas to stand against."

During the nine years of his reign, King Eochy the Fir
Bolg had divided the island of Innis Ealga into five provinces, formalizing the division his forebears had made
naturally according to the topography of the land. At the
time of the division, King Eochy planted a sacred ash tree
on the Hill of Uisnech next to a rock of gigantic proportions, declaring that spot to be the exact center of Innis
Ealga. The tree symbolized all the strength and life that
was in the land.

The Fir Bolg king declared that the province surrounding the sacred tree of life would be known as Meath.
Then he named four provinces to represent the cardinal
points: Ulster in the north; Leinster in the east; Munstser
in the south; and the wilds of Connaught in the west.

The DeDanaans had found the Fir Bolgs' division useful and acting upon Tailteann's advice continued the practice of naming a chieftain to preside over the affairs of
each province or coigedh. That decision now served the
rebels well.

"I was surprised that every single chieftain was willing
to throw in their lot with us," Lugh said. "I was sure that
at least one of them would side with Breas."

"Are they not the ones who have seen most clearly the
hardships of the people? They understand so well what
we must do that not one needed to be coaxed to join our
cause."

"Thank the gods!"

The mist lifted as they neared the broad Nore River
that beckoned them to ride near her banks. They stopped
to refresh their horses and themselves, then turned to follow the river's wide avenue.

"You know, Father," Lugh said, "I was thinking of the
song Cairbed composed about King Eochy and I believe
that as time goes by, people will remember my foster father more for his right governing than for his defeat."

"I think that's true, Lugh, for is it not already told
everywhere how just he was? Your mother looked so
pleased when Cairbed sang the song for her."

"Oh, she was. My foster parents loved each other very

much. She told me that she still misses King Eochy every day of her life."

Cian nodded, understanding too well the pain of a lost love. Lugh guided Anovaar down a grassy hill with Cairbed's song for Eochy running through his head.

Nuad's rebels met up with the coigedh chieftains shortly after sunrise of the third day of the journey and their numbers swelled fourfold. Even if those who sur rounded Breas at Druim Caein chose to stand with him, the young king's ouster was practically assured by such a formidable force. Nuad was hopeful that many in the royal entourage could be persuaded to join the rebel force, leaving Breas with few defenders.

The group rode swiftly to Breas's stronghold near the Brugha na Boyne, arriving under the cover of darkness on the night of the fourth day of their journey. They camped some distance from the Hill of Tara without lighting any fires, willing to risk the danger of wild animals because they did not want Breas alerted to their presence. Nuad believed in the value of surprise.

On the fateful morning, Nuad awoke before the others, aware of a keen longing to have Morrigan at his side. She was a born warrior and had been torn between her desire to go to Druim Caein and the need their babies still had of her. They were so fragile and their demands so great that in the end she was forced to make the difficult choice to stay behind.

Nuad smiled to himself remembering the way his sons' tiny fingers curled around his big ones. The tender feel-ings Ultan and Tadgh awakened in him were foreign to Nuad. He had sometimes felt something similar when regarding Morrigan, but always there was the sexual magnetism between them that overshadowed all else.

He pushed thoughts of his family aside and rose. Qui-etly he went about seeing to his horse, going over the plans for the confrontation one last time.

Cian silently materialized beside him, tending to his own horse. He nodded amiably at Nuad, "Good morning I have high hopes for this day's events."

"I do too, Cian. I feel much as I did on the morning I awoke to learn that we would see Innis Ealga for the first

ime that day. My mouth is dry and my heart pounds
within my chest to think that we are once more about to
ealize the will of the gods."

"Aye. It will be a great day for the DeDanaans when
you are once more our king. We have a terrible need of
eadership, Nuad, and none in our long history has ever
provided it better than you."

Nuad was pleased by Cian's words. He wanted to be
king again more than he had ever wanted anything since
hat day they landed on Innis Ealga. He had let on to the
others that he was leading the rebellion simply to restore
proper balance, but that was not the whole truth.

"Before the gods take me to the Otherworld, Cian, I
want the opportunity to reign over this sacred land of our
people. When I meet my father and grandfather I want to
be able to say to them that I not only followed their
wishes in restoring the DeDanaan people to their proper
soil, but that I ruled in justice and wisdom in the land of
Innis Ealga." He paused to look over the gently rolling
green hills, just emerging from the morning mist.

"I have always felt cheated. How could the gods have
taken the kingship from me just as my dream was realized? I still am not sure why they did it. Perhaps it was
to humble me?"

"I don't know, Nuad. Things like this are what the
priests understand, not warriors like me. All we can do is
take up arms and do as our leaders direct us, but I assure
you, Nuad, that you have no need to be humble. You are
our leader and every DeDanaan will welcome you back to
the kingship with gladness and rejoicing."

Nuad clapped Cian on the back heartily. "Thank you,
my friend. Let us hope it comes to pass. Sound the horn,
Cian, and wake up these lazy rebels. I want to get
started!"

Lugh lay awake watching Cian and Nuad. As Cian
moved off to sound the horn, Nuad, in a gesture uncharacteristic of him, turned his eyes to the velvety green hills
on the eastern horizon, and through the pale rays of dawn,
offered his thanks to the gods for giving him this new opportunity to fulfill his destiny.

The reverence on Nuad's face, when he believed that
no man saw him, was so genuine that Lugh found his soul
deeply touched. He had seen such an expression only

once before, on the face of his beloved King Eochy. He could not put the expression he had seen on Nuad's face out of his mind, even as he rose and prepared for the short ride up the hill to Breas's stronghold.

Nuad rode at the front of the party, flanked by Cian and Macha. She was especially gratified to be returning to Druim Caein to unseat Breas. Lugh rode slightly behind and to the left of the front three. At his side, Mac Lir carried a long staff holding aloft a banner with the symbol of Lough Gur upon it, an interlocking knot of crimson set within a rectangular border of bright green that would identify them to the guards and allow them safe passage up the hill of Tara to the fortified royal compound.

Lugh looked back and caught his grandfather's eye. He was much worried that Diancecht had insisted on coming on this arduous journey, but there had been no dissuading him.

The old physician had uttered not one word of complaint, not even on the second day when they had been lashed by strong winds and an icy rain, but Lugh knew his artificial leg made travel by horseback difficult and painful.

Diancecht winked at Lugh, his eagerness for the confrontation apparent in his bright blue eyes. It had always puzzled Lugh that his grandfather's eyes should look so much younger than the lined face in which they resided.

As the rebels approached the first ditch surrounding the royal stronghold, a group of four warriors came out to met them. They were friendly and their knives remained sheathed. They exchanged curious glances when they saw Nuad's silver hand, but out of courtesy they asked no questions.

"Hail, kinsmen," Nuad said, "I would have an audience with King Breas."

"His lordship is not expecting you," the guard in front replied, frowning. Then a glimmer of understanding spread across his face. He grinned at Nuad and held out his hand. "But you and your party are most welcome here," he said. "We are glad to see you."

Nuad seized his hand in the clasp of kinship, knowing that this man, at least, would offer no resistance to their mission.

The guard spoke to one of the others: "Go to the royal house and announce that visitors from Lough Gur have arrived."

The young warrior rode up the hill and disappeared through the opening in the stone wall, leaving the other three guards to stare in frank amazement at the silver hand Nuad wore. Lugh chuckled aloud as he saw Nuad deliberately cause his forefinger to move. The three men gasped and glanced at each other in confusion.

In a short time the guard returned with two stable boys. "King Breas will be pleased to receive you," he said, "as soon as your horses are cared for and you have had an opportunity to eat and wash."

"Thank you," Nuad said, "we are grateful for an invitation to break the fast at King Breas's renowned table."

There was heavy sarcasm in his voice. The warriors within his hearing did not try to suppress smiles, not even the royal guards, who understood only too well Nuad's bitter allusion.

When they had dined, Lugh said to Cian, "Even though I expected little, I am astonished by the meagerness of that meal."

They had been served the requisite foodstuffs for guests: porridge, sweet milk, and a loaf of newly baked bread, but there were portions enough for one third the number assembled around the turf fires.

"It gives us renewed dedication to our purpose in coming here, doesn't it?" Cian smiled, his eyes looking beyond Lugh, hoping for a glimpse of the captive, Dagda Mor.

A slave came and bowed before Nuad. "The king will receive you and three of your party now, if you please."

Nuad rose, adjusted his cloak deliberately, then turned to his band of rebels. "Cian, you will accompany me, as you will, Mac Lir. Lugh of the Long Hand, I would have you with me, as well."

Lugh was dumbfounded to have been chosen to accompany Nuad into Breas's presence. He knew he did not deserve the honor, having acted badly toward Nuad almost every day since they'd met. He raised his yes to meet Nuad's. The green eyes of the older man were bemused, although the expression on his face was serious. Lugh went to take his place next to the man with the silver hand.

Breas's royal dwelling perched on the crest of the hill almost a mile from the entrance to Druim Caein. As the party walked toward it the sun rose from behind a low bank of clouds, bathing the top of the hill with a radiance that highlighted clearly the construction site of Breas's grand new feasting hall. It was all true, just as they had been told.

None of them had ever seen a hall so large. Men, women, and children were at work hauling bags of dirt to pack around a foundation of stones. Some were shaping saplings into supports while others wove the wattle that would become the walls after daub and powdered lime were applied.

The bones of the new construction were in place, with the roof supports hovering like the wings of a kestrel over the gaunt workers. The sight of it angered Lugh more than anything he had ever seen in his life. The hall was a symbol of evil, built by the hunger and privation of the people. But once the rebels overthrew Breas there was a chance that it could be finished as a monument to the undaunted spirit of the DeDanaan tribe.

Lugh was torn by his desire to be at Nuad's side and the obvious need of his grandfather for support on the long walk to the king's dwelling place. He dropped back to assist Diancecht who smiled a warm welcome.

"Please don't worry yourself with the likes of me," his grandfather said. "Get you to the front with Nuad where you belong, Lugh. Mac Lir will assist me, won't you, Mac?"

The stocky warrior nodded cheerfully. "We have always been friends, we two, and I'll not be leaving you alone this day."

"Go forward, Lugh," Diancecht said soberly. "This event is too important for you not to be beside Nuad. No, please, don't protest. You must trust that destiny has a purpose for you, and it is not back here with a tired old man."

Lugh returned to the front, falling in silently beside Nuad who was striding purposefully forward. Lugh maintained his place by Nuad's side when the four warriors

from Lough Gur were taken into the presence of King
Breas.

Lugh coolly observed Breas who sat upon a stool of
carved oak. He wore a woolen tunic, dyed yellow. Over
it was a cloak of deep purple wool, fastened with the
largest gold cloak pin Lugh had ever seen. Breas wore
new boots of finely tanned deerskin, and carried his knife
in a sheath of matching skin that had been painstakingly
dyed with yellow, purple, and green interlocking spirals
to complement his dress.

Lugh felt disgust at such obvious vanity, and rage when
he looked at the tattered attire of the men from Lough
Gur. Even the servants in Breas's royal house wore old
and patched clothing, only slightly better than Lugh's
own.

Lugh thought that golden locks and fine blue eyes did
not count for much when it came to the character of the
king. It took all of his willpower to step forward and bow
before Breas when it was his turn to be presented. He
bent his knee in respect for the office, not the man who
held it.

King Breas spoke: "I bid welcome to you four, and to
those you bring with you from the settlement of Lough
Gur." His voice cracked unmistakably.

"We have with us the coigedh chieftains and their warriors," Nuad said pointedly.

Breas's heart sank to the toes of his new boots. This
was going to be even worse than it had first appeared.
"What manner of greeting do you bear for me from the
people?" He smiled ingratiatingly, while tapping his fingers nervously against his stool.

Lugh felt the hair on the back of his neck stand upright.
He glanced sideways at Nuad whose strong jaw was set
and determined. Nuad was looking directly at the king.

"The people at Lough Gur are suffering greatly, as are
all your subjects across this island. Each province reports
that tributes are demanded that bring the people to the
point of desperation. There is anger and dismay across
Innis Ealga," he said in a deep and steady voice.

King Breas's voice faltered again as he replied, "I have
been over all of this with your delegation once before.
Surely you can understand the necessity of keeping the

peace in this island. It takes a great deal of wealth to maintain an arsenal and warriors to defend us."

Breas was trying to look confident and majestic, but his power was crumbling and he knew it. He had feared it the moment the messenger told him there was a delegation from Lough Gur waiting to see him, which was led by Nuad, the former king.

Inwardly he cursed himself for the shortsightedness of not having separated the troublemakers at Lough Gur. To have put Nuad together with the council of elders had been folly. Why had he not been able to see that when he sent them out there? But now it was too late. *That damnable white hare! Would to the gods that I had never met it on the path!* he thought. He wished he had invited his mother to this meeting, but he had foolishly wanted to handle it alone.

Nuad dropped all pretense of respect for the king. He had recognized Breas's weakness the moment they began to speak and he sensed that he could move in for the kill right away.

"Nonsense!" he snorted. "You do not protect us. You squander our wealth on bribes to the Fomorians, fine raiment, and feasting halls for your own glory. The people will no longer tolerate it and we have come in their name to demand that you relinquish the kingship."

Nuad paused expectantly, watching King Breas diminish before his eyes. The beautiful king was defeated, pathetically and utterly, although he sputtered and went on at length about his power and the rightfulness of his reign. Nuad let him talk until his words trailed off in futility.

The power of the group from Lough Gur was palpable and as real as the errors of Breas's ways. In the end Breas the Beautiful could not stand against it. He agreed to step down.

Nuad said, "I will leave Cian here to negotiate the terms of your withdrawal. You may have three counselors of your own choosing at your side during the talks. But before I retire from this hall I would know the whereabouts of Dagda, your father by marriage."

It was then that real fear gripped Breas's heart. He did not know what Nuad and his warriors might do to him when they learned how he had treated the tribe's re-

ected wise man. Nuad's hard green eyes forced Breas to
dmit that the wise man was at work on the building of
ae earthen works. Nuad said not a word to him. He
ooked at him with utter contempt.

Breas, in a vain attempt at self-defense, said, "Actually,
e is not working very hard and he seems to enjoy being
utdoors all day."

Breas was on the verge of tears as he babbled on, try-
ag to defend an indefensible position. Nuad would hear
o more; he turned angrily on his heel and motioned to
ugh and Mac Lir to follow him.

Before they could exit, a furious Eri swept into the
oyal dwelling, her cape swirling behind her. She pointed
bejeweled finger at her son: "Why was I not told imme-
iately of this meeting?"

Breas barely had the courage to raise his eyes to meet
er blazing gaze. She did not wait for an answer but
irned to Nuad. In a shrill voice she asked, "What is the
leaning of this? What are you doing here?"

Nuad looked at her steadily as a smile spread across his
ace. "You are too late, Eri. The deed has been done.
our son has renounced the kingship."

All color drained from her face and she looked word-
essly at Breas, feeling faint as she realized the truth of
Nuad's words.

"Not even you, Eri, can prevent the power inherent in
he people of the goddess Danu, from restoring the king-
hip to balance. Your days of power over Innis Ealga
ave come to an end," Nuad said firmly.

Chapter Thirty

Lugh awoke in a strange house on the festival ground, of the Hill of Uisnech on the day of Nuad's second coronation. For a few moments he did not know where he was. He had been dreaming that he was a lad at work with the other Fir Bolg boys, clearing stones from the green fields around Lough Gur. He could almost feel the old familiar aching of his shoulders as he stretched himself awake. He was filled with melancholy for those boyhood friends whom he would never see again.

He went outside to greet the lanky hound who bounded eagerly to his side and licked his hand with glee. Lugh bent slightly and put his face next to the happy animal and roughed his coat with both hands.

"Ready to start the day, Cu?" he asked, looking around at the multitudes of sleeping DeDanaans who had come to the Hill of Uisnech to celebrate a new beginning for Innis Ealga with King Nuad once more at their head. While Lugh was greeting the dog, Diancecht came up behind him and spoke.

"It looks like Bel will attend us today, even after all the rain showers of last night, but I knew he would. Even as I lay awake listening to the raindrops splashing against the thatch, I was confident that the gods would not abandon us on a day of such importance."

Lugh smiled warmly at his grandfather, then let his eyes run over the crowds again. He knew Desheen was out there someplace and the most urgent thing he had to do this morning was to find her. At the base of the hill he could see the cowherds tending their cattle, ready for the fire ceremonies. He wondered if she might be there, helping with the animals.

"I'm glad you're pleased, Grandfather," Lugh answered politely, unwilling to linger.

Diancecht smiled, seeing into Lugh's soul. "I heard that the group from Ulster came in late last night," he said. "They are camped on the western flank of the hill." His grin was broad.

"Really? Oh, thanks, Grandfather! I can't wait to see Desheen."

"One would never have guessed," the old man said dryly. "Well, what are you waiting for? Go to her and stop wasting my time."

His smile was kindly as he watched Lugh run off to seek his true love. This girl had been foreseen by Diancecht as clearly as he had seen Lugh as the king of the peoples of Innis Ealga. The gods' plan seemed to be progressing nicely.

By the time the eye of the Sun God had risen high in the fine blue sky, Desheen and Lugh stood, arms loosely around each other's waists, watching the milling coronation crowd. He ached with desire for her, grateful that she was here beside him. Ulster had seemed as far away as the moon to Lugh, while they had been apart.

She smiled at him and said, "I'm so glad to be here with you, Lugh. Last night I thought our journey would never end. Every step seemed to take as long as a journey of the Sun God across the sky."

He put his face in her hair, inhaling her fragrance. "Lugh, are you paying attention to what I'm saying?" she asked playfully.

"No," he answered honestly, "I'm not. I have eyes only for you. I'm not going to be able to let you go back to Ulster when the ceremony is over." He regarded her solemnly, wondering if he should speak his desire out loud. Would she think his wishes premature? After all, they had known each other only a short time. He decided to risk it.

"Most of us from Lough Gur are going to live at Druim Caein after the coronation," he said, "and I would like you to come there, too."

She was pleased. "I will ask my parents, Lugh, but I'm not sure they will want me to go."

"They would have to agree if we were betrothed."

"Yes," she answered, "if we were betrothed, they would have to say yes."

Lugh took her hands in his and looked into her bright

blue eyes, so clear and beautiful. "I love you, Desheen. If you will agree to be my wife, we won't ever have to be apart again."

As he waited for her answer he found it difficult to breathe. What if she were to refuse him? He was almost certain she had strong feelings for him too, but she might ask him to wait. He felt his heart sink.

"I can't wait," he said urgently. "Desheen, I have loved you from the moment I first saw you. Please, will you do me the very great honor of becoming my wife?"

There on a green hillside in Meath, the lovely, sky-eyed Desheen, above the shouts and whoops of the cowherds driving their cattle between the Beltaine fires, gave Lugh of the Long Hand her answer.

"Oh, yes, Lugh, yes. I love you and would be honored to become your wife."

They fell into one another's arms and kissed the long, slow kiss of lovers whose spirits are fated to intertwine for all eternity. The god in the sky beamed down his approval as did Tailteann and Cian, who could not help noticing the young lovers.

From all those who had served and fawned over him at court, Breas was able to gather only nine men to his side in his disgrace. They rode away from the royal stronghold with him and Eri on the day Nuad was to be crowned toward a small fishing village on the western coast called Dun Dobhrain that was to be their place of exile.

Dark clouds had scudded in from the sea all afternoon, dropping their burdens of rain, then moving off quickly. Breas had the feeling that on the entire island of Innis Ealga, it was raining only on him.

His heart was sore at having to give up dominion over Innis Ealga. It was such a beautiful kingdom and in his own way, he loved it. He thought bitterly of the white hare he had encountered such a short time before.

Breas felt like weeping but didn't dare, not with Eri at his side. A glance her way told him that she was still withdrawn and angry. He sighed. There had been no talking with his mother since he had been deposed. She acted as though it had been his fault, although he knew he was guilty of nothing but ill fortune.

Eri's beauty had once been so great that word of it

spread all over the Northern Lands. Age was upon her now, and her once golden curls were white. But it was not the years that lay on her face, but the anger within her that erased all traces of her former beauty.

She was outraged still, by the easy capitulation Breas had made to the warriors of Lough Gur. The guilty heart of her son that caused him to yield so easily was something she could not comprehend. She was sure it must be the legacy of his Fomorian blood. She had made it a life-long practice never to feel remorse for anything she did. There was no point to it. Remorse made one weak.

Eri never regretted her pairing with Breas's father, even though she had come to feel contempt for him because he was a true Fomorian, lacking all grace and civility. She knew she had been drawn to him as a mare is drawn to a stallion, in the passion of youth. It had meant nothing. *But now,* she thought, *my youthful blunder may prove to be useful.*

In the late afternoon, Breas and his party rode out on a broad green meadow that dipped gently toward the sea, just as the sun burst forth from a bank of clouds over their heads. Eri chose that moment to speak.

"Breas, I have thought long and hard about how you might regain the kingship."

The sound of her voice startled him out of his dour thoughts, and he jumped. "What?"

"Pay attention, Breas!" she said sharply. "I said, I think I know a way for you to regain the kingship."

He looked at her as though she had lost her mind. "I don't think that's possible, Mother. There are only eleven of us. How could we do that?"

Oh, she thought, *he is an irksome boy.* She sighed in irritation and went on as though he had not spoken. "I have never made a secret of your origin, Breas, but neither have I ever claimed kinship with your father, Ethalon the Fomorian. But now, I think the time has come to do just that. Do you still have the ring he gave me?"

Breas eyed her curiously, understanding nothing of what she was thinking, but remembering how canny she had always been in the past.

"Yes, I have it," he answered. "It is in my fes. Do you want to see it?"

"No, I don't want to see it. I want you to take it to your father where he dwells on Tor Conain. I have learned from the Fomorians who visited Druim Caein that he has become a powerful warrior and councilman."

"The gods would have to carry me to Tor Conain on their backs"—Breas laughed nervously—"for surely, I know of no way to get to that enchanted place."

"Don't be difficult," Eri snapped with exasperation, "there are ways. If you were to take the ring to Ethalon as a token, it would identify you as his son and he would be obligated to assist you in an effort to reclaim the kingship."

"But how am I to get to Tor Conain? It is said the island is always shrouded with mist and impossible to locate."

"I think we must make contact with the escaped Fir Bolgs and bide our time with them. Sooner or later, Balor and the Fomorians will come to them again. Perhaps it will be sooner than we think." She paused, her mind weighing the possibilities.

"When news of Nuad's rise reaches them, they will see new opportunities for gain and their greed can be counted on to bring them back to these shores. It we make it known to the Fir Bolgs that we are eager to work with them, who knows what may come to pass?"

"Well, I don't see any reason why the Fir Bolgs would want to assist me. They'd like to have Innis Ealga back and rule over it themselves."

"By the gods, son, think! They have every reason to want to unseat Nuad. He won't be as easily commanded as you and they know it. He stopped all tribute the moment he stole the kingship from you, so they must be desperate by now. You can promise the Fir Bolgs and the Fomorians whatever you have to," she said smiling, "but it should be easy enough to pit them against each other once you are back in power. Right now though, we need their help and going through Ethalon is the only way I know to get it. Do you have any better ideas?"

Breas bowed his head dejectedly. He wished he could go back to being a simple warrior.

High on the Hill of Uisnech delicious fragrances rose from the cauldrons and cooking pits, as the cooks prepared the evening feast that would celebrate Nuad's coronation. Lugh inhaled, and smiled as he completed his grooming. The care with which he dressed after his bath would have astonished Tailteann had she been privy to it, for never in his life had he shaved so closely or lingered so long with a mirror in his hand.

He donned a handsome pale green tunic that Tailteann had embroidered for the coronation. Red and yellow and dark green lozenges traversed the hem of the garment as well as the hem of the long, dark green cloak he put on over it.

It pleased Lugh to be able to dress in fine clothing once more. He sat down on a stone and pulled on new boots of soft tanned deerskin. Even the number of deer the hunters had been able to bring down had increased after Breas's downfall. By the time Lugh reached to buckle on his dagger scabbard, he was humming one of Cairbed's tunes, basking in the joy of Desheen's promise to become his bride.

There came a knock on the door and when he opened it, Queen Tailteann was standing outside, holding a cloak-wrapped object almost as long as she was tall.

"Hello, Mother. What do you have there?" he asked, reaching to relieve her of her burden.

She shook her head and moved away from him, piquing his curiosity.

"What is it?" He laughed. "Have you come here not meaning to show me what it is you carry?"

She laughed too. "Oh, I am going to show it to you, I just want to tell you about it first." She laid her bundle on the furs meant for sleeping, and sat down beside it, patting a place by her side for Lugh. He sat down readily and kissed her on the cheek.

"I have brought you King Eochy's cloidem-mor, Lugh. He called this mighty sword Frega. You know how much store he set by it."

"Frega?" Lugh asked. He had thought the great ceremonial sword of the Fir Bolgs had been lost when his foster father died at Moytirra.

"I have kept it hidden all this time," Tailteann said. "When the tribute collectors grew so bold, I buried it to keep it from them. I have always meant for you to have it, but I wanted to wait until the time was right to give it to you. I think that today, your betrothal day, the time has come."

She lifted the sword from its wrapping carefully and placed it in Lugh's hands. He remembered the golden handle set with jewels and the polished teeth and bones of animals. The blade was of silver and had been engraved by the best Fir Bolg artificers. Now that Lugh had seen what the craftsmen of the DeDanaans could do, he recognized that the sword he held in his hands was not up to the artistic standard of the one Nuad would carry tonight, yet Frega meant more to him than any weapon on Innis Ealga.

His heart was so filled with gratitude and love for Tailteann that he could not trust himself to speak for a few moments. He laid the cloidem-mor across his knees and enveloped his mother in a hug.

"Thank you, Mother. I will treasure Frega and wear it humbly. May it help insure that we live forever in peace and harmony on Innis Ealga." The lump that arose in his throat made it impossible for him to say more.

Chapter Thirty-one

U nder the graceful branches of the sacred ash tree, whose roots reached deeply into the earth in the center of Innis Ealga, Ferfesa and three lesser priests awaited Nuad, the only DeDanaan to be presented before the holy shouting stone on two occasions. On the right side of the tree Dagda Mor, Ogma, and Cairbed the bard, awaited their parts in the ceremony of coronation.

The Lia Fail, the holy coronation stone of the DeDanaans, had been placed directly in front of the tree, its splendid gray surface hard, unyielding, and eternal. The rock encapsulated all the sacredness of DeDanaan kingship. Would the stone shout tonight when a true king of Innis Ealga was crowned? There were few doubters in the crowd.

Next to the Lia Fail was the holed stone through which Nuad would consummate his union with the very soil of Innis Ealga during the Banois Rig rite. It was a profound ceremony, this Wedding of Kingship, and it would seal him forever more to the land and the people of Innis Ealga.

In the dwelling where Nuad dressed for the ceremony, the slave, Brig, looked him over one last time before he left for the Hill of Uisnech. Brig adjusted his master's cloak of royal blue, admiring its hue. The weaving women had labored long to achieve such a deep rich shade from the mussels the sea gods sent them.

The golden embroidery trimming the cloak's edges shimmered in the pale light from a small fire in the center of the dwelling. Nuad's tunic was of the finest linen, bleached as white as his fine strong teeth that gleamed in a triumphant smile. Brig thought Nuad had never looked more handsome, never more like a king, and the majestic silver hand he wore on his left arm contributed greatly to his magnificence.

The silver hand was so exquisite that it seemed no longer a ploy for getting around old rules, but a treasure worthy of the highest office in the land. Brig wondered if future kings would lament never possessing such a marvelous, enchanted thing as Nuad's silver hand.

"You are ready, sir," he said, "to be presented to the people, and it's grand you look."

He was surprised when Nuad gave him a gruff hug, and even more surprised when Nuad said, "I want you to walk up the hill with me, Brig. Come on."

When Nuad and Brig reached the coronation site, two priests fell in beside the king, and Brig stepped aside to take up a position that would give him a good view of the proceedings.

At a signal from Ferfesa, a mighty blast was blown on two huge bronze horns that were used only for royal coronations or funerals. The crowd parted down the middle to make way for the priests, who led Nuad to his place in front of the sacred stones beneath the ash tree.

When the principals were properly positioned, Dagda Mor addressed the DeDanaans. "My people, I welcome you to the coronation ceremony of Nuad of the Silver Hand. For some time a curse has lain upon Innis Ealga because of the hollowness of character that afflicts our former king. As you know, that curse has been lifted from us by the great Nuad, and he comes before us once more to be named the king of the DeDanaans. Let us rejoice together in the warmth of the great god Bel, as the ceremony consecrating his rule begins."

He could feel the warmth of the Sun God, who was nearing the end of the day's journey, on his back as he spoke and was reassured that the god was with them. The high priest stepped forward to address the people, smiling as he lifted his hands toward the god of fire in the sky.

"Fellow DeDanaans!" He shouted, wishing to be heard by the last person in the crowd. "In the season of Beltaine the great god Bel went to do battle with Mot, the evil god of sterility. We know that he has prevailed because the fruitfulness of the earth is being restored. We pray that

Bel's favor will continue to follow us all the days of our lives."

He beamed at Nuad who stood before him in an uncharacteristic pose, with his head bowed and his eyes downcast.

"The health of the DeDanaan people rests on the shoulders of this man, Nuad of the Silver Hand, who presents himself here to receive the blessing of the gods. If he rules in harmony with them, the earth will continue to yield her riches to us, and we will then be assured of seven years of the gods' blessings. Women will bring forth children, the birds and beasts of the green fields will bring forth young, and the earth will groan under the burden of her produce.

"As the gods and the laws of the DeDanaan tribe insist, I ask you now, Nuad, of the Silver Hand, if you willingly present yourself here, unblemished and pure of heart, ready to become one with the holy mother earth and the people of Innis Ealga?"

Nuad raised his eyes and looked directly into those of the priest. His answer came loud and clear and echoed in the stillness of the soft day.

"I do," he said.

"Will you hear the laws regarding the proper conduct of a king and agree to abide by them, for the safety and well-being of the DeDanaan tribe?" Ferfesa asked.

Again, Nuad's answer was strong: "I will."

Ferfesa summoned Cairbed the bard, and Ogma, master of learning and wisdom, to step to the front. Ogma moved slowly, showing his years, and Cairbed took his elbow to assist him to his place. The bard nervously ran his hand over his unruly hair. He had attempted to slick down his red curls before the ceremony began, but he felt them popping up as he stepped toward the holy stones. After a moment of disgust, the import of the occasion pushed all thought of his appearance from his mind as he stopped before the king.

Cairbed addressed Nuad directly. "Hear ye the laws: to be chosen king of the DeDanaan tribe a man must have goodness of form and be free from blemish. He must possess sense and learning, dignity, goodness, wisdom, and strength. He must not use force nor oppression against his people. He must strive to right behavior in all matters. He must have valor in fighting his enemies and he must have the gift of utterance.

"Nuad of the Silver Hand, I charge you with these ancient requirements of kingship: You shall have three chief residences. You will be free from falsehood. You will be free of unworthy conduct toward the people. Hear you, Nuad of the Silver Hand, the laws governing kingship?"

"I do hear," Nuad answered.

Ferfesa placed his left hand on Nuad's white hair, and in supplication to the god prayed. "Oh, mighty Bel, grant this man strength to act in harmony with you and the other gods. Assist him in all things as he goes about fulfilling the requirements of kingship." The priest smiled at Nuad warmly.

The telling of the history of the DeDanaan people was the central part of every coronation ceremony and the honor of reciting it fell to Ogma, long renowned as a scholar devoted to the learning accumulated by the DeDanaan people.

Because Lugh and Tailteann had been held captive during the time of King Breas's coronation they had never before heard the history of the DeDanaans. Ogma related the fate of the descendants of Nemed, the DeDanaan antecedent who had first colonized the shores of Innis Ealga.

Lugh and Tailteann exchanged looks of astonishment because the ancestor of whom he spoke, Nemed, was also the ancestor to whom the Fir Bolgs traced their beginnings.

"This means that the Fir Bolgs and the DeDanaans are related?" Lugh whispered to his foster mother.

Tailteann nodded her head slowly. "It sounds like it, Lugh. Shh. Let us listen to the rest of the story to be sure."

Ogma said, "Simon Breac, a grandson of Nemed, to escape the bedevilment of the Fomorians, led one of three groups of exiles from Innis Ealga into the southern climes, where they were taken as slaves and forced to haul dirt in leathern bags for their masters."

"I knew it," Lugh said softly, "for does not the very name Fir Bolg mean men of the bag?"

Ogma talked on, outlining generation after generation. At last he said, "One group was able to reach the large lands that lie beyond Albion and it was they, our ancestors, who wandered, homeless until the bold Nuad was able to lead the children of Nemed back to our rightful home."

"You're right, Lugh," Tailteann whispered back, "the tale of Nemed has always been in the lore of the Fir Bolg tribe, but since nothing was ever known about the other two grandsons, it was assumed that they had perished in their flight."

She shook her head in wonderment. So, the DeDanaans and Fir Bolgs were cousins. Desheen was looking at her and Lugh in frank curiosity at their whisperings, and Tailteann smiled at her as if to assure her of a full explanation later.

Bringing them up to current history, Ogma told of the death and defeat of the Fir Bolg King, Eochy, at the battle of Moytirra. Even though he treated the episode respectfully, the hearing of it caused Lugh and Tailteann pain. When the scribe had concluded he stepped back and allowed Ferfesa to come to the fore again.

The priest faced Nuad and asked him to raise his right hand. "Do you, Nuad of the Silver Hand, swear on the tombs of our ancestors to observe the laws of the DeDanaan people; to maintain the ancient customs of our tribe; and to rule with strict justice?"

"I do swear," said Nuad, smiling broadly.

Dagda Mor stepped forward and handed him a straight white wand, hewn from a sacred yew tree, as a symbol of the conduct expected from kings who were to be as pure and straight as the wand. Nuad accepted it with reverence. Dagda helped him remove the ceremonial sword and dagger he wore around his waist and placed the weapons upon the ground.

Nuad lifted the white wand high and turned three times around, moving always from left to right, in the same direction the great Sun God himself turned in the sky.

Ferfesa led the king to the holed stone and assisted him onto a small stepping stone that had been placed in front of it. Before he took that fateful step, Nuad sought the face of his beautiful wife, Morrigan. When he saw her, he almost laughed aloud at the lascivious gesture she made with her tongue. She was going to make it easy for him to penetrate the stone. There would be no need of amulets or potions for Nuad.

His loins were undraped by the chief priest and Nuad performed the Banois Rig with gusto. As his seed fell and mingled with the soft rich earth of Innis Ealga, all present heard a mighty shout arise from the sacred Lia Fail. This man was one with the earth, and the holy stone bore loud witness to his true kingship.

When Nuad's loins were covered, he stepped away from the holed stone and turned to face the people. Dagda Mor placed a delicate diadem of gold upon Nuad's white head and held up his silver hand.

The wise man shouted to the crowd. "People of the goddess Danu, I present to you, Nuad, king of the DeDanaan tribe!"

Each priest and chieftain in turn repeated Nuad's name aloud. When the last official had spoken, the crowd erupted, proclaiming Nuad's name again and again in a loud hurrah. He was officially and forever more, their king.

When they finally quieted, an elated Nuad addressed them. "I will, with the gods' help, do all that I have promised this day for your benefit, my people. Together, we will be able to free this island of our most pressing enemies, the Fomorians. I pledge to you that I will hear your concerns and will discuss them with the council of elders and the priests, before taking action.

"Now, as is our age-old custom, I would bestow three boons before we turn to feasting and celebration. First, I would honor my beloved and faithful slave, Brig, who has been at my side for twenty cycles of the sun. I declare that from this day forth he is a free man with all the rights and obligations that such status entails. Further, I name him as my official rechtaire because in actual fact, he has long been my house steward."

Morrigan looked at Brig. He had never been particularly interesting to her. Even though she sensed that he often resented her, she regarded him as part of the household furniture and found it puzzling that Nuad would honor him by making him the royal rechtaire. She regarded the tears of joy streaming down the older man's cheeks with genuine curiosity.

Her thoughts were broken by the sound of Nuad's voice speaking her name. Although he had not discussed it with her, she had been certain that he would raise her from consort status and declare her his queen. He did not disappoint her, and she bowed to him graciously, enjoying the admiration and envy of the other women. She had taken special pains, as Lugh had, to look her very best on this coronation day.

Her serving woman had done up her auburn hair twice, and its intricate twists and coils glinted like copper in the light of the late afternoon. Her cloak of deep green was of soft, washed wool, held at her left shoulder by a golden clasp set with a single polished stone that Nuad gave her when they first came together. The artificers had lingered long over the making of the beautiful golden pin, taking great care as they inset the stone she said was so important to her.

Morrigan was surprised to find her own eyes damp when she raised them to look into her husband's face. His public expression of love for her touched her far more deeply than she thought it would. She gave him her hand and he presented her to the DeDanaans.

"As queen, Morrigan represents the Goddess of the Moon even as I symbolize the great god of the sun," Nuad said.

Lugh glanced up and scrutinized Morrigan carefully, trying to remember his youthful attraction to her. The pull between them had seemed like that of the moon upon the tides. He understood only that the compulsion between men and women was ordained by the gods and that few mortals could resist its power. When he looked at Desheen he was glad that he was among those unable to resist.

King Nuad of the Silver Hand spoke again. "I called the council of elders together for the holy purpose of selecting a Tanist from among the roydamna, those young men in our tribe who are deemed to be king material. The office of Tanist has not been filled in recent times but in light of what happened to us with the last king, we think it is necessary to reach back to the old ways.

"Each candidate was considered carefully and the elders and I are pleased with our choice. He who will be second in authority only to me, is a young man of the highest valor and courage and fair in countenance. But I would caution you to understand that the Tanist does not become king upon my death unless he is chosen by the gods in a proper dream ceremony. He must be elected king in his own right, as though he has never been Tanist, according to the ancient laws of the DeDanaan tribe.

"The Tanist will assist me in all the responsibilities of kingship. If I become ill or incapacitated, he is empowered to order the affairs of the people of Innis Ealga. He is to stand by my side as I conduct royal business, so as to be always informed as fully as I am.

"In the young man whom we have chosen are merged the blood and the spirit of the three peoples of Innis Ealga, the DeDanaans, the Fir Bolgs, and the Fomorians. . . ."

Even though many a DeDanaan turned to look at him as Nuad spoke, the realization that Nuad was referring to him was slow in coming to Lugh. Desheen squeezed his hand as the king said, "I charge you now, Lugh of the Long Hand, to come forward and kneel beneath this holy ash tree, to take the oath of tanisty."

Me, second in line to the kingship? Chosen by Nuad? How could this be? Lugh thought. He felt Desheen release his hand and Tailteann gently nudge him toward the spot where King Nuad stood waiting for him.

Tailteann's heart swelled within her bosom, full of pride and gratitude to the gods for their acknowledgment that Lugh was all that she knew him to be. Tears of joy slid down her cheeks as he watched her beloved foster son walk toward the high king. Lugh had seemed a gift from the gods from the first moment he came to her and Eochy. Now he was to be their gift to the people of Innis Ealga. How she wished King Eochy might know of Lugh's great honor. He would be so proud.

The two kinsmen, Nuad and Lugh, so alike in character and stature, stood facing each other at the exact center of the land beloved by both of them.

"Lugh of the Long Hand, will you bend your knee to me and swear a holy oath on the graves of your ancestors and mine, that you will faithfully serve me and defend this land against all enemies?"

It was surprisingly easy for Lugh to kneel before Nuad and swear allegiance to him. He spoke clearly. "I swear my fealty to you, King Nuad, and will faithfully defend this land against all enemies."

As he heard the priest chanting holy words over his head, he remembered the blazing star he had seen in the heavens over Lough Gur. This moment had the same feeling about it, one of awe at a power mightier than himself. He felt his heart pounding with the knowledge that he had just committed himself, for better or worse, to that power, and was now bound to the soil of Innis Ealga in a compact with the gods.

Chapter Thirty-two

The first six turnings of the moon in King Nuad's second reign went smoothly. Summer had swelled DeDanaan larders and there had been no further contact between the DeDanaans and the Fomorians. Then, late one autumn afternoon, a resident of the settlement in Donegal came staggering into the royal compound at Druim Caein. As soon as Dagda Mor heard his tale, the man was taken directly to King Nuad.

"Well, what is it, man? What happened?" Nuad demanded of the quaking messenger before him. He was not fond of preambles, and wanted to get to the heart of this matter.

"It was a raid, my lord. Most of us at Donegal were in the fields tying up the sheaves for winter when, with no warning, a Fomorian raiding party swept into the compound and slaughtered all of our children and the caregivers who had remained behind in the dwellings.

"We who worked in the fields, heard their cries, and ran as fast as we could to aid them, but it was too late. I lost my own son—" He choked up and could not go on.

Dagda took up the man's tale. "The Fomorians spared no one in the compound, Nuad. This man's son had yet to see his first spring." Dagda's eyes misted over, thinking of his own beloved grandson, Ruadon, born to Brigid such a short time ago. "Balor of the Evil Eye sends you the message that you must honor the bargain that Breas made with him."

"What bargain?" Nuad growled, looking from Dagda back to the messenger whose composure was returning. The man, his voice shaking, answered his king. "They said that Balor of the Evil Eye covets a feasting hall such as the one Breas built here at Druim Caein. To build it, Balor made King Breas agree to send him every

DeDanaan firstborn when they reach their fifteenth summer."

"What?" Nuad roared. "Send him our children! By the gods! The thief is as daft as he is ugly."

"The raiders said to tell you that if you do not send the youngsters willingly, Balor will raid every settlement and take our young ones back to Tor Conain by force."

Nuad's face flushed with fury. He snorted his disgust and said, "If I won't pay him tribute, what makes him think for a moment that I would consider sending him our children? He is mad, he is!"

He sat for some minutes, deep in thought, his chin resting on his silver hand. Finally he spoke. "Dagda, take this man to the baths and see that he gets something to eat. Then gather the Council of the Wise and the Tanist and report back here to me."

He looked at the messenger with great sympathy. "Thank you for making the difficult journey here to tell me of this outrage. You will be rewarded. Would that I had it in my power to restore your son. Please know that you have the full sympathy of Queen Morrigan and myself. Go with Dagda in safety."

The king sat in deep and somber thought long after they left. At his coronation, Nuad had been reminded anew by Ogma's recitation of DeDanaan history, how the Fomorians had tormented even Parthelon and his followers, the first people ever to dwell on the island of Innis Ealga. From that day to this, the people of Innis Ealga had known no peace. Nuad decided that the Fomorians had to be stopped once and for all, if the DeDanaans were ever to realize their full greatness.

The Fir Bolg, Srang, squatted with the Fomorian, Indech, on the beach, hunching close to a small peat fire Srang had built on the lee side of a dune. The afternoon sky was stone gray and sullen, as a bitter wind whipped in from the sea, bending the grasses on top of the dune flat. The two rough warriors were so deep in conversation they took no notice of the chill. Srang gestured emphatically with his fist as he spoke.

"I can see no benefit in it. I am opposed to bringing this Breas to Tor Conain and I told him as much. He is a weak man, so weak that his own people forced him to renounce the DeDanaan kingship, yet he bristles with arrogance. He's lucky I didn't kill him on the spot."

"I'm glad you didn't, Srang, for I see ways in which he could be useful to King Balor."

"Huh," snorted Srang, "how could he be of any use? He has only a handful of supporters by his side . . . and his mother! I think it was she who sent him into Connaught to find me because it was plain in talking with him that he wasn't sure what he was supposed to ask for. He did say that he wants to go to Tor Conain. Can you imagine? He says his father lives there."

That got Indech's full attention. "Did he name his father?"

Srang scratched the thick black stubble on his chin and thought a minute. "No. I don't think he did."

"Did you make plans to meet with him again to give him our answer?"

"I told him we would meet on the northern shore of Lough Erne, the same place I ran into him this time, on the night of the next full moon. He said he'd be there and, by the gods! I suppose he will be."

Indech smiled. "I think I'll go with you. I'd like to meet this Breas and size him up. If he is as weak as you say he is, he ought to be fairly easy to control. You say he wants the Fomorians to help him regain the throne of Innis Ealga?"

"Yes," snarled Srang, "he wants the same thing I want. I'm warning you now that if you ever turn against me and the Fir Bolgs, you won't live to see the next morn." He spit in the sand without taking his eyes from Indech's face.

The Fomorian tribute collector smiled broadly at him and sent a long string of saliva sailing into the same spot. He wiped his chin with the back of his hand.

"Don't worry about that, Srang. King Balor has agreed to help you, hasn't he? What more do you want?"

"I just don't want you messing around with the DeDanaans. I know from experience they aren't to be trusted."

"We don't trust them, Srang, but who is going to tell that to the beautiful ex-king who wants to go to the land of the Fomorians to meet his father? You don't understand the intricacies of our tribe, Srang. If you did, you'd see that Balor will be able to turn Breas into an advantage. Didn't you say that Breas's queen has given birth to a child he's never seen? A thing like that could make a man desperate, willing to do almost anything to get at his son, couldn't it?"

"I guess it could," Srang said, the light slowly dawning on him that there could be rewards in this situation for him and his men. "What have you got in mind?" he asked.

At the Druim Caein bathing compound, Lugh eased his weary body into steaming bathwater and lay back in the canoe-shaped stone basin, letting the warmth of the water cover him. He closed his eyes and let all the tension of the past few hours drain away. He had not understood before what pressures were put upon a king. As a lad, he had watched his foster father at work and understood as a child understands, grasping none of the fine points of kingship. He tried to free his mind from all worry and just enjoy the sensual pleasure of the bath.

"Ahh," came a contented sigh from the next bathing basin. Lugh opened his eyes. His father, Cian, was slowly sliding beneath the hot water. The servant who had filled Cian's basin came and poured more heated water over Lugh, causing a shiver to course through him. He lifted his hand and saw that the heat of the water had turned his skin a bright red.

"You'll soon be boiled, Father, like I am," Lugh said with a smile.

"Ah, I hope so," Cian replied. "I find discussions like the one we've just come from tiring, much more than actual combat. Deciding on any course of action is the most difficult thing we humans have to do. Would that we had the gift to see into the future."

"Grandfather says he has it."

"Sometimes I think he does too." Cian laughed. "Maybe he should have been in the meeting today." He paused. "I'm worried about him, Lugh. He seems to fail more every day. He no longer hears a thing anyone says to him, and I've seen Queen Morrigan leading him by the hand more than once lately. His eyesight is nearly gone."

"Diancecht does seem frail, but his mind is as keen as

ever. If he is looking at you when you speak, he can understand everything."

"I know, but he was always so strong that his decline
makes me sad. It is hard to see my father like this, Lugh.
Someday you will see me in the same way." He laughed.
"When it happens, please remember to be kind."

"I will always be kind to you, Father. Just as you are
kind to Diancecht. All of his children honor him well."

"He has been a wonderful father to Airmead, Miach,
and me. We will be forever grateful to him. I am amused
by the way King Nuad has taken to fatherhood. Have you
seen him with his babies, now that they are old enough to
respond to him? He should have been father to ten children, I think, the way he enjoys them."

"Often Queen Morrigan brings them to Queen Tailteann's house in the afternoon when Brigid is there with
Ruadon. Her baby is as big as Ultan and Tadgh even
though they have seen six turnings of the moon and he
has seen but three."

Cian laughed. "I'm not sure you like the babies as
much as you like the charioteer who comes every afternoon to look in on them."

"I can't deny it, Father. I am mad keen for Desheen
and cannot wait until we can be wed in the new year. You
like her too, don't you?"

"Indeed, I do. She fits in with the people here at Druim
Caein very well. She'll be a good bride for you, Lugh.
You wouldn't want a woman who didn't keep you on
your toes."

By the time the bathwater cooled, Lugh felt refreshed
and raised his reddened body from the bathwater to accept the drying cloth a servant handed him.

"It's about time for the daily adoration of the babies to
begin," he said to Cian. "I think I'll drop in on my foster
mother. Desheen will be there today."

Cian smiled without opening his eyes, and waved farewell to Lugh. He began to wonder how much he had
missed by not knowing Lugh until he was a grown lad.
Those laughing, growing children gathered in Tailteann's
house were a delight to everyone at Druim Caein, and
seemed like the ultimate proof of the gods' pleasure at
Nuad's restoration.

* * *

Desheen was waiting for Lugh outside the bathing compound. Her dark brown hair was still damp and curling around her face for she, too, had refreshed herself in the women's baths, and her cheeks were as red as his.

He smiled happily upon finding her there and slipped his arm around her waist. He bent to kiss her as she stood on tiptoe to reach his lips.

"Umm. You smell wonderful," he said, "like a rose in sunshine."

"Mmmm," she said with a laugh, "so do you! Where have you been all afternoon?"

They clasped hands and set off up the path to the southern side of Druim Caein where Queen Tailteann dwelt, before he answered her.

"We had a long meeting with King Nuad, Desheen. A scout has brought news of a possible Fomorian settlement on our western shore."

"No! Not even the Fomorians would be so brazen as to attempt to build a colony under our very noses, would they? That would be foolish!"

"All we know is what the scout told us, and he says that a sizable number of Fomorians have arrived and are planning to stay."

"Well, that's ridiculous. It can't be permitted, of course. What will be done?"

"Nothing has been decided for sure. The council will meet again in the morning. I hope we can agree on a course of action then."

He looked closely at Desheen, wanting to share his worries with her. He was concerned that he might be speaking of things that should be said only in the council's hearing, yet knew he could trust her. If she was going to be his lifelong mate, he had no wish to be bound by silence when it came to important matters concerning the tribe.

He lowered his voice and stopped in his tracks. "I have reason to believe that King Nuad wishes to stage an all-out battle with the Fomorians. He was already thinking in that direction after he got the message from Balor about sending him our youngsters of fifteen summers, and this news of a possible settlement seems to have confirmed his resolution that they must be stopped . . . once and for all time."

Desheen frowned. "Just a minute Lugh," she said, loosening her hand from his. She was annoyed that she had to tie her hair up again, but the thongs she used after her bath were new and stiff and refused to stay tied.

The sleeves of her garment fell back as she lifted her hands to tie up her wayward locks, revealing graceful arms as fair as new milk. Lugh never ceased to marvel at her beauty. He reached out and took the thongs from her.

"Don't tie it up. I like the way it looks around your face."

She tossed her thick brown curls, saying, "Keep the cursed thongs, then. They are too stiff to be of use to me." She raised her face to his for a kiss and playfully wrapped a tress around his neck.

They walked on and Lugh felt his spirits lifting even though their talk was of a terrible battle with the Fomorians.

"I prefer to stand and fight to the death if need be, rather than be tormented time and time again, with no clear decision as to which of us is the stronger tribe," Lugh declared.

"Yes, but, Lugh, where would such a battle be fought? You know what happened to our ancestors who went to Tor Conain with the same thought of finishing off the Fomorians. Most of them perished, and for those who lived, the long DeDanaan horror of being without a home began at that time. I would want to be very sure such a battle would be fought on the soil of our own Innis Ealga, or I could not support a decision to go to war."

Chapter Thirty-three

The weather turned bitterly cold at Druim Caein and even though the midday dining time approached, the white hoar-frost of morning still lay thick upon the fields surrounding the hill fort. Lugh would not have been surprised to see snowflakes at any moment but he did not feel the cold. A game of hurling always got his blood up and he was excited for the contest to begin.

"May I see your new lorg?" he asked Miach, reaching out for Miach's newly handcrafted hurley stick. Miach handed it to him proudly.

"It is a beautiful piece of work, Miach, you must have spent many days shaping and smoothing this piece of ash, for it is as sleek and pleasing to the touch as a jewel." Lugh ran his fingers over the lorg's striking end that had been flattened and curved to perfection.

"This might not be such an easy win for my team after all." Lugh teased the young physician. "How is Grandfather today?"

"He is better, although he says the cold causes his bones to ache. I don't think he'll be moving far from the fire today."

A ram's horn sounded and the fifteen players who comprised Lugh's team ran onto the frosty playing field, followed by the fifteen members of Miach's team.

From the moment King Nuad threw the liathroid up in the air and the opponents began to strike at it with their lorgs, it was clear that this was a game fought by fiercely competitive equals.

The first liathroid soon had to be replaced, for the small ball of hair lost its leather covering quickly as the teams struck, pushed, and carried it, trying to penetrate into their opponents' end of the field. Driving the liathroid between the two gorse bushes serving as goals would mean victory for either side, and both teams wanted to win badly.

While the men played at hurling, Brigid, Desheen, and Morrigan had gathered in Queen Tailteann's dwelling. The three babies played contentedly on a fur rug spread out on the floor, cooing and gurgling and eyeing one another with great interest. The adults looked on them with quiet affection and chatted of many things while Desheen braided Tailteann's lovely dark hair, streaked now by gray throughout.

Ruadon's little face turned red and he began to howl as though he had been pinched.

"What's the matter with him?" Tailteann asked.

"Just a bubble, probably," Brigid replied, "but he might be hungry. I swear by the gods that this child has an appetite as prodigious as his grandfather's!"

She lifted the squalling baby into her lap and offered him her breast. He took it greedily and the sound of his vigorous sucking filled the dwelling, causing the women to laugh heartily.

"Sounds like he is, indeed, a sapling sprung from the oak of Dagda Mor," Morrigan said with a chuckle.

They talked of the possibility of an all-out battle with the Fomorians while Brigid nursed her son. She had just set Ruadon back on the furs when a commotion arose outside. The shouting drew Morrigan to the door first. She saw flames crackling and leaping into the frozen sky from the thatched roof of a dwelling by the stone wall. She drew in her breath sharply when she saw strange warriors charging across the compound on horseback.

"Fomorians!" she cried. "We are being attacked!"

The raiders brandished torches as they rode toward the second house, intent on setting it ablaze.

"Quickly"—Morrigan shouted to the others—"we must make our way to the souterrain." She bent and picked up Tadgh. Each woman took the baby closest to her. Desheen picked up Ruadon and Brigid took Morrigan's other twin, Ultan.

"Come on," Morrigan commanded, "our only chance is in that tunnel. Run!"

She ran with the infant, Tadgh, in her arms. Desheen ran beside her and she could sense Brigid and Queen

ailteann right behind her. They fairly flew across the
ompound toward the secret entrance to the souterrain.

Queen Tailteann felt panic wash over her as precious
me ebbed away from them and she realized that they
ight not make it to safety. Amid the harsh hoofbeats of
e marauding horses and the war cries of the raiders, she
ttered a desperate prayer to all the gods.

Thick, black smoke whirled into the courtyard from the
urning thatch, making it difficult to see. Tailteann
ounded the corner of a dwelling and saw a horseman
earing down on her. He came so close she felt the damp
eat rising from the chest of his sweating horse. Moments
efore she felt the raider's javelin pierce her chest, she
ooked into his wicked black eyes and recognized Srang,
nce the champion Fir Bolg warrior. His expression
howed surprise and horror when he realized that he had
ounded his own queen.

Tailteann fell, and saw the terrified face of Brigid hov-
ring over her. She screamed, "Save the baby, Brigid,
on't stop. Save the baby!"

Unconsciousness enfolded her in its dark cloak, sparing
er the sight of a handsome blond raider who rode up be-
ide Brigid and tore the infant she held from her grasp.
le thundered off with a triumphant cry.

Trumpets of alarm brought DeDanaan warriors from
e fields and the hurling contest too late to save the in-
ant Ultan. They pounded on horseback into the burning
ompound to defend its residents and fought a pitched
attle with the remaining raiders. The outrage of the
eDanaans enabled them to overcome the attackers in a
hort time. All survivors were taken as captives. Before
ounting up their own dead and wounded, Lugh leapt
rom Anovaar and ran to search for Queen Tailteann and
esheen.

He found his mother where she had fallen and knelt by
er side. "Mother, Mother," he said hoarsely.

She stirred slightly at the sound of his voice and
pened her eyes. The absolute terror that had seized
ugh's heart when he saw her lying on the ground with
javelin protruding from her chest abated somewhat. She
as still alive.

"Miach! Here! Come here, it's Queen Tailteann!" I shouted.

The young physician ran toward them and dropped his knees beside her. A look of horror came over his fac when he saw what had befallen Queen Tailteann. He i spected her wound and withdrew his hand as though l had touched something hot. Her dark red blood drippe from his fingers.

"Help me, Lugh, We must carry her away from th smoke and chaos so I can see to stem the bleeding. Let take her over there, out of the way." He gestured towar the wall where her royal Fir Bolg emblem fluttered in th smoke.

Queen Tailteann moaned when they lifted her, an blood bubbled from her wound as the javelin was jostle Both men were drenched in her blood by the time the laid her gently on the grassy slope. Lugh took her sma hand in his and looked at the fingers he loved so we Her nails were blue. He felt the terror of helplessne again. He raised her hand to his lips and kissed it.

"Oh, Mother," he cried, "don't die. Miach is here an he is going to heal you. Stay with me, please."

Her eyelids fluttered and with a superhuman effort sl managed to say, "Lugh ..." Then she was still. Miac worked over her for a few more moments until both l and Lugh realized that her stillness had become complet Miach reached out and touched Lugh on the shoulde "Lugh. It's over. The gods have called her to them Lugh's beloved foster mother, Tailteann, Queen of the F Bolgs, was dead.

The knowledge entered Lugh's mind slowly, as thoug time had become as heavy as stone, bringing with it a exquisite pain that he had never known before. He imag ined that he could feel the javelin piercing his own ches invading his internal organs, twisting slowly and cruell

Lugh roared with pain and shouted, "No! No! By a the gods there be, No! Mother, Mother!"

His grief was so raw that the physician was frightene by it. Lugh leaped to his feet with a loud cry that mig have rent the heavens in two with its anguish. With h foster mother's blood growing sticky on his hands, l pulled Frega, King Eochy's sword, from its scabbard an pointed it toward the sky.

"Those who spilled this precious blood will pay!" he raged. "I vow by the sun and the moon that whoever committed this crime will pay with his own blood before this day is done." Lugh spun on his heel and ran for Anovaar.

Miach was still kneeling by the queen's body when Lugh came thundering past him and rode out of the gate at a full gallop, bound for the royal meetinghouse where the Fomorian hostages had been taken.

In the dark tunnel Morrigan's anguish filled the space until there seemed to be no air left for the others to breathe.

"They took my baby!" she wailed.

An ashen Brigid said, "It was Breas who took your child, Morrigan. I recognized him. Oh, I'm so sorry. I would have laid down my life to save Ultan. I love him as I love Ruadon." She began to cry. Between sobs she managed to say, "I think Breas must have thought Ultan was my son."

Morrigan's anger now knew no bounds. "You mean my son was stolen by Breas because he thought he was taking his own child? By the gods! I've got to tell King Nuad what has happened to his son. We must find him . . . fast."

She rose, Tadgh still in her arms. The baby's eyes were wide and frightened but he made no sound as he sucked on his two middle fingers.

"No," Desheen cried, grabbing her arm. "You dare not go out there yet. You would not expose Tadgh to the same fate, would you? I'll go. No one needs me as much as these children need the two of you."

The good sense of her words forced Morrigan to agree. "Go then and tell King Nuad that we must organize a search party and head out immediately to find our son before he is harmed. Hurry." She practically pushed Desheen up the ladder that would take her out of the souterrain.

Morrigan, the strongest of DeDanaan women, burst into tears, unable to speak aloud her greatest fear. She held Tadgh tightly to her bosom, and let her tears fall on his little downy head.

* * *

Desheen cautiously made her way to the feasting hall where the hostages had been taken and entered through one of the side doors. There were eleven men, bound and looking hostile, lined up in the front of the long hall. Activity and confusion surrounded them, making it difficult to comprehend the situation at a glance.

King Nuad came striding up the center of the room to his chair at the front, and a semblance of order followed his passage. She could see that there was one DeDanaan captor standing near each captive. The prisoners looked like Fomorians. Desheen could not understand how Breas could have come to be part of a Fomorian raiding party.

King Nuad formed his words so deliberately that she realized he was barely able to contain his rage.

"Who are you and why do you attack innocent women and children?" he asked the hostages.

There was defiant silence from them. "Speak, you!" the king commanded. "We will brook no further insolence from you."

Reluctantly, Cochpar, the leader of the Fomorian tribute collectors, spoke. "We were sent by Balor of the Evil Eye, King of the Fomorians, to collect the tribute that you owe him."

King Nuad snorted in contempt. "Ha! We owe you nothing and even if we did, how could you justify the raid upon our southern settlement? Tell me, what possible reason you could have for such a senseless, brutal raid?"

In a voice barely audible, Cochpar said hoarsely, "It is the custom."

"Custom? What do you mean it is the custom? We have long thought of you Fomorians as savage beasts and now you have the audacity to confirm it by telling me that it is your custom to kill wantonly?"

"Our king commanded us to strike fear into the hearts of our enemies so that we may prevail over them in all things," Cochpar said defensively. The other Fomorians were silent, and stood looking down at the earthen floor of the feasting house, the structure that was so coveted by their king that he had sent them on this mission of death.

Desheen felt her stomach twist with contempt for the captives in front of her. She realized that her fingers were clenched tightly around the beautifully made bronze knife

Lugh had given her. She still felt threatened by these men, even though they were bound and closely guarded.

How could she add to the king's burden by telling him that one of his sons had been kidnapped? She pushed her hair away from her sweaty, dirt-stained face and walked bravely to the front of the hall. Just as she opened her mouth to address King Nuad, Lugh burst through the door closest to her.

The ferocious look on his face terrified her. His handsome features were distorted with rage and he was covered with blood. The captives looked up as he entered with his sword held high and cowered in terror.

Lugh knew he could not identify which of the captives had actually thrown the javelin that took Queen Tailteann's life, so he was determined to kill as many Fomorans as he could in this first moment of surprise.

He ran straight toward Cochpar and struck his neck broadside with a mighty blow of King Eochy's sword. The force was such that it sent the head of the tribute collector spinning onto the floor among the feet of the other captives who jumped back in horror. Blood spurted from Cochpar's neck like a fountain until his still upright body slumped to the floor and spilled its life fluid out onto the hard-packed earth.

"That is for my mother!" Lugh shouted as he raised his sword again and swung at another victim.

Desheen shouted, her voice shrill and all but lost among the clamor in the hall. "No, Lugh! Don't do it!"

He heard her say no, just as King Nuad seized the wrist of his sword arm. "Stop, Lugh," the king commanded, "this is not DeDanaan justice."

Desheen rushed to Lugh's side and took his other arm. The three of them stood that way for some time, the king holding Lugh's wrist and Desheen grasping his trembling arm. Slowly and with great effort, Lugh raised his eyes to look at them.

He said flatly, "Queen Tailteann is dead, pierced through with a javelin thrown by one of these bloodthirsty beasts."

Those closest to the trio heard what Lugh said and repeated it to those behind them. In a very short time the hall was buzzing with the unbearable news that the beloved Fir Bolg queen had been murdered. Many among them wished to put all of the captives to the sword. A cry of, "Let Lugh finish them off!" was heard above the roar of the crowd.

"Are you now able to control your anger, Lugh?" the king demanded.

Lugh nodded dumbly. King Nuad looked meaningfully at Desheen and she acknowledged that she would stay close to Lugh. She took Lugh's hand and squeezed it and was horrified to realize that Tailteann's blood was now on her hand too.

Lugh took comfort from Desheen's presence, although he was unable to look at her or speak to her. His mind was numb. He could no longer think. The rage that had blinded him began to trickle away as the last drops of the blood of Cochpar the Fomorian, trickled from his lifeless body.

King Nuad looked away from Lugh for the first time since he had stayed his hand. A frown crossed his face and he raised his silver hand, demanding silence.

"DeDanaans," the king shouted, "still your blood lust! If we slaughter these captives we will be no better than they. Do you wish to return to the level of savagery that they have so brutally shown us this day? Lugh has acted in a frenzy of grief and rage for they have killed Queen Tailteann, his foster mother. Let us respect the life of this wonderful woman. We would honor her most by refraining from senseless murder. These men will stand before our laws and pay for their crimes. This, I promise you."

The enormity of Tailteann's loss was creeping into Nuad's heart even as he spoke, and he feared his voice might break and betray the depth of his feeling. He, who had so loved a good fight when he was young, now heard words coming from his mouth that Tailteann had once spoken to him.

"We must never let blood lust or revenge win out over reason," he cried.

Lugh hard the familiar words and his heart contracted with pain. He would never hear Tailteann's sweet voice saying those words ... or any others ... to him ... ever again.

He released Desheen's hand and took a step closer to the king. "You are right, King Nuad," he said loudly, then turned to address the DeDanaans. "Queen Tailteann

aught me always to apply reason over impulse and in my
great grief at her loss I failed to do so. I know she would
wish us to judge these men according to the laws. I
should like to do otherwise but I will stay my hand, as
you must. Our strength is in the law and I implore you to
let reason prevail."

"Thank you, Lugh. We will now convene the Council
of the Wise and make our decision. As the most ag-
rieved party here, I invite you to sit at the head of the
able with us to seek justice."

"Wait, my lord, I must speak," Desheen said to King
Nuad. "The raiders have committed another crime against
he DeDanaans. I regret deeply that I must tell you that
hey have stolen your son, Ultan, from Brigid's arms as
he ran for safety. The raiders have ridden out of the compound with him. Brigid has identified the kidnapper as
her former husband, Breas. She believes that he has allied
himself with the Fomorians and that he thought he was
stealing Prince Ruadon."

King Nuad took an involuntary breath. "Where are the
queen and Tadgh?" he asked in a trembling voice.

"I left them in the shelter of the souterrain. Not knowing if the raiders were still attacking, we thought it better
I came to seek you out alone."

"Are they hurt?"

"They are not, King Nuad."

"By the gods!" Nuad swore. "We must start after the
kidnappers immediately and get my son back. Guards! Go
to the souterrain at once and bring Queen Morrigan and
he others here to the feasting hall. Watch my wife and
my son with special care. Move!"

Chapter Thirty-four

Morrigan ran into the feasting hall, her long auburn hair undone and streaming behind her, clutching Tadgh to her bosom. "Nuad, Nuad," she screamed, "they have stolen Ultan. We must mount our horses and ride after them before the trail is cold."

"Come here," he demanded. "Let me see you and Tadgh." He reached out for the baby and took him in his arms. The child looked at his father and gurgled happily, flailing his tiny hands as he tried to seize his father's nose, innocently unaware of the peril his twin brother faced.

Nuad took a deep breath filled with relief. The child was unharmed. He handed him back to his mother. "You are not hurt?" he asked Morrigan, measuring his tone to keep his fear from showing. His eyes told her all that he was feeling.

"I am wounded to the core, Nuad. They have stolen our son! Don't you understand? There is no time to stand here talking. We must ride at once to find him and bring him back."

The mantle of kingship lay heavily upon Nuad's shoulders. He knew that delay could not be tolerated, but his duty to the tribe demanded his presence at the Council of the Wise.

"Morrigan, try to understand that my heart urges me to ride in search of our son, but duty demands that I not leave the people without a leader in this terrible chaos.

Her earth-dark eyes flashed with anger. "I shall ride without you then, Nuad. Who will come with me to find the stolen DeDanaan prince?" she demanded of those in the hall.

Cian stood and said, "I will go with you." Others followed.

Lugh did not volunteer to accompany Morrigan, not even when Desheen agreed to go. He had to stay with the council to seek justice for the slaying of his mother, and to plan her funeral.

Macha and Neimain were by Morrigan's side, ready to ride with her search party, when Brigid and Brig approached the queen.

"Give Tadgh to us, Queen Morrigan," Brigid said, "and ride like the wind after Ultan. We will see that your son is well cared for until you return with his brother. I will nurse him as though he were Ruadon."

Brig held out his arms. Morrigan hesitated a moment, but finally, she placed her son in Brigid's care. "Thank you," she said.

She whirled around to leave but was stopped by Nuad's voice.

"I will join the search as soon as the council adjourns, Morrigan. In which direction will you ride?"

"Northwesterly." She eyed the prisoners. "Is that not the direction in which your thieving comrades have gone?"

Two of the frightened men nodded yes. Before Nuad could speak again, she and her sisters were out the door, running for the horse pens.

At the end of the meeting of the Council of the Wise, the Dagda Mor announced their consensus to the surviving Fomorian raiders. They would be escorted by a DeDanaan war party to the coast of Donegal where their boats lay waiting. They would carry the head of Cochpar back to their king, as proof of the DeDanaan's ire and power. They must present it to him and tell him that there would never be another tribute paid to a Fomorian so long as a DeDanaan drew breath.

The terrified captives cowered before Dagda's words, knowing that as fragile as their well-being was in the heart of the DeDanaan tribe, they would be in even greater danger when they arrived on Tor Conain bearing Cochpar's severed head. Balor's rage was too awful to contemplate.

"Listen carefully, Fomorians," Dagda concluded. "You will give your king notice that we, the DeDanaan tribe, do hereby declare that a battle to the death will be fought against the Fomorian tribe on the Northern Plain of Moytirra, on the day of midwinter after Samhain."

Lugh nodded his head in approval of the pronouncement, a grim look on his face. No DeDanaan should ever again have to suffer the grief that filled his heart to overflowing. For that, Lugh was willing to lay down his life.

He glanced at King Nuad who sat in his chair at the front of the hall, glowering at the captives. The king's impatience with the proceedings was obvious. He wanted to join those already out searching for his son.

Dagda warned the hostages. "If any Fomorian should be so foolish as to launch an attack against us before the appointed time, be assured that it will be repulsed without such mercy as has been shown to you here today. Look around you at the DeDanaans and you will know that we are ready to fight a holy war against the wrongs your people have done us. The great gods will assist us because our cause is just. Make no mistake about that."

"Morrigan, we've got to stop," Macha implored. "It's too dark to go on. We'll be putting the horses at risk if we try to ride farther tonight. Please, be reasonable. I promise you that we will be off at the first light of day."

"She's right, Morrigan," Neimain called from behind them, "we have to stop."

Morrigan rode on without answering them. Her rage had carried her this far and she was afraid to stop, afraid to let herself imagine what fate might have befallen her infant son. Her horse stumbled and she lurched forward. She had to grasp his mane for balance.

"How can I stop, Macha?" she asked bitterly. "Tell me how a mother can rein in and do nothing while beasts have her child. Tell me that, will you?"

"If we don't stop, Morrigan, we will have little chance of finding him at all. Those who took Ultan will have to stop for the night and rest, too. They can't see in the dark any more than we can. I'm sure we will be able to make up ground in the morning. They can't be too far ahead of us."

Macha pulled her horse in and stopped. Those behind her did the same. Morrigan rode on but halted when she realized that the others were no longer following. She surveyed their location on a broad treeless plain and turned to address the others.

"All right, but we can't stop here," she said. "As soon as the moon rises we will be seen too easily. We must make for the woods." She pointed to a jagged black outline on a rise to the left of the party.

Riding that far in the darkness was against Desheen's judgment. She had fear that one of the horses might be injured, but she decided to say nothing for she had no wish to know the sting of Morrigan's temper. It had grown worse with every moment away from her son.

On the morning of the second day of the search, King Nuad, Lugh, Dagda, and seven others left Druim Caein and rode hard in a northwesterly direction, hoping to catch up with Morrigan's party.

Before the sun was high in the sky, Lugh urged Anovaar into a trot alongside the king. "I've been thinking, my lord. Perhaps we should fan out and cover more territory instead of trying to meet up with Morrigan's party. You said yourself that we lost the Fomorian tracks back there by the bog."

Nuad frowned. He had considered the same thing. "What you say has merit, Lugh, but what would a handful of warriors be able to do if they did find the kidnappers? I think we are stronger if we stay together. . . . We don't know how many of them there are. We don't even know why they took Ultan, for certain. I wouldn't be surprised if a ransom demand is at this moment being delivered to Druim Caein."

"But Brigid and Desheen were almost positive it was Breas," Lugh said, thinking that King Nuad did not want to face the truth.

Lugh was sure it would have been easy for a man of Breas's character to ally himself with the hated Fomorians. A man who beat his wife could be expected to do such a dishonorable thing.

Nuad was strangely silent, so Lugh pressed on.

"I can think of a compelling reason why Breas would join up with the Fomorians," he said. "He wants them to help him regain the throne of Innis Ealga."

King Nuad looked at Lugh curiously. He could be right but it was something he would have to think about another day. Right now nothing mattered but his family. He was afraid Morrigan wouldn't use good judgment if rage alone propelled her. He was glad that Cian and Desheen were riding with her because both of them were of careful, reasoning natures. But he also knew how powerful Morrigan's personality could be; he would not rest easily until he found her.

"Maybe, Lugh, maybe. I don't know. Right now, I have to find Morrigan and together we will rescue our son."

Lugh struggled to hide his exasperation.

"Would you object if I were to take, say three warriors, and ride north?" he asked deferentially. "We can set a time and place to meet you. I have such a strong feeling that we need to spread out and cover as much territory as possible that I won't be easy until I try."

Nuad sighed. He felt so emotionally weary that he did not want to have to make another decision. "All right, Lugh, go ahead. Meet us tomorrow before the sun goes down, on the eastern shore of Upper Lough Erne. I'm sure the Fomorians are making for the coast. Either they'll try to get back to their new settlement or to their boats on the western shore. I warn you, though, that if you aren't at the lough by sunup of the next day, we will have to ride on without you."

"I understand, my lord, and thank you. We'll be there. May one of us have your son safely in our care when next we meet."

Lugh pulled Anovaar about and went back to the others to recruit three comrades to ride with him. He knew Dagda would be willing because he had expressed a similar wish to widen the search.

At Druim Caein the physicians, Airmead and Miach, were preparing Queen Tailteann's body for the royal funeral that would be held as soon as the searchers returned.

In the house of Dagda Mor, Brigid and Cairbed bent their heads together late into the night composing the funeral song he would sing for the Fir Bolg queen.

Brigid had felt timid about going to Cairbed with her poem, but she reasoned that the words, which came unbidden into her head, must have been sent by the gods. The rhyme had shimmered within her imagination even as tears of grief fell down her cheeks. Her sorrow at losing Tailteann was so profound that she knew she could not have consciously composed anything.

Cairbed received her poem warmly and began to put it to a tune.

He plucked at his harp, frowned, and stopped to adjust the wooden pegs that held the gut strings taut. When he was satisfied that the tone was true, he plucked the strings softly and began to sing her words.

"Sure, the world won't be seeing the likes of Tailteann in it for many and many a year," she said to Cairbed as the last notes from his harp faded away. She wiped a tear from her eye and smiled sadly at him. It was lovely to have him here with her in her house while all the world slept around them.

"Don't weep now, my dear Brigid," Cairbed said. "When I go back to the bard's house it's not a sad woman I want to be leaving behind this night. The funeral day will dawn soon enough and there will be plenty of tears then."

He felt a lump rising in his own throat at the thought of a final farewell to Queen Tailteann. He reached out to comfort Brigid and was almost as surprised as she was when the gesture ended in an embrace, followed by a shy kiss.

When Cairbed finally slipped from Brigid's dwelling into the star-sparkled night, he walked in wonder across the compound toward the guest house, leaving Brigid alone to marvel at the events of the day.

Her heart was too full to permit slumber. She had not thought to find love in her lifetime, especially not in the midst of sorrow, but there it was. She loved Cairbed and he loved her. He said he always had. Why had she been so blinded by Breas's shining good looks when she'd had a man of solid gold next to her all the time?

She stepped outside the dwelling and looked up at the night sky, thinking how strange were the ways of the gods. "Do you toy with us mortals for your own amusement?" she whispered. She drew her cloak a little tighter about her shoulders, and returned to the warmth of her fire. She knew there would be no answer.

Chapter Thirty-five

Dagda's belly rumbled from hunger. "By the gods, Lugh," he said, "I'm going into the woods and fire an arrow at a wood hen. I can't keep going without food and we've had none all day."

"What do you mean? There is still bread left in our bags."

"You call that food? No, I must have meat to turn upon the spit. There is still light enough to hunt. I'll be back in no time."

The thought of a decent meal was appealing to Lugh and the others as well, but Dagda's stamina amazed him. It had been a hard day's ride without a single sign of the Fomorians. Lugh was dejected and coming to believe that he should have heeded King Nuad and stayed with the others. He shrugged. "All right," he said, "but don't go far and be sure to get back here before darkness falls. We can't go searching for you, too."

"I'll be back with food for our bellies in no time at all." Dagda laughed and turned his horse to ford a small creek that flowed between them and a tall stand of trees in the distance.

After a short ride across a rocky plain, he led his sturdy brown steed down a steep descent toward the river Uinnius, balancing precariously as they negotiated the difficult terrain.

Suddenly, there came the loud clatter and beat of horses' hooves as four strange warriors swooped down upon him. They rode straight toward him with upraised swords, uttering ferocious cries. Startled, Dagda pulled his horse sharply to the left, causing the animal to lose his footing and stumble. He lurched sideways and fell with a resounding thump against sharp stones.

The only weapon Dagda had on his person was a dagger. He knew it would be of little use against the superior swords being wielded by the warriors, but as he lay on his belly he slipped the knife from its sheath and slid it beneath his leg wrappings. If he willingly yielded up his arrows and the sword hanging on his horse, perhaps his attackers would not search him too carefully.

When he realized the men surrounding him bore the dark, grim visages of Fomorians, he feared for his life. Their leader leaped from his horse and commanded, "Get up if you can, old man, or be stuck through where you lie." He brandished his sword menacingly.

Dagda did as he was bid. Every bone and sinew hurt and his thigh burned where the stones and gravel had scraped the skin way, but he struggled to his feet.

"Identify yourself. Who are you and what are you doing in these parts traveling alone?" demanded the warrior.

Dagda thought fast. He would have to lie to protect the others who were riding abroad in this area searching for the baby.

"I am Dagda the DeDanann. I am in these parts because I have been visiting my son, Bove the Red, in Ulster. My manservant was taken ill while I was in my son's residence so I travel alone back to my home. My son has so few settlers that I declined to take another servant from his colony believing, wrongly I see, that I would not be in danger."

"Bind him," the war chief Conan said. "We will take him to our camp and see what Indech wants to do with him."

He turned to Dagda the Wise and asked, with a wicked smile on his thin lips, "Are you the Dagda of great girth, the man known for the size of his cauldron and his gluttony? By the gods, I do believe you are! Men! We have captured the great glutton of the DeDanaans, the man about whom jokes are made and whose excesses amuse all the peoples of the northern lands! I think there will be merriment in our camp this night."

Dagda was shocked and offended that he was known to these savages, not for his wisdom or standing within the DeDanann tribe, but for his huge appetite. He made no reply to the taunts of his captors, refusing to speak more than his name and tribal connection.

* * *

Thirteen warriors, men and women, all dark and fierce looking, were sitting around a fire eating and drinking, when the small Fomorian watch party rode in with the captive Dagda.

The warriors were excited by the diversion and stopped eating to watch the newcomer. Many mocked and jeered at the sight of his great belly. All recognized him as a DeDanaan. The leader, Conan, silenced them with a menacing gesture and they went sullenly back to their food, keeping their eyes on Dagda.

The Fomorian chief, Indech, stood to greet Dagda. He was short but powerfully built. His upper arms were so big they bulged against the sleeves of his dirty tunic. He wore a long dark beard, streaked with gray. Around his forehead was a greasy leather thong tied in back, to keep his filthy black hair out of his face. A long copper dagger was thrust in his belt and on his back he carried a quiver of birch wood arrows. Dagda felt fear ripple though his belly even as the delicious aroma coming from the cooking cauldron made his knees weak. He knew he was in a perilous position and had to keep his wits about him; this was no time to think of food.

When Indech determined that the DeDanaan before him was indeed the renowned Dagda, and that he was not going to get any more from him than his name and tribe and some phony story about his presence here, he asked, "Are you hungry, old man?"

For a moment, Dagda was hopeful of humane treatment. Feeling limp from hunger, he nodded yes.

"Prepare a plate for our guest then," Indech said to Conan. Dagda's bonds were loosened, and he was handed a wooden bowl filled to the brim with boiled fish, oatmeal, and wild leeks. He tried to eat slowly without seeming eager, but his hunger was great. When he finished, he was offered a beaker of ale. Gratefully, he accepted it and downed it in one long gulp.

"Would you have more then, Dagda?" asked Indech, narrowing his small dark eyes and baring his teeth in the semblance of a smile.

"Yes, thank you," Dagda replied. He looked around the fire at the cruel, expectant faces of the Fomorians and realized that he was being offered not hospitality, but ridicule. He was confused about what to do next. He had to bide his time and go along with them if he wished to get out of this predicament alive.

Some hours later, the Fomorians, led by Conan, dumped Dagda unceremoniously along the banks of the river Uinnius. "Tell your fine new king what he can expect from us if he fails to honor the bargain your previous king struck with us. Our mighty King Balor insists on having his due. We will ride to the DeDanaan royal enclosure at a day and an hour of our own choosing.

"On that day we expect to collect all the tribute a subservient people should be grateful to provide, including your firstlings of fifteen summers. Tell your king we send our regards!" With that, Conan and his laughing comrades wheeled their horses and rode off.

They had forced Dagda to eat until his already great belly was as distended as that of any woman ready to give birth. He was sick and filled with great anger at having been made to suffer such humiliation at the hands of these brutes.

He was also glad to be alive and had made no sound of protest when they stole his horse and all of his belongings, leaving him only the tunic he wore and his leg wrappings. They had even stolen his leather boots, jesting that there was enough leather in them to cover an entire fleet of curraghs, and they would be useful on their journey back to Tor Conain.

He heard them ride off but he was too ill to lift his head. He rose to his hands and knees on the sandy strand where they discarded him and retched and retched until every morsel he had been forced to eat was purged. The effort left him weak and longing to bathe in the river, but the sun had long since set and the night air was cold. Without a cloak to warm him he was already shivering violently. He knew he had need of shelter and had to find it fast.

He staggered a short distance down the bank until the rising moon revealed a sandbar in the middle of the river. He reasoned that he could probably pass the night safely there. He tested the depth of the water with an ash branch he found on the ground. He drew his knife from its hiding place and used it to cut an armload of tall grasses grow-

ing along the shore. He unwrapped his leggings and
tucked the bindings under his belt. Then he turned up the
skirt of his tunic and tucked it under his belt as well.
Gathering up the fragrant grasses, he stepped gingerly
into the icy water. The cold penetrated to the bone and his
legs were numb before he reached the sandbar. How he
longed for the gift of fire. It was unlikely that wild boar
or wolves would cross the moving waters to seek him
out, but fire would warm and dry him, and give him comfort against the darkness of the night.

Dagda slept fitfully, believing that the night lasted
longer than any he had ever known. He awoke with the
first light of dawn in the crude bed of grass he had made
for himself, thirstier than he had ever been in his life. He
made his way to the edge of the sandbar and lay down to
drink his fill from the cool, clean waters of the Uinnius.
When he sat up he was disgusted by the rank odors of
vomit and smoke that were on him as reminders of last
night's humiliation.

He removed his tunic and shivered in the morning air,
regarding it closely. There was no help for it. It had to be
washed and so did he. He soaked the garment in the water, rubbed it deftly with sand, and rinsed it again, then
spread the tunic across a small hawthorne tree that had
somehow taken root in the sand. He glanced skyward.

There were a few wispy clouds moving overhead and
the strong golden rays of the sun illuminated their under-
sides. *Thank the gods,* he thought, *the sun is going to
smile upon me this morning.* It seemed only fair after
what he had been through.

Bracing himself, he entered the river and forced himself to seek a deep enough spot in which to bathe. At last
he was covered to his neck with freezing water. *By the
gods this wakes a fellow up!* he thought, and quickly
scooped up handfuls of black sand filled with silver
specks from the bottom of the river to rub his skin vigorously. After he washed his face and hair, he sat back and
let the soothing waters flow over him where he was stiff
and sore from his fall. The water felt good now, moving
against his badly scraped and bruised thigh. He wondered
if the water might have healing properties, just as the
many sacred wells throughout Innis Ealga did.

Finally, he left the water and strode, naked, back toward the sandbar.

He had been so sure that the Sun God was going to reveal himself fully this morning that he was surprised to see a heavy mist curling up from the river. He could no longer see the sandbar. *What a fine cauldron of stew this is,* he thought. *How is a man to find his only tunic in such a fog?*

"Ho there, you are a grand figure of a man, indeed!" came the bold cry of a woman from the riverbank.

Startled out of his solitude, Dagda turned his great head and strained to see who called him. As if by sorcery, a break in the fog allowed a shaft of sunlight to stream through, illuminating the figure of the most voluptuous woman Dagda had ever seen. So dazzled was he, he did not wonder how it was that she could have seen him through the thick, mysterious fog.

She was short and dark skinned, standing with her feet far apart, her hands on her hips, staring admiringly at his nakedness. Dagda made no move to cover himself for indeed, his large appetites were not limited to food and he was long accustomed to taking pleasure wherever it was offered.

He looked at her heavy breasts straining against a tunic that looked as though it had not been washed for many turnings of the moon.

"And you, lass," he called, "are a grand figure of a woman, indeed you are. If you would care to come closer I will be pleased to show you just what manner of man I am."

He was delighted when she raised her hands over her head and pulled her tunic off in one graceful motion. She stood and allowed him to look at her, as brazenly unashamed of her body as he was of his.

Those are fine strong thighs indeed, he thought. *They will provide a fair welcome for the likes of this big fellow.* He patted his penis and his thoughts were translated into action as it stirred to life and rose, fully erect.

The sight of it seemed to inflame the dark beauty making her way toward him through the water. She tossed her long black hair, like a colt frolicking in a meadow, and came to where he stood.

When she reached Dagda she touched his manhood

gently, then fell to her knees in the water and kissed it. "By all the gods in the heavens, I have never seen anything like this in all my days," she said approvingly.

He took her, the first time, right there in the river. By the time the Sun God was high in the sky all signs of the morning's fog had cleared away. Dagda carried the woman to the strand known as Eda, and there they coupled many times.

"If we do this once more," she said at last, "I think you might thrust your way through my body and carry us both to the land of the gods, for mortals are not allowed to know such joy."

When their passion seemed spent they lay touching and talked for the first time. She told him her name was Dedecha and that she was the daughter of Indech, the greatest of all Fomorian champions. Dagda choked. Was that not the name of the chieftain who had humiliated him last night?

"I am a map maker," she told him, "sent with the tribute collectors to get the lay of your land. I was working yesterday and went too far to get back to the camp in time for the evening meal, so I just stayed where I was for the night. I often do that. My father does not like it, but I can take care of myself."

Dagda was glad she had not been there to witness his degradation. "Sure and it fills my heart with sorrow that you are a Fomorian," he said truthfully, "for I am known as Dagda the Wise and I am a Dedanaan, a sworn enemy of your people."

"My heart too, fills with sorrow at the enmity of our peoples, but it does not mean that you and I must be enemies," she said.

He picked up her small brown hand and brushed it with his lips. "Enemies, you and I? Never. I feel the hand of the gods in our meeting. Surely you must feel it too?"

"I do," she said laughing. "Who but a god could have dreamed you up? I have never in all my days seen a creature such as yourself."

"Perhaps we two can be of use in bringing about a lasting peace between our tribes. Your father is a powerful warrior and I am not without modesty when I say to you that I have some influence in King Nuad's court."

He could see her eyes cloud over with doubt. She had

no wish to betray her people, yet she was eager to please Dagda. He saw her hesitation and caressed her firm pink nipples. They rose to his touch like ripening strawberries yearning toward the sun.

He pulled her upright, and placed her astride him. Coupling this way, her passion rose to a new high, to match his own.

When Dagda Mor rode toward the place where he had left Lugh and the others, he was sitting upon the back of Dedecha's small pony, carrying her leather fes filled with food. He could still smell her scent upon his skin and the memory of her caused his indefatigable member to stir. By the gods! How he hoped they would ordain another meeting with her. He had never known such coupling, and he was a man of considerable experience. Surely the gods would not bring her to him only to deny them another meeting.

He whistled as he rode on, sexually sated and happy in the knowledge that he had invaluable information to pass on. He was barely aware of the awkwardness of trying to ride with his feet wrapped in soft green mosses that had grown in the shady places beside the river Uinnius.

Chapter Thirty-six

Morrigan's anxiety turned to frenzy as time passed and they found no tracks of the Fomorians who had stolen her son, Ultan. The others in her party were profoundly relieved when they saw King Nuad and his warriors riding toward them.

Nuad galloped straight to Morrigan's side. He leaned across the distance between them to embrace her and kiss her. "My beloved one, we have knowledge of where our son has been taken. Dagda was told by a Fomorian map maker that Breas has indeed, taken up with them, in hopes of regaining the throne. He stole our son, believing Ultan to be his own child, and he has taken him to the place on the western shore where the Fomorians would establish a colony."

"Let us be off then. There is no time to waste. We have searched too long already and fear eats at my heart for our son," Morrigan said.

Nuad saw the dark circles under her lovely eyes, the pallidness of her fair skin, and he knew she was pushing herself beyond mortal endurance. How he wished she could have been spared such anguish.

"We must cool our horses before we continue. Dismount and Dagda will tell you all that he has learned, won't you, Dagda?"

"Of course, sire," he said.

Many miles later, the DeDanaans, led by bone-weary Nuad and Morrigan, came over the crest of a hill and saw below them a rough, makeshift settlement, barely more than a camp. King Nuad held his hand up cautiously, and the party slowed to a stop. No smoke rose from the huts.

"It looks deserted, Nuad. What if they have taken Ultan to Tor Conain? We'll never get him back if they've done that," Morrigan cried.

"I don't see how they have had time. Lugh, Cian, will you scout this place out? I don't want to ride into a Fomorian ambush. Go around to the south of the camp and take the last few lengths on foot. Be careful not to be seen and get back up here as fast as you can. We'll wait behind that thicket of pine trees," the king said.

"Be careful, Lugh," Desheen whispered. "Oh, please, don't take any chances."

"Don't worry," he reassured her. "As much as I want to see those savages brought to justice, I'm not going to do anything foolish." He leaned over and kissed her. "Besides, I know you'll be waiting for me. That's all the incentive I need to be cautious." He covered her hand with his own, then looked at Cian.

"Ready?" he asked.

The two of them rode silently to the Fomorian settlement and the waiting group of DeDanaans uttered silent prayers for their safety.

When they returned, Cian spoke to the king and queen. This camp is deserted. Could we have come to the wrong place?" A worried frown creased his face. He addressed Dagda. "You're sure this is the settlement the map maker told you about?"

"It looks like it," Dagda answered, "but she said nothing about the Fomorians leaving. She said they meant to establish a permanent colony."

"We have to be sure," Morrigan said, whipping her horse and riding toward the camp. Nuad wheeled his big stallion around and followed after her.

"I wish she'd let one of us go first," Lugh said, exasperated by Morrigan's headstrong and reckless behavior.

The rest of the search party caught up with Morrigan and Nuad as they crossed the ditch surrounding the small settlement. The queen jumped from her horse and ran into the compound. She knelt at the first fire she came to and felt the ashes. They were cool on top but warm underneath.

"It hasn't been so long since this place was occupied," she said. "Quickly . . . search every dwelling." She wiped her hands on her tunic and turned to commence the search.

Lugh and Desheen found the infant Ultan in the second house they searched. Lugh spoke not a word as he looked

down at the broken body of the baby, but he felt his hear
turn to stone within him.

"Oh, it can't be!" Desheen cried and moved to pick up
the still, small form.

"No," Lugh said, reaching out to restrain her. "don'
touch him. He's dead. His parents must see for them
selves what has been done."

Desheen shook her head. There was horror in her eyes
"No, Lugh, I think they should be spared this sight. I
would be unkind to make them look upon it."

"How else can they know what it is that we mus
avenge when we stand in battle with the Fomorians?"

"We can tell them, Lugh. They don't have to see thei
baby like this."

"They must. I'm not being hard, Desheen, believe me
but I know that what one can imagine is far worse thar
the knowledge of what really happened. Remember Aibe
and her imagined demons? Reality, no matter how hard
is better when faced head-on."

Desheen was not convinced, but she was willing to
concede the point. "We will go together to tell them?"
she asked.

Lugh nodded and took her hand. They left the dwelling
and had gone but a few steps when Desheen began to cry
"I can't bear all of this, Lugh. First your mother, and now
this innocent baby . . . ," she sobbed.

Lugh held her and tried to comfort her. Although hi
eyes remained dry, the pain in his heart was as great, per
haps greater than Desheen's. "Somehow . . . by the grace
of the gods . . . we must get through this, Desheen. I an
glad you are here. Your presence lightens all my bur
dens."

"And I am grateful for you, Lugh," she sniffed. "I
don't think I could stand it if I had to face this alone.
love you." She dried her eyes. "Come. I am composed
now. Let us go to the king and queen."

The shriek Morrigan uttered when she saw her baby
shook the leaves of the tallest oaks and caused the wrens
to leave their nests. She beat her breast and rent her cloth
ing, screaming out her pain. Nuad stood transfixed, star
ing down at his son, motionless and silent as stone. He

alone, of the entire search party, seemed deaf to his wife's cries.

At length he bent down and picked up the broken body of their son. He examined it carefully, much as he and Morrigan had done when Ultan was born. This time he was not looking in awe at his child's tiny fingers and soft whorls of hair as he had then; he seemed to be memorizing the child's every injury.

There were large purple bruises on the side of the baby's face, and several of his ribs, as well as his left leg, were broken. There was no blood, no puncture wounds anywhere to be found. Nuad bent close to the little pink lips that had so recently begun to smile at the world around him, and inhaled. There was no scent of poison, just the sweet familiar smell of his son's soft skin. The child had been beaten to death.

Nuad held Ultan tightly to his chest and bent his shaggy white head protectively over him. Morrigan's anguished cries reached him as though for the first time and he turned to her, with tears streaming down his rugged cheeks. He put his silver hand around her, pulling her into a circle with him and Ultan. She soon quieted into a soft keening and together the mother and father wept, allowing the tears of their grief to fall upon the head of their slain son.

They buried Ultan on the crest of a hill overlooking the sea. Dagda Mor said holy words over his grave and the DeDanaans left the infant there, in the bosom of Innis Ealga. When they had gone, the only sounds on the hilltop were from the waves beating against the sandy strand, the whitecaps shimmering gold in the late afternoon sunshine.

Lugh had felt numb all the way back to Druim Caein, and he still had not recovered when dawn came washing over the green hills of the royal stronghold with a light hand, painting the frosty hills a soft rose-gold. It was Tailteann's funeral day. Treetops stirred before the breeze and although the air was cold, a few winter birds sang a welcome to the sun.

Lugh heard the compound come to life, everyone preparing to pay homage to Queen Tailteann, but he lay on the furs looking up at the roof of his dwelling without seeing. From the moment he and Desheen had found Ultan, the earth had lost its clear colors and sharp edges for him. His heart was heavy and bruised inside his chest, and all sensory information seemed to come to him as though wrapped in newly carded wool.

Thinking of this last farewell to his mother, he was bereft, feeling more alone than he had ever felt in his life. He had mourned for King Eochy and missed him still, but even that awful sorrow was somehow less than the deadening pain of losing his foster mother.

Desheen's light and familiar rap came at his door. He listlessly turned his head and called, "Enter." Through the dullness of his being he realized that she alone was the only person he truly wanted to see.

He struggled to sit up. Wordlessly, she came and knelt beside him and drew his head to her bosom, as a mother would a child. She held him lightly and stroked his head, soothing his tortured spirit with her touch.

He wept then for the first time since he had found Tailteann on the ground near the souterrain. All the grief that was pent up in him poured out in tears that Desheen wiped away.

When at last he gained his composure he realized that his limbs were no longer as heavy as standing stones and his heart felt lighter.

"I can get through this day now," he said in wonderment at the easing of pain the tears and Desheen's present had brought.

"I know you can, Lugh, you always could. You are strong because you are Tailteann's son."

"Not only can I get through it," he vowed, "I will give my mother all the honor and respect she deserves."

"You were very fortunate to have had her as a foster mother, Lugh, as I was to have known her. I doubt that your natural mother could have loved you more . . . or taught you better." She kissed him. "Come now," she said softly, "it is time to prepare for the ceremony."

It had been decided that Queen Tailteann would be cremated at the Brugha na Boyne and her ashes interred within the great temple tomb that Parthelon's people had built so many generations ago as a last refuge for those of royal blood.

In a single row the priests crouched down and entered the long tunnel that led into the large central chamber made of stone. Once inside they were able to stand upright. They shone their torches toward the niches that lay on three sides of the central chamber.

The chief priest, Ferfesa, glanced upward and saw that the corbeled stones that made up the domed roof were undisturbed. *The gods are good,* he thought. *All these years and the stones do not move, no moisture finds its way into this holy place.*

Tailteann's funerary urn would lie upon the flattened basin stone in the niche on the left. Old bones, that had been stripped clean on some mountainside long ago, lay in the niche to the right, awing the DeDanaans with their antiquity. No one dared to speak in the presence of the ancestors.

Ferfesa dusted the basin that was to receive Tailteann's ashes. The others inspected the stones and swept the earthen floor of the central chamber with short brooms made from fragrant boughs.

When all was in readiness, Ferfesa placed a candle scented with sweet oils in a stone cup and set it on the waiting basin stone. He lit a rush from one of the torches and touched it to the candlewick. The light flickered, then burned steadily, a symbol of the light the DeDanaans hoped the Sun God would send into the tomb on midwinter's day as a blessing upon Tailteann's spirit.

The ancients had built a slot in the front of the tomb, to invite him in on the shortest day of winter if he chose to renew his promise of rebirth. Some years he did not come, but it was unthinkable to those who had loved Queen Tailteann that he would not honor her goodness by shining upon her.

When all the tasks were done, the group followed Ferfesa out of the tunnel and back into the daylight, blinking at its brightness. The great kerbstone that had sealed the entrance to the tomb lay beside the opening, its deeply carved triple spirals offering reassurance to the bereaved. Two guards stood watch over the open tomb that was now in perfect order to receive the ashes.

* * *

Tailteann's body was dressed in a long gown of white linen and boots of the softest skins, and was laid out upon a wooden platform some distance in front of the huge circular tomb. Her eyes were closed and if it had not been for her awful stillness and the bloodless hue of her skin, her face was so composed that one might have thought she was only resting. Her small, delicate hands were clasped across her breast, as if touching the spot where the javelin had claimed her life.

Every DeDanaan in the vicinity had come to witness her final journey to the Otherworld. Silent crowds stood back a respectful distance from the platform. Ferfesa and four lesser priests were positioned around her bier, awaiting the arrival of her bereaved son, Lugh, who was to be accompanied by King Nuad and Queen Morrigan, themselves in deep mourning.

Lugh and Desheen came down the path to the burial site ahead of the king and queen. The curious, searching their faces for traces of grief, found it plainly etched there.

Lugh's brilliant green eyes were glazed with a pain that was almost physical. His face appeared to have hardened, his carefree youth gone forever. Desheen clung to Lugh's left hand, willing her love and strength to flow into him. He wore a yellow tunic, to honor the Sun God, and the cloak that Tailteann had embroidered for him to wear to Nuad's second coronation. His right hand rested upon the hilt of Frega, King Eochy's magic sword.

He felt his spirit tremble inside him as he approached the place where his mother lay. He could not bear to see her there, so still, so silent, yet, he could not tear his eyes away from her small form.

The king and queen were seated, staring straight head, Morrigan looking as though she were carved from ice.

Ferfesa called upon the Sun God. "Oh, mighty Bel, god of the sky, attend the DeDanaan tribe here today where we have gathered to send the spirit of a high queen back to her home in the Otherworld."

There were prayers and the sanctification of Tailteann's body by water, followed by still more prayers. Then Cairbed stood to sing the funeral lament that Brigid had composed.

He plucked sad notes from his harp and sang Brigid's

words with grace and simplicity. DeDanaans wept openly long before he came to the end of the song. Lugh had chosen those whom Tailteann loved especially well to carry the kindling wood for her funeral fire: Brigid, Diancecht, Dagda, Ogma, Cairbed, and Desheen. To Tailteann's everlasting honor, King Nuad, himself grief stricken, rose to place the last piece of dried wood upon her pyre.

When all was in readiness, Ferfesa handed Lugh a cresset of flaming pitch. He accepted it, his hand shaking mightily, but the man who had been fostered by King Eochy and Queen Tailteann of the Fir Bolg tribe, spilled not a drop as he set Tailteann's body ablaze.

"Go on the wings of a wren, my mother," he whispered, "I will see to it that our people never again suffer as I do now from the hand of a Fomorian. I promise you this."

With an enormous rush, the platform burst into flames. The last Lugh saw of Queen Tailteann through the fire were her small brown hands, folded as though in supplication to the gods.

Chapter Thirty-seven

The night before the second battle on the Plain of Moytirra, a shower of stars fell over Innis Ealga. The holy men of the Fomorians, as well as the DeDanaans, testified to their leaders that it was an omen of victory sent by the gods to fortify them and give them strength for the battle. Only King Balor of the Fomorians believed it. King Nuad believed in the strength of planning by his war council.

Tension was high in the DeDanaan camp on the eastern shore of Lough Arrow, as they awaited word from their scouts about the arrival of the Fomorians to Innis Ealga.

King Nuad spoke in low tones to his comrades. "I think they will land at Mag Scene, but I could be wrong. Our scouts are stationed up and down the entire northwestern coast though, and runners will bring us word of Balor's troop movements shortly after the Fomorians put ashore."

Lugh looked at King Nuad's beautiful silver hand. It was a worry to him that Nuad had not confided in him about how he planned to participate in the battle. As wondrous as the silver hand was it did not afford Nuad the ability to control a horse and fight at the same time.

Lugh understood in his bones that the physical presence of a king on the field of battle had always been necessary to rally fighting forces. The lore of both the Fir Bolgs and the DeDanaans was full of what happened when kings were killed during battle. Troops almost always lost heart and often lost the fight as well. Had not the determination of the Fir Bolgs cracked when King Eochy was struck down?

Lugh knew King Nuad recognized this, but if he had a

plan for overcoming his handicap, why had he not spoken of it?

"All is in such a fine state of readiness that there is not much for us to do now, but await the arrival of the Fomorians," the king was saying. "You warriors might as well get some rest now. There will be no time for any after the fighting starts."

The king dismissed his forces and retired to his battle tent where Morrigan awaited him. The iciness that engulfed her after Ultan was killed had not left her, and few DeDanaans but Nuad could bear to be in her company. Nuad had confided his worry about her to Lugh, but believed as Diancecht had told him, that time would thaw her frozen heart.

Lugh ambled off to look for Desheen, whom he had seen driving her chariot over the broad green Plain of the Pillars, sometime earlier. He hoped she might be through with her practice maneuvers by now.

Before he reached the horse pens he saw her come clattering up to the smithy in her chariot. One of the wheels was bent at an awkward angle. She climbed down and spoke a few words with Gobinu, then unharnessed the horses.

Lugh bounded toward her, reaching her just as she set off to stable her team. "Hello, Desheen," he called, "what happened to your chariot?"

"Hello, my darling." She smiled. "It's nothing too bad. I feared I had broken an axle, but Creidne says it is only dented. He can pound it out this afternoon. I hit a large stone, so covered with moss that it blended right into the grass. I just didn't see it." She wrinkled her nose in irritation. She did not like this waiting any more than Lugh did and she knew her own impatience had made her careless.

She rose on tiptoe to kiss him. "What were you doing? Going over the plans for the battle one more time? By the gods, Lugh! There cannot be a single thing you and Nuad haven't thought of. Are you nervous?"

"No, just eager to get this battle underway. Until it starts there is nothing to do but worry about details. I have too much energy and there is no way to expend it until the Fomorians get here."

"I know. Everybody seems to feel the same way except

Dagda Mor—and your father. I think he'll be much happier when the fighting is behind us ... odd, since he is such a skilled warrior."

"My father always prefers to negotiate differences. He's a lot like Dagda Mor in that regard. Neither of them realizes that there are some people with whom it is impossible to reason. How could one negotiate with a tribe who would beat a tiny baby to death?"

"I'm sure I don't know," Desheen said, "but we don't have proof that the Fomorians killed Ultan. Perhaps Breas did it to get even with Brigid. Whoever did it was a low beast, that's for certain."

She changed the subject. "Come on, I'll show you how Gobinu, Creidne, and Luchta have set up the forge. I think they have done a fine job."

"Your idea of setting up a forge on the battle site is such a good one, Desheen, I wish I had thought of it. Mending the chariots and the weapons on the spot is bound to give us a tremendous advantage over the Fomorians. When their weapons break they will just be out of luck, but we will be able to fight on as long as there is a warrior left standing to hold a sword.

"Diancecht said the other day that battles don't always turn on which tribe is the most powerful. Broken weapons held by the strongest hands are of no use."

"I hope the forge works as well as we think it's going to," Desheen answered, trying to combat her genuine fear.

They were inspecting the forge when a blast from the bronze battle horns split the air. "That's it!" Lugh cried. "The Fomorians have landed! It won't be long now! Even as we speak they are advancing toward Moytirra." He could barely contain his excitement.

"If they landed at Mag Scene it will take at least a day for them to move their warriors and supplies down here to Lough Arrow. Let's go to the battle tent and find out more," Desheen suggested.

By the midday dining hour of the next day the DeDanaans were able to watch the Fomorian warriors as they set up their battle camp across the field of northern Moytirra.

* * *

"What is it, Father? You sigh as sadly as if the weight the earth were upon you," Lugh said as he came to and beside Cian.

"I was thinking about your mother, Lugh. I don't suppose it's likely that Balor would let her come this close to e . . . or to you. No doubt she was left back on their remote island."

His words did not get the sympathetic reception from ugh that Cian had expected.

"We can't afford to be distracted," Lugh said sternly. We have to keep our minds on defeating the enemy, othing else."

Cian looked at Lugh sharply. There was a hardness in s son's voice he had never heard before. "Is it revenge ou're seeking, or victory? They are distinctly different ings, you know."

"I know it, Father. But I need to harden myself for this attle because I will be standing against my own grandfaer. The gods know that I have no soft feelings for King alor, after what he has subjected us to over the years. ut we do carry the same blood in our veins, and I fear at such knowledge could cause me to falter if he and I ould come face to face."

"I understand your concern, Lugh, but the man is a rute. You owe him nothing now, nor have you ever."

"I know, but still he is the father of the woman who ave me life. He is her flesh and blood . . . and mine. Will have the courage to raise my hand against him if the eed should arise? And will the gods punish me if I do?"

Cian put his arm around Lugh and spoke, looking traight into his son's green eyes. "I am certain no god ould wish to punish you, Lugh. I have watched you row into a man as tall and straight as a javelin. There is o doubt in my mind that you will conduct yourself with onor and valor in this battle. Try to put such doubts beind you. You know what your duty is. You know where ight lies and you will do what you must do. Think no ore about it, son. The gods are watching over you."

Dagda physically ached with longing to see Dedecha, aughter of the Fomorian champion, Indech. His loins ingled and his head felt muddled from the wanting of er. If she were across the plain with the Fomorian war-

riors, she was certain to raise arms in combat against hi
and his people.

He knew what he should do if he came face to fa
with her in battle, but he honestly did not know if
could do her harm.

On the evening before the battle, a group of four F
morians made their way across the plain of northe
Moytirra holding aloft a white banner tied to a javelin.
was the custom for the challenged warriors to call up
the challenging king to agree on the rules of battle. Su
a call was not expected from the Fomorians, who nev
followed proscribed rules in any other areas of conduc

King Nuad sent Lugh, Cian, Miach, and Macha out
meet the party and escort them back to his battle te
"Be especially wary," he warned them, "this may well b
a trick."

The two parties met midway between the battle tents
their leaders and the chief Fomorian spoke first.

"Hail, DeDanaans. I am Indech, champion of the F
morians."

Lugh and Miach recognized his name from the tal
Dagda the Wise had told about his encounter wi
Dedecha, Indech's daughter, and glanced knowingly
one another. Lugh introduced himself. "I am Lugh, t
Tanist of the DeDanaans."

The disheveled, dirty warriors inclined their heads :
acknowledgment of Lugh's status and allowed him
lead them into the DeDanaan camp. They found Kir
Nuad and Queen Morrigan seated outside the battle te
in the gathering darkness, next to a newly kindled fire

The royal DeDanaan couple did not rise to greet the
visitors. Lugh spoke: "King Nuad, Queen Morrigan, ma
I present Indech, champion of the Fomorian tribe an
spokesman for his king, Balor."

Lugh towered above the Fomorians, who were to a ma
short and stocky with black hair and swarthy skir
Indech's small eyes narrowed when he looked into Kir
Nuad's face, as though he were squinting into the sun.

To the Fomorians, Lugh said, "This is King Nuad (
the Silver Hand and Queen Morrigan, rulers of the ar
cient tribe of DeDanaans."

Indech nodded his head curtly. His thin, pinched face ave away nothing.

"We bid you welcome to this meeting," King Nuad aid. "It is the hope of the DeDanaan people that blood-hed might still be avoided. I offer you the opportunity to urrender peaceably to our superior force. If your king is greeable we will prepare a treaty that will enable us to ive in peace with one another without the spilling of ›lood."

They were hollow words, spoken only because of cus-om. Neither side had any intention of pulling back from his battle, and they all knew it. Indech looked at King Nuad blankly, as though he had not understood his words.)ne of his party spat upon the ground. Silence hung heavily between the adversaries.

"The only blood that will be spilt upon this earth will ›e that of DeDanaan warriors," Indech said at last. "My ing will not bend before a man with only one hand, nor ›efore his warriors. We will meet you in full combat on he morrow at the first hour of the sunrise."

"So be it." Nuad grinned. "We shall meet you in the center of the plain when the cock crows. Do your people observe the ancient rules of combat that allow for the safe removal of the wounded and dead?"

"We do," Indech answered, but something in his tone made Lugh's skin prickle. The man was lying, he was sure of it. Queen Morrigan realized it too, and her large dark eyes bored in on the Fomorian until he was forced to lower his gaze.

"That is all then," Nuad said. "Tell King Balor that we intend to win this battle and put a stop to his marauding forever more. Tell him too, that we know of the prophecy by your priestess, Birog, that he will die by the hand of one of his own blood."

Grinning broadly at the effect his ominous words had on his callers, Nuad went on. "And then tell him that Lugh of the Long Hand, son of his only daughter, Ethne, will go against him in battle. Good evening, gentlemen.'

King Nuad stood up and offered Queen Morrigan his hand. She took it and they turned their backs on the vis-itors as a sign of contempt and walked unhurriedly back to the royal battle tent.

* * *

Across the field, King Balor sat in his tent with h
new and distrusted allies, Breas the DeDanaan, and Sran
the Fir Bolg, who hated one another so intensely that the
could not be left alone together. Stout Queen Kathlen s:
at Balor's feet on a crude stool.

He spoke to her. "The taking of Innis Ealga will giv
us a springboard for new conquests . . . maybe even in
Albion. I cannot wait for the morrow. They will offer u
a compact of peace, of course."

"Of course," she sneered, "what else could we ex
pected from them?"

They both laughed as though she had made a witty re
mark. Breas looked at his feet, embarrassed, then glance
at Srang. As always, the Fir Bolg's face was hard and im
passive. He stared straight ahead. He had demonstrate
his evil nature so clearly when he and Breas had quar
reled that Kathlen was surprised when Balor taunted th
Fir Bolg.

"Did your honorable King Eochy make the same offe
to the DeDanaans when they came to steal your land
Srang? Too bad he didn't take them up on it since h
wasn't strong enough to stand up to the invaders."

Srang's jaw clenched and Breas could see the muscle
moving beneath his skin, but the Fir Bolg maintained hi
stony demeanor and his silence.

Kathlen laughed aloud, throwing back her head. "Oh
Balor! That's a good one," she cackled.

Breas was repulsed by these people whom he consid
ered rude savages. He wished he did not have to rely or
their help to get his kingdom back. It had cost him too
much already. He could not bear to think of what Srang
had done to his son. He felt his stomach turn as Balo
moved and he caught the scent of his person. They af
fronted him continually; he wondered if he really needec
these savages as much as his mother thought he did.

King Balor grew serious and addressed Srang anc
Breas directly. "I expect you to comply with my bat
tle orders. I want one Fomorian warrior against each
DeDanaan warrior. But first we will soften up King
Nuad's forces with a barrage of Fomorian arrows. Do you
understand?"

Breas and Srang had tried to tell him that the
DeDanaans fought from sophisticated strategy and that

uch chaotic hand-to-hand combat would fail against
iem, but Balor refused to listen. He was still angry that
iey had dared to argue with him.

"My people have warred like this since time out of
iind," he said, "and it has always worked for us. I would
e a fool to change the way we do things now. I'm warn-
ig you for the last time. You will fight my way or you
ill be eliminated before the fighting begins."

Srang tried to protest but Breas, who prided himself on
ecognizing when further talk was futile, said nothing.

Indech's voice came from outside the tent, interrupting
alor's tirade. "I request permission to enter, sire."

"Come in, come in," Balor bellowed. "What did our
ine friends have to say?"

He hoped the wild and unkempt appearances of Indech
nd his companions had struck fear into the hearts of the
)eDanaans. He knew his men looked ferocious, with
heir tangled hair and ratty animal skins, even unarmed.
Ie smiled when he saw Indech.

"We turned down their offer of a peace treaty as you
nstructed, my lord. We said the only blood that would be
pilled upon the morrow would be theirs. In truth, the
ing with the silver hand seemed pleased with this. He
ppears eager to do battle."

"Ho! We'll see how eager he is when the arrows start
o fly," snorted Kathlen. "Let's see how brave the one-
anded man is then!"

Indech went on: "We agreed to engage in combat when
he cock crows at down. We will meet in the middle of
he plain and at a signal from the hornsman the fighting
vill begin."

King Balor of the Evil Eye nodded his great, bull-like
ead.

"That's it then, men. Get some sleep. The dawn comes
uickly." He rose and placed his powerful hand on
3reas's shoulder as the former DeDanaan king stood to
o. "Stay," he ordered.

When the tent was emptied, Kathlen rose and blocked
he flap with her square body, folding her arms over her
mple bosom. Her sturdy legs were planted like oaks
where she stood. Breas grew uneasy. There was no mirth
n the loose-lipped smile she gave him.

King Balor addressed him, "You understand, Breas,

that when we succeed in taking this land from th
DeDanaans you will owe the Fomorian people a grea
debt?"

"Yes, I understand that, my lord. I am grateful for you
help when my own father refused me. I will be more tha
generous to you when I am once more king of th
DeDanaans." He flashed his brilliant white-toothed smile

Balor ignored it. "Queen Kathlen and I have bee
thinking that the best way you could show us how grate
ful you are would be for you to take our daughter, Ethne
to bride."

Breas gulped. He was sure Ethne had been pretty once
but now she was old and bitter. He'd had enough of plair
women with Brigid, who had been so distasteful to him
that he still marveled how he had ever been able to ge
her with child.

Every fiber of his being wanted to refuse Balor and
Kathlen, but he knew he was the supplicant in this alli
ance and not strong enough to say no.

"King Balor, Queen Kathlen, I am honored beyond be
lief that you would choose me to be the husband of you
daughter, but do you not know that I am wed to Brigid
daughter of the Dagda Mor?"

He did not tell them that by stepping down from the
DeDanaan kingship he had paved the way for Brigid to
appeal to the council of elders and have the marriage dis
solved.

"We know," Balor said, "but when we win, it will mat
ter not. There are ways to eliminate unpleasant obsta-
cles."

Breas felt his heart sink. Why would they want him to
wed their daughter? She, who had remained unclaimed all
these years, why now and why him?

"Yes, of course, I see," Breas said, nervously wiping
his sweaty palms on his tunic. "Yes. Well, that would
please me, of course."

"Fine, then we are agreed?"

"Yes. We are agreed."

He didn't want to touch the hand Balor held out to him
to seal the pact, but he had to. Breas wished he possessed
his mother's cunning. She would understand what these
two were up to. He had wanted to bring her to Lough Ar-

y with him, but Balor insisted that she remain behind his tower dwelling on Tor Conain.

Kathlen chuckled gleefully after Breas departed. "Well ne, my love. He hasn't the courage of a kitten, has he? nat a fine, handsome son-in-law he will make us! When is honestly wed to our daughter, our claim to Innis lga will be as strong and legitimate as his. Breas will easily controlled, I have no doubt. You saw how he cked down from Srang after he killed his son."

Balor grabbed her and nipped her on the neck, patting r rump as he did so. "It went well indeed. Did I not tell u that Breas was sent to us by the gods? What a tool y have given us, all golden and pretty!"

Just outside the tent flap, Indech called softly, so as not be heard by anyone but Balor and Kathlen. "May I me in, my lord?"

King Balor was annoyed by the intrusion. He released thlen and held back the tent flap for Indech to enter. "What is it now?" he snapped. "I thought I sent you to t some rest."

"You did, sir, but there is something else I must tell u and I did not think it wise to say it in front of the oth- s."

"Well, what is it, man? Speak."

"King Nuad bid me remind you of Birog's prophecy at you will be sent to the Otherworld by the hand of one o carries your blood in his veins."

Indech hesitated. He saw Kathlen's face go white under e grime.

"That is just a scare tactic, like war witches," Balor id. "You know that, Indech. I am surprised that I have remind you of it. Is this what you disturbed me to y?"

"No, sir, there is more. The DeDanaan king said to tell u that your grandson will go against you tomorrow, the n of Ethne and Cian, the DeDanaan captive. He is lled Lugh of the Long Hand."

"By the gods, man, you are a fool!" Balor boxed dech's ear. "Get thee from me, idiot. I don't need to ar such drivel on the night before an important battle. ut, I say, and don't come back. May fleas lie in wait for u in your bed."

Indech awkwardly backed out of the tent, holding his

smarting ear. Kathlen went to Balor's side and grasp[ed]
his arm, her eyes full of terror.

"Oh, Balor! I told you we should have killed th[e]
mewling infant when it was born, but no, you had to be[nd]
to the wishes of our daughter. You should not have do[ne]
it. A girl so dim as to get with child by a DeDanaan ca[p]-
tive was not to be listened to. Now that boy is going [to]
fulfill the prophecy. Oh, Balor!" she wailed.

The one-eyed king dismissed his wife's concern [by]
telling her she was a foolish old woman, but when [he]
climbed beneath the furs to court sleep, his heavy fram[e]
was wracked by fear and trembling. He thought he cou[ld]
feel the cold chill of the Underworld on his neck. Slee[p]
came to him just moments before the crow of the co[ck]
rang out across the northern Plain of Moytirra, signali[ng]
the start of the battle day.

Chapter Thirty-eight

On the point of the highest hill near the Plain of Moytirra, thin, pale rays of the rising Sun God shone directly through a break in the fast-moving clouds, onto the gray stone burial cairn of King Eochy that rose from the green grass to meet the sky.

In the soft morning light Lugh could feel the dead king's presence. He raised his hand in a silent salute to the spirit entombed beneath the cairn's stones and walked to the edge of Lough Arrow, determined never to let his beloved foster parents down. He would act with reason and compassion, but he meant full well to defeat their ancient enemy in the battle today. That would be the greatest honor he could offer them.

He splashed ice-cold water on his face and his thoughts turned to battle strategy. This was the day in which he would meet his destiny and he could feel the thrill of it in his bones. The atmosphere of tension and anticipation permeating the camp reminded him of the first battle of Moytirra, only this time he was going to be a full participant.

He met Desheen at the fulach fiadah and together they ate their morning rations, sitting close enough to touch but finding no verbal expression for their deepest feelings. They spoke of strategy and weapons and the readiness of the DeDanaan army in hushed tones and avoided looking directly at one another until there was no time left.

Lugh took her in his arms, inhaling the deliciousness of her, and she clung tightly to him. She murmured his name, and whispered, "I love you, Lugh, with all my being. Please be careful and come back to me."

"I will be careful, as you must likewise be. I love you

too, with all my being. My only wish is to grow old with you by my side."

He wanted to say more, to share what was in his heart. "I am surrounded by spirits here on this Plain of Pillars where King Eochy lost his life, and I cannot help remembering all that has gone before . . . His words trailed off, there was too much. Too much feeling, too much history, and too little time.

"Never mind," he said, "the future is what concerns us now, a future we will face free of the threat of the Fomorians. We must take leave of one another now to fight for that freedom."

The young lovers rose from the stone upon which they had been sitting, embraced one last time, then wordlessly moved apart. Desheen ran to her chariot and Lugh moved toward a restless Anovaar, who seemed to sense the combat in the air.

Outside the royal battle tent, Morrigan fretted that she had not chanted the old spells over Nuad that would guarantee his safety. She would have to depend on Diancecht to make certain the remaining ancient rituals were followed. Once there had been a time when she had acknowledged the old physician as her master in the old faith, but it had become clear to both of them as time went by that she was now the superior practitioner of the ancient arts.

Through the early morning mist she could hear the enemy troops moving into battle formations across the plain. Lough Arrow lay still and silver in the dawn, but she failed to see its beauty. The agony of losing her child blocked everything else out, driving her on to avenge his death. She had even pushed Tadgh away from her, allowing Brigid to care for him almost exclusively. Being near him exacerbated the pain of losing Ultan, and she could not bear to hold her growing, animated son while her other child lay stone cold under the earth of a faraway hill.

If she could inflict pain and suffering upon the Fomorians, she hoped it would free her spirit to become, once more, mother to Tadgh. She knew that nothing else would work.

"It is time, Morrigan, the hour of battle is upon us,"

Nuad said, stepping from the battle tent. He took her hand, and looked at her bitter dark eyes. He was deeply concerned about her and had been from the day they laid young Ultan in his grave. It was as though the woman he knew had been stolen by the gods. Her familiar body still lay beside him at night, but there was no spirit left in it.

"Take no foolish chances, my love," he said, and drew her into his arms and kissed her.

"Nor should you, Nuad. I want you to come back from this battle untouched," she said dully.

At that moment two water fowl swept down to glide on the waters of Lough Arrow, leaving a V-shaped trail behind them, and Morrigan looked up. She saw the mating pair of fowl as a good omen. She reached up to kiss her husband.

"I do not doubt that we will emerge from this war victorious, Nuad, but we must be realistic and speak of the future if one of us should be killed in the fighting. Tadgh is still much in need of a mother. I love my sisters dearly, but neither Macha nor Neimain has the temperament to raise him. I have thought about it for days. If I don't come back from this fight, I want you to ask Brigid to be his foster mother."

King Nuad looked at her intently. He was surprised that she was able to speak of their son, but he could see that she was serious.

"Of course, my darling. I have not thought you wished to speak of such things or I would have broached the subject to you earlier, for I too have thought on the matter. I love our son above all things and there is much I wish for him in this life. If I should be the one to fall in the battle, you must rouse yourself from this melancholy and once more become a mother to him."

He squeezed her hand and turned to her for one last embrace before the battle. Then he lifted his silver hand to the sky and vowed, "I swear by the sun and moon, the sea, the dew, the colors, and all the elements, visible and invisible, that the sovereignty of Innis Ealga shall never be taken from the children of Nemed."

He strode off to mount his golden charger and Morrigan watched him go, her heart full of love that she wished she could express. A white owl, returning from its nocturnal rounds slid silently through the dawn, back to its perch in the oak forest. She was so intent on watching Nuad walk away that she did not see it fly over his head. She ran to don her battle armor and take up her weapons; the thawing of her heart had already begun. Revenge was at hand.

DeDanaan priests ignited the huge fires they had built with painstaking care over the past four days, as the curved horns sounded the first of three calls to battle. Lugh had always disliked wearing the battle helmet with bull's horns on either side and he still found the DeDanaan headdress unsettling. He adjusted his helmet and took a deep breath, trying to subdue the fluttery feeling in his chest.

He saw King Nuad riding deliberately toward him. Suddenly it seemed as though the very air around him trembled with expectancy. There was purpose on the king's face. He held the reins in his right hand, hailing Lugh with the silver one that reflected the pale rays of the rising sun. He came alongside Anovaar.

"Lugh," he said, "I want you to take my sword, Claimh Solais, from its scabbard and make it your own. Trade me Frega, King Eochy's sword, for my sword of light. I cannot fight with one hand, so I honor you now by asking you to take the leadership in the fighting.

"I will ride in the battle formation as king of the DeDanaans but I must needs rely on you to raise Claimh Solais against the enemy. What I am unable to do you must do. Much glory and fame will be yours."

"My lord, you do me the greatest honor," Lugh said, "but I care little for glory or fame. I will gladly do it for you, and for the memory of my foster parents who struggled so long against the Fomorians. I give you my solemn vow that I will use all the gifts the gods have given me to bring the DeDanaans victory and to act as nobly as you . . . and they . . . would have me do."

King Nuad nodded, gesturing toward the scabbard hanging from his horse's neck. Lugh leaned over and slipped Nuad's sword of light smoothly from its resting place. For a moment, he saw reflected on its gleaming blade the twin images of himself and the king of the DeDanaans.

The battle horns sounded a second time. Hurriedly

Lugh removed the sword Queen Tailteann had given him and slid it into King Nuad's now empty scabbard.

The two men smiled at one another and clasped hands. Each then turned his steed around and rode to his assigned place within the battle formation. The sword of light rested easily against Lugh's thigh.

King Nuad's heart was heavy at the loss of his own prowess. *Vain man,* he thought, *why is it not enough for you to be remembered as the king who restored the DeDanaan people to their homeland? Why must you want more? Always more.*

The sword of light had been passed to Lugh. Nuad thanked the gods to have one so worthy of the responsibility. As he watched his loyal warriors gathering into the battle formation, he marveled anew at their stamina and bravery. He shook his head in admiration and a lump filled his throat.

By the gods! I do love this land and these people, he thought, remembering once again his beloved father and grandfather. *None but the gods can stop the DeDanaans from claiming their right to live on Innis Ealga free from all threat.*

A line of DeDanaan spear-throwers stretched across the great width of the Plain of Moytirra, four rows deep, their javelins held high and straight. The battle horns sounded the last call and they lunged forward. The archers followed. Behind them came the swordsmen on horseback, then the charioteers who hauled yet more weapons as well as food and water.

The leather-covered bronze shields protecting the DeDanaan warriors were brilliant in the early morning light. Some were gaily colored, some whitewashed with lime in the hope of blinding the enemy with their brightness.

Lugh felt his pulse pounding in his neck as the distance from the Fomorians narrowed. He urged Anovaar forward with his knees. His moment had come. He experienced only a flicker of doubt about using an unfamiliar sword. It was after all, King Nuad's magical sword of light that no one could resist. He knew with a certainty that it could not fail him.

The DeDanaans advanced to the center of the field,

pounding on their shields with short swords, shouting loud war cries. From the corner of his eye Lugh could see the Fomorian war witches, their faces painted with bright blue woad. They screamed and gesticulated like madwomen along the sides of the battlefield, bringing curses down upon the heads of the DeDanaans, imploring their gods to destroy their enemy with thunder and lightning and great suffering. The din caused the hills and valleys of Innis Ealga to reverberate with the fury of humankind in conflict.

Lugh caught a glimpse of the three sisters, Morrigan, Macha, and Neimain, in the ranks of the mounted DeDanaan spear-throwers, who moved forward in a wedge-shaped formation. He looked for Cian and realized with alarm that his father had joined the last line of foot spear-throwers, the group that would take the brunt of the Fomorian charge. Without thinking, Lugh uttered a silent prayer for his well-being.

Next to Lugh, King Nuad rode tall. He appeared calm, but Lugh knew he must be feeling the same heightened sense of reality that he himself was feeling. Colors, smells, sounds, all seemed sharper and more intense than he'd ever known them.

The two sides clashed and Lugh wielded his long sword with skill. He was soon separated from King Nuad in the fierce fighting, but when the Fomorians fell back to regroup because of the high number of casualties they had sustained, Lugh knew that he and Nuad led the superior force. Feeling satisfaction, not pride, he was glad to be able to call himself a DeDanaan.

There was hardly enough time to get back into formation and catch his breath before the Fomorians, with wild war cries, rushed toward the center of the DeDanaan's shield wall. For a moment it seemed to Lugh that their attack might break through, thwarting the battle plan. The center of the shield line buckled and fell back and the Fomorians rushed in headlong ... but it was a trap.

As the Fomorians pushed against the center of the line, the DeDanaan sides lengthened into flanks commanded by Dagda on the left and Ogma on the right. The flank troops moved forward and rapidly enclosed the Fomorians within their ranks. Lugh galloped forward to meet the hapless enemy warriors, his sword of light slashing and thrusting in a blur of speed.

Smoke from DeDanaan bone fires swirled across the battlefield, propelled by a stiff western wind. Over the heads of the combatants it mingled with the smoke from the Fomorian fires and the sky grew dark. Lough Arrow was as choppy and black as the clouds that even now were forming over the great western sea and advancing steadily toward the Plain of Moytirra.

The spear-throwers, led by Cian, hurled their javelins at a brace of mounted Fomorians, which included Breas. He wielded a Fomorian sword against his kinsmen with a growing sense of panic. He could see that the coolness and superior organization of the DeDanaans was causing the foray to go against his new allies.

The fighting rapidly grew more fierce, and many men and women fell to their fates. Some were trampled into the blood-soaked earth by horses and chariots from their own side, but in the heat of battle little could be done to prevent it.

The holy men stoked the bone fires. Red and yellow flames leaped into the ever-darkening sky, higher than the treetops of the forest that surrounded the Plain of Moytirra on three sides. The combatants felt the intense heat as they fought. The sounds of sword clashing against shield, men cursing and shouting, and the thud of warriors and horses colliding, filled the Plain of the Pillars. It was push forward, fall back, flanks forward, charge ahead; each bloody encounter followed by yet a bloodier one.

In the thick of the fighting Desheen's chariot thundered by Lugh, giving him a glimpse of her strong slender arms, controlling the direction of the vehicle that carried more weapons to the front. Sleek, accurate javelins rained down on the Fomorian warriors who still fought with stone battle-axes.

The sight of the primitive weapons angered Lugh. In close quarters, axes could be just as deadly as the DeDanaan's superior bronze weapons, but the use of them seemed to make the enemy less worthy of the terrible effort it was taking to defeat them.

Lugh hoped that the Fomorians believed that the DeDanaans had an endless supply of javelins and swords.

It was not so, of course, but the smiths were working so swiftly as to make it appear true. A broken weapon was repaired and returned to a warrior's hands in no time at all. Ominous black clouds scudded in front of the sun, casting large dark shadows across the fighting field. A cold wind rose to a howl out of the north, sweeping across the opposing warriors.

During a lull, the DeDanaans, at King Nuad's command regrouped into a formation with a wedge of swordsmen positioned behind a shield wall. Behind the wedge came three formations of warriors; each line smaller and tighter than the first. Dagda and Ogma commanded the flanks of the second line in whose center King Nuad rode, surrounded by bodyguards.

Lugh commanded the tightest innermost line, depending on Cian and Neimain to oversee the flanks. At the rear of the flying wedge and the three formations, rode the charioteers.

The DeDanaans were still organizing into this complex pattern when, before the battle horns sounded, the Fomorians charged in one wild, screaming, painted mass.

The DeDanaans reacted instinctively, quickly closing ranks in the shield wall and the wedge. They rushed forward to meet the charge. When the enemy was almost upon them, those in front stopped abruptly at Nuad's shouted order, and knelt behind their shields. They planted the dull ends of their javelins firmly in the earth, the points jutting outward at an angle. Within moments the running, screaming Fomorians were impaled upon them.

The second line of Fomorians could not stop in time and went crashing headlong into their fellow warriors who were writhing and dying on the DeDanaan javelins. The Fomorians were confused and horrified as they slid about in the spilled blood of their kinsmen. The sheer weight of their numbers caused the crouching line of DeDanaan spear-throwers to buckle and it began to fall back.

A third wave of Fomorians, who'd had time to assess the situation, moved quickly to take advantage of it, pressing forward with all their might.

The right and left flanks of the first DeDanaans moved up to assist those in the wedge, and the onslaught of Fo-

norians was slowly pushed back. Suddenly they broke
and signaled a retreat, giving the DeDanaans time to regroup and tighten their formation.

Lugh caught a glimpse of Morrigan's angry, tear-
stained face and saw that her beloved sister Neimain lay
dead at her feet. There was no time to think on it, for the
Fomorian horse warriors were charging down upon them
at full gallop, led by Indech, the father of Dagda's lover,
Dedecha.

The DeDanaan flanks, led by Dada and Ogma, successfully beat them back, only to see them surge forward with
renewed strength. Indech led his army in a frenzy of killing. His sword caught the breast of Ogma and he plunged
it into him with gusto. The learned DeDanaan leader fell
and was no more.

Breas was bravely holding his own in the fray when he
saw Macha, the beauty he had once wanted for his queen,
riding toward him brandishing a short sword. She rode
close enough to recognize him and he was mildly surprised to see the hatred blazing in her eyes. He turned his
horse abruptly to avoid her sword thrust and in so doing
found himself looking directly into the disgust-filled face
of his Fir Bolg ally, Srang.

Humiliated to have been seen avoiding Macha's blow,
Breas turned his steed back to meet her thrust but he was
too late. Srang had moved forward and was even now
plunging his javelin between Macha's milk-white breasts.
She fell from her horse with a thud, her sightless eyes
staring into the sky from which an icy rain had begun
to fall. Breas saw blood trickle from a corner of her
beautiful lips before the onslaught of another wave of
DeDanaans distracted him from her death.

A large DeDanaan was knocked from his horse to land
at Breas's feet. The blow sent the fallen man's helmet flying across the field and Breas recognized the warrior as
Bove the Red, son of the Dagda Mor and Brigid's brother.
The big red-haired man lay sprawled directly in Breas's
path. Remembering his downfall at the hands of Bove's
family, Breas screamed a bloodcurdling oath at the
downed warrior, slicing viciously at him with his sword.

Bove, already wounded, was unable to escape Breas's
weapon and sustained grievous wounds. Blood spurted
chest-high onto Breas's horse. Satisfied that he had

wreaked revenge upon Bove for forcing him from th
DeDanaan kingship, Breas reined his horse to the righ
pounding into the fray, his battle lust high.

Brigid, standing on the side of the battlefield ready
nurse the fallen, saw Bove knocked from his horse. Sh
had many reasons for hating her former husband, bu
when she saw Breas deliberately slay her helpless brothe
all of them welled within her. Acting almost purely on in
stinct, she slipped a stone into her leather sling, wound
up above her head, and let it fly. Straight and true, th
stone found its mark, and an astonished Breas felt himse
knocked from his horse onto the field amid the mud an
dangerous horse's hooves.

He was not mortally wounded and could have re
mounted and continued to fight, but Srang, the Fir Bolg
saw him lying on the ground and galloped toward him
As casually as spearing a piece of meat, Srang threw hi
javelin though Breas's body, pinning him to the eart
where he lay. The spear quivered from the impact an
Srang smiled, well pleased to be rid of his chief rival fo
Innis Ealga, and knowing that in the chaos King Balo
would never discover who had done the deed.

Raindrops turned rapidly into hail, hard pellets of ic
that bombarded the combatants mercilessly. Harder an
harder the hail fell until both sides were forced by its fur
to signal a retreat. The intensity of the storm obscured ev
ery warrior's vision, making further battle impossible o
the slippery, ice-covered field. Hailstones bounced furi
ously off the bodies of the battle slain as though the
were being hurled from on high by gods angered at th
waste of their creations. The sky was black and lightnin
cracked like a whip across the expanse over Lough Ar
row.

Lugh and King Nuad conferred during the respite
holding their shields over their heads to protect them
selves. Nuad had to shout to be heard. "I think the tim
has come to stop this terrible slaughter, Lugh. We mus
request single combat with King Balor. I cannot do it. Ar
you willing to act on my behalf? Before you agree I mus
warn you that it will be dangerous, Lugh. Balor is a fero
cious fighter and you have never before gone agains
such a one as he."

Lugh was badly shaken by the destruction in which he had participated, but he said simply, "I am ready," and wiped the rain and the sweat from his eyes with the back of his hand.

A image of Desheen passed through his mind, but he could not allow himself thoughts of anything but the current challenge. Word of the single combat was quickly passed among the warriors.

As the fury of the storm subsided, DeDanaan priests, bards, and musicians positioned themselves atop the large stones that lined the eastern side of the lough, ready to beat the bodhrans and chant the ancient words that had called kings to single combat since time out of mind.

Brig brought King Nuad his splendid dark green cloak and a fine helmet of bull skin ornamented with horns of cast gold. Nuad put on his regal finery and rode to the front of the DeDanaan troops sitting erect on his golden horse, the muscles in his jaw taut but otherwise appearing calm and in control. His green eyes sought the face of his beautiful wife as he rode. He saw her, dirty and scratched, but unharmed. Their eyes met and their spirits communicated. The king rode on without flinching at the sudden, loud beat of the bodhrans calling Balor of the Evil Eye to meet him.

Lugh moved up with the front shield carriers, tense and ready to be called forth as soon as Balor was informed of the arrangement.

There was a flurry of activity on the Fomorian side, then warriors parted to allow the biggest black stallion Lugh had ever seen to pass between them. On it sat King Balor, as broad and black as the horse upon which he rode. He wore a boar's head helmet and black armor of poorly tanned leather that matched his eye patch. His face was painted with grotesque designs of blue and red. In his right hand he carried a battle-ax. The large handle of a short sword protruded from beneath his thick belt. The earth shook as horse and rider approached Nuad in the center of the field. The Fomorian king stopped and fixed his adversary with a baleful stare.

"Hail, King Balor," shouted Nuad in a strong, unwavering voice. "I am Nuad, King of the DeDanaans and son of the Sun. The time has come for single combat between us." He held up his hand of silver, careful to show only the back of it to his enemy. "The DeDanaan champion, Lugh, will wield my sword of light against you on this occasion as my designee."

King Balor sat silently on his horse as King Nuad spoke. When he was through, Balor leaned his massive head back and roared with derisive laughter. In a boar's eye would he do single combat with a designee. He turned his face to the side to peer at Nuad with his good eye.

"So, the brave DeDanaan king would send a lad to do his work for him, would he? I fight single combat with kings only," he growled.

"Our champion, Lugh, is a man of royal blood from both our tribes," King Nuad said. "He is the natural child of your daughter, Ethne, and has bid me salute you as a kinsman. We offer you, once more, the chance to surrender peacefully. Will you yield to DeDanaan superiority or will you risk the truth of your own prophecy by going against a man of your own blood?"

Nuad saw Balor pale under his paint at the mention of Lugh's birth. "I told you, man. I fight only kings," Balor snarled, raising his battle-ax and throwing it with tremendous force at King Nuad's head. Before the DeDanaan king could react, the force of the blow shattered his skull and toppled him from his big golden horse. Morrigan's scream pierced the very heavens over the plain of Moytirra.

The shock on both sides of the field at the barbarity of Balor's act was palpable. Lugh alone acted. He hoisted a javelin and took calculated aim. With unerring speed and skill, he threw it with all of the strength at his command. It pierced the crest of the Fomorian and the dark hulk of King Balor fell to the ground, dead instantly by the hand of his own kinsman.

Seeing the prophecy of Birog of the Mountains come true silenced even the war witches of the Fomorians, who looked helplessly to their priests for guidance. Receiving none, they muttered in hushed confusion, not knowing what to do next. The Fomorian troops were in a similar disarray.

"Re-form in the wedge and prepare to attack!" Lugh shouted to the DeDanaan warriors. Queen Morrigan rode to Lugh's side, her eyes red-rimmed and wild. "Lead on,

Lugh, I would avenge Nuad and Ultan!" she cried, brandishing her sword.

"As would I," Lugh answered.

The Fomorians fought furiously, but without King Balor at their head, their forays lacked all direction. They attempted to fight one on one, as he had directed, and were at a loss when entire lines of DeDanaans moved upon them.

Indech tried to seize control, and was shouting orders without much success when Cian's line of swordsmen surrounded him. He tried to hit Cian with his battle-ax, but missed. He lost valuable moments fumbling for his sword. As Cian drew close, his short sword ready to strike at Indech, the Fomorian's war chief, Conan, rode up behind Indech. He saw his companion's peril and hurled a stone ax that sent Cian's sword hurtling from his hand.

Indech seized on his good fortune and struck Cian a mighty blow across the shoulders. Cian felt a warm spurt of blood gush from his wound. As he fell from his horse he caught a glimpse of Desheen in her chariot, then all went black.

Desheen drove her chariot close to Conan and threw her dagger at him. It stuck firmly in his neck. He grabbed wildly at the knife and with great effort pulled the blade from his body. Before he could throw it at her, he was toppled from his horse by the broadside of Dagda's sword.

When Dagda realized whom he had struck, he was glad. It was the man who had humiliated him in the Formorian's camp. Desheen stopped her chariot, leaped down, and with superhuman strength managed to lift the wounded Cian into the conveyance. She jumped in beside him and skillfully turned the horses around in the midst of the melee and drove him to the sidelines where the physicians and Brigid were waiting to treat his wound.

Dagda fought on with the mighty Conan and was soon getting the worst of it, tiring and fearful that he would be the next DeDanaan sent to the Otherworld. From somewhere to the left of his head, he heard a battle-ax whir past him. It struck Conan on the side of the head and the big man fell from his horse just as the voluptuous Fomorian, Dedecha, rode up beside Dagda.

"Pretend to fight me," she said, waving her sword at him. Gratefully, he did as she asked. They clashed sword blades harmlessly.

"One of us will have to feign injury," she said.

"I'll fall," he told her.

"No, I will," she answered.

"Let's both go down," he suggested with a wink, carefully nicking her arm.

"All right," she agreed, and drew a thin line of blood from his arm with her sword.

At the same moment, they each plummeted from their horses. Dagda was the first up. He caught his horse and rode off the field to seek the assistance of the physicians for his wound, his heart gladdened that Dedecha was still fond of him. Because his back was to her as he left the field, he failed to see Cairbed's javelin run Dedecha through the middle just as she remounted her horse.

Morrigan rode as though chased by demons, into the thick of an oncoming line of Fomorian warriors. She fought with abandon, no longer caring if she lived or died.

A circle of warriors protecting a formidable old woman gave Morrigan to know that this must be Kathlen, the queen of the Fomorians. She focused her frenzy on her.

All the rage that Morrigan felt found cruel expression as she bore down on the woman who became the symbol of all she and the DeDanaans had lost. She slew three of Kathlen's guards before she could get close enough to the queen herself.

"Take this!" she cried, striking the enemy queen's knife from her hand with her first blow. She slashed wildly at Kathlen's terrified face, shouting, "These wounds are for your Fomorian treachery, for wounding my heart by killing my baby."

Blood bubbled around Kathlen's lips as the light of understanding dawned in her eyes. "Stop!" she shrieked. "It were no Fomorian what killed your baby. It was Srang, the Fir Bolg. He done it to keep Breas from having a prince!"

Her words had no effect. It was too late to stay Morrigan's fury. She plunged her blade into Kathlen's chest, screaming, "This is to avenge the killing of my king of the silver hand!"

When the Fomorian queen fell dead at her feet, orrigan wheeled her horse around looking for more enmies to slay. Those who had been witness to her frenzy ed from her, back to the relative safety of the sidelines. heir departure triggered a full-blown retreat.

Thus it was, that the second battle on the Plain of oytirra drew to a close before nightfall, the carrion circing the killing ground, awaiting their share of the fallen ead.

Chapter Thirty-nine

At the waxing of the midwinter moon, the Council of the Wise met at Druim Caein to choose the Tarbfeis dreamer. In a holy sleep, he would learn who the new king was to be. The silence of the dead stretched all the way from the Plain of Pillars to the royal stronghold, because the bones of too many DeDanaan heros had been left behind in new wedge tombs at Moytirra; tombs whose huge roof stones slanted toward the west so the Sun God would shine on them each evening, granting them his silent blessing.

The council members went at their task with heavy hearts. They ate of hazelnuts that had been gathered from a sacred tree of knowledge that grew near the Well of Conla. Buoyed by the belief that the gods guided their selection of the dreamer through the consumption of the nuts of wisdom, it was an easy matter to agree that Brig, King Nuad's house steward, should be the impartial dreamer. He could be trusted to receive the Imbas Forosnai, the knowledge that illuminates, in an enchanted sleep brought on by drinking broth made from the meat of a scared white bull.

The news that he was the chosen one for Tarbfels was brought to Brig at Queen Morrigan's house. Word of Brig's selection spread across the settlement quickly and had just reached Lugh and Desheen where they were grooming their horses, when Cian called out to them.

"Lugh! Desheen! There you are. Thank the gods I have found you. Come with me quickly, for your grandfather has been stricken, Lugh. He is very, very ill. Hurry. There may not be much time left."

Lugh, reacting to the fear on his father's face as much as to his words, whirled and tore off toward Diancecht's house with Desheen and Cian right behind him.

* * *

The only light in Diancecht's dwelling came from the fire in the middle of the round house. Miach was kneeling beside the still form of his father, who lay on furs pulled close to the fire. Diancecht's bronze leg lay apart from him, reflecting the dancing flames. *The presence of death is in this house,* Lugh thought. *I can feel it as keenly as I did during the battle.*

His grandfather's lips were colorless and his brilliant blue eyes were closed, leaving his aged face pale and transparent. The old physician's chest rose and fell violently with each tortured breath. His hands, gnarled and disfigured by age, lay limply at his sides. An insistent thought formed in Lugh's mind that he must call for Morrigan. It grew so strong it could not be denied.

"I will be right back," he whispered to Desheen, and slipped out the door.

He ran as fast as his legs could carry him, to the royal dwelling. Without knocking, he burst in, almost knocking Brig down. Morrigan looked up from where she tended Tadgh, startled by Lugh's intrusion.

"Come with me," he said to her. "Diancecht is dying and he needs you."

With no questions, Morrigan rose from her stool and handed her son to Brig. "Take him to Brigid," she said. "I don't know when I will be back."

She went directly to a peg on the wall where her medicine bag hung and took it down. "Has Diancecht called for me?" she asked.

"No," Lugh said. "I knew that you had to come. I don't know why, but I had to fetch you to him."

I know why, Morrigan thought, *the gods would have him home but not before the old rites are said over him.*

She slipped the medicine fes around her neck, and said, "Come on."

"Uncle Miach, Aunt Airmead, I have brought Morrigan," Lugh announced. "She can help Grandfather."

Miach's eyes flashed with resentment and he started to protest, but Airmead stopped him. "Let her try, Miach. You know there is nothing more you and I can do. What can it hurt?"

"Fetch me a beaker of water and a flat stone," Mor-

rigan ordered. She handed a small piece of limestone to
Lugh saying, "Take this chalk and mash it into powder
for me. Hurry, there is no time to waste."

After Morrigan had worked her magic, the old physician's eyes fluttered open, and he whispered in a raspy
voice, "Has the Tarbfels dreamer seen the new king?"

"No, Diancecht, not yet, but you will live to hear news
of the next king. I promise you that," Morrigan answered.

While Diancecht's family kept their vigil over him that
night, Brig laid himself down to dream on the newly
flailed hide of a white bull under the silver shadows of
the moon and the watchful eyes of the priests. He slipped
into a slumber filled with all the colors of the rainbow,
swirling in rapidly descending eddies, spiraling down,
down, down, to the very center of Brig's spirit.

The gods came to him then, in quick succession. He
saw waves crash against the rocks standing sentinel by
the sea, each impact sending up higher and higher silver
sprays. Slowly, the silver solidified and coiled itself into
the same concentric spirals as those carved into the kerb-
stones in front of the great necropolis, the Brugha na
Boyne. The spirals rose into the sky and hovered there as
from the sea there came a rumbling sound, growing in intensity until it blotted out the black sky and its silver design.

Standing stones from ages past burst from the surface
of the sea, rows and rows of them marching away until
they disappeared across the line of the horizon. Still more
came, and Brig understood that they were the spirits of
mankind from time out of mind, leaving their sepulchers.

The gray stones came to a halt and the dome of the sky
overhead grew purple. Lightning crashed and fear was
unleashed. The stones leaned toward one another seeking
comfort from the face of evil that loomed over them, filling the dome.

The beat of a bodhran could be heard, then the sweet
soft tones of a golden harp sounded and reverberated
across the sky. A vibrating, golden line stretched from horizon to horizon, as taut as a fisherman's rope with a full
net.

With a sharp crack the line frayed, then broke apart in
the center. Golden sparks flew, illuminating the purple

night, before they fell into the sea and were quenched. Overhead the two parts of the golden line moved, forming into two faceless figures.

A great burst of pure white light washed over the scene, causing the golden figures to throw their arms across their eyes to escape its terrible brilliance. The sounds of the harp and the bodhran grew louder and were joined by pipes. Louder and louder the music grew as the musicians marched toward the dreaming spirit. They were led by King Nuad who walked slowly beside his golden steed, holding the reins lightly in his silver hand. He was smiling his old familiar smile, his strong cleft chin jutting forward. Through his transparent body it was possible for the dreamer to see legions of warriors who had lived before his time, marching in step as though they were one.

A blinding golden light, a thousand times more intense than before, shone down on them, and the dreaming Brig knew that the Sun God himself was behind him. He dared not turn to gaze upon the mighty god. He could hear a spring breeze rustling new leaves on unseen trees and he could smell the sweet scent of new-mown hay. A long way off, he heard the cry of a newborn child. The Sun God spoke without words and Brig knew the next king of the DeDanaans was to be Lugh.

Diancecht's family had stayed by his side all night and as dawn approached it became clear that there was no strength left in the old physician. The life force sat upon him as lightly as a delicate fledgling upon a tree branch, ready to fly into the Otherworld.

Morrigan could feel her powers slipping away from her and still word did not come about the Tarbfels ceremony. Even the old spells could not thwart much longer the will of the gods. She felt a tingle even before she saw Dagda enter the dwelling and go to Lugh's side. He placed his hand on the young man's shoulder and whispered in his ear.

Lugh went to kneel at his grandfather's side. He placed his lips close to his ear. "Grandfather, I am the one. The gods have chosen me."

Diancecht opened his eyes, the piercing blue eyes that had always seemed to see into Lugh's spirit. He looked there now, and smiled. "I know, my son, I know," he murmured, "but I wanted to hear it from your own lips."

He withdrew his hand from Lugh's. Using his thumb he made the secret sign of a cross within a circle on Lugh's forehead. The effort cost him the little strength that was left to him and his blue-veined hand fell back weakly to the furs.

What happened next would be sung of by bards and written about by poets for as long as humankind walked upon the face of Innis Ealga. In Lugh's mind and in those of all the persons assembled there, a vision of another time and place formed slowly, then found sharp focus, mesmerizing them.

Lugh watched his fourteen-year-old self lying by the edge of a stream as an old man with hair the color of new milk approached the glade. They saw Lugh leap behind a tree with his dagger drawn, and they heard the old man's words after Lugh had confronted him: *You are the man who will heal the wounds of the invasion and become our champion and our king ... My words will stay in your heart until we meet again, although I must remove them from your mind for a while. When they are needed you will remember every detail of our meeting.*

Lugh did remember, with a clarity that made the scene as real to him as the one he was living at the moment. He heard his grandfather tell him that he must mind the Stone of Destiny, that his place in time was secure. The words, *You will be king, you will be king,* echoed in the dwelling. The vision faded, and they were all in the present once more.

Diancecht struggled to speak. "Yes, Lugh, you are the one. You have always been the one," he whispered.

"Grandfather, you came to me by the stream so long ago. You told me then. How did you know this would happen?" Lugh asked.

Diancecht moved his fingers feebly and said, "The gods are good."

He smiled and with those words, yielded up his spirit to the Otherworld. He had done the gods' will, and all things in the heavens and on Innis Ealga were as they should be.

Lugh stood looking down on the lifeless form of his

grandfather for a long time. Then he stood and reached for Desheen's hand. She gave it to him gladly.

Lugh looked at Morrigan, his father, Cian, Airmead, Miach, and the great Dagda Mor, and he smiled. When he and Desheen stepped from the dwelling into the light, the eye of the Sun God was shining full upon the land of Innis Ealga. Lugh turned to Desheen and knew that the human heart is capable of feeling great sorrow and great joy at the same time.

Glossary

Banois rig	The wedding of kingship, referring to the ritual with the holed stone.
bast	Cloth made from the inner layer of oak bark.
Beltaine	May 1st. The festival marking the beginning of summer when cattle are sent to higher pastures. The name comes from the Phoenician sun god, Baal.
bodhran	A round hand drum of bent oak, covered with goatskin.
boon	A blessing or gift bestowed by one in authority.
boroma	A cow tax. Also called *Boru.*
cloidem-mor	A type of broadsword.
Coigedh	The clan chieftains from the provinces.
cressets	Metal cups on poles, in which pitch is burned.
curraghs	Wicker-framed long boats covered with ox hides.
duilesc	An edible seaweed served at feasts.
fes	A leather bag worn at the waist to carry personal possessions.
filach fiadah	A horsehose-shaped cooking pit near water
Imbas-Forosnai	"The knowledge that illuminates," sent by the gods in an enchanted sleep.

kerbstone	A large, often elaborately carved, entrance stone placed in front of chambered tombs.
liathroid	A hide-covered ball used in the game of hurling.
lorg	A shaped ash stick used in the game of hurling.
lough	A lake.
lozenge	A zigzag design used for ornamentation.
Rechtaire	The house steward of the king—an honored position.
roydamna	Those considered "king material," from whom a king is chosen.
ruam	An herb used to make cheeks pink.
souterrain	A tunnel dug under the courtyards of hill forts for food storage and protection during attack.
torque	A heavy metal neck ornament, open in the front.
wattle wall	Construction of woven wicker over which daub, a mixture of dung and mud, is applied.